The Hero's Apprentice

The Hero's Apprentice

essays by *Laurence Gonzales*

CHRISTMAS 1997

DAD —

THIS MAY NOT BE A
JOHN GRISHAM OR A TOM
CLANCY BOOK, IT'S A "FEEL
GOOD" BOOK. I HOPE YOU
ENJOY IT. AFTER ALL, YOU'LL
ALWAYS BE A HERO'S
APPRENTICE IN MY EYES.

LOVE YOU ALWAYS,
JAN

The University of Arkansas Press
Fayetteville   1994

98   97   96   95   94   5   4   3   2   1

Designed by Gail Carter

The paper used in this publication meets the minimum
requirements of the American National Standard for
Permanence of Paper for Printed Library Materials
Z39.48-1984. ♾

Library of Congress Cataloging-in-Publication Data

Gonzales, Laurence, 1947–
    The hero's apprentice : essays / by Laurence Gonzales.
      p.   cm.
    ISBN 1-55728-360-5 (cloth). — ISBN 1-55728-361-3 (paper)
    I. Title.
  PS3557.0467H47   1994
  814'.54—dc20   94-3676
                                 CIP

for my mother

boss i went
and interviewed the mummy
of the egyptian pharaoh
in the metropolitan museum
as you bade me to do

—archy and mehitabel

Even our misfortunes are a part of our belongings.

—Antoine de Saint-Exupéry

Acknowledgments

For their heroic efforts, I owe thanks to a number of fine editors, among them, Peter Bloch, Michael Korda, James McKinley, James Morgan, Christine Newman, John Rasmus, and Kerry Temple. Thanks also to Jan and Don and Marc and Noa. Special thanks and love to Paula Ketcham.

These stories originally appeared in somewhat different form in *New Letters, Notre Dame Magazine, Men's Journal, Chicago Magazine, Whittle Communications Special Reports,* and *Penthouse Magazine.* The essay "Rites of Spring" was a finalist for the National Magazine Award.

Contents

Introduction

When I was a boy, kicking around the dying oil fields of southeast Texas with my grandfather's .22 rifle and a stolen package of Chesterfields, I had the idea that the highest achievement in coolness would be to fly an airplane upside down. I don't know where the idea came from, and I don't know either where I first heard of the Pitts Special, a small red airplane designed to fly upside down. But by the time I was in the fourth or fifth grade, both the idea and the airplane had become thoroughly mixed up with my idea of who I was.

Short of being abducted by aliens, there was very little chance that I would get to fly in anything. My parents had no money for such things as airplane rides, and I didn't know any pilots. There wasn't even an airfield within biking distance. Nevertheless, the conviction that I should fly a Pitts—and above all the conviction that I should find some other way to be cool—persisted. I didn't even know what being cool was. I just knew it was something to strive for.

I remember watching my father and falling under his spell. It was 1951, a world of heroes, stars, and spies. My father, a dashing and handsome officer, had been gravely wounded by the enemy, and his wounds persisted into my childhood. He smoked Chesterfields, and I'd sit and watch him by the hour. There was nothing more cool than my father smoking a Chesterfield. He had a moustache and an Errol Flynn way of working the circles of blue smoke by some sort of telekinesis, holding the delicate white cylinder of the cigarette with such satisfaction, and then delivering its ash with a tap of his index finger to the glass receptacle on the table by his newspaper. It was a dazzling magic show for me when I was four: The wounded warrior. I knew what had happened to him: He had gained his character, his validity, and those heroic qualities by flying an airplane and being shot down. He had gone out to meet something terrible, and he had mastered it and had come back to be treated like a king by all those around him, to sit and smoke and to be suave, disdainful, smart, and handsome. Most important, I understood in some dim way that the fact of his *not* reacting to any of this was the key. To be cool was the ability, the instinctive ability, not to react to danger. He was the hero and I was his apprentice, and that is what I learned at his knee.

I knew there was little hope that I would ever be so noble. Certainly he would never give me the recipe. But it was irresistible even to a child to try to decipher it, to steal my share of whatever he had.

Children don't understand everything, but they see everything, and whatever they don't understand, they store up for later. When they are up to it, they process the information they've stored, they decode it, and they find out what it meant. I took in the lesson he was teaching me. I fell under his hypnotic spell: Even at the age of four, I was a budding fighter pilot. I knew it for a while. I reveled in it. I knew what I'd be when I grew up. But then the noise of a troubled childhood forced me to bury it, and there it lay for thirty years.

■ ■ ■

My father was one of those combat vets who didn't want to talk about the war and didn't know anyone from the war. He had left it behind completely (he thought) and never looked back until one day in 1987 when a Colonel Barryhill walked into a shopping mall in San Antonio, Texas, and struck up a conversation with a woman behind a jewelry counter, who told him about her nephew who had been a pilot in the war. The conversation triggered a series of events that led someone from the United States Air Force 398th Bomb Group to contact my father and inform him that he was going to be promoted and awarded the Distinguished Flying Cross for his service in 1945. In 1988 we all went down to Randolph Air Force Base for what turned out to be an elaborate ceremony in the hallowed rotunda of the building the fliers there call the Taj Mahal. He wound up on national television.

I had never seen my father in the company of a military man.

That's how completely he had detached himself from the war. Suddenly now at the age of forty, I was watching this remarkable thing: My father drove onto an enormous air force base, and at the gate was a sign welcoming him by name. Colonels treated him like somebody really important. It wasn't his rank. He was only being promoted from lieutenant to captain. No, it was that he'd *been there.* Some of them had been there, too, and they recognized what they were seeing. He was a hero. It was a stunning experience for me, like finding out that my father was a spy for the Russians. Why hadn't he let me in on his secret? I think I know now: It was a secret from him, too. It had been such a terrifying experience, that he'd had to wait almost half a century before he could deal with it. And the four decades he waited just happened to be my whole lifetime.

Those events triggered something in both of us, then. For him it opened the door to dealing with his war experience, coming back to flying, getting in touch with his pilot and warrior nature. He went to reunions and found people he'd flown with. He reopened and healed some old wounds. He went back to the place from which he launched his planes and the place where he finally crashed, and there he resurrected the little boy who had become the dashing pilot, whose life was snapped in two. He gave up being cool and became warm.

For me the experience was something that should have happened when I was ten years old: The old man takes me to the temple and says: "Son, today I am going to show you your destiny. Because you are no longer a little boy, you are lost. But don't worry. This is what you are going to be now. It's what I am, and it's what you will become. You are no longer lost. This is your path. This is your legacy." But that's not the way it happened. I knew nothing about this until I was forty and walked unsuspectingly into the Taj Mahal at Randolph Air Force Base, and then all at once I understood what I had to do.

■   ■   ■

It was the middle of winter, and I was making the final push to pass the exams: There was some flying involved, but by the time a pilot is ready to become a flight instructor, flying the airplane is second nature. The big question is: Do we know all the rules? There is a sort of Talmudic rigidity in the FAA's vision of flight instruction. We are expected to know everything and to be able to explain it in the government's own words—no other explanation, however sensible, will do. So we study and study and pore over the books, trying to unscramble the bad prose and commit two dozen volumes to rote memory and hold onto them for just long enough to get past that infuriating oral exam.

One regulation explains that a pilot must undergo a flight review by a flight instructor every two years. In other words, a pilot's license is no good after two years unless we go up and fly with an instructor and prove that we can still fly. One day my instructor, Kurt, and I discovered that (according to a strict interpretation of the regulations) a flight instructor could go blind and still legally conduct that biennial flight review for another pilot. We all knew that the FAA's game was inherently silly. Yet we had to submit to it. It was like being in the air force. So our only comfort was to delight in such monuments to FAA absurdity. "The Blind Flight Instructor" was a real find, we thought, and we went around telling everyone who would listen.

That sort of gaff is not just the result of bad grammar. It's also a great example of the government's misguided compulsion to control something that won't submit to control. There is an element involved in flight—in certain kinds of flight more than others—and it can't be named. It is a spiritual element, and although it's obvious, it has no name, and so it remains invisible. It gives FAA gurus fits trying to devise a rule, and then another rule, to pin it down and make it mandatory, but since they won't admit that it exists, they can't name it, and it remains beyond the reach of their rules.

If they could admit that it exists, it might read something like this: Rule #10,001: You must be cool.

The FAA finds it difficult to state the reason, too: You must be cool, or *else you will die.* Any experienced flight instructor can tell if another pilot has it or not. It's an easy test. You don't even have to fly with someone; you can tell by the way a person moves.

In fact, as Kurt and I discovered, the reason that you can be blind and still give flight instruction is that what you really need is this spirit of coolness. After all, I had never seen my father anywhere near an airplane.

■ ■ ■

I went to California to study aerobatics with Randy Gagne, the Canadian national champion, and a member of the U.S. Aerobatics Team. We met at Van Nuys Airport north of Los Angeles to fly his Pitts Special. As he was briefing me on how he wanted to conduct the flight, he mentioned certain things he wished me to do and not to do in order to keep from getting killed, and that led to a discussion of aerobatics accidents and of whether or not the whole business was just inherently dangerous. I wanted to own a Pitts Special, but I had never flown solo in one.

"Since 1981, I've counted an average of six pilots a year we've lost in aerobatics," Randy told me. "But a lot of them have just had it stamped on their forehead—" And here he made as if he were putting a rubber stamp on himself, bringing his fist to his forehead: "'I Am Going to Die in an Air Crash.'"

Randy was short and thick with untamed curly brown hair and a smile that made it look as if someone had tickled him from behind. It was hard to stay dead serious around Randy. He had genuine and original pilot style. He smoked Marlboros incessantly in that pilot-style of smoking that is so unbearably cool, as if to say: "Yep. Take a good look: I'm on fire, and I don't even mind it." When he explained the physical act of flight, his hands made the most remarkable *pas de deux*, transforming themselves into different shapes and flying past each other with speed and grace to illustrate a point (with smoke coming from his Marlboro).

I asked him what it was that he'd seen in those people who had the stamp of death on their foreheads.

"It's just an attitude," he said. "They don't listen. They don't learn. They know everything. You can't teach them anything. They're not open."

He'd hit on an important idea. If we're open, we can receive. If our cup is full, then anything that's put in is wasted.

I began to understand why the FAA could not write rules about these things. The FAA was a government bureaucracy that had been set up to administer the activities of people who were on a spiritual quest. In unlocking the puzzle, we are faced with an answer that seems like a paradox. Government bureaucracies deal in linear equations, and this was curved space. If you know everything, you know nothing. Ignorance is wisdom. Safety is danger.

■ ■ ■

On our first day out, we climbed through a layer of broken clouds to get the altitude we needed to practice ten-turn spins. As I found a hole in the cloud deck and pointed the nose toward sunshine, Randy took the controls and said, "Let me show you something." He sat in front and I sat in back of the tiny red biplane. We spoke through the intercom headsets we wore.

Randy demonstrated how, by putting the airplane between the sun and the cloud and by tilting it just so, he could make a perfectly circular rainbow, refracted by the thin oboe reed of our wings, and projected down onto our shadow, right on the frothy surface of the clouds below. We flew along, dancing with our rainbow, and he said, "Isn't that neat? When the top of the cloud is flat, you can make a big rainbow and then spin down through the center of it."

I came for what I thought was technical flight training, and here I had found a peculiar little wizard who wanted to teach me to spin down through the center of my own rainbow. What imagination could have guessed at this lesson? Was it genius? Wisdom? Lunacy?

It was the temptation of the Buddha: The trick is to overcome fear, to let go and see the beauty and transcend the instinct to hold on tight. Joseph Campbell, in describing the three temptations of the Buddha, said, "Then the Lord of Lust turned himself into the Lord of Death and flung at the Buddha all the weapons of an army of monsters. But the Buddha had found in himself that still point within, which is of eternity, untouched by time. So again, he was not moved, and the weapons flung at him turned into flowers of worship." The Buddha, in short, was cool. So Randy had showed me how to turn my fear into rainbows. We were learning the first lesson of the fighter pilot, the stunt pilot, the aerobaticist: The lesson in coolness. It's not a lesson in *acting* cool. It's a lesson in *being* cool. It's a lesson in turning a twisting anxiety into a calm awareness.

When we were ready to spin, Randy said, "Okay, now bury the stick."

In order to spin, I had to stall, and in order to stall (at least upright) I had to pull the stick all the way back. In other words, bury it in my gut—to draw something to me, to take it in without flinching. It was a motion like hari-kari—putting a sword in my gut. Hence: Bury the stick. And there was something final and peaceful about it. The engine power was at idle, the airplane was stalled a mile above the earth, and we just dangled there for a moment, inexplicably, before dropping into the violent world of a spin.

An ordinary spin was enough to make anyone dizzy, but Randy had more and better varieties of spins to confound and terrify the unwary. I was no stranger to spinning airplanes, both in practice and in competition. But Randy taught me ways of winding it up that felt like certain recipes for suicide. The world—the blue dome of the sky and the green dome of the earth—twirled into a brown primordial slime. And when the spins stopped, we'd be pointed straight for the ground, and when I'd pull out, my vision would go gray as the leech of centrifugal force turned my blood to liquid lead and drew it from my brain.

Just as the Eskimos have two hundred distinct names for snow, we have as many names for spins. On the third day of training, we practiced inverted flat spins. Randy called it "Mr. Toad's Wild Ride." The inverted flat spin is the most profane and sinister menace of any old-time flying movie—we've all seen it—where a plane is hopelessly whirling and diving toward the ground, while an officer in the tower calls desperately into a microphone: "Pull up! Pull up!" Indeed, once Randy showed me how to get into the inverted flat spin, I found that I could pull the stick, push the stick, kick the rudder right or left, and the plane responded about like a donkey pushed out of a cargo plane. It just kept tumbling stupidly toward the earth.

I glanced out the window. The world looked like cookie dough. My throat was sealed with the diphtheria of panic.

Until a few years ago, this would have been the end of us both, just as it was in the movies. No one understood how to get out of inverted flat spins, and there were all sorts of mystical schools of thought on the subject. Randy told me, "Eight years ago the inverted flat spin was just black magic. Pilots thought that when you got into an inverted flat spin, gremlins came out and danced on the wings to tell you it was your day to die. Nobody knew exactly how it worked or how to get out of it. Everybody had a different technique. And people died from it on a regular basis. Only now, since Gene Beggs has publicized the correct method, do we all know the same thing for the first time in history." Gene Beggs was an aerobatics pilot who went back and rediscovered a foolproof method for recovering from spins. He discovered it accidentally, by doing it and by being aware and calm enough to remember what he had done in that moment of facing the whirling demon, his own death.

The very concept stopped me in my tracks: that throughout the development of powered flight, of fighter planes, through World War II, through the process of sending people to the moon, through it all we had never learned the secret of the inverted flat spin. Not until, more or less by accident, some accidental hero figured it out in the mid-1980s. I especially loved the idea because it was not a victory won by science. It was a mystical epiphany, born in the wild and racing terrified brain and heart of a lonely pilot, discovering first principles as he spun to his death. Then somehow he was snatched back and had the presence of mind—the spirit—to remember what he'd done.

Well, the secret was out, and Randy taught it to me: Chop the power to idle. Let go of the stick. Then—and only then—kick the rudder. Like the combination to a safe, it won't work in any other order.

No wonder it took us so long to learn. It was the opposite of everything we were after. We wanted absolute control, and this was the most confounding and unthinkable paradox: If you haven't been truly out of control, you haven't been truly in control.

"Now, you just saw how disoriented you can become, and I had prepared you for what was coming," Randy said. "Can you imagine having this happen when you're not expecting it? You'd hit the ground before you could figure out whether to take a shit or tip your hat."

I understood the lesson: To regain control, we have to let go. Randy put it another way: "Anytime you find that you're fighting the airplane, the airplane's going to win. Let go."

One day my seven-year-old daughter, Amelia, came to me after watching a Coyote and Road Runner cartoon and asked me why, when the coyote ran off the cliff, he didn't fall until he looked down. Moreover (she wanted to know), why didn't he just refuse to look down, and then he could go, "wherever he wanted to go?" By asking why the fact of being afraid made the coyote fall, Amelia had hit upon a universal principle. To show fear, even if we show it only to ourselves, is to fall from grace, to fall physically, to fall spiritually, to die.

In *Snow Leopard*, Peter Matthiessen points out that in the language of Nepal, the word for "falling off" and the word for "clinging" are cognate. In other words, if we hold on too tightly, we may squander our energy in vain and be unable to save ourselves. Put it another way: Attitude is everything. To stay cool is the ultimate achievement. So then there was truly something of substance in my childish craving to be cool like my father. A nervous pilot, like a nervous mountaineer, is lost.

■ ■ ■

One day I met an old man out on the ramp, and we struck up a conversation. His name was Will, and he was dressed in blue cotton work pants and a colorless old corduroy shirt. Will was tall and thin and his face was deeply lined. He had sad eyes and a mouth that seemed too wide and moved in such a mobile fashion that it almost seemed he wore a rubber mask. One side would smile while the other frowned. He was filled with passion, which he held at bay as if it were an animal he could barely control. Incipient tears of joy and sadness sparkled in his eyes as he recalled learning to fly in the 1930s in a Curtiss Jenny when he was sixteen years old.

Will said, "My instructor was an old barnstormer. He did wing walking, parachuting—a little bit of everything." Will had "done a few takeoffs and landings, I guess. Then one day we were out flying, when I felt a tap on my shoulder and looked around just in time to see him climbing out of the cockpit."

His instructor leaped clear of the plane, and Will saw a parachute open.

"I guess that was my first solo flight," he said, and he seemed perfectly willing to leave his story right there, with the sixteen-year-old boy suspended in air, while his instructor floated to the ground.

"Well, what happened?" I asked. "Were you scared?"

"I was terrified," he said. "Of course, I was scared."

"What did he say when you landed?"

"'I see you got down all right,' was all he said," Will told me. And then he walked away.

I called after him. I wanted to know more. But he turned and gave me a sad smile and was gone. I never saw him again.

I'd like to say that flight instruction has come a long way since then, but it hasn't. On the fifth day flying with Randy, we were working on landings, talking to the control tower, coming in, landing, going around again, landing again, around and around, when finally on the approach, he said, "How would you feel if I got out on this next one and let you take it around yourself?"

There was a long silence before my answer, because there was something stuck in my throat. The Pitts Special S2B is a 260-horsepower rocket sled, and it rides on three tiny wheels that are so close together that it can turn in tight circles just as easily as it can go straight. It's impossible to see the runway while landing—the engine's in the way—so it's all done with feel, faith, and finesse. I had been doing it, to be sure, but somehow Randy was like Dumbo's feather: taking him away was sure to make me fall. I was Wiley Coyote about to look down. When new pilots make their first solo flights, there is a ceremony, and shirttails are ripped and inscribed with the date. The Pitts Special is so difficult to land that it's the only aircraft for which a second solo celebration is considered appropriate. I've seen thirty-thousand-hour airline pilots get their shirttails clipped after soloing a Pitts for the first time.

I landed and taxied up to the tower, and Randy got out. The tower controller wondered what we were doing, so Randy told him that he was soloing a student. When Randy was gone, and I was taxiing out toward the end of the runway, the tower called me and said, "Sir, is this your first Pitts solo?"

"Affirm," was all I said. I was concentrating hard on being here now. My older daughter, Elena, and I have been writing a document we call *The Rules of Life* and that is our first rule: Be Here Now.

When it's time to fly alone, it's as if we feel a tap on the shoulder and look around to see that our instructor has leaped out. What a harsh and beautiful and lonely place that is. I pushed the throttle forward and the right rudder in, and the airplane erupted down the runway, gobbled up the white line, and was gone in the air before I knew what had happened—Randy weighed two hundred pounds, and I had lost my ballast.

I took the gleaming red airplane around just the way we'd been doing. It felt so good. It was so cool. And when I greased it on and rolled out on the high-speed taxiway, the tower controller called me and said, "Nice job. Congratulations."

How transcendent is the feeling when, using what we have learned and by our own skill, we save our own skin and cause ourselves to be reunited with the earth and its people. Then we have truly done something.

■　■　■

I flew with Randy for a week and came to know him as a modest master. He never did anything to show off, but only to make a point that might help to open my perceptions. The world of aerobatics is just one big optical illusion anyway, and often Randy would tilt my world on its axis so that I could get a look at it from another angle. It would suddenly pop the illusion, and I'd see the way things really were: It wasn't a black picture on a white background; it was a white picture on a black background. That happened a lot while we were upside down, where up is down and left is right.

Once he had qualified me to recover from inadvertent spins and to land the airplane safely, we concentrated on sharpening my technique for an upcoming contest. Competition aerobatics is considered the best way to perfect flying technique. It is judged according to the precision with which pilots fly a dozen figures in sequence—spins, loops, rolls, hammerheads, Cuban 8s, Immelmans, and so on.

I flew the sequence a few times, and Randy said he thought I could place in the top five if I didn't lose my concentration during the stress of competition. He gave me a few tips to help improve my scores. The maneuvers involved a lot of climbing and diving. I was pulling a lot of G's, flipping over on my back, tumbling down, up, and backward. By the time we'd been through it several times, I was tired and my flying had started to become a little ragged.

Randy took the controls, and said, "Let me show you something. I'm going to fly the sequence the way it's supposed to be flown." *Great* thought. I wanted to see it done precisely so that I could imitate what I saw. Then he added, "Only I'm going to fly it with my eyes closed and my head down. Just tell me when we're vertical."

Instinctively I reached out for something to hold onto, but there was nothing in that bubble-canopy Pitts. Hanging up there five thousand feet above the ground north of the Santa Susana Pass, the small tan river of mud snaking through the valley below, green mountains rising on either side, I suddenly felt a terror grip my heart. Randy was going to fly the entire sequence with his eyes closed? This seemed to me to be the height of madness and certain to end in one of those violent spins to the ground. And yet I felt that, in keeping with this spirit of coolness that we had developed, I could hardly refuse to go along with him. A bond of trust is forged between instructor and student—but perhaps *trust* is the wrong word. It's more like the hold a charismatic cult leader has on a new convert: It's so strong that the student would follow the instructor anywhere, even to certain death.

As my mind raced, searching for some logic in this situation, which seemed to defy everything I had struggled to learn up until that point, I remembered being back home with my instructor, Kurt, laughing and discovering that legally a flight instructor could be blind. I watched Randy bow his head down low, as if in prayer. I thought: This is *insane*. Maybe the FAA knows something I don't know. Maybe it really is all right to be blind.

Back in the sixties, a friend of mine used to say, "A blown mind is an open mind." Now as Randy began the sequence, my mind was completely open. And utterly blown.

The aircraft rolled inverted, and I forced myself to let go and relax. The mountains slid down one side of the canopy and sneaked up the other as smoothly as if stage hands moved a scrim.

I looked at the back of Randy's head. He wasn't peeking. Anyway, I had come to know him well enough to feel certain that he'd never cheat at such a thing. I could trust him: He would die first.

Split S. Loop. Immelman. How did he do that?

I was watching lovely competition maneuvers being done by a blind man. I began to relax for real now. Giving myself over to the madness of it, I laughed out loud. Nothing in my fifteen years of flying could have prepared me for this.

A level 360-degree turn doesn't seem like much of a feat, but he started out pointing west and ended up pointing exactly west, and that's akin to driving the family car around the block blindfolded. Spin-and-a-quarter: Right on heading. I called the vertical line for him on the way down.

He pulled the nose to the horizon, and I found that we were headed straight for one of those green mountains at eyeball level. Rather than telling him to watch out for the mountain, I found myself laughing. Was this true chaos, or had we reached some new pinnacle of transcendent order? In those few maneuvers, I had somehow developed a complete faith in Randy's ability to fly aerobatics blindfolded.

I could see cows and power lines, but sure enough, before we hit the mountain, he pulled up to a hammerhead. Once again I called the vertical line for him on the way up. He turned on a wing tip and found the precise vertical line down.

Working up to the finish, he drew a figure called a fish hook, in which he angled upward, rolled inverted, and then dove straight toward the ground. There is no sensation quite like being a passenger in an airplane that is pointed straight at the ground, going 160 knots, piloted by a man who insists on keeping his eyes shut.

Perhaps more remarkable was that he pulled out exactly at three thousand feet, where we were supposed to be. Almost as an afterthought, as we headed for that mountain again, he completed the last figure, a two-point roll—bam: inverted. Bam: Upright. Dead solid perfect. Had it been a contest, he would have easily placed near the top.

"Your airplane," he said, handing me back the controls. I could barely fly I was so shaken.

"So you see," he went on smoothly, as if nothing at all unusual had happened, finally raising his head and looking around, "you do need to watch the horizon and look at your reference points, but it's really a matter of feel more than anything."

■ ■ ■

Several years ago, before I met Randy, before my father's reawakening, before I flew a Pitts, I had started out to write a book about what I was calling "dangerous professions." But after a while some strange subjects began to creep in: My friend Roberta, the brain surgeon. Or me: Upon a mountain in Montana, down in a nightclub in Austin, or in a hospital puzzling out how to deal with cancer. I began to see that it wasn't danger that defined my quest. It was something inside of us. I've been calling it coolness, a cool place in the heart, a place where we can be calm and aware while doing something difficult, something that would be impossible to do without that inner place of coolness from which to think and function smoothly.

The essays that follow represent encounters with people on a quest for that place. Most are not heroes. After a lifetime of being the apprentice, I believe that heroes are made by events that we can't control. We can only control our readiness for events, and even then we can't know if we are preparing for the right event. That's why we play games with such passion. It's one time when we can prepare for a predictable event, master it, and achieve the sense of becoming a hero.

Glacier National Park

on the Last American Wilderness

Already we could see a snowstorm forming at the higher elevations. Mountain peaks dissolved and reappeared inside the clouds. Ducks glided in by twos and landed on the rain-freaked surface of Swiftcurrent Lake. The view exerts a supernatural pull, and soon we were off on what we thought would be an easy mid-morning walk in a landscape that provides what many experienced backpackers consider the best hiking in America: Glacier National Park.

Half an hour out, the trail divided. We could take the short "nature walk" around the lake, or we could go up into the mountains. "It's not raining *that* hard," I said.

"Let's go up," Paula said. "We can always turn back."

This then is how it happens. This is how it happens to those who invite it to happen, and this is how it happens to people like us who do not. Here on this gentle trail a number of streams run together, and what starts as a trickle of good intentions gradually grows to a torrent of inevitable consequences.

We ascended the high trail in heavy forest. We'd been hiking the trails of Glacier for almost a week, and the soreness was gone. Now there was this new misty view of everything, as if the woods had caught fire and the smoke was blowing two ways at once. The dreamy effect drew us in. Each step felt lighter than the last. With each step I felt myself thinking that just one more step would be sufficient. It was not, and like a drinker late at the saloon, I moved steadily onward by trifling increments.

It did not seem as if we had walked that far, but soon we came upon a sign for Grinnell Lake; and although it lay five kilometers away and in the wrong direction, that became our new destination. We were in a dark wood. A virgin forest of firs and pines and cedars rose black and dripping on all sides, hung with the mossy bunting of silver-green mists. Occasional piles of bear scat, dissolving in the rain and pebbled with berries, reminded us that here on the Canadian border we were in the last stronghold of grizzly and mountain lion, and that whatever else we were doing, we were trespassing.

Grizzly bears (*Ursus arctos*) are the most dangerous land animals in the world, their only rival being the polar bear. Even a cursory pass through the naturalists' reports on encounters between bears and humans will make us believers: "Nearby was a piece of lip and scalp with hair still attached. The bear apparently pulled Fredenhagen out of the tent by her neck. . . . Fredenhagen's body was found 250 feet from the tent. Quite a bit of her soft tissue had been eaten."

The following is from an official park report about the attack of a grizzly on a couple camped near Granite Park Chalet, not far from where we stayed:

> While in a sound sleep [Roy Ducat] remembered being awakened by Julie [Hegelson] who was nearby. She told him to pretend he was dead. Roy stated that he and Julie were suddenly knocked about five feet outside of their sleeping bags by a blow. He recalled being on his stomach facing down. Julie was about two feet away. The bear "gnawed" into his right shoulder. Roy made every effort to remain still and kept his eyes closed. The bear then went to Julie and chewed on her, but soon returned and chewed on Roy's left arm and the back of both legs near his buttocks but he did not once utter a sound. The bear again returned to Julie and chewed on her.

The bear eventually dragged Julie away and killed her. Roy survived his injuries to tell the story. Bears were an important influence in our decision to stay in a hotel and not in a tent. Glacier has the worst record of any national park for bear attacks.

■ ■ ■

The way parted ahead. Sunlight reflected off of something metallic, and suddenly we had stepped out of the forest and onto the shores of a hidden lake. I had been worrying about bears, and yet, standing still now for a few moments on the edge of Grinnell Lake, I began to realize that bears had little to do with the precarious nature of our circumstances. Our $3.99 ponchos were not holding up very well, being nothing more than glorified garbage bags. Waterfalls undulated like Arabian horsetails against the black and shining mountain walls, which rose abruptly from the lake and vanished into gray vapors. Only now could I appreciate the tiny white pellets bouncing around in crazy patterns on the ground as the rain fell. I stooped down. Water poured from my hood. I touched the ground.

"I think it's called hail," Paula said.

A faint rumble of thunder, a mocking laugh from up the mountain, told us the rest of the story. "Are you wet?" I asked.

"I'm pretty wet," she said from under her blue poncho.

We started back as the reality of what we had done descended. We'd been doing fifteen-mile hikes in high alpine territory, but the weather had been fine so far. We'd become complacent—disdainful, in fact. Anyway, we had planned this as a twenty-minute walk around the lake. Now the cold began to rummage in my bones, and I could feel myself shivering. We had no packs, no water, no food, inadequate clothing. I recalled the story of Ranger Pierce, who died while walking from the town of Cut Bank to St. Mary's ranger station in 1913. He was caught out by the weather. One report of his death said, "When at last he sat down beside the trail to wait for death he placed his snowshoes' points upward in the snow beside him. He sat there, and the snow came down and covered him. They found him the next day by the points of his snowshoes."

We decided to jog. Splashing in the freezing mud, suffocating now in the smells of rotted pine and rain and cold vinyl, I understood the treachery of the mountain that had seduced us.

■ ■ ■

We ran what seemed a very long and icy way through the forest, with thunder rolling off the mountain and hail falling all around (big hail now, clattering through high branches) and water squirting through layered socks. Eventually we found ourselves panting at a fork in the trail, trying to decide which way to go.

"Let's go back the way we came," she said.

"It may be shorter the other way," I said.

We were on the point of arguing, actually, when we heard human voices. Listen: Salvation or ridicule? Should we hide from them or approach and show our pitiful selves? Most of us would rather die than be embarrassed. "It's the boat dock," Paula said.

She was right: We had walked a wide half circle on cliff sides around the long and skinny lakes that filled this glacial valley. Returning, we had come straight down, and now we'd stumbled onto the Josephine Lake sightseeing boat. It was screened from us by only a few yards of forest.

We plunged through the woods and burst into the open at the dock, where a group of tourists in colorful rain gear boarded a boat. We skidded down the embankment, ran up the plank past the startled face of a park ranger, and leapt aboard just as she cast off. A moment later we were underway—the last boat of the day, as it turned out. Halfway across the lake, the hailstorm set in with a purpose, hammering like machine-gun fire on the wooden hull. Soon it turned to freezing rain, sleet, and finally to a wet, heavy snow that came at us sideways and stuck. The front window of the boat was obscured by ice. The pilot put his head out the side to see.

I doubt that we would have perished if we'd missed the boat, but I'm sure Ranger Pierce doubted he would perish, too, when he set out. It showed us how fast the weather could turn. Each small step seems insignificant, but in the tumbling geometry of those mountains, the steps can add up quickly. One experienced hiker said, "I've never hiked in Glacier that I didn't get some hairs on the back of my neck standing up somewhere for some reason—weather, bears, *something*..." The park is a Rorschach. It never reveals its own nature, but it can tell us a lot about ourselves.

■　■　■

Months later now, I can still feel myself being drawn back. I'm afraid I'll just pitch everything one of these days and get on a plane to Kalispell. Anything can set me off: the first flurries of snow at Thanksgiving, the sight of a trail rising into woods and darkness, even the scent of pine and fur caught on the wind. Suddenly I'm out of the Midwest and back there, standing in a place where you can spit straight down three thousand feet into a lake on one side, and on the other side you can throw a stone that will simply vanish without ever hitting anything at all. The Northern Rockies of Montana. This is the end of the world, the place where weather is manufactured for the rest of the country; the great engine of these mountains whips it up like gray meringue and sends it howling down on toward Minnesota and points east. The last stand of wolf, lion, mountain goat, and bear. There's even one ten-thousand-foot peak that's never been climbed. (Glacier does not invite technical climbing; the billion-year-old sedimentary mudstone simply comes apart in your hands. It's like trying to climb up the side of a giant mushroom.)

Glacier is some of the last true wilderness, a place of strange, beautiful, even dangerous, gifts. Two children, one in 1990, another in 1991, were attacked by mountain lions while walking with their parents. Only one road goes through the park, a scant seventy-six miles of paving, as against the more than seven hundred miles of trail. We take satisfaction in the knowledge that we can still get killed here, even in a time when Going-to-the-Sun Road leads from Canada to the K-mart in Kalispell.

Glacier National Park is bisected by the Continental Divide. The eastern side is alpine. The western side is rain forest. On both sides there are lakes large enough to have whitecaps on them when the wind is blowing, which seems to be most of the time.

Visitors who arrive by airplane or train will find themselves on the west side of the park. There, the Village Inn at Apgar commands a view of Lake McDonald that is worth the entire trip. We first saw it early one morning when the mountains were white with snow. Clouds had descended over the lake and hung in a billowing fleet just a few dozen feet off the water as if the white mountains were calving icebergs of vapor.

Travelers who arrive by car from the east will see no foothills. The mountains rise so abruptly it appears as if the earth caught fire and flames of rock leaped to the sky in tongues of blue, red-tipped and hoary with snow, while their smoke is made by the clouds of a storm in perpetual approach. Undulating formations of rock gyrate upward. Fringes of copper green climb and dance the ridges. Walls of red smoke work their way up, where the wind grabs the fleece of snow and spins it into endless bolts of blue sky.

Although it has always seemed to draw people inexorably inward, Glacier was never hospitable. The tourist season is essentially June, July, and August. By September crews are removing the road signs, which would be flattened by one-hundred-foot snowdrifts if they were left out. Even before Europeans came, the Indians, it appears, only ventured in with caution or under duress or on eccentric errands of magic. Blackfeet braves, as part of their initiation into manhood, went into the wilderness to fast and pray until they received a medicine vision. This was known as the warrior's sleep. A buffalo skull, presumably from such a ritual, was found atop 9,066-foot Chief Mountain, a place where no bison could go.

Our first experience there was a sorcerer's sleep. We flew from Chicago to Salt Lake City to Kalispell, where we rented a car to cross Going-to-the-Sun Road from Belton to St. Mary—possibly the most beautiful drive in the United States. The trail head was right out in the hotel parking lot; within an hour we were fording a waterfall atop a cliff that descended into a gorge, where a cataract sprayed white noise and icy water up the rising wind that probed the canyon.

We reached Iceberg Lake at an elevation of six thousand feet. Above the cliff the sun was dissolving like a luminous tablet in boiling clouds. A five-hundred-year-old glacier hugged the mountain, gradually melting into the aqua-green of a lake that was just on the point of freezing solid like a chemical sapphire.

That night there was a tornado. It left the hotel standing, but it shook the old timbers until the building swayed back and forth. On the banks of Swiftcurrent Lake, looking up the sharp slopes of the Lewis Range toward the Continental Divide, the Many Glacier Hotel is built like a Swiss chalet, constructed from local stone and trees that were taken straight out of the surrounding forests in 1915. The workers must have ripped the branches off and roughed the trees down to their present thirty-inch girth with hand tools. The ones in the main lobby create a vaulted hollow nave four stories tall, with the rooms arranged on balconies all around. In the middle of the night the timbers swayed like fishing poles, and the furniture moved. Old-timers said the hotel hadn't shaken like that in seventy-five years.

■　■　■

From the first, everyone wanted to own this land, and in the end, no one has been able to maintain a hold on it. In 1670, Charles II gave the Hudson's Bay Company possession of all the "waters which flow into Hudson's Bay," which is to say, about half of what is now called Waterton-Glacier International Peace Park, a 724-square-mile tract of mountain wilderness set aside as national park land by Canada and the United States and joined by treaty in 1932. In the 262 years between those two dates, everyone who saw the place tried to make it pay, but no one could, and no one ever has.

In 1886 oil was discovered in the area, and for a while it was thought that Glacier would finally pay its way and justify its existence, but the gushers quickly turned to a trickle. Similarly, in 1890 copper was found at a number of locations, and there was a brief mining boom, during which the east side of the park, which had been given to the Blackfeet as a reservation, was hastily bought back by the U.S. Government and opened to mining—not to let them keep anything of value. Altyn and St. Mary became boom towns, but the mines petered out. Nothing, it seemed, could make those mountains pay. Even today, the hotels operate at a loss.

Like the search for the Northwest Passage long after it ceased to have any commercial value, the struggle for possession of the Glacier area continued. By 1891 the railroad had pushed through to Kalispell. It is literally possible today to get on a subway in Manhattan, take it to the Grand Central Station, board Amtrak, and get off two days later in Belton, right across the way from Glacier Park Lodge. From there it's all on foot; the trails lead directly into the mountains.

George Bird Grinnell was an eastern aristocrat who liked to hunt big game in Glacier. He used his political influence to start the movement to dedicate the park. In May 1910 President William Howard Taft signed into law a bill that would attempt simultaneously to create and destroy Glacier National Park, proposing as it did that the park be "protected" and "developed." It was not altogether different from Charles II's gesture in giving the land to the Hudson's Bay Company. As one of the first journalists to go there in 1916 wrote, "I object to the word 'Park' ... A park is a civilized spot. . . . [Glacier] is the wildest part of America. If the Government had not preserved it, it would have preserved itself."

■ ■ ■

The second day we were there, a black bear put its paw through a car window to get food. "It feasted on the tortilla chips," Park Ranger Bob

Arbogast told me, "and then finished it off with a bag of marshmallows. Then it took a box of pasta and hid it unopened behind a building for future use. The bears are extremely smart." All that morning Arbogast listened to the rangers whispering on the radio across the mountains. A number of rangers wanted the bear's life spared, and they were trying, as he put it, "to bend park policy a little and have the bear relocated." (In the death of photographer Charles Gibbs, the sow that attacked him had not been killed. Recognizing that Gibbs had been at fault, the foremost bear expert in North America, Stephen Herrero, said that was "a courageous management call.")

Gary Gregory, the park's supervisory natural resource management specialist, made the distinction between the sow that Gibbs had surprised with her cubs and a bear that's after human food: "Those are food-conditioned bears. They cannot be allowed to stay in the park. The first six fatalities in Glacier were by food-conditioned bears, as are most injuries from black bears. Back in the thirties and forties there were multiple injuries every year when the bears had access to garbage and people fed them along roads." Until the 1960s, the garbage from the millions of visitors was kept in open dumps, and the bears fed there freely. Moreover, people fed the bears, thinking that their begging behavior was a sign of tameness. The bears simply made the connection: *You can get food from people.* This often translated into: *If you're hungry, attack a person.* Gregory said, "You can read the ranger logs from back then and see that nearly every day there were injuries. Bears became camp marauders. For years those bears were relocated, but now everyone recognizes that they're too dangerous." Moreover, relocation doesn't necessarily work. One park ranger at Glacier, who lived in a cabin in the woods, found a bear sleeping on his porch. After a few days, the rangers relocated the bear seventy miles across the park. The bear was back, sleeping on the porch again, six days later.

Arbogast said, "Once they've gotten that human food, they've got one thing on their mind forever more when they see people, and that makes them dangerous sooner or later."

People who hike the back country often are surprised by the strictness of the rangers, who see their job as protecting the bears and the park, not the people. When a bear attacks a hiker or camper, it is the human's fault. If a bear gets so much as a candy wrapper, chances are

that the bear will eventually have to be shot. As Bob Arbogast put it, "A fed bear is a dead bear."

"The policy has worked," said Gregory. In the years between 1958 and 1977 there were an average of 28 incidents of property damage per year by marauding bears. During the period of 1985 to 1991 the new policy regarding garbage and feeding reduced the rate to 1.3 incidents per year. The rate went up again during 1992. "We had a rash of problem bears," Gregory said, "as everyone in Montana did this year." The reasons seemed to be a shortage of the bears' natural food supplies, a general failure of the huckleberry crop, and a growing bear population. The bears have been protected successfully and they are thriving.

Grizzly bears generally attack when people stumble upon them by accident. Just before we arrived, a couple encountered a female with cubs on the Swiftcurrent Trail and the man was mauled, the most common type of accident. But sometimes bears simply feed on humans for no known reason. Now as we hike these trails, we understand that we are in constant contact with the bears—they see us all the time; they are everywhere, and we're trespassing on their land. It's up to them whether we see them or not.

■ ■ ■

We had just come off of several days of hiking when we found the Park Cafe in St. Mary. It's easy to miss. Paula happened to notice the sign that says "Home Made Pies" and the potted plants on the whitewashed porch and pointed out that whoever had taken the trouble to hang those plants would have taken some trouble in baking those pies as well.

Inside we found classical music playing softly. Homemade curtains hung on the windows. The servers were friendly, well read, and well scrubbed. I asked a waitress who I might thank for the miracle of blackberry pie in these austere mountains, and a moment later Kathryn Hiestand came scrambling out of the kitchen. Without warning she sat peering at us through the pencil-line circles of her spectacles. She said nothing as she waited for us to explain our presence.

Kathryn had sharp, clean features. Light brown hair rose cleanly from her thin face, rounded the summit, and descended in the steep rappel of a pigtail to the middle of her back. We told her that we wanted to know where the best hiking was, and she looked at us incredulously.

She took a sharp inhalation of breath, and I thought for a moment that she would answer the question. Then she shook her head and bolted. She was gone.

It took days and a lot of persuasion, but Kathryn eventually told us a little bit about herself. "Starting when I was twenty-two years old," she said, "I wrote the Blackfeet man who owned this place every year until he got old enough and gave in and sold it to me. I didn't want the gift shop next door, but that was part of the deal." Neal Miller, her husband, fixes and maintains things. He and Kathryn live in a canvas tepee out in back of the cafe.

We came to understand that Kathryn was a human image of the place. She had become the expression, in flesh and blood and affect, of Glacier—its sharpness, its moody propensity for abrupt change in weather. Kathryn and her followers formed a cult of the park, a cult of secret trails not listed on the charts. I began to see why she had abruptly left the table when we asked about the best trails. Even if she had wanted to tell us, her trails had no names; the destinations appeared on no map. Our hikes took us fifteen miles out and two thousand feet up. Their hikes began where we turned back.

While Kathryn was reluctant to tell us where to hike, one of her servers, Joseph, was more than happy to oblige. Joseph was a Minnesota premed student, working his second summer at the Park Cafe. Joseph had a quiet laugh and seemed perpetually amused by something. When we asked his advice, he hunkered down on one knee by the table and said, "We're going to climb Heaven's Peak tomorrow if the weather holds. It's going to be Fan-*Tas*-Tick." He said we were welcome to come along, describing it at length and mentioning very casually and only at the end that the best part was "Class Five. Fan-*Tas*-Tick! It's a pull, and there's going to be a lot of bushwhacking and scree scrambling, but you can do it." *The Climber's Guide to Glacier National Park* by G. Gordon Edwards, which is the bible of the Park Cafe, has this to say: "Class 5. Severe. High rock work where pitons may be used and climbers should be roped for safety."

That night we were having dinner with a park ranger. I told him about our invitation from Joseph to climb Heaven's Peak, and he practically blew dark roast Sumatran coffee through his nose. "You got advice from Joseph!" Then he lowered his voice and leaned in

confidentially. "That boy is trying to get himself killed," he said. "*Never take advice from Joseph.*"

Fortunately, a blizzard helped us to decline Joseph's invitation gracefully. But the following night he knelt beside our table, having just come off the mountain. He was red and grinning from the cold. He told us about leaving his group during the snowstorm and hiking alone to the top of a ridge, beneath a waterfall that was trying its best to freeze, and then finding himself wet and cold and stranded, cut off, with no way to get down. Snow swirled around him. His gaiters and Gore-Tex filled with melting snow. Clouds descended. He yelled and yelled until the group found him and helped him down.

"How was it?" Paula asked.

"I thought I was dead. It was Fan-*Tas*-Tick."

I told Kathryn about a 150-mile bicycle route Joseph had recommended to me as "A great ride. You'll love this. It's quite a pull, but it's Fan-*Tas*-Tick." It wound its way up into Canada and back.

She said, "Yeah, did he tell you he broke his collarbone doing it?"

■ ■ ■

We started with the easy trails and worked up. From Lake McDonald on the west side, hiking to Avalanche Lake was a good workout requiring no special endurance or skill, through giant cedars that had been saplings during the Crusades. The terrain was gently mountainous. Along the way we passed the turn-off for the Mount Brown Lookout, which by contrast is a steep and strenuous walk. While the trail to Avalanche Lake climbs only five hundred feet in two miles, the trail to Mount Brown Lookout climbs more than forty-three hundred feet in five and a half miles. The only difference is which fork in the road you take. Of course, all the rules change if the weather changes, which it does—and rapidly. One park ranger told me, "When you go hiking, pack as if you're going to have to spend the night."

From the Many Glacier area on the east side of the park, the hike to Iceberg Lake is alpine in character (i.e., rock trails instead of forest paths) but easy, even though it climbs twelve hundred feet in five miles. The Grinnell Glacier hike involves more exposed climbing on naked cliff side and therefore more impressive vistas, more vertigo, and a few slippery spots where a misstep would leave a person hanging in mid-air over a two-thousand-foot drop to nowhere. That is no small consideration. The mountain goats have a 50 percent mortality rate in the first year of life. The number-one cause of death is falling. In fact, the number-one cause of accidental death in Glacier is falling. (Number one of all is heart attack.)

Despite the obvious risks involved, Grinnell Glacier is only five and a half miles with a sixteen-hundred-foot climb. But the vertical ascent figure is *net;* sometimes we had to climb and descend an additional one thousand feet.

The trail to Cracker Lake climbs fourteen hundred feet over 6.1 miles, but there are no cliff-side trails—it's all open mountainside or high pine forest, crossing several beautiful rivers and streambeds along the way. The day we went to Cracker Lake the weather was warm and sunny. We had been crossing boulder fields and rolling slopes below the cliffs of Allen Mountain, when far below our trail the lake appeared so suddenly that it had the quality of a bright and shimmering blue-green hallucination. The peculiar color of the lakes in Glacier, like nothing else found in nature, is caused by finely powdered rock suspended in the water. This so-called "glacier flour" was left behind by the grinding work of glaciers ten thousand years ago.

We reached a precipice above Cracker Lake and climbed a rock outcropping that was overgrown with wind-sculpted pines and covered with a soft bed of moss and grass. There we were able to get out of the wind and rest in the warm sun. We made a picnic lunch with our feet dangling high over the lake. After an hour of resting together, we dressed again for the six-mile hike back. Since the trail head was literally in the hotel parking lot, we were able to shower and change clothes before going out. On either side of the park, visitors can stay in comfortable hotels (Glacier Park Lodge even has a nine-hole golf course) and still be within an hour's hike of extreme wilderness. The special gift of Glacier is that it allows us to move so quickly and seemingly without transition from comfort to peril. The special trick is to pay attention.

■　■　■

Although part of the mystique of Glacier National Park is the alluring notion that we may die in some romantic fashion, quite naturally we don't really want to die. We want the safe illusion that we can come close and walk out unscathed from this place where others have perished. That illusion of mastery and special dispensation sustains us and gives flavor to the walks we take. Even on the lower western side, we'd find evidence in piles of bear scat as big and black as twisted car mufflers, lying and sometimes still steaming in the middle of the trails. One day we were able to watch a bear rip apart a mountain ash no more than ten feet away. That was before we learned that no sensible person should come that close by choice. But good sense seems to have little to do with it. Like the park itself, the bears can exert a hypnotic pull on people, against which we are defenseless. Some people scuba dive with the sharks at Sharm Al Shek, too.

Charles Gibbs found himself one day with a rare opportunity to photograph a grizzly sow with her cubs. Gary Gregory told me, "He had been around bears a lot and ought to have known better. He came too close. He was alone. Being alone is a bad idea anyway. We know a lot about his situation because he took about forty slides before she attacked." It seems that when the bear beckons, we come ahead, no matter what we know. Gibbs's vast experience as a nature photographer didn't help him. If anything, it may have made him complacent.

That same year, 1987, a lone hiker was killed camping off-trail in a remote wilderness area, but no one knows what happened. He wasn't found for over a month.

A teenage couple was killed in 1980 not far from our hotel. Like Kathryn's people, they were part of a youth cult who came to work in the hotels for the chance to hike. "The bear might have approached the teenagers because of odors from sexual intercourse," Herrero wrote in his excellent book *Bear Attacks*. "Both had been partly consumed. Early the following morning [July 25], Blackfoot Tribe members shot a grizzly bear near the site. Careful autopsy of the bear revealed identifiable remains of the victims still in the bear's digestive tract."

If good sense makes no difference, neither do precautions. Here is an account of a group of women who were sleeping out of doors not far from the Many Glacier Hotel:

> All of the women were experienced campers and hikers.
> They were concerned about bears. They had a clean camp,
> no food was in their tents, they had no deodorants, per-
> fumes, or odorous materials on them, and none of them

was menstruating. They had even left their unlocked car ten feet from their tent as a refuge in case a bear did bother them. . . . Despite their precautions, at around seven in the morning of September 23, Mary Pat Mahoney was dragged from her tent, killed, and partly devoured by a grizzly bear.

Another couple slept with a loaded 30.06 rifle and .44 magnum revolver beside them, and the bear simply ripped a slit in the tent, picked up the man by the head, and dragged him off into the forest. No shots were fired. We might be tempted to think that if guns don't work, maybe brains will: It would stand to reason that nobody ought to be more cautious around bears than a bear scientist, and yet Dr. Gilbert Barrie was very nearly eaten by a grizzly. Seeing Dr. Barrie gives the business of bear attacks a kind of vivid reality that most of us would rather not have. For one thing, half of his face is missing. It is a pale and concave swath of wrinkled scar tissue, like a dead flower, topped by a black eye patch and goggle-like spectacles. The left half of his mouth was ripped away by the first bite.

But despite all the evidence of their ferocity, our fear of bears goes beyond the rational. Statistically, a visitor is more likely to be killed driving through Glacier than hiking. The ranking of deaths by number are heart attacks, falling, drowning, auto accidents, and bear attacks. Not long before we came, a woman leaned out for a better look over a waterfall, and the invisible force just sucked her right into empty space. Cause of death: Falling. Kathryn told us of an experienced mountaineer who was killed by a falling rock while climbing. He was even wearing a helmet. And a couple drowned right in front of the Many Glacier Hotel when their canoe tipped over. They weren't wearing life vests, and the glacial green lake water, enticing as the emerald city of Oz, is too cold for swimming even a short distance.

Even so, those dangers can't inspire the kind of terror that a grizzly bear does. Every gift shop in Glacier sells "Bear Bells," and the tourists wear them in great dangling bunches, although the park rangers assured us that they're not very effective. (The joke among rangers was this: How do you tell the difference between black bear shit and grizzly bear shit? The answer: Grizzly bear shit has bells in it.) The bells I think, like the red warning signs at the trail heads, are a tribute to the bear, not a totem against it. The bear is the spirit of the park—hairy, drooling, capricious, irrational, and hungry—and the signs and bells are part of a ritual. The bear is symbolic of the conflict we feel about wilderness—the wilderness out there, and the wildness within. Still, Glacier is one of the few places where we might actually be eaten (or at least dragged around a bit) by a bear.

"I've never seen a bear on the trail," Kathryn told me. "Not in twelve years."

"How do you avoid it?" I asked.

"We make a lot of noise," she said.

I asked one park ranger to demonstrate how he avoids bears, and he walked down the trail shouting, "Hey, Bear! Yo, Bear! Coming through!" He began singing and whistling and clapping his hands, making a complete fool out of himself as he went. It was preposterous and silly and seemed to go against the contemplative mood of the forest, but he had never seen a bear on the trail either. Soon we found ourselves doing the same.

■　■　■

We hiked to Grinnell Glacier, six miles in, six miles out. The trail was straightforward, but it was cut into the side of the near-vertical face of the mountain with a few places where a slip could result in a real fall. We scrambled over shale stair-step waterfalls, which dripped off into space and were transformed into a rising mist. Halfway up, we saw the bending of rock we'd read about. Under the extraordinary pressure of tectonic movement, rock becomes malleable like wax, and it bends. Here was a pastry braided out of magma, limestone, and marble. Here a whole cliff side, like wood that had been steamed and bowed to make a violin body—great swirls and French curves and boat-hull shapes— had been extruded out of stone. And here the still-born red rock prow of a phantom ship had emerged from the mountain and crumbled.

The story of this bending rock began before the atmosphere of earth contained enough oxygen to support even the simplest animal. More than a billion years ago these were flatlands, which lay beneath a shallow ocean called the Belt Sea. Through hundreds of millions of years, layers of sand, mud, and carbonate sediment (up to thirty-five hundred feet thick in places) were compressed under their own great weight and transformed into shales, limestones, and mudstones.

About 65 million years ago one slab of rock began to slide up over another. The result was the Rocky Mountains. Under the tremendous pressure of its grinding upward slide, some of the rock grew hot and softened like wax and bent into the beautiful shapes we see on the trail to Grinnell Glacier. During the last great ice age the park was completely immersed so that only the highest peaks protruded. The ice flowed, carving the rock.

The Grinnell trail grew slick with newly fallen snow, now melting in sunlight, and yet the hike had warmed me, and I stripped down to a T-shirt. The vertigo was almost erotic at times. The final pitch was a steep field of talus boulders, and as we climbed out of the protection of the rock, we exposed ourselves to the open wind, where the trail vanished in blinding snow. We went from T-shirts to parkas in a few hundred yards, fighting our way to the foot of the gray and jutting glacier. As the last rise in the land dropped away before us, it revealed a startling green lake half-stilled by smoky pancake ice, like the half-blind eye of an old, old cat. The wind picked up clouds of snow and made radiant ghosts across the gloomy crepe-and-asphalt cliffs. High thin clouds drifted against the blue iridescence of the trembling sky.

Nearby, lashed to a rock, was a steel box containing supplies—ice axes and ropes—for people who walk out onto the glacier and fall into a crevasse. A ranger told me, "The crevasses are usually fifty or sixty feet deep, and they get narrower at the bottom. Usually if you fall in, you get wedged in the bottom there in such a way that you can't breathe. You die of suffocation. But if the fall doesn't kill you, hypothermia will finish you off."

"So we're not allowed to go out on the glacier," I said.

"Oh, no," he assured me. "You can go out there. You can go anywhere you want to. *I'm* not going out there, though."

■ ■ ■

Before we left the park, we went to check on the black bear that had been jailed for stealing Tostitos and found that it had been shot. Gary Gregory said, "Nearly every land manager today is unwilling to accept that kind of bear." But even though park policy may kill a few, the bears still own Glacier. Shortly after we left, a lone hiker—John Petranyi, forty, of Madison—was lured back in there off the trails and surprised a female bear and her two cubs at close range. She knocked him down, and he should have stayed down. Investigators learn to read the tracks, the clawing, scratching struggle, the drag marks, and the trail of blood. John Petranyi got up and moved twenty feet before the sow knocked him down again. Once more, he should have stayed down. She was leaving or starting to leave, but John got up again. He made it about six hundred feet down the trail before she came down after him, running in that amazing way only a grizzly can run—it's like a gold mountain leaping off the earth and falling toward you, it's so fast and huge.

"The bears ate him," Gregory said. The three bears were killed. They said it was because they would now have an inclination to attack for food. "If they'd just killed him and moved on, nothing would have been done to the bears," Gregory said. But I think the bears were sacrificed for other reasons.

When a bear kills a human—and especially when a bear eats a human—a momentous transfer of spiritual power takes place that upsets all the assumptions we make about our world. It has the same terrible inverting sense that we get from the crash of an airliner, when the principles we trust to protect us are shattered by the immense power of randomness and chaos. All the bear experts in academia were convened in plenary session when they found John Petranyi. Numerous agencies were involved. The community of bear naturalists (bear worshipers might be more truthful) forms a network like a fine spider web, and this touch of death will make it tremble for years to come. Eventually a report was issued, but it didn't tell us much. We can't know, for example, how the man saw his final moments, as that great wall of muscle rose before him. The report can't tell us what it smelled like to be smothered in the greasy robe of grizzled fur. And it doesn't say this: That bears are intelligent. That when a person goes into Glacier to hike and sleep outdoors alone, it is a strong suggestion to the bears that something is wrong and that the person needs to be eaten. I think the three bears were killed to atone for what we can't say.

Biologists are speculating now that it will be another active year. The bears denned with below average fat, not in as good condition as at the end of a normal year. They're going to be moving around more than usual, looking for food. "But I've been trying to predict for a long time," Gregory said, "and I can't do it. They're very unpredictable."

This then is our difficulty: We want the wilderness served up on a platter. We want that original paradox of the law that created Glacier National Park: We want it wild, we want it safe, we want it all, and we want it now. In other words, we want to be in a Coke commercial. Meanwhile, those who have been captured by the lure of the park, who walk into it every day of their lives and live there as the Blackfeet once did and still do—they understand something that we can't understand in a visit or two or three. And if we try to go in and pretend that we know everything already—if we throw ourselves without humility against the weather, the heights, the bears, the waters—we end up with our very own panel, convened to determine what hypnotic force, what invisible undertow, yanked us from this womb of civilization.

■ ■ ■

We sat in the Park Cafe one night and watched the snow make patterns like spider web in the incandescent parking lot lights, while Kathryn talked about sitting at that same table during a forest fire a few years earlier. "It jumped the lake. It was an incredibly jumpy fire. It was in September, and the wind was high." She thought about that for a moment. "Well, the wind's always high on this side. There were fires everywhere. It was like Montana *closed* that year. We could sit here and see trees explode."

Kathryn finally decided to pass on to us one of her secret trails. She became animated as she talked, as if she were telling me an old family tale. "Okay. Look. Swiftcurrent Pass, there's a slope of huckleberry. Go up through it to the ledge, then find the waterfall, climb the rocks there to the high plateau, and you'll be above Shangri La. Then you can climb down to Iceberg Lake, about half an hour down, and you already walked that way, so you'll know your way back from there."

Paula looked up from the pad on which she was taking notes. We looked at each other and shrugged. I told Kathryn that her secret was safe with us. We were lost, and we hadn't even left the cafe.

Kathryn hung her head as if we were hopeless. "Look," she said. "You've just got to come into the park and spend some time here. You've just got to spend some time."

The Work of the Giants
on Building a Building

The stories about death were like casting a spell. After I had been working on high buildings for a time, I came to understand that the construction workers tried, unconsciously, to transfer death and all its grisly trappings to the newcomer. By telling it, they gave it away—the more gruesome the tale was, the better for warding off danger—and like a game of tag, whoever was "It" had to turn around and give it away again. I got splashed with blood like that, metaphorically speaking, just as soon as I got on the job, and now I'm obliged to pass it on, too.

Skip Reston, a truck driver, was killed when a crane fell on him in the steel yard at Calumet City. Skip was delivering a tall crane on a flatbed truck. He parked in back of the steel mill, and the crew gathered to figure out how to get the crane off the flatbed. The men sipped coffee and laughed as the summer sun grew high, sucking up the crane's long shadow, like blood soaking into the brown earth that had been turned for years by the studded heels of rolling stock.

Suddenly the crane's shadow began to get longer, and the men looked up to see it tipping over. The abused earth had given way beneath the truck's tires, which listed to one side now, spilling the crane off the flatbed.

Most of the men were too stunned to move, and they simply let events move around them. But Skip panicked and ran. The crane boom was now creaking as it came down through the air like the long neck of a brontosaurus. Skip ran a kind of zigzag pattern at first, the way ants run when you kick an anthill. It was as if he could see his own fate stalking him, as if he had driven all the way from home that morning with fate at his heels and had mounted the cab of his truck knowing that Death itself was drawing a bead on him while he sipped his coffee.

Then he straightened his path and ran flat out, as hard as he could. He ran right into the shadow of the dinosaur, where man merged with darkness, and the earth swallowed him.

One of the ironworkers ran to Skip and turned away as soon as he saw what had happened: A length of intestine had come out of Skip's mouth. The crane boom had cut him in half.

It took three hours of hard work in the hot summer sun to get the crane lifted off the corpse. "We picked him up with a number-sixteen banjo shovel," the ironworker told me, fashioning for me the gift of these images, casting out death with his spell of word pictures. "Skip turned black lying there in the sun. The smell was so bad it coulda gagged a maggot."

The story was one kind of initiation, but it wasn't long before I was crawling around on the half-completed building and death was happening for real. Right on Michigan Avenue in front of the Drake Hotel, a material tower on top of a new building was lifting a bucket of cement. The bucket had reached the fortieth floor, when it caught on the lip of the building and tipped over like a cream pitcher, pouring a ton of wet concrete to the street below, where it crushed a taxicab, killing the driver. The vehicle, now bearing its grim cargo, continued to roll along in the slow traffic lane, until a passer-by reached inside and pulled the parking brake. The flat vehicle, bearing the flat man, came to rest in front of the doorman at the Drake Hotel, who almost held the door open for a couple who'd been waiting, until he realized what he was seeing.

■ ■ ■

On construction sites accidents are an almost continuous occurrence. Just because they're not happening to any particular individual doesn't mean they're not happening.

Until I saw it happen, it was impossible for me to imagine the energy that even a small object can gather while falling. I had reached the sixty-sixth floor one day, and I was just about to leave the protection of the elevator, when somebody let go of a bit of junk up on seventy-one. It was nothing, really, a square of plywood smaller than a coffee

The Work of the Giants

saucer with a bent nail driven through the center, but it came licking down the wind like tongues of fire and nearly bit my arm off. It landed on the gangplank where I was about to step, and it went off like a rifle shot. When it ricocheted off and away, it looked as if someone had cut the plank with a fire axe.

One day on the Sears Tower, the wind came along, sucked up a whole sheet of plywood, and flew it away like a toy kite. In the caverns of the city it spun and spun until it was revolving like a Skil-saw blade. Surfing and descending on a cushion of air, it gained momentum. The eight-foot-long sheet of half-inch plywood rode all the way to street level, where it cut a man's head off. He was not a construction worker, risking his life for twenty dollars an hour. He was an undertaker. He just happened to be walking by. (I almost said, "At the wrong time," but no matter when we come, we're always on time for death.)

Then we all share the risk, even if we're just walking through town after lunch, like Flitcraft in *The Maltese Falcon;* most of us simply never get the chance to realize it. If we're hit, we're dead. If we're not, we live in happy ignorance of our peril. After a while, I began to feel safer on top of the building than on the street below. At least I knew I wasn't going to jump off. That was before the helicopters started coming and trying to blow me off.

■　■　■

I stood in the basement of 311 South Wacker Drive with a city engineer named Jimmy Orlando. We were four stories beneath the earth, looking at the underpinnings of the world's tallest reinforced concrete structure. The air was wet and dark with that musty chemical smell of new concrete. Jimmy paused in what would one day be underground parking, and looked around with respect, as if we were in one of the great cathedrals of Europe. Jimmy's job was to inspect new construction in the city of Chicago, so that must have been a familiar sight; yet he shook his head in quiet amazement and said, "That's what's holding her up," pointing to the square pillars all around us in that wet cave, which was so vast that we could not see its farthest corners from where we stood—they simply vanished into deeper shadow.

A building is a living thing. The unimaginable crushing weight of it stands in equilibrium with the muscle of the earth itself, and together they tremble, pushing against each other, like the motionless wrestling of equal Titans. Standing in the narthex as we were, I could feel the tension; I could hear the chimes of wind in the building's lungs above. Those muscles of concrete exhale the building's wet and labored chemical breath; and the forces, which have not yet settled (and which will not settle for another fifty years) are still so new and close to the surface that I had to ask myself: Who will win, earth or axe? And: Will it hold?

"She's heavy," Jimmy said softly, echoing my thoughts. "She's really heavy." I liked him for having such respect for that place. It was just another pink marble office building, but it was the work of the giants. Jimmy knew that he didn't have to tell me it was heavy: It was the same stuff that had buried that cab driver. In fact, the cost of massive construction was measured not only in dollars but in lives as well. The old-timers used to say, "A man a million." One man would be killed for every million dollars spent. But costs went up, and the modern equivalent became, "One man for every seven stories."

Jimmy took me into the construction office, where I was introduced to the quality-control engineer. I asked him a question about safety, and he laughed. "The developer couldn't care less if we built this building out of blood," he told me.

To get on top we rode a plywood box suspended on a cable. At different floors, men got on with materials—stone or wood or metal—and others got off. All the workers had on hard hats and balaclavas, gauntlet gloves, and well-ripped quilted suits and work boots scuffed to a greasy pale suede softness. A naked light bulb above us provided eerie illumination, now and then flickering and going out, leaving us in blackness to listen to the railroad whistle of the wind sucking up the shaft and out the unfinished levels of the skyscraper.

A big man got on and someone asked him, "You working, Crozier, or are you just jacking off?"

In response, Crozier pounded his chest, and a cloud of marble dust formed around him. "Nah," he said, "I just roll around in the dust." His hard-hat graffiti read, "Pissed On/Pissed Off." There were guys in there named Beetle Juice, Bunyon, and Maximum Sperm Buildup. The air was heavy with plywood and testosterone, acetylene and boot leather, wet cement and cigarette smoke. Everyone smoked all the time, as if one kind of death were not enough.

It seemed as if a lot of them were trying out for the part of the macho construction worker in a movie. Hard words were so common that one had to be truly poetic to raise even a titter in that crowd; mere profanity would not do it. Everyone had heard *everything* before, and if someone died or was injured, the tribal ritual of exorcising death called for a callous and indifferent commentary that belied any real emotions.

At level forty-six, a guy got on with a can of gasoline, and several people lit up Camels and Marlboros, as if to say: *Oh, yeah? You can't scare me with that shit. Watch this, motherfucker.* I couldn't help thinking of the two elevator workers on the Sears Tower, which was next door (tallest office building in the world), who were down in the shaft, hanging on ropes, cleaning the tracks with solvent. Someone, who was welding above, had dropped sparks down the shaft. The solvent ignited and the two men were burned alive, hanging in the chimney. Referring to one of the dead, I heard a man say, "That stupid asshole was my best friend." Then he picked up a hammer and began hitting the board where he'd been working. There was no nail there, but he kept hitting it anyway.

■　■　■

Three-Eleven, as they called the building, was seventy-one stories tall, and when I first went up, I was too afraid of falling to notice my surroundings. My focus was all *out there* in some undefined middle distance, and I was never sure what precisely I was looking at. I think I was looking around so fast, just checking to see if I was still alive, that I never fixed on anything at all.

We become used to barriers that screen our view of the world—windows, walls, trees, the crowd on the street, the house next door, but up there, every time I turned a corner, I was flung into the air above the river, into the misty fires of civilization gnawing on the shoreline of Lake Michigan. Blood rust and brown tracks, the Cartesian nightmare crisscross equation of transmission lines and relay towers, smokestacks and counterweights of rusted, ancient bridge scaffolding, and the slate-green lake meeting the bright winter sky somewhere out in the air-brushed distance. Far below I could see the mountains of rust in an auto junkyard, where all steel dreams came to an end, and gulls wove helical gyres above it, swirling in ascending spirals up toward the energy of the sun.

I'd be walking down a naked metal staircase, and suddenly I'd clear a barrier and that view would open up, and I'd grab hold of whatever was nearby to assure myself that I was still attached, lest I float away. One day, standing up there in the wind on an open gangway nearly a thousand feet in the air over the city of Chicago, I found myself with an unattached two-by-four in my hand, as if that could save me.

I was standing next to a great disordered pile of lumber, wire, conduit, tile, insulation, and discarded bolts. A carpenter came up the stairs at that moment, and I must have been squinting hard at the far distant *thing* out there, because he did a take. Then he said, "Don't get blowed off up here," smiled knowingly at me, and walked on by, pushed along by the wind that was a raw and constant fact of life.

Another man, who'd overheard, said, "That's sage fucking advice." And *he* walked on by, too. (I later learned that people didn't want to be near a guy when he fell, because it might reflect badly on them.)

I think that was the day I finally got myself up on that building in spirit as well as body, the day I learned to forget about the great void, which I'd been watching way too hard, as if it might snatch me away without warning. I laughed and threw the two-by-four down and began to relax. Yeah, I thought: Don't get blowed off up here. There's nothing magical or special about that void. It's the same void that surrounds us on the ground. It's just that, when we're up there, the junk is cleared away, and we can *see* it. That taxi driver, that undertaker—they never even got to look it square in the eye before it got them.

■　■　■

I always thought there was something mysterious about building these big buildings, but after a while up there, I came to understand that it's all just men and plain work. The hand, the wrench, the eye. There is no secret. It's just like me in my garage on a weekend, clutching a claw hammer. Plywood, two-by-fours, Sawzall, and pocketknives. The insulation is the same stuff you can buy at the hardware store. There's just more of it.

I stood on sixty-nine and watched a man in coveralls set up a scarred and paint-stained wooden ladder against a stick of aluminum that would one day be a window frame. The ladder leaned against that thin aluminum strut, beyond which was nothing—the mind-sucking

　　　　　　　　　　　　The Work of the Giants

view, the city shrouded in vapors—and then he climbed up the ladder to the top and stood, wobbling there, with scudding clouds passing below him and wind whipping his hair. He let go with both hands and began to bang furiously on a nail.

Strange things happened from our perspective: Each time he scuffed his toe over the edge in a puff of concrete dust, his Red Wing work shoe appeared to cover up a city park, crushing trees and obliterating play equipment. His fist, with which he held onto a steel brace, seemed to demolish an office building. His head annihilated a section of freeway, and cars appeared to stream in one of his ears and out the other.

Beside him now: a crew on a scaffolding, an equally precarious spot, an arc welder working, a cascade of sparks, hallucinations of a woman's hair. The phantasmagorical cataract flowed down the side of the building, swirled in eddies, and was carried off by the wind.

The wind had come up in earnest. It was an effort for me just to stay in one spot. I had heard from the men that sometimes the wind got up to 70 mph and ripped nailed-down plywood sheets away from wooden studs buried in concrete and tore guard rails free from their moorings. I sat down on a concrete block, trying to ignore the sensation that I was being sucked out into the air, when I noticed something that had escaped my divided attention up until that point: I was the only one up there without a safety harness.

■　■　■

One morning a group of us stood waiting in the dank chamber of the basement, where curds of concrete had been troweled to look like the icing on a cold and melancholy cake. We were waiting to go on top, and I passed the time watching a woman named Barb, who was engaged in conversation with a young carpenter. She sat on a wire spool, and he sat on a cinder block. They were just bullshitting, waiting for the eternal elevator. He had a Sawzall in one hand and a circular carbide saw blade in the other. Every once in a while as they talked, she'd whallop him on the leg with a fine punch that would have raised a welt on pine. She wore a hard hat and spectacles. A Marlboro was gripped in her teeth. With her head down like that she spouted a continuous string of invectives. I might have mistaken her for one of the boys. But at one point she took off her hard hat and stood up. She had short hair and regular features and bright, laughing eyes. I could see her shape moving inside her coveralls; she was all muscle, too, and had narrow hips and sinewy arms.

She sat back down and put her hard hat on again, and as she talked about her "fucking old man," she absently tore up bits and scraps of materials she found in her immediate vicinity. I could see how shy she was beneath the bravado, and how lonely it must be on a job like that, not just for her, and not just because she was a woman—although certainly that must have made it more intense. It was lonely for everyone.

When it seemed that no one was listening, Barb's voice softened and she talked intimately with the young man at her side.

"It's windy as shit up there today," he said.

"Yeah, I hate it when it's like that," she said.

"Yeah, I hate it," he said softly, sadly.

She reached over and coyly stuck her finger into the hole in the middle of his carbide saw blade and gingerly took it from him. That was a man who would not ordinarily give up his carbide saw blade, not without a fight, but I saw him look up at her and smile. She smiled, too, and there was a moment, a connection, and he averted his eyes shyly, looking at her finger in the hole.

Then the tenderness seemed to loom between them like a danger even bigger than the building that surrounded us, and he seemed to come suddenly to his senses.

"Hey, look out with that," he said gruffly. "Those cost a dollar-ninety-nine at Wal-Mart." And he reached for his saw blade, but she pulled it out of his reach.

"Oh, yeah?" she said, suddenly back on her guard, and she spun the blade on her finger and lunged at his crotch with it. He whipped up his Sawzall to defend himself.

■　■　■

One of the construction workers had fallen, and I went to the hospital to be with him. He had not fallen far, maybe forty feet. It was not a spectacular accident by any means—most of them aren't. His name was Lawrence Goers, and he was a big man. My first impression of him when I saw him in the trauma unit was that he'd been in an explosion:

The Work of the Giants

The waistband of his jeans, with thermal underwear beneath, was all that remained of the wonderful warmth we wear up there—the overalls, T-shirts, plaid flannel shirts, and then the Wall's Blizzard Pruf quilted oversuit. All of that lay in tatters around him, revealing his powerful body. His naked white skin now rose and fell with tortured respiration, as he struggled to overcome the terrible indignity heaped upon it by gravity. Everything was broken—his lungs, his ribs, his face. His eyes were swollen shut, his nose and mouth covered with blood that oozed around the tubes and right out of his ears. Beneath the hammered mask of his face, his brain was damaged, too. A piece of bone had come out through his leg and severed a big blood vessel. He'd lost a lot of blood, and his face was smashed. Even his heart was broken.

As the dozen or so trauma doctors and nurses worked on him, a radio someone had placed upon a counter played the Beatles, softly singing, "If I needed someone to love, you're the one that I'd be thinking of."

I visited Lawrence Goers in the intensive care unit several times after that. He never regained consciousness. All he knew was that he went to work one day in the usual way, and then he was flying through the air above the city. On the fourth day he died.

■　■　■

We were on the roof at 311 South Wacker. We called it "71," because there were seventy-one flights of stairs between us and lunch, but it was actually the roof. I looked down on the airplanes landing at Meigs Field. There was no railing, just our fragile perch in the sky.

I had been out there since before dawn, when the city lights were spread before us like an arcade game of heroic proportions. At night the total darkness of the air and sky, the flickering yellow lights below, and the crisscrossing of the sky by the white landing lights of jets, made these measureless distances seem make-believe. We froze, but we froze in a dream, and in the dream we hoped for morning.

Most of the men had been up there all night in a desperate attempt to unbolt the great material tower—those are the cranes we see like T-squares on top of most skyscrapers that are under construction. They grow out of the center of the building as the building grows. With block and tackle, they lift things up that men cannot lift.

Now the material tower had to be taken away, and the deadline for doing so was today. Everyone was tired and irritable and hurrying to meet the schedule of a helicopter that would arrive at 8 A.M. to pick it off in a spectacular move that would draw police and crowds and FAA officials.

The men who would remove the material tower—physically detach it and take it away—were ironworkers. The ironworkers are the grand circus performers of the construction world. They climb the highest. They don't tie off. They work without nets. When you see men high on man-made structures, you can be sure you're looking at ironworkers.

At sunup we cast a shadow that put a whole neighborhood in darkness. The day rose bright after the storm of the previous day, but the sun was not going to melt the ice that had turned the building into a seventy-one-story Popsicle and that circular concrete roof into a treacherous skating rink. Only the day before, four men were almost lost up here when they tried to remove plywood sheets in a 65 mph wind.

Now the horizontal boom or jib of the crane, which extended some 150 feet from its counterweights to its far tip, was swinging toward us, and I was watching the hands of Dave, the operator, in the glass-enclosed cab, as he flicked the levers with his skilled fingers. No one begrudged him his warm cocoon, his leather chair with the arm rests, his tape deck playing music. Our lives depended on the flicking of his fingers. Most certainly did the lives of two ironworkers who were balanced out on the very tip of the great yellow openwork cantilevered jib, as small as barnacles clinging to the tip of that heroic tentacle.

The trolley that moves back and forth along the jib, bearing the block and tackle, had carried two intrepid men out there almost an hour ago, and as it carried them out, they used their eight-pound sledge hammers to knock several thousand pounds of ice off the open metal framework. The trolley had them motored back in, leaving them stranded out there, suspended over thin air and a nine-hundred-foot drop to the street, and from their perch they dismantled cables and worried pins out of frozen holes and stood on iron bars that were covered with an inch of ice, all the while clinging to life with nothing other than a free hand, when they happened to have one.

A supervisor stood at the roof's edge and shouted at them in a crescendo of ascending expletives, telling them how to do their work.

It was pretty obvious to all involved that he was out of line. There's always one man on a job who panics, who can't stand the stress, and everyone knows he's more than a pain in the ass—he can cost you your life, too. Furthermore, it was obvious that the men were embarrassed for him, for how transparent his fear had become. But it was the two men out on the jib who were in the most immediate danger, and one of them finally stood up on the web work of icy steel, and with outstretched arms he called the supervisor out: "Hey, you fat, loud-mouthed motherfucker! Yeah, you! You come out here," he shouted across the empty air. "If you don't like the way I'm doing this job, you come out here and do it your fucking self, or else just shut the fuck up." The supervisor quietly went away, and we didn't hear from him for the rest of the morning.

I had started to look around for a place to hide as soon as I realized that the men were ready—the chopper was coming. I could hear its idling engines from the earth far below. The police had blocked off the streets, and the helicopter had landed in a parking lot. I tiptoed to the edge, taking care not to slip on the ice. Peeking over, I saw that the helicopter had left its detachable fuel tanks on the ground, to carry as little weight as possible. The section of jib it was picking up was thirteen thousand pounds on the first lift (the first "pick," they called it), and the pilot did not want to carry anything he didn't need.

I found a man who worked for the company that leased the cranes, and I asked him where he was going to be when the helicopter came up. "Get your back to something," he said, putting his back against an aluminum strut that stuck out of the circular concrete floor right at the very edge. I found another aluminum strut, which had a horizontal cross piece and when I put my back to it and stretched my arms out, I must have looked like Christ in a hard hat. I braced my foot against a heavy steel object in front of me on the deck. I could feel the aluminum bar behind me move, and I wondered how strong it was. I made the mistake of looking around behind me to check and saw that there was nothing between me and the drop to Franklin Street except that piece of aluminum. I was on the very edge, and the aluminum cross suddenly seemed flimsy indeed. I was reconsidering my strategy, when I heard the helicopter coming, and I knew it was too late to move. If the helicopter downwash caught me while I was skating on ice, I'd be blown off.

There is no sound in nature that carries the premeditated malevolence of a Sikorsky Skycrane Helicopter, the savage mechanical scream of its jet engines, the malicious, whistling invective of its rotors, and the soundless pealing waves that tear our clothes and snatch our eyeglasses away. As the stupendous orange and green contraption peeked over the rim of the concrete roof, it rose into our sightline like a hotrod from hell. It was stripped down to stark essentials. No polite decorative cowling adorned its unclad engines, whose tubing and drive shafts were visible in all their greasy, smoking reality. The only frill was the name someone had taken the trouble to paint on the nose, "Incredible Hulk."

The approaching rotor sucked up chips of ice, grains of sand, bent nails, and bits of concrete from the roof surface and flung them at us like rifle fire. The wind beat against us, furiously trying to dislodge us from our feeble perch.

The forces involved are not to be imagined. Despite the fact that it was a clear, cold day, the rotating wing actually creamed the air until a steaming white froth of water vapor surrounded the great circle of the six blades. That condensation turned instantly to ice crystals and that breath of frozen mist hung there and dissipated as she rode on her own copious blast.

The moment the helicopter had appeared over the rim of the roof, several men had fallen flat on their faces and hugged the icy concrete for dear life. A few feet ahead of me, a man lost his hard hat in the rotor downwash, and it went past me like a white cannonball and disappeared over the side. It was all I could do to hang onto the aluminum crucifix to which I was nailed by the column of air that stood like an elephant in the center of my chest.

But none of that was as amazing to me as the ironworkers, who stood fifteen feet from me, alone, unsupported, who leaned with all their weight into the wind and worked, while all I could do was to hang on and cringe. One man, incredibly, still stood on the jib, whanging away at a recalcitrant four-inch pin with a sledge. His only safety harness was his gloved hand, wrapped around a yellow steel support, which glittered with an inch of ice.

A moment later, the pin popped out and the great jib cut loose and floated in air as if by magic. The man leapt free to the roof, and the helicopter lifted away, bearing its magnificent load tilting and rotating

The Work of the Giants

in the whirl of wild momentum. Then the beast and the sound were gone, and I stood trembling on the edge, looking down at the cars creeping past below us and thinking this was too much, way too much, for a Saturday morning.

■ ■ ■

At a quarter to seven in the morning, the whole building was working. Only the topmost stories remained completely open to the wind. That was where I was headed. The elevator went to sixty-six and it was stairs from there on up to seventy-one. As the doors opened on sixty-six the wind caught us and sucked us out of the plywood box and onto the concrete apron, and we were thrust very quickly face to face with the city, stretched below and howling. It was the middle of winter and a blizzard was on its way. Coming to work in the morning, I'd see people bundled up, hurrying along, pulling their coats around themselves for warmth against the wind, and I'd wonder if they knew what real cold was like, with fish hooks in the wind.

Climbing the open metal stairs to the top, I passed a few men working, a welding unit flared, spilling a cataract of sparks out over the city mist. A man stood on a wooden ladder, hanging over the street like he was practicing some kind of circus stunt, hammering a nail upside down. I trudged on, watching the sky, the whirling skirts of that dark dancer, descending on us slowly from the northwest. I turned another flight, then another, passing by the remnants of the giant yellow crane, which had been put together with bolts the size of my forearm and nuts far bigger than my own.

I climbed and climbed on exposed steel stairs toward the summit, and as I went, I met workers coming down. I was looking around, marveling at the fact that I could put one foot in front of the other now, sixty-eight, seventy stories above the ground, with nothing separating me from the whistling air. I had been terrified of heights before this job, but now I had become . . . well, not used to it, but resigned to the idea of facing it anyway. At the end of each day, I'd feel an elation that I'd done it again, cheated the Devil, as they say. I let go of the handrail as I reached the top steps. I was a baby, learning to walk.

Now suddenly all partitions dropped away, and I was climbing narrow metal stairs that were naked in the sky, open to the mind-sucking view of the city and the lake shore, the minute insect automobiles below. Low clouds, the hem of a skirt, passed beneath me as I worked my way higher and higher.

I was so distracted by the view that I had ceased to notice something when I passed a certain point in my ascent: No more workers were coming down, and no more sounds of working reached my ears. The final staircase was half the width of the others, and the railing had not been bolted to the concrete structure, so it swung out away from the building as I climbed and swayed there drunkenly in the breeze. I learned new rules for life almost every day up there. This one was my favorite: Don't lean on anything, because it might not be attached.

So it was that I discovered, as I reached the very top of the building, that I was completely alone up there. All the other workers had fled downward, because it was too windy to keep working. At least five floors below me were now abandoned, and I was standing on a circle of concrete no bigger than half a tennis court, with nothing but the darkening, snowy sky above me.

I sat up there for a long time, just me and the concrete and the wind. The open floors below were like a whale's baleen, and the wind strummed them until they sang a deep, vibrating song. I heard a siren calling from the snow-blind city.

There are not many places where we can look our own death right in the eye, but this was one of them. I think it was D. H. Lawrence who said that every year an anniversary passes unnoticed: It's the anniversary of your death. Here I could celebrate that anniversary. I could walk right to the edge and look at it.

I stood against the wind. With shuffling steps, I traversed the ice to the building's edge. Now I saw the winter storm coming in upon us, and I stayed to watch as Nature lifted her skirts and squatted on this cold erection. The wind picked up and snow began. The silver lady on top of the Chicago Board of Trade vanished in a white whirling vortex, and the dancing fabric of snow now blew straight up, twisting into the sky above me. I heard the whimsical, indifferent song she played in the reeds of concrete below me and understood that I was in the icy organs of the sky now. I had been swallowed, and the willowy silver folds of flesh moved and shifted about me until the whole city—and the lake

The Work of the Giants

as well—had disappeared from view and nothing but whiteness remained, whiteness and Mother Wind.

We stayed like that for an hour or more—she held me there—and when she withdrew, only the tufted ice of her pubic hair remained upon the building. Her slick saliva hung like a frozen confection from the crossbeams and stuck in my hair and beard. Now she shook out her skirts and moved on across the lake, leaving me spent in her wake.

The Hero's Apprentice

on Competition Flying

High brush-stroke clouds of gray and silver colored the sky. Across the runway a thick green carpet of corn, wreathed in glittering heat waves, rose gently toward a hill to the east. I wandered out on the ramp, waiting for my turn to fly in the contest. It was July Fourth, and every corner of the airport ramp was jammed with aircraft, mostly red Pitts biplanes, although here and there I could see even more exotic flying machines than that—a Stevens Akro, a Rebel, even a Bücker Jungmann.

A man equipped with a hand-held radio walked urgently up and down a line of airplanes. The pilots sat in them awaiting the starter's signal. Out on a patch of scorched grass between the runway and the ramp sat the five judges on lawn chairs, shielding their eyes from the high sun with the sheets of paper on which were printed the aerobatics figures we had to perform—ordinary rolls, spins, and loops, as well as impossible-sounding maneuvers with descriptions that defy the imagination: "Pull-pull humpty with an outside snap-and-a-half up, push out inverted."

As I watched an aircraft overhead, I tried to imagine what the pilot was doing in the cockpit. Flying itself is not a difficult mechanical skill to learn. I've seen instructors teach the basics of flying in forty-five minutes. For example, the ailerons are like fins on the trailing edge of the wings. They deflect in opposite directions; when the stick is moved left, the left one is up and the right one is down.

As I watched the airplane in the sky roll, it looked so simple, like walking the tightrope. How would you give directions for walking the tightrope? In order to roll an airplane, the pilot must perform a continuous, subtle blending and changing of control movements—left stick, right rudder, left-back stick, right rudder, left-forward stick, left rudder. . . . Meanwhile, the green earth and blue sky are sliding off the frame of references and pitching away, enormous weights are thrown on our legs and shoulders, as blood gushes from stomach to head and then rushes away to pool in our feet and hands. Where are we?

We're upside down. The old references no longer apply. If we try to speak of up and down, we have to accept that up is green and down is blue, and our brains, worn in ruts of long habit and in conflict with our senses, rebel and betray us. Instead we think of movement in relationship to ourselves. The reason I don't get dizzy when I do those corkscrews is that I view the maneuvers as taking place around me, while I am "the still point in the turning world," as T. S. Eliot put it. We are truly the center of the universe. If I pull the stick toward my nose, the airplane's nose comes to me; if I push the stick away from my nose, the airplane's nose goes away from me. Right aileron, like an oar put into the water, pushes me to the left. After a while it's no harder than crocheting. An observer on the ground sees us as inverted, but within ourselves we are always upright. Well, always is a long time. It is possible to become disoriented and be unable to untangle all the knots we tie. Then we come tumbling to earth in an unraveling ball of yarn.

I made my way over to the fuel pumps and found a place to sit and watch as pilots took on fuel and pushed away. Beyond the ramp, I could see that families had spread their blankets on the grass by the primitive terminal building. A set of wooden steps ran up the outside of the frame building to a second-floor meeting room, where women were serving lunch at cafeteria tables. A line of people climbed the stairs, went past the tables, and then descended in a human conveyor designed to move paper plates of barbecued pork and potato salad. People in colorful shorts, their backsides up in the air, rummaged with their paws in tubs of iced-down Pepsi and Mountain Dew. Some took their plates out onto the ramp and unfolded lawn chairs in the shade of an airplane wing.

Farmers from the area came to gawk at the airplanes, which could be heard for miles around. They stood, those rough, unshaven men, big in the beam, wearing threadbare overalls, scowling and squinting suspiciously. Most of them knew the airport only as a place where crop dusters parked and fueled and where the vile and mysterious chemicals were kept that blessed or hexed their fields. But now overhead came some ungodly machine, painted as if it were a joyful thing to fly; this Red Devil, hot-rod device came, having split the bonds of earth, emitting a hell-fire smell and smoke and a hideous shriek. As if that were not enough, it came barrelling over their heads flying upside down. The women who had prepared the food (neatly dressed women with styled hair, women who looked as if they had stepped out of the pages of *Ladies Home Journal,* the wives of certain pilots, who seemed to go from contest to contest) offered those gawking farmers coffee and barbecue and cake and a place to sit, but the farmers just squinted harder at the inverted aircraft overhead, its pilot dangling like a hideous incubus in a sparkling amniotic bubble. One of them said, "Well, I just don't know . . ." and walked back to his truck and drove away.

■　■　■

Competitive aerobatics is not a glamorous sport. We perform for a panel of judges, usually in some remote place. It's not an air show— we fly too high to make it interesting to those on the ground. No audience comes to watch. We stay in the worst motels, dark, boxed-in places that smell of after shave and tobacco smoke, with rattling air conditioners and water that tastes like the first fire-and-brimstone days of creation. The contests take place during summer in places like Wisconsin and Iowa and Illinois and Michigan, so when we emerge from our icy little cells, we are hit by a blast of heat that knocks the cattle in the fields unconscious.

The previous day I hadn't even finished parking my airplane at Clarinda when a little fellow wearing a safari hat and a small moustache came up and told me of a pilot he knew with a similar airplane who had flown the same contest the year before. "Yeah, he took off out of here after the contest and went on up to Broken Bow for some gas. And you know how it is: Some line boy at the ramp says, 'Hey, why don't you show us some stuff?' And somebody else chimes in: 'Yeah, why don't you do some flips or whatever they're called—some *stunts.*' And the next thing they know, this pilot takes off out of there—gee, I can't remember his name now, it'll come to me. Anyway, he turns back toward the runway. Now this guy has just come from our contest, see. He didn't fly too bad, come to think of it. And he's got his back seat

　　　　　　　　　　　　　　The Hero's Apprentice

and his luggage compartment just jammed full of stuff. I mean, he even had a lawn chair in there. But here he comes, back over the runway, and you can hear he's at red-line speed, just screaming in there. And what does he do? He tries a snap roll right over the field."

"What happened?" I asked.

"He did a split-S right into the ground. Went in upside down."

As I tied down my airplane, I watched the fellow vanish back into the scenery: eight acres of hot concrete in the middle of the cool green and rolling miles of shoulder-high corn, forty Pitts Specials and kindred aircraft, and the pilots pushing them around, checking parachutes, and lining up to take off and rip around the sky doing things that airplanes ought not do, not over God's green acres, anyway. As I watched the spectral figure go, I began to take his point: What do we want here? Exactly what are we attempting to conjure with all this bother and ritual? I have been there now, and I think I know: We conjure ourselves. There, out across the ramp: I see a woman I know, Jan Jones, polishing her red biplane like the magic lamp it is; the genie that jumps out will be her.

I know what we want: We want someone to watch us. We want to be seen.

■　■　■

The earliest fairy tales I heard were told to me by my mother, and they were about my father's last flight in a B-17 Flying Fortress heavy bomber over Düsseldorf. That was my childhood mythology. It's what I had instead of Hansel and Gretel, and the air force fight song was what we sang instead of "Three Blind Mice." My father, the hero of those stories, was forever going off into some wild blue yonder, and there was no suggestion that I might ever go, too.

My father's flying story was filled with improbable clashes of fate and irony. When I was a teenager, I decided that it was all lies and ceased to believe it. In my twenties I wrote it into every novel and short story I composed, and I began to think of it as simply fiction, something I'd made up or stolen. But then in my thirties I really began to believe it. I demanded the real story from my father and anyone who might have known him. At the age of forty I went to Germany and California to track it down. I began to understand how real it was—not only the details I had heard from my mother, but other details I'm sure she didn't know and didn't want to know.

I met a very famous movie producer in Los Angeles. His list of credits was enough to make a free-lance writer swoon. He lived in a glorious, fairy-tale house, and when I arrived, Telly Savalas was standing by the pool to greet me, along with a cast of characters that made it look like a convention of late-night television actors. The producer had flown with my father, and I asked him to tell me about it, and he laughed and said, "Well, I can remember one time before a mission Freddy was teaching us all how to say, 'Will you go to bed with me?' in French, because he believed that we'd have the war won in a week or two and be drinking cognac and relaxing in France very soon."

My father was a Gregory Peck kind of aviator, with a moustache and his hat cocked rakishly to one side, daring the Devil to take him. With a thirty-six-hour pass, he could permanently disrupt the social fabric of any town. After twenty-five missions as one of the best pilots in heavy bombers, he was about to graduate to P-51 Mustang fighters and become the ace that God and Destiny had always meant him to be. Instead of spreading death from above without discrimination in fairy rings of fire over towns and factories and fields, he could go canopy-to-canopy with the enemy himself, a German pilot, a boy like himself, barely twenty-three years old. And kill him, of course.

His left wing was shot off on that last B-17 mission, and my father never got to see the inside of a Mustang. He was very nearly prevented from ever seeing his fiancée again, too.

He was approaching the target at twenty-seven thousand feet when an anti-aircraft artillery shell burst close enough to rip off most of the left wing. Almost immediately the aircraft went inverted and began to spin. My father tried to talk to his copilot, who happened to be the Old Man that day, a Col. Frank Hunter. It appeared that he was either dead or had been hit or had fainted—something was wrong, because he would not respond. Suddenly my father was the Old Man, and he understood that he could either perform or die. That's the way it happens: You're a little boy, walking along holding the Old Man's hand, and everything seems secure. Then one day you look up, and everything is different. It's the same hand. It's the same walk. But now you're the Old Man.

As he wrestled with the controls, it became obvious that there was nothing he could do to right the plane. Although he couldn't be certain that the intercom was working, he gave the order to bail out, and then unstrapped himself. The minute he unstrapped, he was pinned against the instrument panel by the tremendous G-forces. He rode the airplane down. It entered the clouds, and somewhere in that other world, forces we cannot see tore the plane in half, and it plunged in pieces to the smoky winter earth.

No one survived except my father. No one knows how he managed, though there are some who say he made a pact with the Devil. Perhaps it was just some exotic maple-seed fluttering motion of the cockpit, which still had a wing and a half attached, and maybe that motion slowed his descent at just the right moment. Perhaps the wreckage slid down the snowy railroad embankment where he was found. Perhaps a spectral hand reached out and grabbed him by the hair and jerked him rudely back at the last moment, because every bone in his body was broken, more or less, except his scrawny neck; then a German soldier got up on the wing and found him in there, a crumpled bloody ball of canvas and Wildroot Cream Oil, as if some demon had blown his nose and tossed away the rag.

The German soldier pulled out his Parabellum pistol to put the poor American animal out of its misery, but the gun jammed. My father woke up long enough to feel the barrel pressed against his temple and hear the click that didn't fire. The German soldier was cursing. My father laughed, because he was delirious and thought it was all so funny, this German brown-shirt saying, *"Swinehundt!"* just like in a movie. The laughter made the German angrier, but by then a crowd had gathered— of Germans, civilians and soldiers alike—and somehow it was decided that the American pilot had to be taken prisoner and questioned if possible and that anyway, if they were going to shoot him, it wouldn't be good form to do it in front of all those farmers, who had come with pitch forks and sour looks and the thought of perhaps sticking some additional holes in the pilot for reparation.

This was truly the stuff of dreams. Yet it was real. When I went to Germany with my father in 1988, people who had been teenagers and children at the time of his crash were able to verify the story, even if they disagreed on the details somewhat. Someone produced a photo of children playing in the wreckage—it was summer by then, a year or two later, and weeds grew up through the torn fuselage, and when I saw the forlorn look on the face of the little boy, I recognized myself, playing in the wreckage of the broken bomber.

During my lifetime, my father never flew. My mother shopped at the military base, but we hung around no airfields. No mention was made of flying. Sometimes I found things that excited old memories: An old uniform stuffed in a cedar chest beneath the other clothes. A pair of silver air force wings in a dish of cuff links on his dresser. If I saw any sort of airplane, I began leaping around like a dog catching a long-forgotten scent, but I never saw my father gaze longingly at the sky when a biplane rattled past overhead. How could he have been so passionate as to give his youth and life for aviation, and then not even be moved to look? It was as if something had died inside him in that fall. Now I am a pilot, out on a hot swatch of concrete in no place I've ever wanted to be, following the daylight moon across the sky in search of something I cannot name.

■ ■ ■

I stood up from where I sat at the fuel pumps. I passed a man sitting in a Christen Eagle, a high-performance biplane painted with a rainbow feather pattern. I wondered what he was pretending to be, so small in there, tucked snugly into his remarkable painted bird. His was one in the line of planes that were waiting to go up. With only his head visible, he looked like a male siren, with the head of a man and the body of a bird. As I passed close by his open canopy, he stared straight ahead as if in a trance, repeating over and over, "Focus, focus, focus . . ."

As I crossed the ramp, I caught sight of myself in the terminal window: parachute slung over my shoulder, sun glasses reflecting a piece of the sky. These days I see that I'm walking the walk and talking the talk—that slow walk that old fighter pilots get, because everything's just moving too fast. I see the same slow walk in old aerobatics pilots: If you move too fast you'll make a mistake, and there's just no time to correct mistakes, no time to hurry. I see that I'm wearing the same soft clothes and soft shoes that those old pilots come to wear, my father's shoes, my father's battered jeans, a plain cotton shirt that's been washed too many times. If those pilots survive their days of being sharp, they gradually become softer and softer like that old shirt. I crossed the

The Hero's Apprentice

ramp and stepped up onto the wing of a machine so improbable—a gleaming blue engineering confection of spun sugar and molten glass—that it looked as if it could only exist in a dream. It was my turn to fly.

■ ■ ■

Flying is like being in one of those nightmares when the fever runs high and things are either way too big or way too small. When I first flew I was terrified of everything. More than once I sat on the end of the runway, unable to push the throttle forward because I was gripped in the tetanus of my fear. Nothing was more humiliating than taxiing an airplane out to the end of a runway, talking to the control tower, and then finding that I didn't have the nerve to go. I would have to call the tower to get taxiing instructions back to the ramp. I would go home and drink. I hit new lows during that period. I had to rebuild myself literally from the ground up. I was never certain of precisely what filled me with such terror. It's not a fear of heights. Fifty feet is just frightening; but *altitude* is truly mysterious.

The world becomes a vague and misty place where everything is taken on faith. The known world is transformed into an undifferentiated vista, endless smears of color, as if someone has spilled a great paint set on a page with no edges. Is it earth? Is it sky? Uncertain, we grab for a hand hold, but gravity doesn't work anymore. The bottom drops out from under us. We float. We become heavy. We float again. Our senses make no sense. The noise is so loud that we can't talk to each other. Have we gone deaf? Are we having a stroke? Did someone put acid in the coffee? And if we're at all claustrophobic, well, we're locked into something no bigger than the inside of a refrigerator, and it smells like gasoline and urethane.

Then there is the infernal radio. Phantom voices confer in scratchy mutters, a committee of ghosts, locked in the amber of some other dimension: "Wah-wah-wah-wah-wah?"

"Wah-wah-Two-Three-wah-wah-wah."

"Wah-wah-wah-Number Two."

"Wah-wah-Roger."

Anyone who is the least bit subject to panic goes into afterburner under such conditions. I have heard pilots say that just by getting near an airplane we get 40 percent more stupid. No wonder.

But there's more: I was not afraid when the instructor was in the plane. The plane was the same. The earth and ether were the same. I was the same. Why then should it frighten me to leave the earth alone?

There is nothing quite like seeing the surface of the earth drop away—everything we hold dear and familiar, our whole world in effect, folding back as if it had been a scrim in a play. It's as if I had lived in the center of town all my life, and one day somebody pushed real hard, and all the buildings toppled over, and I saw that they were only painted on a card.

As the details of that world fade and shrink, the concerns of that realm shrivel, too. That was, in effect, the place where I finally met myself for the first time—no bottle, no jokes, no bullshit, no clever evasions—just me and . . . what?

Here was my epiphany: that I had never known responsibility before. Suddenly I understood why I was comfortable with an instructor on board. I wasn't afraid of dying; I was afraid of living.

It took me years to begin to feel at home with the ghosts, the vapors, the spirits of that world. But now I think I've begun to understand what I'm doing up there anyway. I am recreating a rite of passage that I never had, forging a connection, a pathway from one world to the next, from the world of my childhood, where I was just a bag on my father's belt, to the world of my adulthood, which hardly ever seems to have the stamp of reality that his world had. I am snatched away and thrust into an alien place—a cave, a jungle, a river, or now this nothingness I've found. I am put through a series of tests, and the peril is real; my life depends on how I perform. I am annealed in the blue flame of the burning sky. Finally, I can stand up and walk away.

Well, flying . . . flying is one thing. Flying upside down is another.

■ ■ ■

I first flew upside down on a magazine assignment in an air force jet fighter trainer. The experience was for pilots the unspeakable, the nameless, the ineffable. If simply leaving the earth was to meet myself for the first time, then flying upside down was the first step in beginning to celebrate myself. Flying isn't the only way to do it; everyone can have the experience. I think Walt Whitman flew upside down.

I began my studies as an acolyte aerobatics pilot in an old and weathered Bellanca Citabria, an airplane made of tube and fabric, designed for teaching loops and spins and rolls. Although I had gotten used to flying, when I turned to aerobatics, I had to go back to the beginning and learn everything all over again. The business of turning upside down brought back all the old panic. When I was flying with my instructor, I was all right. I was dangling from my father's belt. But going out solo I'd be paralyzed again. I was convinced that I'd get stuck upside down or go into an uncontrollable spin. Frantic, I would land the plane and stand on the ramp shaking my head. The airplane was an inert object. How could it defy me so? And yet I knew that within its greasy retort a curious alchemy took place. It took me a long time to understand that I was the spirit of animation within it; I was the only genie that could ever jump out and grant my wish.

As I worked on the figures, gradually the fear was battered down under the hammer of my persistence. I moved into high performance airplanes, and the whole question of confidence reared its ugly head again. The Citabria is a relatively docile airplane. The Pitts Special was different. It wasn't even fair to call it an airplane, because that fire-engine red biplane broke so many rules of airplane design that it could be dangerous to assume that it worked the way other airplanes did. I met a man at the Iowa contest who had just bought a Pitts. The following weekend I saw him at a contest in Wisconsin, and he told me that he'd crashed on landing—broke off one landing gear and ripped up the whole lower wing. Many first-time Pitts pilots weren't nearly as lucky; at least he walked away from it.

Like Hell's Angels on motorcycles, the Pitts is *meant* to cause trouble. It's unstable, because that characteristic makes it more prone to aerobatics. An ordinary airplane, like a toy glider or a kite, will right itself if you let go of the controls. But a Pitts Special flies as well upside down as it does right-side up; it won't right itself. It likes to tumble. Similarly, if it's put into a spin, it may just stay in a spin—all the way to the ground, unless you know precisely what to do to get it back under control. You don't have to be a novice to kill yourself in a Pitts. Our act is like Houdini's, who would shackle his hands and feet and tie himself up and lock himself in a coffin and then have himself thrown into the bay. He had to undo everything he'd done before he ran out of air. One of the world's most famous air show performers, Art Scholl, died in a Pitts

Special after getting into a spin from which he did not recover. He just couldn't untie all the knots he'd tied and undo all the handcuffs. He ran out of air. He was involved in the filming of *Top Gun* at the time.

■ ■ ■

In any airplane the maneuvers can be confusing. An airplane spins when one wing is stalled and the other is still flying. The Pitts' swept upper wing makes that easier to do. The smooth flow of air over a wing produces lift. When we stall a wing, we break up that smooth flow and the lift vanishes, just as a soap bubble vanishes when you touch it. We pull the throttle back in order to slow the airplane's progress through the air. But we try to maintain the same altitude. With less power pulling us through the air, there's less airflow over the wings. We have to point the nose up higher and higher just to stay up. The airplane struggles to fly now, shuddering and complaining as the engine pops and backfires. Finally the air over the wings begins to burble and tumble in turbulent eddies until all lift is gone. The airplane, now fully stalled, sinks toward the earth.

If we push the right rudder suddenly, the nose will slue to the right and the right wing will swing backward. But at the same time the left wing comes forward, which gives it a burst of smooth airflow, a shot of lift. The left wing leaps for joy to be flying again. But the right wing is dead, and the nose has somehow pointed itself almost straight at the earth, while the happy left wing, oblivious of our plight, flies around and around. Now we are spinning. And we'll continue spinning all the way to the ground unless we reverse the steps we took to get into this fix (i.e., left rudder to stop the rotation, forward stick to break the stall, power back on to fly the hell out of there). In a few seconds a Pitts can crank itself into a prodigious rotation, and after a few turns our eyeballs tend to revolve in their sockets like wind-up toys.

■ ■ ■

I'll never forget the first time I climbed into such an aircraft. My friend Mark Peteler had just bought one, and he let me sit in it. It was like dropping into a cool metallic hole. My eyes barely looked out over the canopy rail. It was very close. My legs fit into holes at the end of which my toes found the rudder pedals. The stick was short and solid between

The Hero's Apprentice

my legs. My shoulders almost touched the sides. I could see that in a crash I would bash my face to pieces against the flat, sharp metal instrument panel a few inches before my eyes.

I reached up and slid the canopy closed. I felt as if I had violated some code of intimacy, burst through some invisible curtain that keeps men at a safe distance from one another. It was as if I'd gone into Mark's closet and put on all his clothes.

I felt the electric impulse of neurons flowing down the stick and out through the fuselage to the wings. It was sexy. The airplane seemed a living thing. I was becoming part of the airplane, or the airplane was becoming part of me. I could read in the sharply contrasting aromas a story that had been played out in here: Mark's fight with himself, etched in sweat, his old dread and joy fixed like lacquer in the nylon and leather, the smell of grease and gas and paint and smoke. Reading those scents, I could relive his experience, the tremendous and treacherous power to which we connected ourselves through this forbidden lycanthropy. And suddenly I was no longer in sympathy with Mark's ordeal. I wanted my own. I felt myself overcome by greed and lust.

I was overcome by this mad idea: There was Mark, my brother, my friend, at the nose of the airplane, innocently putting screws in the spinner. *I'll kill Mark*, I thought. *I'll flee with his airplane. Perhaps if I simply start the engine, the propeller will hack him in two, and I can taxi away, leaving the grass spattered with his blood, as I fly off with my little red Pitts.* For such were the extremes of emotion that this mysterious contrivance of sticks and cloth excited in the breasts of pilots, even just sitting in it, parked on the grass by the hangars. But Mark trusted me.

The amount of trust involved is always a source of amazement for me. The first time an instructor gives me the controls of an airplane, I can always see that he knows he's handing me his life. He passes control to me as if passing a brimming cup. I love the process. We look into each other's eyes.

Now, as I climbed into the cockpit for the Clarinda, Iowa, contest, Scott Robertson watched me carefully in order to gauge exactly how stupid I really was. I had scarcely met Scott the day before. He was a corporate pilot and the owner of this airplane, and he had somehow agreed to let me fly it in the contest.

I had arrived at Clarinda the day before in my Citabria, looking for someone with a Pitts who would agree to fly with me. Because of insurance regulations, we can't go into competition alone unless we own the airplane. I had introduced myself on the ramp the day before, and Scott greeted me coldly, squinting at me as if I had come to borrow his wife.

Scott was neat, serious, youthful, and still had that sharpness about him that you see in young fighter pilots. But I could see that he was mellowing: He wore soft clothes and moved deliberately, with a distinct smoothness that set him apart: no hurry, no twitching, and no startle response. I knew what I was looking at before he even told me that his father had been a military pilot. Scott had the fighter pilot look and the wary coolness of long experience.

So the day before the contest, Scott grudgingly let me get into his airplane, and he took me up for a practice session. It was a test for both of us. His job was to trust me enough to let me fly, but to catch me before I killed him. My job was to calm down and fly so well that he'd let me compete the next day.

The Pitts is an awfully uncomfortable airplane and harder to get into than bicycle shorts. It's like mounting a horse. It's easy for an instructor to see how much experience you've had just by watching a rider get on and off. If you can't get on the horse, you haven't been riding long enough to get into the ring. I had to step onto the left lower wing, take hold of a handle cut out of the center of the top wing, and then lift my right foot higher than my belt buckle in order to clear the canopy rail and step in. Standing on the seat would seem contrary to manners, but it's the only way to get into a Pitts. I lifted my left foot over the rail and lowered myself gingerly into position. Scott watched me carefully and seemed satisfied that I had at least climbed into a Pitts once or twice before. Then he watched me strap in, making certain that I fastened my harness correctly. Duane Coles, a famous air show pilot, tells a story about his days as an instructor of air force pilots during World War II, flying an open-cockpit Stearman. Duane took a student up and demonstrated a loop. The student fell out at the top when the airplane was upside down three thousand feet above the ground. The student had forgotten to fasten his seat belt and Duane had failed to check.

■ ■ ■

The Hero's Apprentice

I was whipping around up there during our practice session, sending the Pitts into spins, loops, and rolls that took place so fast it was like flicking the pages of a book. During one pull-out, I yanked on the stick so hard that my headphones peeled off from the centrifugal force and ended up around my neck. As I stitched up the sky with my maneuvers, feeling like a hot shot, I heard nothing from the intercom and began to wonder if Scott had died back there. Finally, I pressed the red button on the throttle and said, "Could you give me some comments on my flying?"

"Well," he said, "that instructor of yours isn't doing you much good."

■ ■ ■

On Saturday when Scott climbed into the back with me for the actual competition, I wasn't at all sure what I was in for, and I'm sure he wasn't either. An aerobatics contest sounds like an air show, but it's not. The airplanes fly high for reasons of safety, and they are hard to see. In fact, only a trained judge can tell what the airplanes are doing. It seems that the horrible, clattering, coughing, buzzing, rattling noise they make is everywhere, like the heat and the sun that bakes us, and yet sometimes we can't even find the tiny airplane in the sky.

The day had worn on and on, with airplane after airplane flying overhead, while panels of judges lay afflicted with heat prostration in their lawn chairs. I had worked as an assistant on the judging line for a while, and the waves of heat pouring in off the ramp made me sick. I had to sit in the air-conditioned terminal building and rest before I flew just to make sure I didn't faint during the competition. By the time Scott and I sealed ourselves into the plexiglass canopy, the temperature was nearing one hundred, and I was sunburned and feeling cross-eyed. As we sat and waited in line for our turn to fly, the sweat poured into my ears and ran down my shoulders. The parachute on my back felt like a great nylon-and-Velcro leech, sucking the fluid out of me.

As I watched the starter send off the aircraft ahead of us, I had this thought: It's about the hand. It's about passing something from his hand to my hand. Scott's not very happy about that prospect—not yet. He's stewing back there, probably regretting that he ever agreed to let me compete in his airplane. I admit I talked him into it—conned him, I suppose—by mentioning names of pilots I had flown with, pilots I knew he would have to respect, such as the coach of the U.S. Aerobatics Team.

Now there seemed to be something in the air like the powder on butterfly wings, drifting, shifting colors. I threw my head back and sighed with the heat. I looked at the sky: Pastel clouds, fractal mountains of light, layered like the many temperaments of snow, seemed to cast a new and portentous darkness down on us. I yawned hugely. Suddenly I felt like going to sleep. I realized that I was afraid.

When I was first learning to fly a Pitts, I told my instructor that I wanted to gain enough experience to feel comfortable. He said, "You mean *confident*. You'll never feel comfortable. Not if you're smart."

■ ■ ■

There are five categories of aerobatics competitors, and Scott had been consistently placing near the top in Advanced, the second highest category. I was merely a beginner in the Basic category. Even if I did something as stupid as Scott expected me to do, he was poised to save us. And yet, when the starter, with his radio and his hand signals, cleared us to take off, I looked out on the ramp and saw my friends waving, noticed my old pal Jonas snapping my picture, and beyond him the ranks of judges awaiting my performance, and I felt small and inadequate, a kid being pushed out on stage for a role he hasn't quite learned.

Scott performed the take-off. Just a few inches forward of my feet there was a Lycoming six-cylinder engine, and when he opened the throttle, there was an immense clattering explosion that suddenly wiped out all sensory perceptions. It was so loud that it was like a wall of sound, slamming me back in my seat.

The only thing separating me from that engine was the twenty-five-gallon fuel tank in my lap. It was made of thin aluminum, like a water balloon filled with one-hundred-octane gasoline.

Scott had said beforehand that he would not talk to me once we left the ground. He said he would allow me to make any mistakes I was going to make except ones that would kill us. And so as we lifted off, Scott said, "Your airplane," and I reached out to take the stick, but the acceleration was too great, or else I was overcome by the pastel sleeping powder that was floating in the air. It seemed as if my hand moved in slow motion. I remembered then my father's journey back to earth

　　　　　　　　　　　　　　　　　The Hero's Apprentice

in 1945: With his left wing shot off, his airplane rolled over on its back and entered a spin. Soon the spin accelerated to such a pace that the world was just a blur, and my father tried to reach out to bring the airplane under control, but his hands were frozen in some invisible medium that held him there like an insect preserved in amber. Einstein was right: The faster you go, the slower time goes.

I finally reached the stick and took control of the airplane. My eyes felt heavy. I yawned again, whipping the little airplane around to the right and pointing the nose so high that all I could see were the swirling clouds with breaks to the blue above. As I came into the holding area, I could see the judges down there. I found the white markers for the box and then looked out over the Iowa farmland. The airport with its long north-south runway was in a river bottom with low hills to the south side and a town to the north. Farther out, rivers ran in darker green designs, like veins on the back of a giant hand. But as I climbed, those details dissolved and became insignificant.

Flying reduces the world to its primitive state again, both the world within and the world without. There are no road signs, only the vast, disordered, unpartitioned landscape, raw, voracious, world without end. We are all squashed in here inside of ourselves, where we have been holding everything in all these years, and now the open spaces and the rubbing of the wind on our wings can release the genie. I feel as if I've been pushed through the airlock of a ship in earth orbit, and now the great vacuum of space is causing me to explode. I see that I am not substantial enough to hang on a thread and a spark like this. The Zen part is the waiting, but I have to keep busy.

A signal from below: Red panels are flipped over to white. A white signal means I can enter the box. It's my turn.

I bend time around my wrist, and the hazy line where sky and earth meet tilts precariously. I am flying through the ragged base of the boiling clouds, and as I tear the fabric, I get a sense of my terrific speed. All sound is gone. The obliterating, savage noise of the engine is the equivalent of silence now, because my ears are swollen shut; I am deaf. Everything grows heavy as I pull around into the zone where I will perform. I rock my wings to signal the judges: I begin the sequence.

I cut the power, and the world goes more silent than the silence I thought I knew. I am shot. This is a game of cowboys. I reach up and clutch my heart, throw my head back, and pull the stick to my stomach, as the airplane slows to stalling speed. Using the rudder pedals, I keep the wings level. I watch the altimeter to avoid climbing or sinking. I hang there for a moment like an insect on a pin and wait for the stall. I feel the buffet, the shudder, the break, and then I jam my foot into the left rudder pedal, and the airplane rolls over on its back as we enter a spin. Soon the spin accelerates to such a pace that the world is just a blur. I try to reach out to control the airplane now, but my hands are frozen.

■　■　■

That night I sat in the bar, watching the pilots drift in after a hot day of flying. They had all gone back to the motel and cleaned up, and now wore pressed sport shirts and slacks. In a back room of this restaurant two very long tables had been set for about eighty people. I was pensively drinking a diet Pepsi, thinking about what a dismal showing I had made, when Scott came up behind me. I turned to see him standing there with a big grin and his hand stuck in my face. "Congratulations," he said.

"For what?" I asked, shaking his hand.

"You took fourth place," he said proudly, pumping my hand. "Not bad. Not bad." And he pulled up a chair and sat down and we talked.

It had been a tricky flight, at least for my midwestern aviator's brain. The problem was that we get used to flying with the section lines, which form a wonderful Cartesian grid aligned with the cardinal points of the compass. It's how we learn to stay straight during maneuvers: We line up with a road. But the whole Jeffersonian world fills our peripheral vision, and our hands and feet respond automatically to realign us with the great grid of the universe. For example, as I pull up into a loop, I pull the stick straight back, about 4.5 G's. As soon as the great Pitts nose comes up, all I see is sky—no referent to tell me if I'm straight or crooked. I look out the left side, and I can watch the sky and earth revolve around the calipers of my biplane wingtips. As the lower wing comes up past the vertical and starts over the top, I throw my head back, easing off on the stick a little (I'm slowing down as I go up, so I don't want to pinch the top of the loop and turn it into an 'el' instead of an 'O'). As I throw my head back, I pick up the horizon behind me.

But at the same time, I pick up the whole world, the graph paper of farm fields, and without any effort, my hands and feet put me straight with it.

Well, for some reason, the box at Clarinda had been aligned with the runway, but the runway was not aligned with the section lines. Consequently, we had to fly all the figures off on an angle—that is at an angle to the whole world. So each time I had gone upside down during practice, I'd see those section lines, line up with them, and come out of the loop twenty degrees off heading with the competition area—the box.

The following weekend I flew in the Great Lakes regional contest at Burlington, Wisconsin, and the box and runway and world were all lined up. My friend Mark Peteler came, but his little Pitts Special—the one that had turned me to a murderous fantasy, was broken, and he couldn't fly. A friend had brought his two-place Pitts for me to fly, and now I told Mark, "You ought to ask him. He'll let you use his Pitts, I'm sure of it."

"Oh, that's okay," Mark said.

"No, go ahead," I said. "You ought to fly."

I took second place at Burlington. Mark was the only pilot who beat me that day.

■ ■ ■

Going home, my friend Jonas did barrel rolls around me with his black Italian fighter plane. I know what it's all about: It's doing those amazing tricks for each other. I can go up with a perfect stranger like Scott, someone who doesn't even want to like me, and I can *show* him what I can do. In the end, he has a grin on his face. It's about proof.

Now as Jonas rolled around me, it was the same thing. It was a thing that can get us killed, too, but I was grinning—I was laughing at his antics. He's good. He's a really good pilot. I tried to talk him into competing, but he doesn't have anything to prove. He just wants to have fun.

His plane zipped past just above me, a dark and lethal-looking silhouette, and then went straight up, vertical, rolling. He cut back in on me and dove. Jonas was dog-fighting. He pulled up beside me, slowing, and I could see him grinning in his bubble canopy, half man, half bird. He pulled out a camera and snapped my picture.

I hit a button to transmit, and said, "You want to go in formation? I can go about ten knots faster, if you can go about fifty knots slower."

"Nah," he said. "I think I'll punch it and go."

"Bye-bye," I said.

I saw his hand go down to the throttle. There was a stitch in the fabric of time, a shuddering explosion of power, and he was gone, a black dot rising ahead of me.

■ ■ ■

At my last fuel stop in Centerville, a man crossed the ramp to look at my humble old Citabria. He said he had one just like it and had been intending to compete, "but my instructor got killed."

"How?" I asked.

"He was doing some low-level rolls for a photographer, right over the runway. He caught a wing tip. Actually, he didn't die in the crash. He broke his neck and died a few days later."

As we were talking, an airplane pulled up to the pumps for fuel. It was two Frenchmen on a race around the world. They had started in Geneva, and already they had crossed Russia and the Pacific. That very morning they had flown non-stop from Fresno to Centerville, Iowa. Their airplane was decorated with stickers like an old camper truck.

"Why?" I asked.

He smiled and shrugged and looked at his companion, who smiled and shrugged, too. "Why not?" he said, and when they climbed in and waved and flew away to Paris, I flew home.

I had grown to realize something new: I suppose there may come a time when everyone I know is dead and I'm ninety-nine years old, and I am the Old Man myself, the only Old Man, never destined to be the little boy again, but I doubt it. I remember when my grandfather Agustín was dying, I went to visit him. He had been in the Mexican Revolution at the turn of the century. Here was a man who had been through rites of passage that I could never hope to know. Agustín's father was a real cowboy rancher, who raised cattle and rode a horse with a rifle in his saddle until the week of his death. All his life Agustín had been in the shadow of that man, and I had been in the shadow of my father, who was in the shadow of this amazing old warrior, who had shot his way out of Guerrero at the age of fourteen and had come to the United States to make his way with only three words of English to his name: "Guaranteed all wool."

I took Elena and Amelia, my little daughters, to see him, and with their marvelous lack of self-consciousness, they stormed the citadel of his darkened room, where he lay dying. They leaped all over him, that grizzled old man with bad breath and false teeth, kissing him and hugging him and stroking his fine white hair, saying, "Pepo, I love you!" And Agustín, who was blind and almost ninety and could no longer even speak, started crying, he was so happy. He made little moaning sounds of pleasure, a big smile broke out on his battered face, and tears streamed down those parched cheeks, which had suffered such a long drought of weeping. He lifted his hand out to the girls and touched their faces. Even the Old Man wasn't the Old Man anymore.

House of Pain

on Brain Surgery

The first time I saw Helen,* she was sitting up in bed, her almond eyes looking at me inquisitively. A girlish pout informed the expression of her full red lips, and her extravagant black eyebrows gave an intelligent cast to her broad forehead. Her Greek nose was fine and straight, and her olive skin was clear and veiled in a soft light that cast reflections on tiny hairs, which glittered on her outstretched arm. I kept expecting her to yawn and smile and greet the morning sun out there beyond the ice crystals on the windows. It was a gorgeous day. But all she did was breathe in and out and stare at me. Her lips moved slightly as she breathed, and Dr. Roberta Glick, the neurosurgeon, said, over and over, "Helen? Hello, Helen? Can you squeeze my fingers? Helen? Hello, Helen? Squeeze my fingers, Helen. Squeeze my fingers."

Dr. Glick turned to me. "She may hear us, but she can't respond." It was only then that I saw the curving horseshoe scar that circumscribed half her skull—bone removed for surgery. In the middle of the scar was a dark and ragged hole, no bigger than a nickel, where the bullet had gone in.

Helen's hair was beginning to grow back—it was about Marine recruit length now—and I could see that she had been well cared for here, clean and groomed and fed, and well cared for by her boyfriend, until he hired someone to shoot her in the head. He was a drug dealer, and Helen was going to inform on him, because she was pregnant and needed to change her life. Now she was going to have her baby in

*Helen's name and certain others have been changed.

68

peace—Cook County Hospital was going to keep her alive that long at least. There was no name on Helen's chart, and her whereabouts was a closely guarded secret because the boyfriend was still after her.

As we continued rounds in the early morning hours—Dr. Glick, the brain surgeon, with her entourage of surgical residents and medical students and nurses—we passed others like Helen. "We're going to see the train wrecks of the night," Dr. Glick had told me on the way to the hospital. She had also told me, "Our motto is: See no evil; hear no evil; smell no evil." At first I mistook her flip remarks for cynicism, but I didn't understand. The truth was that Roberta Glick worked at the edge of the universe. As a top neurosurgeon, she could have been making five hundred thousand dollars a year fixing slipped discs. Instead, she was working at Cook County Hospital on Chicago's west side. A neurosurgeon in private practice might actually open someone's skull ten times in a year. Dr. Glick, getting paid a pittance by comparison, performed the same operation a dozen times in the single month I spent with her.

At first I wanted to know every story. But after a few months of going on rounds, I learned that there was always something more tragic than the last story I'd heard. In the pediatric ward, we visited an eight-year-old boy whose spine had been severed by a gang bullet. He was paralyzed from the neck down. "You should have seen me when I had to tell his mother that he would never walk again," Dr. Glick said. "It was so sad. So sad." And then she moved quickly on to the next subject. She never spent too much time in one place in quiet contemplation. It was too risky. If she was going to be able to do these people any good, she couldn't become emotionally crippled by the horror. But my curiosity still had the best of me then, and I hung back to watch the eight-year-old boy.

I stood by his bed and watched as the nurse suctioned out the breathing tube that had been surgically implanted in his neck. He had dark Latin eyes and soft, shining black hair, and he wore Nike athletic socks that would never run a step. Each time she detached him from the respirator, he started to suffocate, and a look of panic overcame his gentle, handsome face; his mouth worked to gulp air, as the nurse spoke soft words of encouragement.

I began to regard morning rounds as a test, to see what the world was made of. It was harsh stuff, diamond hard. As we walked down the hall, Dr. Glick told me about one of her patients, a woman who had a fatal form of brain cancer. No one would operate on her. Most doctors would have given her up, told her family to take her home and let her die. But then, that's Dr. Glick's speciality: Hopeless cases. You see, the fact is, malignant brain tumors are almost always fatal, so why bother doing surgery? The patient's going to die anyway. On the other hand, Dr. Glick can sometimes take a comatose patient and, by carefully removing as much of the tumor as possible, give the family someone they can talk to, someone who can say goodbye, maybe even someone with a few good years left.

After the intricate and tedious operation, this particular woman survived for three more years. In fact, there was an unforeseen benefit from the operation. She had gone through a hideous divorce from a very bad husband, and when Roberta removed the tumor, she also inadvertently removed the part of the woman's brain that contained her husband. "She had absolutely no memory of him, nor of the messy divorce. It was kind of a bonus for her. She was happy. She was doing fine. But then she caught on fire and burned up," Dr. Glick told me. The woman was making coffee when her robe caught on fire. "Her mother came in and watched her burn to death." I could see the pain in Dr. Glick's face when she thought of the paradox of losing this woman, whose life she'd saved, to fire. All Dr. Glick could do was toss it off with a remark. Otherwise, if she became too involved with it, then all her pursuits would seem futile. The whole practice and all her skills would seem a grim joke, and she'd have to quit and go into a cushy private practice.

There was a man who made a study of which qualities might predict who would become a good neurosurgeon. He first went to the seminary for advice on how they chose priests, but they were of no help. Then he went to United Airlines to ask them how they found good pilots. United told him, "Well, there are pilots who will get you from A to B every time and never do anything interesting, and then there are test pilots. There's not much in between."

"Which one are you?" I asked Dr. Glick.

"I'm a test pilot," she said.

So she was. She took the cases that no one else would touch. Once two little girls were brought to Chicago from Honduras. They were both terminally ill, and no one would operate on them, not Children's Memorial Hospital, not Northwestern, not the University of Chicago. They did not want the blood on their hands. Besides, they wanted paying customers. Dr. Glick took them for free at Cook County. She performed both operations. She kept a photograph of herself with one of them on her office bulletin board. The picture showed Dr. Glick, smiling, her arm around an eight-year-old girl whose head was all bandaged in white. The little girl was smiling, too, and her parents were smiling. Everybody was smiling.

"How did they do?" I asked.

"She lived," Dr. Glick said, pointing to the smiling girl with pretty brown eyes. "The other one died."

And so, as we made rounds, I began to understand what Dr. Glick thought about when she'd say something like, "Oh, this is all lightweight stuff. This is routine." At other times, she'd hunker down inside herself and whisper something like this: "In one day there is so much drama, there's such intensity, you have to go home and numb out. Sometimes I get home from a case, and it's two in the morning, and I've been up for days, but I'm not even tired anymore—I'm beyond being tired— and I just sit up watching 'Ben Casey' or something moronic. It's what I call the Never-ending Search for Boredom."

I commuted to work with Dr. Glick, and every morning we'd get into her dusty black Honda Civic and ride to downtown Chicago, stopping at McDonald's on the way to get coffee and orange juice, and sometimes a plain biscuit. Dr. Glick liked to try to sum up neurosurgery for me, but we both knew that she never could. She'd say, "Neurosurgery is the most fun you can have with your clothes on." Then she'd think about it and say, "No, that's not right. Neurosurgery is . . ." But it always came out sounding like something Charlie Brown would say on a greeting card. And then a summary of her world would come down out of nowhere, like the day we were driving home and her beeper went off. Dr. Glick called the hospital on the car phone that she kept on the floor under a knitted cap. The sun was going down, and along the lakeshore the waves were crashing in a bloody running sunlight. I heard her talking, then she turned to me and said, "One of my patients is DOA in the hospital. Listen. I'm on hold." She put the phone to my ear. I could hear elevator music playing. "Isn't that great music to hear when you're waiting for someone to tell you your patient is dead?"

So sometimes we just rode in silence.

One morning there was a long period of silence, and I knew she was thinking about "Neurosurgery is . . ." Finally, she said, "Nobody wants to touch the brain." She was not being flip. She was making the observation that the brain is a holy place, a dangerous place to be, and that most doctors are afraid of it, just as most pilots are afraid of flying upside down. I waited, as we cruised along the lakeshore, watching the waves curl and disintegrate in the winter sunlight. Then Dr. Glick said, reverently, almost in a whisper, "We're going to touch the brain today."

There are very few arts that can make a grown man faint. But when Roberta Glick first uncovered the human brain and showed it to me, I broke out in a cold sweat, and I had to put my head between my knees.

■　■　■

Coming out of surgery, I always felt dangerously contaminated, as if I'd been working with plutonium. In part it was the constant threat of AIDS when we were sprayed with the patient's blood. In part it was the smoke that seemed to hang continuously in the warm, moist air of the operating room during brain surgery, the toasty smell of flesh from the cautery knives, an odor that seemed to cling to me for days, no matter how many showers I took.

People who have never spent any time in one may speak of operating rooms as the epitome of cleanliness, but when I turn my mind back to surgery, I see the piles of bloody sponges through a curtain of blue smoke; I see the burn-blackened flesh of the scalp that is pinned back to the blue bunting with black threads and silver clamps; and I see a fragment of someone's skull skittering across the cracked linoleum floor and disappearing underneath the silver-painted radiator in the corner.

My first time, a sense of panic overtook me as we went in. Even before we got through the amazing fortress of the skull to the actual brain, I felt I was being suffocated, as I watched Dr. Glick lift the scalp and peel it back and cut through facial muscles just over the patient's eye socket. Dr. Glick was a vegetarian, and I began to understand why. People are made of meat.

My panic was rooted in a deeper sense of what was going on. To begin with, it takes time to disengage; during my first few operations, the patient's flesh was my flesh. I could feel each scalpel stroke; I was wide awake, and they were operating on me. The danger was so palpable then—that this human form was coming undone before my eyes, as if we'd pulled the keystone out of the great Building of Life. I knew that we were creating a grave emergency with each new step we took, plunging deeper and deeper into the unknown, and yet on we went. Indeed, what Nature had so wonderfully stitched together, molecule by electric molecule—this beautiful, fanciful, dimpled smoothness, this robust living tissue—was being jerked apart, and there was no hope that it would ever go back together again, not the way it was, and maybe not at all.

The problem now before us demanded this sort of desperate action: It had been there for some years, though no one could have known. The woman looked and acted normal enough, until she came in one day complaining of a weakness in her right arm, and then someone took an X-ray of her head, and there it was: A tumor as big as a tennis ball in the center of her brain.

Now on a steel cart I saw her hair in a plastic bag. "It's the law," Dr. Glick told me when I asked why they had saved it. "In case she dies. To return all the parts to her family."

As the knife cut, blood vessels burst like grapes; and as they broke, they trickled, and the trickle of red life flickered white in the light, like a molten magic metal that was sometimes red and sometimes silver. The head—the object of this elaborate and daring ritual—was at chest height, clamped in steel points, like a sculpture on display. Beneath the head a large clear plastic bag hung down to the floor and filled with gore as the operation proceeded. The skin is an amazingly tough and resilient fabric, able to take terrible torment, but under the gleaming silver blade of the scalpel it pops submissively, parting along a neat line down to the white surface beneath: the skull. The skin is thick and its edge is white with fat, but immediately blood would ooze forth, and Dr. Glick touched the vessels with electric forceps to cauterize the bleeding.

Each surgery followed the same pattern: Once the thick scalp had been pulled back from the bone, the thin membrane that covered the skull was removed with electric knives. The first time I saw clouds of smoke rising from a human skull and watched the two blue-shrouded surgeons' heads (Dr. Glick and her chief resident) bobbing with their work—the headlights they wore dancing in the smoke and making odd reflections on the silver-red blood pouring down the drapery below the patient's head—I could not help thinking of primitive rituals of human sacrifice. I understood that we were about to enter into the heart of darkness, armed here with little else than our wits and fire and a few metal implements.

We were in an alien world. A foreign language was spoken. "What's her crit? Give me twenty of Decadron. Cushing retractor." Sometimes after surgery, I'd go back into the world and find it difficult; surgery was a strange dream, a kind of madness: Constant noises hurt our ears, high-pitched screeching sounds, the hiss and hum of fans and the roar of machinery, both near and distant, and the intermittent bells, whistles, tones, and sirens, all underlay with the throbbing heartbeat and breathing of the mechanisms that kept the patient alive as we worked. Usually a beat-up old radio played music from somewhere in a far corner.

A nurse wheeled a black tank of compressed air into view beside the patient, rolling it out on a black dolly with dirty rubber tires. It looked as if we were preparing to weld. On the far side of the patient, a wall of wires, tubes, and monitors hid the anesthesiologist, who was back there chemically manipulating the patient's life functions. Now and then I could see the dark eyes, the Indian brown skin, the red cosmetic dot in the center of her forehead, as she peered over the blue draping and looked out at the theater of surgery from behind her mask.

"Who was the first person to operate on a meningioma?" Dr. Glick asked as she worked quickly and carefully. Neither of her residents knew the answer. "Durand in 1895," Dr. Glick told them. As one of the senior neurosurgeons at Cook County Hospital, it was her job to teach as she worked. "It's amazing how many neurosurgeons," she had told me, "don't even know gross anatomy." More than once I'd seen her send residents back to the textbooks because they could not identify major landmarks within the brain.

The black tank of air was hooked to a pneumatic drill with a drill bit inserted in it—a large one. The helical silver screw skated for a moment on the white surface, then bit and caught and began spewing out curlicues of bone, like holy candle wax. It took all of Dr. Glick's strength to keep the drill biting. I wondered what it sounded like inside the secret vault of that woman's head when they applied the screaming silver drill to her skull. (Could she hear? Once, during surgery, two residents were making jokes, and Dr. Glick stopped them, saying, "You know, they say that even anesthetized patients can hear what we say. Have a little respect.") The chief resident, using something that looked like a basting bulb, splashed salt water on the drill bit to keep it cool. It was a bizarre baptism of holy water and steel. The white bone that was being screwed up out of the growing skull hole mixed with water and blood and ran like semen down the blue surgical drapings into the long clear plastic bag. One of the residents kicked a bloody sponge down between my feet. As the growling drill gnawed into the patient's head, I saw the brown eyes of the anesthesiologist peer out at me for a moment, then disappear once again. A Mozart chorus played from a speaker somewhere.

Blood, like fine silver, tarnishes to a black metallic sheen if it's left in the open air. Blood is metal; it's crystalline; it is the life force. It can also be the kiss of death. One morning Dr. Glick forgot to put on her goggles and only remembered when she hit an artery. The spray of blood caught us all in its shower, but it hit Dr. Glick directly in the eye. She leapt from the operating room and ran to wash her eye. A couple of weeks later, she said to me, walking down the hall, "I still haven't gotten myself tested for HIV virus," the AIDS virus.

Now Dr. Glick withdrew the drill, and the scrimshaw of her art showed clearly: A nickel-sized hole, beneath which we could see the *dura mater* covering a living human brain. "Do you know what *dura mater* means?" Dr. Glick asked. "It means 'tough mother.' And this is one tough mother."

The bone was not only tough, it was alive. It bled. It was also surprisingly thick. I found it difficult to believe that anything could crack my skull without also killing me. The chief resident was drilling the second hole now, and it took all his strength, too. He got up on his toes and leaned down with elbows out and an expression on his face of fierce concentration. While the drill was passing back and forth between the two surgeons, making its siren sound and its dental smell, I caught sight of a man, reflected in the glass of a cabinet where surgical supplies were kept: He wore clear plastic goggles (to protect his eyes from flying bone chips and spraying blood), a blue surgical mask, a green hairnet, and swamp-green scrubs. His eyes were wide with amazement at what he was seeing; the skin of his face was pale with shock. It took me a moment to realize that I was looking at myself.

Finally, all six holes were drilled, and the air was thick with the smell of burned flesh and bone, as Dr. Glick called for the geelee saw guide. "Do you know what this is used for?" she asked. "It's a French safecracker's tool," she said, waving the thin strip of spring steel at us.

Dr. Glick inserted the geelee saw guide into one of the holes to pass it between the skull and the *dura* so that it came out the next hole. Blood flowed at each hole as she worked, while the chief resident worked at a steel cart, fitting a cutting bit onto the pneumatic drill head. The phone rang, and a nurse held it to his ear so that he could prescribe medication for one of his patients without contaminating his hands.

Taking turns, they cut with the pneumatic saw blade from hole to hole. "Like cutting plywood," Dr. Glick had told me. Only it was nothing like cutting plywood. Bone is alive, and beneath all the blue draping was a human being, ensconced in the form of a towering sarcophagus. A steel platform was suspended above the patient, on which all the surgical tools were laid out, and a scrub nurse stood on a riser above us to reach them and pass them one by one to Dr. Glick. "Surgery is all ritual," she told me one day.

Now the whistling saw was spuming forth its white froth of spermy bone, giving off a smell of sea wrack and rotten weed and burning flesh, as Mozart played along. ("We play rock-and-roll when we're closing," Dr. Glick said. "It makes it go faster.") As the buzz saw rounded the corner to the last hole, the bit slowed down, the tone went down, and the music stopped as the skull fell open. With four hands, they lifted the tea saucer of bone and splashed it into a stainless steel bowl of water, a move that made me think of the sacraments. It was difficult not to, with the vestments, the incense, the ritual nature of surgery, and even the music.

Now through the semi-translucence of the bloody *dura*, I could see a dark and forbidding blue-gray shade, like building storm clouds, the matter of thought itself, beating and rising with the tide of life, which lay unraveled now in bloody streamers.

Dr. Glick plucked the membrane with a stainless steel pick as fine as a sewing needle, and then cut it with the tip of a scalpel—the slightest

House of Pain

touch of the blade parted the tissue. Then, guiding the instrument care-fully, she slit the *dura* all around and peeled it back to reveal the naked brain.

"No one wants to touch the brain," she had told me more than once. "The general surgeon will do almost anything, but no one wants to touch the brain. It's too mysterious." What she meant was that it was too risky. There is no wiring diagram for the human brain. Sometimes, they could take enormous pieces of it out, and the person would remain completely normal afterward. Other times, they could nick a blood ves-sel and render a patient unable to speak. Moreover, it takes a lot of blood up there to keep things going. That tidal surge of blood collects at the top of the head—the saggital sinus—which is not so much a blood vessel as it is a virtual canyon of blood. From there it flows back out of the brain and recirculates. When doing brain surgery—going in with the drills and saws and then puncturing the *dura*—it is crucial not to start the sinus bleeding, because then it's like the dam has burst. There's no way to stop it, and it comes roaring out of there until there is no more. Once I saw it nicked ever-so-slightly, and we were awash in blood. One morning a chief resident came out as we were going in, and he was shaken and pale and saying, "I'd begun to think I should do neurosurgery wearing rubber boots."

And yet, just when I thought I had heard or seen the strangest thing of all, Nature had another surprise in store for me: One day, after surgery, after we had closed and were back in her office, Dr. Glick asked me, "Did you see how the brain started looking all red and angry at the end there?" I said I had. She explained that sometimes the brain will take the abuse of trauma, and sometimes it will not. Now and then when they opened someone's head, the irritated brain simply swelled up, overflowed the boundaries of the skull, and continued swelling right out of the patient's head.

"What do you do then?" I asked.

"Lop off as much as we have to, and close 'em up," she said.

I found it difficult to accept that there was nothing more, not some secret answer, some maneuver, some last incantation that would save the day. But it was just a measure of how primitive our methods were. And it was a reminder, lest we forget, how costly mistakes could be, whether they were Nature's mistakes or our own.

on Brain Surgery

As soon as the brain was exposed, Dr. Glick called for the laser and asked, "Is everyone wearing goggles?" She held the laser gun poised over the patient's beating brain. Dr. Glick took up a wooden tongue depressor and pointed the laser gun at it and fired. A wisp of smoke curled into the air. A neat black hole appeared in the wooden spatula. "I guess it's turned on," she said with a laugh.

As the laser reduced the tumor to ashes, the two surgeons chatted about doctors who had set patients on fire. One surgeon got the nickname "Torch" because he set several patients on fire with a laser, and I wanted to say, "Shh! The patient might hear you."

The tumor began to glow from within. I don't think I'd ever seen anything as strange as that. The tumor was a fatty, convoluted, red, angry blob, like special effects in a bad horror film, only it was real, and it was inside someone's brain. There is no limit to the Great Imagination: One day we went into a lady's brain and found a fungus ball, a mushroom-shaped growth the size of a bonsai tree right in the center of her head. It was no wonder people believed in voodoo, hexes, and the presence of the devil. How else to explain such a gleeful, malicious, and devious trick of Nature that would cause a mushroom to grow in one's brain?

Now the glistening fatty blob, which was the size of a baseball, was being reduced to brown ash from the shimmering caustic laser light inside it—our cancer within the cancer—fighting fire with fire. The chief resident wanted to crank up the laser and blaze away, commando-style, but Dr. Glick took it slowly, inch by smoking inch. The field was flowing with bright hot lava. The anesthesiologist started a unit of blood.

By the time of that particular operation, I had been at it for a while, and I'd become somewhat inured to the vicissitudes of surgery, the blood and smoke, the smells and sounds. I found myself yawning there, exhausted from weeks of work, and somewhat hungry, because it was afternoon, and we'd been there since seven. It was nothing for Dr. Glick—she could go fourteen hours.

Early that morning, during prep, she had stopped in the staff room for a cup of coffee, and I watched as she poured the plastic cup full of milk and added a teaspoon of coffee. I had wondered why she did that, until I watched her operate and realized that she didn't get to go to the bathroom between seven in the morning and seven at night. When I would go home to have dinner (or even wimp out and go to bed) sometimes Dr. Glick would call me at eleven or midnight and I'd hear her cackle madly on the other end of the line and say with a kind of goading, prideful levity, "I'm still in the O.R., Laurence. You want to come down and watch some more?"

I began to realize that they took pleasure in the pain of exhaustion, these surgeons. Also, I began to understand the paradox of what might seem—to the casual observer—their callous attitude, when compared with the actual depth of their passion and compassion. For no matter what they said, no matter what jokes they made or what hard remarks, they always did it while they were saving someone's life. I'd seen the same attitude among fighter pilots, who would say, "It's not your day," when they meant, "This will kill you." A surgeon would no more say, "I love this patient," than a fighter pilot would say, "I'm afraid of dying in a crash," although both of those statements would certainly be the truth.

There's a certain class of people who aren't called to show up for work unless someone has already hit the panic button, and Dr. Glick was certainly one of them.

One day while I was at the hospital, a construction worker fell off a building, and then a piece of heavy equipment fell on top of him. Everyone was called in, because that poor man had something wrong with every part of him. His head was smashed. His left leg was crushed. His left lung had filled with blood. His heart was bruised, and at first they were concerned that he might have torn major blood vessels off of it. ("Have you ever seen an emergency chest crack?" Dr. Glick asked. "Oh, you've got to see them crack his chest if they decide to do that.") She was called in because of the head injuries, and when she first laid eyes on him, she said, "Ooo, God, that's yucky."

Indeed, I had never seen anything like it. I stood over him in the Angiogram Room, where they were taking X-rays. The man's face was blown up and distorted until it was unrecognizable, except as purple meat. Bubbles of mucus and sputtering blood percolated out of his nose and mouth around the tape and tubes, shunts and silver clips and clamps and colored lines, red and yellow and green. There must have been a dozen people around him, experts from every field, and while one of Dr. Glick's people was drilling a hole in the man's head, others were running metal probes into his arteries and still others were connecting him to a variety of devices I had never seen before. Every few moments someone would shout a warning that they were going to shoot, and we'd all scurry behind a screen to avoid being irradiated by the X-rays. There was much gaiety and joking about deformed babies.

When they had moved the patient to a trauma unit bed, I stood by him for a long time, waiting for him to die. I wanted to write down what I'd feel when he died. His family was across the hall, and the trauma surgeon had set his chances of living at two-in-ten, which Dr. Glick said was optimistic. He was a big man with reddish-blond hair, and when I came in, his jeans were still on him—what was left of them after the paramedics and surgeons had cut them away to get at the flesh beneath. A nurse brought in his construction boots in a plastic bag. They were filled with blood. Dr. Glick's intracranial pressure monitor was screwed into his head now like a piece of plumbing, and an optical lead from it fed a digital instrument that read the pressure in his brain. His brain was swelling because of the hard blow he'd taken in the fall. That alone could kill him. If his other vital signs stabilized, then Dr. Glick could put him in a drug-induced coma, which would reduce the swelling until his brain could settle down.

More wires and tubes ran into and out of the fallen construction worker than I have ever seen—he was more a device now than a human being—and yet when the trauma surgeon pulled back his eyelid (so badly swollen that it took two fingers to open it) there was a small hazel iris in there and a dark pupil—life. I couldn't help thinking about him on this Friday morning, kissing his wife and children goodbye and going off to work with his lunch pail, thinking about what a great weekend he was going to have. By afternoon, here he was—beside an old Carrier air conditioner by a dirty window overlooking a ventilation shaft in the county hospital. And suddenly I didn't want him to die. I didn't want to see it.

I watched across the aisle as a grandmother stroked the head of an eighteen-year-old boy who had come in with multiple gunshot wounds and was now in a coma. The nurse told me, "He is technically dead, but his family won't give consent. His head is rotting, and his feet are rotting. It's terrible." A surgical resident shook his head, saying, "Yeah, isn't it terrible when they start to decompose on you before they're dead?"

Yet the House of Pain had many carpenters. The construction worker did not die in the night, and by morning, things were looking up. When Dr. Glick and I came in at eight, we saw the trauma team marching in a phalanx down the hall, and we stopped to watch. They were young men and women in green scrubs, and their hair was all in disarray, and they were covered with sweat and blood. They looked like athletes—or more properly, like gladiators—and they were smiling. They had made it through the night with a man that no one thought would live. Of course, they were exhausted, but they looked happy. I thought: Now here's a new TV series, "Trauma Team!"

Dr. Glick paused at her office door to watch. "Look at them," she told me with a laugh. "Look at them. They love it."

We stopped by to see the lady Dr. Glick had operated on the previous day, the one with the tumor the size of a tennis ball. She was sitting up in bed, a youthful, pretty woman with an open smile. I was amazed at how well she looked. There was no sign that she had undergone a traumatic experience, except for the bandages on the back of her head.

"How do you feel?" Dr. Glick asked.

"Fine," she said.

As we walked away, I asked how the woman would do.

"She'll be completely cured," Dr. Glick said.

Making rounds, we passed through the pediatric ward and saw a baby that weighed five hundred grams. "I've never seen a baby that small," Dr. Glick said. She told me how she had recently become very sensitive about things that happened to children. "I can't stand it," she said, "with children. It kills me."

We walked up the stairs and down the hall to stop by and see Helen, the pregnant woman who had been shot in the head. She was sitting up, too, or someone had propped her up, her vacant eyes staring out the dirty window at the little park across the street. Her mouth was working, and bubbles of saliva grew and popped and grew again. "Look at that," Dr. Glick said, explaining that sometimes coma patients move their mouths like that before they start to come out of it. "She might wake up. Good morning, Helen."

Austin

on the Blues

The night I arrived in Austin there was a benefit blues jam at Pearl's Oyster Bar. Pearl's is a big room with lazy ceiling fans turning over an endless stretch of bar stools. Long black tables on a contemporary black-and-white tile floor give the place a clean look that sets it apart from most Austin nightclubs. As my brother Gregory and I walked in, Dave Sebree, up on a small raised stage, was walking his vintage Fender guitar into a long, explosive dirge introduction. There'd be a whining expulsion of guitar notes, an alien voice trying urgently to talk, word by painful word. Then a sudden streak of flickering sound in sixty-fourth notes would spill over like an electrical discharge from cloud to blackened cloud. All of this rode on the back of a bass drum beast, ride and snare and high hat clattering upon its saddle. The drummer's set was painted with purple hippos and other mutant zoo animals.

My brother Gregory has been a Texas nightclub musician ever since tragically discovering rhythm and blues in his first semester of a full-ride math scholarship to Rice University almost thirty years ago. Between his saxophone and his singing, he's managed to work with everyone from Johnny Winter to Willie Nelson and in every knocked-together joint from the Louisiana oil fields to the Pecos River. Now he dragged me to the front of Pearl's and pointed out his friend Bob Kniffin up on the stage. A curly-haired man in his late thirties or early forties, it would not have seemed out of place to find Bob selling cars or insurance or teaching college English. There he was, though, singing and playing rhythm guitar behind Dave Sebree's solo. He sang a chorus and then tore into his own solo that left the sallow, buck-toothed keyboard player gaping in disbelief at the sounds he was hearing.

Kniffin was notorious all over southwest Texas as a truly psychotic guitarist, as likely to break into licks from Ornette Coleman or Archie Schepp as to fall back on the Austin tradition of Stevie Ray Vaughan's blues, which Sebree was carrying on. Kniffin's bands themselves have caused eyebrows to raise in Austin and San Antonio in recent years. Gregory was a member of Kniffin's "One Quarter Human." Before that, there was "Bob and the Sea Monkeys," which actually released a tape called "Hung like a Donkey." The label showed a donkey with a rope around its neck. Southwest Texas is famous for local bands like these, and as I walked around Austin, I saw posters everywhere for bands with names like Liquid Mice and Billy Bacon and the Forbidden Pigs, whose new album "Dressed to Swill" appeared to be generating some enthusiasm around town.

Even though it was only a Monday night, Pearl's was jammed, not only with people who wanted good seafood and beer, but with musicians from all over town, come to pay their respects to Mark Long and his family. Mark was a waiter at Pearl's. He was murdered the week before. Mark was young and sweet and everyone loved him. He was found dead in his car, shot through the head. I had known the violence of Texas when I worked there as a traveling rhythm-and-blues musician in the sixties. I remember seeing a sign in the window of a dry cleaners across the street from the courthouse in San Antonio that advertised: "We re-weave bullet holes." I understand that Austin hasn't become that violent yet; but when you hear about "The Travis County Cooler," don't think it's a wine-and-fruit-juice drink: Mark was apparently the victim of a Texas traffic disagreement that ended with someone pulling a gun—no one knows who. Now Pearl's and musicians from all over Austin were getting together to help Mark's widow with what little money they could collect, and the atmosphere was, if not festive, at least energized by the grim urgency of life along the Colorado River. Several couples were dancing on the cramped dance floor, as Kniffin wrapped up a solo that was hampered only by the mangled fingers of his left hand, which he'd crushed in a door earlier in the day and which had grown black and swollen during the set.

Kniffin came off the stage and the three of us gathered in the back of the club to watch the procession of singers, bassists, drummers, guitarists—the music never actually stopped, as musicians changed places, new ones arriving and exhausted ones leaving throughout the night. It was a true jam in the grand old style, and there are only a few cities left where we can still witness that kind of performance. As in the gold rush days of California, all you have to do is show up, and the treasure is yours. New Orleans is certainly one of those cities. But Austin has more music per square foot than any place I've ever been. As in New Orleans, there is a large local musician population in Austin, as well as a style of music that runs like plasma through the veins of the city. Everyone speaks a common language. The local musicians know each other, of course, but they can also walk into a bar and sit in and pretty much know what the songs are, the correct key, the signals, and even where the drum solo goes. A finger pointed at the right moment, a nod, a wink—it always sounds as if they've rehearsed, but they're just members of the same tribe. It's like sandlot baseball: You don't have to ask the rules.

Now Gregory, Bob Kniffin, and I huddled at the back to listen, as a studious-looking drummer with a cigarette dangling from his lips and a terrific rhythm-guitar player named Glen Rexach tried to drive a locomotive through that old Peavey Classic 50 amp, while a singer with a long-neck in hand split the air with a rough blues lament.

I asked Bob if he thought Mark's murder was a sign that Austin was becoming more violent like San Antonio and Houston had become.

In customary Texas style, Bob said, "I don't know," and then embellished the thought with a story. "I remember one night I was playing here and some guy yelled at me, 'Why don't you get a real job,' and I just went off. These fucking people don't recognize what you're playing unless you're imitating Stevie Ray Vaughan or Willie Nelson. I just grabbed the mike and yelled back, 'I've got a real job: Fucking your mother. Only what makes it such a hard job is that the bitch is so fucking ugly.' The guy went out in the parking lot and waited for me for an hour and a half. I don't know. People just get crazy here."

Rexach switched to bass, and a short, fat, bearded fellow took center stage to sing. So it went all night long, with the dirty little guy being replaced by a big clean collegiate guy, who played like Jimi Hendrix.

At the back of the club, Gregory watched for a while, rubbed his grizzled beard, and said, "Ahh, I played all them notes before."

"Yeah," Bob said, "but not in that order."

"Yeah, and not that fast either," Gregory said. "Well, anyway, it's not *that* much fun."

"All they need is a singer to hold them guitar solos apart," Bob said.

And then they fell to reminiscing about the time Gregory was playing a gig and Bob happened to come up to the stage to hassle him and shouted something obscene, to which Gregory made a professional comeback, to which Bob responded, "Tell it to your mother," to which Gregory said, "You can tell her yourself. She's sitting right next to you." And Bob turned around to see my parents, who had come down to Texas to hear their son play in a band.

Bob said, "I mean, there was no mistaking it. It was your mother and father. I about died."

Now as Gregory and Bob began gossiping about their drummer, who'd managed to get himself shot not once but on two separate occasions, a whole new band took the stage, one whose members were shaved all over. One was a woman singer/guitarist with reddish-brown dreadlocks, wearing snakeskin boots and bicycle shorts. She was accompanied by a bass player who looked like an angry tennis instructor on a six-state murder spree—Big Dogs and Nikes. The drummer was so young he couldn't see over the ride cymbal, but when they started playing, Gregory and Bob looked up from their gossip and took notice.

"They're doing something there," Bob said.

"They're together," Gregory said.

"That's that waif-on-lithium sound."

"I like some of that shit."

As we talked, more musicians came up the street like parking-lot refugees. Gregory and Bob shrugged and went back to their talk: Oh, well, it's just Austin. Music here is like the Northern Lights in the Arctic Circle: The locals like it all right, but it can blind you if you're an outsider.

"I've got to get home," Bob said. "I can't be too careful. My wife's a full-blown coon-ass."

"Yeah? Well, how did they feel about their daughter marrying outside the family?" Gregory asked.

Then Bob tried to kiss Gregory, and as Gregory was struggling to get away and while all these Texas men in cowboy boots with long-neck beer bottles in their fists watched the scene unfold, Bob shouted, "What's the matter? Are you afraid to kiss an old man in a Texas nightclub?"

Late in the evening, guitarist Van Wilks showed up, "A well-known Austin stalwart," Kniffin observed as Wilks took the stage, his bald head shining in the spotlight. He was one of those serious, studious-looking musicians you see all over Austin. He hardly cracked a smile, but his fingers were flying, and as he built momentum, he blew that little oyster bar right out onto U.S. Highway 183.

The remarkable thing about the evening was this: Hour after hour, all night long, they came up the street and sat in. And they were all *really good*. And they were all white. Where did they get all these really accomplished blues musicians who look like college students or their professors? Well, a lot of them (like Gregory) were actually college students (or their professors) who came down to Texas on some other errand and became irredeemably infected with the blues. Some of them were what we had instead of surfers.

■ ■ ■

A visit to Austin is best begun by checking into the Four Seasons Hotel along the Colorado River, which is one of the best hotels in the United States. Almost every room has a view of the river, where crew boats and geese can be seen slipping along through the day. The grounds are breathtaking. The atmosphere is casual and elegant. The Four Seasons is so secure in its own image that it will let you have your big old slobbering and shedding Labrador retriever in your room. The Four Seasons is an adult hotel.

Because music in Austin ends at 2 A.M., breakfast in bed comes about noon. A swim in Barton Springs in the afternoon is a good way to exercise in Austin because it's the only outdoor place in the city that's cool; the water is sixty-nine degrees year round and topless bathing is okay for not just one but two genders. "It's hotter than Africa here," one local told me, and he'd been to both places; he owned one of those hill country game preserves where you can contract to shoot a Walia Ibex. Sometimes in the summertime you can see the large black buzzards drop off the high tension lines where they roost and begin a slow and hopeful meandering trail that follows the few joggers who are stubborn enough to persist against the dangerous midday heat. But as the sun goes down, the heat rises away to the upper atmosphere, and the goat weed gives off a strange alluring aroma, like the inside of an old cedar closet; and soon the towering cumulus clouds that have threatened to explode all afternoon begin to thin out and stretch away to the pink horizon. That's when people like to gather in the parking lot of the Austin *American Statesman* newspaper under the Congress Avenue bridge and set up cameras on tripods and let their children run around, screaming and laughing as the sun goes down. Everyone there watches the underside of the immense concrete bridge with the flushed, exhausted, yet hopeful expressions of people who've just spent the day in a steam bath.

Just before full dark, the bats come out. Austin has the largest population of bats in the United States. In 1980 when the city rebuilt the Congress Street bridge, an engineering artifact left sixteen-inch crevices all along the underside, which made perfect roosting and nesting places for migrating Mexican free-tail bats. If you've ever wondered what a million dollars would look like flying out the window, this is the place to see it. For more than half an hour these wallet-sized mammalians come flickering out and fly east over the river to form a black and undulating ribbon, which slithers along the horizon as far as the eye can see and then gathers itself into a mysterious black cloud in the distance, and finally disappears like a line of music—gone in the air.

I joined my friends Chris and Gerry Goldstein, and we headed up Lamar Boulevard to Threadgill's for dinner. Gerry, a criminal lawyer who teaches at the University of Texas Law School in Austin, was telling me about the locally famous "Fighting Cocks on Cocaine Case," which won the coveted Most Humorous Defense Award. "Our client," he said, "was arrested by the feds with a kilo of cocaine, and possession of any drug is only a misdemeanor under federal law. He claimed that the cocaine wasn't to sell, nor even for his own use but instead for his fighting cocks. It seems that he'd blow the cocaine into their nostrils during the fight and revive them at the crucial moment."

Ed Wilson, who owns Threadgill's, joined us as we ordered a table full of his famed vegetable dishes, along with some chicken livers for Chris and "Texas Caviar" (a black-eyed pea salad) for Gerry. Ed Wilson has appeared in numerous rock-and-roll concert contract riders, because the musicians insisted on home cooking the way only Threadgill's can make it: meatloaf and chicken-fried steaks, fried chicken, and the famous "bronzed catfish."

Ed has many special gifts—food and music being two of them. Talking is another. Especially talking about the history of his legendary Armadillo World Headquarters, or what he calls "The roots of our permissiveness," which others call, simply, the sixties. So much of what we now call the sixties began in Austin (not San Francisco) that it's difficult to separate the two as cultural phenomena. And it's impossible to separate the food from the history when having dinner with Eddie Wilson.

The Armadillo (and by extension Ed) is credited with changing Austin from a thumb-dick Texas college town into one of the world's most important music cities. As Ed put it, "We was blamed for getting overrun with people. But the clean-room freaks came and built a lot of stuff and fell on their faces, too." He's right about the computer people; Pearl's Oyster Bar is on a street called Research.

Now he's trying to undo some of the damage by giving interviews that bad-mouth the town. During my visit, he was on a radio talk show, telling people that "there are cracks in the street big enough to suck down a whole family in a Cadillac, and that there's a million bands here but not one of them plays in tune." As Gerry, Chris, and I wolfed down mounds of vegetable and jalapeño jambalaya, he explained that the standard of living is bad, there's crime, there are gangs, and there might even be pelagra, too. He suggested that people not even slow down as they pass through Austin. "When I started here, a beer license cost thirty-six dollars. Now you can't hardly open a nightclub without getting strangled by red tape."

In 1972 Eddie Wilson got up on stage to announce the first Willie Nelson concert at Armadillo. Frustrated by the blank stares that greeted that historic proclamation, he grabbed the microphone and shouted, "Well, he's only the Bob Dylan of country music, you hippie assholes!" Now, more than twenty years later, Eddie Wilson sits at a yellow Formica table in Threadgill's, another Austin institution he has created (re-created, actually, out of a 1930s gas station where Janis Joplin got her start). He takes a long look out over the landscape of cultural history before assessing it this way: "The last big hump in the rolly coaster is coming up. It had better be good."

While we ate what most people in Austin admit is the best home cooking in Texas, Houston White sat in a corner, sipping iced tea. Gone all gray now but sporting the same familiar beard, he is still unmistakably one of the Fabulous Furry Freak Brothers created by cartoonists Gilbert Shelton and Tony Bell in their legendary *Wonder Warthog Comix,* which were a seminal Austin influence in the underground press movement of the sixties.

After an enormous meal of Texas chili beans, sautéed squash, red beans and rice, cajun-Italian eggplant, and the delicate and spicy bronzed catfish, we went out into the parking lot. The temperature had settled down to a comfortable eighty-five or ninety degrees, and there was a couple making love in the bed of a sky-blue pickup truck in the shadow of an old tree outside the orange circle of sodium vapor light. We drove down Guadalupe Avenue to Antone's, perhaps the most famous nightclub in Austin, owned by Clifford Antone. The scion of a well-known Louisiana Lebanese family of restauranteurs, whose empire stretches throughout the Gulf Coast basin and points west, Clifford dabbled in a number of experimental business ventures in the bad old days and finally settled on promoting music as a way of having more fun without the risk. Gerry is his attorney. Clifford's ultimate success in Antone's has been given the stamp of approval more than once, perhaps most recently when Willie Nelson celebrated his sixtieth birthday there last year.

The room was cavernous in the grand style of the Whiskey in Los Angeles and numerous other serious music joints, where decor seems to be the result of a recent fire-bombing incident that was never quite cleaned up. The walls were black. The ceiling was black. The lights were off. The concrete floor was scummed over with some sort of resinous gick. The stage was low and crude. And the only evidence of frivolous adornment was a single word made from large and roughly cut white cardboard letters on one wall. It said: BEER. No brand. No price.

When we arrived, singer/guitarist Sue Foley was already playing, accompanied only by John Penner on bass and Freddy Pharoah on drums. She was really ripping it up on her pink Stratocaster. With her reddish-blond hair, in black jeans and T-shirt, and her big white-girl smile, she looked like a Dove Bar ad, but she played this dirty, vagrant, and deeply disturbing blues. Her voice was as sharp and shiny as the wire in her hands. She had a Prohibition-era sound that was hard to reconcile with her wholesome good looks. When she burst forth with a guitar solo, she slashed the Fender neck around as if she were trying to kill a rattlesnake that had her by the thumb and wouldn't let go. She made haunting sounds of captured panic that I still hear sometimes when I'm driving fast on a dark road.

After the set I went to the back room to talk to her. I asked how old she was, and she said, "Mid-twenties." Pharoah said, "Twenty-two." Penner said, "Twenty-four." Then Sue lit up and said, "Yeah, twenty-four. It's twenty-four."

She told me that I could call her if I wanted to know more, "But not tomorrow. I'm going fishing tomorrow." It was an Austin kind of message: I'd like to be famous, but it's going to have to wait. I've got to go fishing first. Her record *Young Girl Blues* is available on Antone's label at Antone's Record Store across Guadalupe Street from Antone's.

■ ■ ■

It was midnight when we arrived at Zona Rosa, a kind of Day-of-the-Dead hallucination in a renovated garage, where the roll-up doors were still rolled up, only now they were painted with alligators and monsters from hell, which appeared to crawl up the wall and across the ceiling over our heads. Hubcaps wired to the high chain-link fence outside spelled out "LA ZONA." The backdrop of the paint-peeling wooden stage was corrugated steel, and a dancing skeleton had been assembled into a mosaic of broken mirrors high on one wall. The featured singer was Sarah Elizabeth Campbell, a large woman with a clear, soft voice. Sarah looked as if she'd lost her children at Sea World and had wandered in here by accident in her flower-print stretch pants and battered Bass leather sandals, but she sang just as pretty as Emmy Lou Harris and was accompanied by mandolin, bass, guitar, and keyboards—one of those amazing Austin pick-up bands (the next night I saw the same mandolin player doing bluegrass at Threadgill's 6:30 Wednesday night jam). The group sounded eerily like The Band, all back-in-the-woods somewhere where it wasn't cold yet, but it was going to be. She had another one of those serious Austin guitarists. He wore a long-sleeved white dress shirt with the cuffs buttoned and he never smiled, because everything he had was concentrated up in the tips of his fingers, and there's no business like show business, no business at all. Just picking.

Sarah ran the gamut from country to torch song, "Since I Fell for You," and her own original compositions, which sounded a little like the work of J. D. Souther. All the songs were so sad that I began to wonder whether we were going to read about her in the paper the next morning. But then during a break between tunes, she reminded us that Tuesday night was Bummer Night at La Zona. "And here's another sad song," she whispered. "Can I please have a Dr. Pepper?" Dr. Pepper is what people in Austin drink instead of Evian.

And again, when that song ended: "This is one of the saddest songs ever written," Sarah announced. "It's about a dead whore. May I *please* have a Dr. Pepper?"

■ ■ ■

When I awoke early the next afternoon, I slid down Lavaca Street to the Texas Chili Parlor in the shadow of the pink Capitol building for breakfast. On the way I passed Flamengo Automotiva and Sombrero Rosa. ("Close," said the sign on the pink architectural sculpture of an immense round Mexican hat, whose windows had been boarded up.) The Chili Parlor was a dark bar with scarred old wooden tables and heavy wooden chairs. An over-amped collection of junk burst forth from every corner, and a big sign scrawled in red letters hung over the bar:

No Lone Star
No Checks
No Amex
No Fries
No Foo-Foo Drinks
No Talking to Imaginary People

Another sign informed customers that "Tipping is not a place in China." When she came to take my order, the waitress only asked, "Regular, medium, or hot?" and when she brought it, I found that I could turn the heavy white ceramic bowl upside down, and the chili wouldn't fall out. It was served with a mound of jalapeños and onions large enough to open a roadside taco stand, and the medium I ordered was bordering on too hot to eat. But the flavor was right, that Texas acid-whiskey bite and a rich undercurrent of sweet dark flavors that come from using chili pods, not powder.

■ ■ ■

Each evening, as the sun went down, something seemed to be nagging at the back of my mind about Austin's architecture, and finally that day I realized what it was: I had the sun in my eyes no matter what direction I went. Austin in daylight looks like a geode that's been cracked open, and all the projecting spires of glass make it seem utterly artificial.

Moreover, there seems to be a definite low-rider influence in the architecture. As the evening grew dark, lights came on, and I could see that numerous skyscrapers were fringed with blue or red neon, the spectrum-shifting kind those Mexican gang bangers put around the license plates and under the rocker panels on their cars. By the time it's full dark, there is a kind of cheap festive atmosphere to the city that is created in the sky by illuminated buildings twenty or thirty stories tall, hung there like great piñatas.

■　■　■

"Since they changed the drinking age to twenty-one, the Sixth Street scene is dead," Gerry had warned me. But I went anyway, just to see for myself. *Dead* is not exactly the word I would choose. In fact, it's wall-to-wall teenagers, and there are five or six bands to every block, most of them playing in bars that have no cover charge. Gregory told me, "Some of these bands make only three hundred dollars for playing until two A.M. Some of them work for tips." Indeed, at the foot of the stages I saw plastic buckets here and there with signs that said, "Tips." That was their livelihood. The remarkable thing about the Sixth Street scene was that many of the musicians there were the seconds, the rejects, the ones they swept out of the street at night, and they were really good. Austin has such an embarrassment of riches in music that it's practically impossible to walk into a club where there's live music and be sorely disappointed. And if you don't like the style, you can walk next door. As an experiment, I went from bar to bar, listening to one or two songs, and I heard a dozen bands an hour. There's crawfish by the platter and jazz at J. C. Clark. Maggie Mae's is an old stand-by club that features good young bands and dining on an upstairs deck under the stars—or at least under the neon glare of low-rider architecture, which glows like the trail of an electric snail as it crawls across the skyline. Chicago House, just off Sixth, is set up with raked seats like a Chicago theater and features quiet folk music, which was a bizarre, if welcome, change after a dozen electric blues bands. Lovers lay draped across each other in the darkness. It was cool, and there was no smoking.

The best group on Sixth Street that night was Black Pearl. It was no coincidence about the name: singer Lisa Tingle had taken a few pages from Janis Joplin's book, and her guitarist had studied Stevie Ray Vaughan, and her drummer had that fat-back grin, like: Nothing's ever going to be more fun than this. It was midnight, the place was packed, and they were really good.

Lisa was blond and beautiful, and that made it more amazing when she stepped up to the microphone and did "Cold Sweat," a James Brown number that demands a lot from any singer. It wasn't just show, either. She reached way down and ripped something out of herself that didn't want to let go. When she finally worked it up to a screaming finale, the crowd went wild, and people out beyond the picture window on the street stopped to hear what seemed to be an impossible sound coming from this pretty woman who leaped around as if she'd been set afire.

I stopped by Antone's to catch a set of what they call "front porch blues," which is something like "Dueling Banjos" in that scene from the movie *Deliverance*. A large man named Rubin, who had giant arms that were decorated with giant tattoos, played upright bass fiddle, and even his instrument was tattooed with stickers. He wore cut-off jeans and great high-top tennis shoes and a stained T-shirt. His hair was awry and he had a crazed look, and when the banjo player nodded at him for a solo, the man simply went insane with an eruption of string-slapping technical wizardry.

With acoustic guitar, harmonica, and four-string banjo, they played "Stealin'" and similar songs. The banjo player's name was Danny. He was tall and had very long, stringy blond hair—almost albino in appearance. In fact, he looked a little like a Texas musician I played with in the sixties, Johnny Winter, when I lived there and worked as a musician, traveling the country with my brother Gregory. And I realized that here I was seeing the very reason I had quit. These musicians had been doing this all their lives, and they really knew how. They were not trying to "make it." They didn't want to be Jerry Jeff Walker or Willie Nelson. This was as far as the road came, and that was fine with them. As I was having those thoughts, Danny sang a song he wrote called "Going to Brownsville," and I understood that as far as he'd ever dreamed of going was to Brownsville, about 250 miles away.

．　．　．

I took Gregory to Jean Pierre's Upstairs, which along with the Inn at Brushy Creek, is about as close as Austin comes to a big-city restaurant. They had table cloths, for one thing, and the owner, former Peruvian race-car driver Jean Pierre Piaget, had paid someone a lot of money for decorating and for the American native art that hung nicely framed on the walls. Evidently, he also paid a chef, because the food was comparable to some of the nouvelle creole restaurants I'd found in New Orleans, only with a distinctly southwest flavor. Seafood sausage over a bed of saffron fettucini with garlic and chili. Red tortilla soup. Poblano battered shrimp. Pheasant breast over tamale dressing with chipótle demiglaze. Nut soufflé with wild berry sauce: Checkmate. Dinner for two with no alcohol was about eighty dollars.

Most people can eat to satiety at Threadgill's for ten dollars, or certainly at the Texas Chili Parlor. A complete dinner at Ruby's Barbecue, including coffee and dessert, costs only slightly more than that—and this (along with Sam's) is the best barbecue in the state, certainly the most convenient, situated as it is right behind Antone's. One table top at Ruby's was laminated over with testimonials from local musicians. Van Wilks wrote with typical understatement, "Hot beans and coleslaw—thanks." Another scrawled out: "Ruby took my cherry— 6-30-91."

．　．　．

Since the Sixth Street scene exploded and fragmented all over the city, music is no longer centralized, but the Continental Club on South Congress is more out of the way than anything else in Austin, except perhaps Sneakers up in the north nineties on Lamar. The Continental is a small, dirty club with murals of gay Paree (or maybe it was once a bad Italian restaurant, and that's actually Venice). With red upholstered stools and those small high drink tables that are designed to let those fall down who are inclined to fall down, the whole place smells sweet and sharp of urinal disinfectant. In fact, from the moment I walked in,

I recognized this club from my youth. It was just the kind of place we used to play, a real hole. And yet when I had asked Clifford Antone for recommendations of clubs other than his own, the first words from his lips were "Continental Club." Elsewhere in town, when I spoke to musicians, they all said, "Guy Forsythe is playing there tonight. You'd better go see him. He's very authentic."

Authentic? I wasn't sure what that meant. As he got up on stage, I saw just another college kid playing the blues. From the back of the club where I sat at the bar sipping a Coke, he seemed clean cut and had regular features. He wore baggy black pants and a gangster-style silver watch chain. His rhythm guitar player had a gold-medallion Texas tie and a black shirt. I noticed a big plastic jar labeled "Tips" at the foot of the stage and wondered if his band was even getting paid for this late-night gig. (Two other bands had already played earlier in the night.) Guy played one song, and I thought, Wow, this man is really good. By the time that he and his rhythm guitarist were trading licks back and forth at the end of the first song, I was on the edge of my bar stool. I slipped off and pushed through the crowd to get closer.

When I say "college kids," I don't literally mean they were U.T. students, although many of them (such as Janis Joplin) were. But even the others . . . well, they were just kids, white American kids, and they started out wanting to play the blues.

Now, the blues is a shadowy thing, we are told. It's a black art, an occult practice, like divination or alchemy, and its outcomes are uncertain and dangerous. Yet these kids practice the blues. They lock themselves in little rooms all over Texas and practice on ninety-nine-degree summer days and late into the night by turning on window fans, and some of them eventually cross over the line, and an inner change takes place like a deep chromatic shift. Then they are no longer themselves, no longer those college kids with pale, open faces. They look down one day, and they have the hands of a monster, and there is a fulminating sound coming from the instrument. The monster comes roaring out at them and consumes them, and from then on the blues is all they've got. They're destined to wander around inside of it for the rest of their lives.

Guy Forsythe had crossed over the line. There were no breaks between songs in his titanic set that night. It was as if he'd grabbed a live wire and could not let go, even though it burned him. His instrument was never out of tune, and the faint, bemused smile on his face changed only now and then to an Edvard Munch sort of scream. He sang "Can't Be Satisfied" from Muddy Waters's famous record, a seminal piece about killing his girlfriend, the very essence of the blues. Oh, Guy Forsythe loved that one. He danced and smiled and yelled and jumped as he sang: "I feel like snapping a pistol in her face. I'm going to let some graveyard, Lord, be her resting place."

His jubilance was so boyish and genuine, so immediate and spontaneous, that it was infectious and became part of the whole performance. Yet it was menacing, too, a devil dance. Now and then as he creased the air with astonishing and spectacular sounds, I could see him look down at his own hands in disbelief: Even after all these years, he could hardly believe he was making that music. I had finally worked my way right up next to the stage, and I could see his short-sleeved shirt hike up to reveal the edge of a tattoo and the grizzled look where he hadn't shaved, and I felt a twinge of pain as I understood what a sound like that had cost of his youth, and what price it would continue to exact in the years to come. I saw the green glass of a cut wine bottle neck on his little finger, flying as he played slide guitar: He had the dynamics, real dynamics, unlike so many bands that have one volume: LOUDER.

Now Guy danced a fiendish dance, shaking and whipping around and crying out as the drummer pounded a vengeful rhythm, casting a spell deep into the morning hours.

I kept trying to go home. I had a headache and a brutal two-hour drive ahead of me to meet my kids in San Antonio, where my relatives live. But I couldn't leave. He had me pinned there. And when he put on his ammo belt of harmonicas, I knew I wouldn't leave until he did.

He played like that, with a wanton, seductive abandon, until after two A.M., and then I walked out into the dead, wet night air, remembering all the nights of playing Texas clubs with Johnny Winter and others, the night terrors, the acoustic tremors, the endless road, and the deadly roach motels where we passed our mornings in coma sleep. We had been like the bats under the Congress Street bridge, flickering into the falling evening on our endless errand.

Austin

In the Belly of the Whale

on an Off-Shore Oil Rig

When the crew boat arrived at a little past dawn, I saw no way for us to get from the deck of the boat to the main deck of the rig. There were no stairs. There was no elevator. Yet the off-shore oil-drilling rig towered above us and blotted out the sun, a skyscraper teetering on three enormous steel pilings driven into the surface of the heaving sea. The slick pilings, shooting right out of the sea, offered no handholds, so the entire question of getting on and off the rig remained mysterious to me. The crew, which had been sleeping in rows of aqua-blue Naugahyde chairs in the dark cabin below decks ever since we left Galveston several hours earlier, had come out, all sleepy and yawning, with hair matted and eyes crossed, and those rough, dirty men in T-shirts and jeans and construction boots carried their sea bags onto the rear deck of that ancient one-hundred-foot diesel boat and stood there on the greasy wooden planks as if God himself were about to come down and lift them up to the deck above so that they could go to work.

I had been waiting to meet the man in charge, Bud Cole, but he had been asleep below during the whole trip, and now I saw him standing on the deck ahead of all the other men, his sea bag at his feet—first in line, it seemed (though in line for what, I still could not imagine). I crawled across the planks of the deck, the blackened-with-oil deck, all worn to a supple, oily suede by years and years of shoes and gear. I stumbled over chains and wooden crates to get to Bud, and when I finally stood beside him, I gazed up at the amazing edifice of gray steel, which we faced in our tiny boat, bobbing on the open sea. There was a pile of brown rope at Bud Cole's feet. It was in the center of what looked to be an oversized orange life ring, and its purpose, if it had any, evaded me, as everything else about this trip had so far, ever since the twinkling lights of Galveston Island had withered and vanished on the dark horizon behind our churning green wake in the dead of night.

Bud wore a blue jumpsuit and was built like a Rottweiller dog, the kind of man it would be difficult to knock over, because he was wide and had a low center of gravity. I was to learn that natural selection would favor that quality on an oil rig: Speaking strictly in terms of Newtonian physics, a man like that is already down when he's standing up, and so he would be less likely to fall off. Bud was looking up and away from me, so I poked him in the arm to get his attention, and my fingertip met something the texture of an inflated truck tire. It was Bud Cole's tricep muscle.

I introduced myself, and it became immediately apparent that no one had told him that I was coming onto his oil rig. He turned his scowling, incredulous rage upon me: a visage that was reticulated with the complex carvings of sea wind and time, like a face on a crumpled hundred-dollar bill. He wore a hard hat, and beneath its brim were the small and venomous spiders of his eyes, peering at me out of their agitated web of wrinkles.

"I'm a writer," I said by way of explanation.

"Oh," he said, his face breaking into the smile of a guard dog. "A writer. Just what we fucking need." And with no goodbye or further warning, he stepped onto the big orange life ring near his feet. The rope that had been piled within its circumference straightened up as if by a magical force and created a woven basket in the air, standing by itself without any evident reason why it should, except that there were unknowable forces all around us, and this evidently was one of them.

The boat pitched and rolled with the sea, and Bud grabbed hold of some of the rope standing inexplicably among us. Three other men grabbed hands full of that same black rope creation, all matted and slick with grime and the secretions of some dark process. Each man placed one foot on the orange ring, and then, with the rope taut and singing in the sea wind, they all rose amazingly into the sky, like the trapeze lady does before her circus act, a hand trailing languidly in the air.

Because of having pushed my way to the head of the line to talk to Bud, I found that I was next, I and three companions. The man to my left must have seen the look of horrified incomprehension on my face when Bud ascended into the heavens, because he tried to explain to me how to take the ride. As the open-work basket was coming back down, empty now, I began to understand the mechanism by which we were expected to get onto the oil rig from that pitching boat, which was holding itself steady in the running seas by means of its diesel engines and the skilled hands of its captain at the throttles. Now I began to put together pieces of the puzzle: I could see far above us the red Link-Belt crane, perched atop the fifteen-story structure and swiveling and grinding as it lowered the cable on which dangled the woven-rope basket with the orange ring at the bottom.

The man to my left was now speaking to me with the intent, perhaps, to save my life. He was thin and wasted beyond recognition as a human being. His teeth had turned black, and his skin was creased into a mummified, corpse-like appearance, and his moustache dangled like a false moustache, fashioned for Halloween effect out of a handful of horsetail clippings. He wore a hard hat and squinted at the sun now rising higher, and he said with a Cajun accent so thick I could barely understand him, "Keep one foot on the deck, so you can get off if the boat pitches out from under you. You don't want to be caught up on the basket until you're ready to go. Then just hang on."

"What?" I asked. I didn't understand what he meant. But the three men standing with me had thrown their sea bags into the middle of the orange ring, which had a round piece of canvas lashed onto its circumference, like a trampoline, to accommodate cargo. I saw now that the outer ring was a circle of steel pipe with orange polystyrene padding, and the man who was trying to talk to me grabbed two hands full of rope and put one construction boot on the iron ring. I threw my bag in the center with the others and took hold of the rope and put my steel-toed boot on the circle. I inferred from what they were doing that, contrary to my instinct of self-preservation, we were to hang on outside the basket rather than crawl inside the cage it formed, which seemed to be a superfluous display of machismo under the circumstances.

"Now, what did you say?" I asked. Before he could answer, I was jerked off the deck, up and away from the gentle lapping of the ocean green, and I was swinging and floating in the air—now five, now ten stories up—over the tiny boat below and all the other crewmen down there, gawking up at me and grinning in their peculiar way that I would learn was a kind of detached and malicious delight at the mortal plight of another human being.

I found myself above the very rig itself. Suddenly and as if by a powerful magic I scarcely understood, I was looking down on the chaotic angularity of the great gray derrick and the vast and cluttered Texas deck, which was strewn with sharp objects and welding tanks and hoses and drums, churning black gears and whirling red machinery; and I understood that the greasy rope in my hand and those four pale fingers that I used for nothing more strenuous than hoisting a pencil now and then were all that stood between me and something I was not quite ready to face. Infinity, I suppose. All at once, I understood that this was a test. The stepping onto the basket had been a profound test, a first combat Rorshach, when we are expected to reach into the dark grab-bag of the soul and come up with a big surprise—in a matter of a second or two everything is all decided. We find out what we're made of, and there's no time to plan it. It's not show, like so much of life on shore. I was surprised how comfortable I was up there, dangling like a toy in the sky over the jagged metal jaws of the rig. I was almost sorry when the ride was over, because it was such an interesting vantage from which to view the work we do with our breathtaking arrogance.

When I alighted from the basket (and just when I should have felt safest) I understood that I had been delivered into the far greater peril of the clanging, churning rig itself, as if I'd been a tender bit of carrot, tossed into the teeth of a blender.

■   ■   ■

We were out in the Gulf of Mexico, in thirteen fathoms of water, for one purpose and one purpose only: To make money. The men were there because no one would do that kind of work unless it paid well. The pay was good, of course, because no one would take all that trouble if there wasn't a lot of profit to be made by the parent company. We were there to take oil and gas out of the earth.

The type of rig we were on is known as a Bethlemen jack-up rig. It was made by Bethlehem Steel, and the mechanism by which it is jacked up is peculiar to that company's design. The main deck and all the great steel structure of the thing, which is about the size of a down-town office building in St. Paul, Minnesota, is designed to float in the water. It has three immense steel legs running through it, like the legs of a stool. The rig can run itself up and down the legs by means of hydraulic power and steel pins inserted in holes in the legs. Thus the building can crawl up and down those legs. With the legs above the water, the rig floats like an inverted stool. The rig is towed out to sea. There the hydraulic mechanism ratchets the legs down into the sea. The legs meet the immovable ocean floor and then the rig continues to jack itself up. Pushing against the sea bottom, it lifts out of the water. Thus it climbs to the top of the legs and balances there, like a Brad Holland painting of a man on stilts standing mysteriously in the waves.

One man who'd been working those rigs since they were invented told me that when they first appeared in the Gulf, "People were scared to death to work on jack-ups." He said they just seemed too weird, this whole building hiking itself up three steel pilings in the middle of the ocean and being expected to stay there. People thought it was crazy. Some still do. Approaching those rigs out in the open sea, there is certainly an eerie sense that one is seeing a very bad idea made manifest.

Once the platform is in place, and the legs are fully extended, the actual rig (the derrick we have all seen in films) is extended out over the ocean on a cantilevered mechanism, the size of which defies our ability to comprehend. The everyday machinery of the oil business is beyond the scope of ordinary experience: Everything is extremely large. Men on the rig are but slivers of skin. The off-shore rig is a world of immense gravity, of moving steel in quantities that ordinary men are not used to seeing. When the cantilevered derrick assembly slides out, it is as if an aircraft carrier has gotten underway, only it is underway in mid-air, with no waves of water cleaving on its prow. It glides out on gray steel tracks lapped with black grease until it hangs fifteen stories out over the ocean, and then the deck on which the twenty-story derrick sits becomes analogous to the West Texas desert floor, and drilling begins at that point downward into thin air and then farther downward through green sea water and on below that into sea mud and finally into the black skin and muscle and bone of the very earth itself.

I landed on the rig in the midst of talk and work that I did not understand. Men were coming off the basket four at a time, jumping down to the steel deck and tossing their sea bags off and sitting on them to await instruction.

"You the new tool pusher?"

"Feels good to be home again, doesn't it?"

"I don't even know how to start an SKD-4, let alone pump one."

"You know the difference between a fairy tale and an oil-field story?" someone asked me. "A fairy tale begins, 'Once upon a time,' and an oil-field story begins, 'Now this ain't no shit.'"

Not long after I got there, someone told me, oh, by the way, there's no medic on board, so don't get hurt. It's a long wait for the helicopter. "Say, you got any gloves, or what?" It had been a warm autumn day in Texas when I left, and I had none.

Now all around us on this topmost deck of the rig, I could see the chaos of the audacious effort we were here to undertake: The stealing of natural gas from the very lungs of the earth. The only clear, clean, and uncluttered area I could see was the cantilevered helipad, which balanced out the leaning weight of the cantilevered derrick on the far side of the rig. An orange wind sock waved high above it on a mast. Every thirty seconds I could hear the bel canto singing of the foghorn attached to the oil well. It went like that around the clock. Near us one of the giant columnar legs of the jack-up rig stuck out of a circular hole in the steel deck floor and was shimmed all around its circumference with great buff-gray aluminum wedges.

On my left and right were a matching pair of red Link-Belt cranes, one of which had picked me from the deck of the boat and had carried others from the rig down to the boat during the crew change. The off-shore crews worked seven days on the rig and then had seven days off. Each man worked a twelve-hour shift, from six to six. The rig ran twenty-four hours a day. There were approximately thirty-five men on the rig when I was there (a complete crew was forty-nine).

The available deck space consisted of multi-leveled steel platforms, many football fields in size, open to the sun and air and connected by a maze of steel-mesh staircases like fire escapes, with yellow pipe handrails, so that, in an attempt to cross from one end of the rig to the other in a straight line, one would walk down a level, then up a level, then up another level, then down three levels, migrating in this fashion as if over mountainous terrain. All of that deck space around us, as far as the eye could see, was cluttered with the mess and wreckage of the oil business. Mesh baskets the size of Lincoln Continentals, formed out of red-rusted steel, were filled with trash, pipe, wire, hose, paint cans, and discarded styrene coffee cups. On a lower deck I could see skids of chemicals and sand and cement in brown paper sacks, all wrapped around in clear plastic sheeting against the weather. Red oil drums with black grease streaks sat here and there with no apparent order. Cooling fans in heavy sheet steel cases that protruded ten feet above the deck seemed to ring around us, breathing hot air and a constant roaring noise that made it difficult to talk. Dirt collected everywhere, mixing with grease and oil and forming a black coating on hands and clothes and boots. The incessant wheeling roar of machinery seemed to stalk us, and foul odors amplified the hugeness of the rig and the hugeness of its purpose.

Everywhere I turned, the yawning drop to the sea confronted my movements, and often there was little more than a piece of chain between me and the concupiscent tumbling arc, the downward plunge that would prang the deck with my bones. The highest catwalks were made of metal mesh, like fire escapes, and always through them I could see the dimensionless ocean ten or twenty stories down. At the highest dizzying point of a catwalk, I turned a corner and found myself face to face with a ten-foot-diameter blue fan creating a cyclone of air and trying to blow me off and hurl me fifteen stories to the waves below. I looked down: Lines of pipe lay on a wooden platform below, and ropes and hose were everywhere distributed in chaotic coils and heaps. From one side of the rig, exhaust stacks released coils of smoke into the Gulf air, while blue cooling fans roared beside them, and black tanks of hydrochloric acid below gave off a smell like electricity. Everything—whether tank or pallet or pipe rack—had clevis holds for attachment and was moveable by crane. It had all been disgorged here temporarily, for the purpose of work, and it would be taken away when the work was done.

Some rigs never find a thing for all their drilling, but this one had located a well, and the morning I arrived, someone slid a slick and waxy explosive charge down the hole and fired it, perforating the well casing. Natural gas came vomiting up. It was the modern-day equivalent of a gusher. It looked as if, for all its trouble, the parent company might actually see some profit out of this sea-going erector set.

The derrick itself was a relatively small part of the whole operation. It stood like a rusty Christmas tree in all its ringing steel glory out on the plate steel floor of the cantilevered platform, suspended fifteen stories over the ocean, which was licking the yellow-painted pilings below with a lazy green tongue.

Now I walked out onto that platform. There's something about walking on a surface made of two-inch boiler plate steel. Nothing else in my experience felt that way, not concrete, not dance floors. Out here we were made to match our flesh with steel, and it was cold, and it didn't give at all. I stood between the legs of the derrick to watch the three roughnecks work the pipe and the winch man operate the levers and the derrick man, who hung ten stories above us, perform his astonishing feats of agility.

A thirty-five-thousand-pound yellow steel block and tackle—the "elevator"—was lifting pieces of pipe up out of a hole in the platform floor. Sections of pipe made up the shaft. On the lower end, somewhere beneath sea, was the bit that did the drilling, and now they were drawing it up, section by section.

The roughnecks danced around the block and its snapping "elevator" jaws, which grabbed the pieces of pipe as they came. They'd lift one out of the sea, unscrew it, then send it skyward on the block and tackle, opening and closing the jaws each time. Their eyes were wide with attention, three ordinary-looking young men, who might have been mistaken for fraternity brothers at some state college if they hadn't been covered with oil and mud, if they hadn't been in the middle of the ocean sixty miles from the nearest land. When they attached a section of pipe to the block, it was whisked high into the air, where the derrick man had to catch it and put it into a rack. As the block turned loose of the one-hundred-foot pipe, the derrick man lassoed his end with a piece of rope and a casual, cowboy furling of wrist and arm, taking advantage of the only moment when several tons of steel, balanced on a pencil point, would yield to such an insignificant tug and fall obediently into the rack.

Everything was done at a rapid pace, the way football players run scrimmage at practice, blocking dummies and crushing bone. The roughnecks on this rig were playing without pads, though, and they were playing against steel. While all that action was taking place, everything moved at once and in different directions: The entire platform swayed back and forth with the wind and the force of the waves against it, and so the twenty-story derrick was in a constant state of twisting and torquing. The block, which the winch man raised and lowered like a conductor directing an orchestra with the baton of his lever, was always turning, swinging, and making one-hundred-foot excursions up and down its cables. The men were continually setting and removing the slips, steel shims hinged to fit around the pipe so that it wouldn't slip down the hole and fall into the sea. (In that way, while a length of pipe was fixed in position with slips, the crew could remove the elevator jaws and reposition them for the next pull—the next length of pipe.) Everything was always moving, including the men. By necessity, there was no let-up.

Each time they pulled a section of pipe out of the hole, a piece of pipe ten stories tall was suddenly set free. It literally came alive, wriggling wildly in the air, held by nothing more than the tiny man and his rope high up on the derrick. The marvelous thing that he was doing up there was wrestling on high with a many-ton piece of wild wriggling steel, and all he had to work with was a greasy piece of hemp rope.

He hauled on his rope, and the pipe struggled and whipped away, and I saw him come way out over the side of his little perch up there. For a moment, I thought he was going to take a ride like a minuscule pole vaulter, out into the blue air over the green and churning sea. The metal whip made by the pipe could flick him like a speck of snot into the sharky sea without even slowing the pace of its gyrations. But the man was working with the forces contained in the pipe. He was playing the kinetic energies of the pipe against its own weight, I could see that now. He wasn't fighting the pipe, but more he was gentling it over, over, and it almost walked now, the way a fisherman plays the fighting tarpon with a piece of string—and then when the propitious moment came, he reeled in his rope and the pipe was landed and clamped securely off to one side in its rack.

Now once again, the tip of another length of pipe protruded from the hole in the platform floor, held in place by slips. The roughnecks wasted no time in fixing the elevator jaws to it so that the whole ballet of steel and kinetic energy could repeat itself again and again, until all the pipe has been drawn out of the sea floor or until the shift had run its brutal course.

I had never seen anything quite like the eyes of the roughnecks as they handled all that metal. Theirs was a dance within a dance. They had, in effect, thrown themselves into the moving jaws of this machine, and their job was to stand on its tongue and pick its teeth while it chewed, like the tiny birds that groom a beast.

A fellow came to stand next to me as I watched. His name was Dave, and he had advanced up the ladder from roughneck to rig mechanic. He now had a pretty good job, and he laughed softly to himself as he watched those young men dance. I noticed that he was missing a finger on his right hand, and I asked him how he'd lost it. He smiled and cut his eyes in the direction of the well head. "Doing something just about like that there," he said. So as they worked, I understood that what the roughnecks avoided was more important than what they met head on. They did not have to fight so hard and close to the moving metal—they could have stood back; but they did so anyway, the way a bullfighter fights close to the bull; and their feet and fingers were always in play, as if all day long they cast dice, betting with their very own bones.

Occasionally the pieces of metal came clanging together in an unhappy way, by an accident of the myriad motions—the sea and wind, the derrick and gravity, winch cables the size of my wrist, writhing like a pit full of electric snakes, and the swaying of the block. All this now and then added up to the great ringing of a gong, which made for grisly results if a man was not paying close attention to his job. At one point Bud Cole, the tool pusher, came up to the floor. He had been working on off-shore rigs for twenty-three years, a feat of remarkable endurance. Remarkable not just for the peril and the stress, but for the tedium; to bear the rig so long would seem to be intolerable. What would become of the longing for human contact? Maybe there would be none left.

In a boat, your very progress through the water makes for a kind of variety, and one piece of ocean real estate can look so different from another, that it can be as varied as driving through the countryside, especially when you anticipate the appearance now and then of dolphins or perhaps the far-off sight of an unknown bit of land. But on the rig, we were marooned, and not even the idea of motion was there to relieve the monotony of the blue and infinite sky, which seemed locked in a neatly ruled line against the green and moody sea. There

In the Belly of the Whale

was no comfort or distraction there in those two desolate hemispheres, and we could not even entertain ourselves with the hope of change, because any change in sea or sky would be a change for the worse (weather being the one great enemy of the precariously balanced rig).

So as Bud observed the work with the ten-story sections of pipe, I watched him with a certain wonder at his tenacity. He wore yellow-tinted safety goggles and an aluminum hard hat, and he squinted up at the wild black pipe, standing on its point and undulating like a licorice stick. He admired it for a moment and then grinned at me with the most malevolent enjoyment I had ever seen.

"You got that fuckin' book wrote yet?" he asked.

■ ■ ■

Dean Reeves was in the film *Thunder Bay* with James Stewart. In 1951 he happened to be a roughneck on Kerr McGee's Rig Number 37 when the film crew showed up. He worked with that thirty-five-thousand-pound steel block and the ninety-foot lengths of pipe, and the boister-ous, swinging song of metal against metal. When I found him, he had risen to the rank of "company man," and he was sitting in his office on the oil rig, which was part of an enclosed area within that city-on-the-sea. The indoor area contained the galley for feeding forty or fifty men, the sleeping quarters, showers, recreation room, other offices, copiers, file cabinets, fax machines, telephones, and the like.

Reeves's office walls were painted a sort of corpse beige. The floor was brown-speckled linoleum. There were gray steel lockers against one wall and his bunk against another. Reeves was a heavy man with a broad beam and a nose like W. C. Fields's. His hard hat was hung on the side of a locker. It was covered with stickers from the companies that supply equipment and services to oil rigs. He sat at a steel desk with a phone at his elbow, and he was chewing tobacco and spitting thin brown streams of what looked like molten brass into a tin vegetable can from which the label had been removed—a metal man in a metal place drooling metal like a castle gargoyle.

"I lost a man in the early sixties," he told me. "He was inexperi-enced. He had just started. He stuck his head in the wrong place." The very hunks of metal I had seen those roughnecks dodging up above on the floor—block and pipe and elevator and slips—two of them had come together, and the man's timing was off. He was not in step with the dance. His head was crushed flat in no more time than it takes to clap hands. "He was dead before he hit the floor," Reeves said, spitting into the can and shaking his head sadly, as if it had just happened yesterday. "And there was nothing you could do about it. It's just an empty feeling . . . blood running out of his ears."

I asked if it was inexperience that got most people in trouble on these rigs. "Your best hand is the one that gets his fingers cut off and what-not," he said. "The guy who stands back with his hands in his pockets, he's not going to get hurt." I felt a certain sense of relief in hearing him say that, since it described precisely what I intended to do with my time on the rig. But his reminiscence seemed to get him talking about the dangers of the rig, and he went on.

"I had one old boy who was walking around on the Texas deck, not looking where he was going, and he fell through an open hatch. Fell eighty feet to the deck below. And he lived." I asked how a man could survive an eighty-foot fall. "I don't know. The waves were lapping over the lower deck, and maybe he hit it just right, but he was holding onto the bars when we got to him. He never worked again, though. He was pretty badly busted up." The main equipment deck on older style rigs was called the Texas deck, because it was so big, and perhaps because, like the state of Texas itself, if you could find a way to drill far enough through it, you'd probably strike oil. On newer rigs, all the equipment is scattered about on different levels, pumps, generators, mud room, Haliburton unit, and pipe racks. There's no actual Texas deck, though some people still use the term.

It goes without saying that while working or even just walking around on the decks, it is very easy to get hurt very badly in so many ways that they are impossible to describe in detail. (Reeves told me about a scuba diver who was poking around a capped well below the surface when they pulled the cap off by a cable from above. "The oil level had dropped and created a vacuum," he said. "And when they pulled that cap off, it just pulled him right down. Sucked his guts out. It was terrible.")

And yet there were graver perils still, and they were all tied up in the very nature of our endeavor here: To draw gas and oil out of the earth. Pockets of gas and oil don't just sit down there in neat geological

In the Belly of the Whale

formations, waiting to be sucked up. They are under tremendous pressure—ten thousand pounds per square inch was a figure I heard bandied about a lot. The pipe that was lowered into the hole was hollow, and a chemical preparation called mud was pumped through it to create enough weight to hold the pressure of the gas or oil that would otherwise come spewing up the well head. The more pressure the gas or oil exerted to get out, the more mud one had to pump in to hold it down. It was that balance of the natural pressure from below the earth and the artificial pressure from above that allowed control of the flow once the surface was punctured.

Once it was drilled, the well was essentially a casing, or a hollow pipe, down into the earth, like a straw sticking into a coconut. It was the straw that was filled with the chemical mud, which was made from a substance called barite, a white powder that crept around the rig and got on our skin and caused itching and burning and ate leather like acid. One worker, looking at my feet, said, "It'll make the toes of them boots look up at you and smile." Concealed within the bowels of the rig was a great machinery—a plant—for concocting and storing and pumping the mud. One day I walked across the metal mesh strung over it in a dark, noisy room that smelled strong enough to dissolve bones. Below our feet was the brown swirling glue of barite—acres of it, like a science fiction film conception of the primal ooze. This, then, was the life blood of the rig. Without mud to hold back the gas and oil, the alternative was a blowout—the wild, uncontrolled spuming of gas and oil out of the ground and into the air—a gusher like in the movies. In movies, people always get happy when the well blows. In real life, they would dive into the ocean rather than stay on the rig during such a catastrophic event.

Sometimes a blowout just happens. The unimaginable pressure of gas will simply cut through the steel casing or a ring gasket, and then there will be the sounding of the great whale of commerce, and it will go down burning. In fact, for all the safety briefings I did not receive on the rig, there was one thing they bothered to tell me: If there's a blowout, you've got about four minutes before the steel pilings and gird-ers melt down and flow into the sea. "So get in the lifeboat if you hear the general alarm," the man named Dave had told me.

"I'd leap over the side if it came to that," said Reeves, who had experienced numerous blowouts in his time. Sometimes the tool pusher can cause a blowout by hurrying, pulling the pipe out of the hole too fast and creating an effect they call swabbing. As the pipe comes out, it causes suction below. If the suction starts the mud flowing upward too fast, it can draw gas up after it. Momentum in the wrong direction begins the blowout. Even a small amount of natural gas, once ignited, will provide sufficient rocket power to start the whole well going. "Then you got a burnt-up rig," Reeves said. Shallow gas wells, he informed me, such as the one on which we sat so pleasantly chatting at that moment, were most susceptible to the swabbing effect.

"We lost one at Chesterfield," he reminisced, "a little old shallow well like this. Swabbed it in, but it didn't catch fire for some reason. They called me, and I said, 'Keep your suction and pump your heavy mud.' I figured it would slow it down, and the water mixed with the gas would lessen the chance of catching fire. We finally killed it with heavy mud." That blowout had started because the pipe going up and down had simply rubbed a hole in the side of the well casing.

"I lost one in Dilly," he went on. "Shut in and locked up and we had a leak, a small one, and about the time they got ready to pump it around, one of these little old Texas lightning storms come up and set this thing on fire."

"What did you do?" I asked.

"Got the hell off of there," he said. It burned his rig up.

He told me about another incident in the late sixties in which "we'd run out of mud and had one bottled up and leaking and nothing to pump. Everybody was running around with life jackets on. It was pretty tight there for a while, until the boat came with more mud."

One of the worst disasters, Reeves told me, could result from a salt-water flow. Sometimes gas wells contain a lot of salt water under extreme pressure, and once that gets away from you, it's like tapping directly into a volcano. First the salt water comes out like a rocket—uncontrollable by mud or any other means. The steel well casing the men have placed in the hole simply falls into the yawning earth; then as the salt water gushes out of the lower bowels of the earth, it drives the sand of the ocean floor away, creating a larger and larger crater, until the very foundations of the rig are undermined and the whole platform, legs and all, falls into the sinkhole created in the floor of the ocean. In other words, for their audacious affronts, the Dragon of the earth swallows them whole, as men, machines, ambition, and all go tilting into the sucking sea.

The phone rang at Reeves's elbow while we were talking. He picked up his tin can, spit into it, then set it down and picked up the phone. "We got it killed," he said to someone in Houston, "and we eased on out of the hole with that packer and I'm just getting back in the hole with a scraper now and of course we had a crew change right in the middle of all that. I'm fixin' to go to two-and-a-half dual round." When he hung up, he told me he planned to get a gravel pack in there and then put the Christmas tree on it, and for the first time I understood the mechanics of an oil well: It was like giving blood, a metal hypodermic stuck in the tender flesh, held there by friction. The gas or oil follows the path of least resistance, through the tube rather than around it. A gravel pack around the tube assures no leakage. With a flow manifold on the end of the tube (the Christmas tree, he called it) one could then turn the gas on and off and meter it and steal it away and sell it, like blood.

■　■　■

I was standing on the platform one day, and several men were standing nearby. There was a pause in the action, and I had taken out my black notebook to write something. I noticed the men looking at me in a peculiar way, not saying anything, just looking, watching me as if I were some kind of curiosity in their otherwise routine day. I don't know what made me turn around, perhaps it was the flick of their eyes—perhaps I noticed that they were watching not only me but something behind me as well. For whatever reason, I looked around, and there was a craneload of pipe, moving slowly but implacably toward my head. It was not exactly a close call, though closer than I would have liked. I stepped aside and the four-ton rack of pipe was set on the floor, and that was all. I looked back at the men, and they weren't laughing or anything, but one of them glanced at me in a peculiar way, with a little smile, like: *Well, it didn't get you this time, but maybe next time.* Maybe I was just getting paranoid from all the noise, but I understood at that moment how truly grave was the danger I was in on that rig. For not only were the mechanical facts of the rig inhospitable to life and limb, but the men themselves seemed singularly incapable of empathy or altruism. I now understood something about the men and their work.

Nothing escaped their vigilant notice—a shift in the wind, a chance remark, the tinkling of machinery, a sudden odor from somewhere—because all of those things could signal the beginning of the end, and the man who noticed what was going on first was the man most likely to survive it. Men, machines, nature, they knew from hard (sometimes deadly) experience, were not to be trusted. Fate was a hand-made affair, knocked together and roughed out from whatever materials were at hand. The rule was fixed: Opportunity plus Will equals Fate. To the extent that I was new and unknown, they regarded me as coldly as if the magical Link-Belt crane had lifted another rack of pipe off that boat and set it on the deck for them to trip over and fall one hundred feet to their death. I understood why Bud Cole had been so displeased to find me on his rig. I couldn't possibly help, so therefore I was a liability. And in an emergency, I'd be worse than worthless. Someone would have to save me. It was a job no one wanted.

What I saw of those men was real, because each man was working hard every moment for his own survival. They did not have the energy or the time for poses, for subtle or clever deceptions, or for social gamesmanship. What I saw on the surface was a man pitted against something that would kill him if he did not dominate it now and without any protracted thinking-out of his strategy. Everything on the rig was a test, and the men had to react instantly; and so what I saw in those men was raw nerve and muscle, all on the surface, where there was no leeway for deep thought or introspection. I don't think those men were actively trying to get me killed, but they were not very actively interested in preventing my death, either. Moreover, I got the distinct impression that they would have been mildly amused if I had been maimed by my chance meeting with the moving machinery of their lives. (When I got back, I talked to my brother, a native of Texas, who still lives in San Antonio, and he said, "Aw, that's just east Texas. Everybody in east Texas is like that. Of course, everybody in east Texas works on oil rigs, too . . .")

On the other hand, I had to remember that they were doing something that no one else would do. They were risking their lives so that I could be warm. The gathering of oil and gas is a battle for survival. We need oil. Oil is heat. Oil is motion. We cling to a rock in the sea, quite literally to save our lives. Those men are the forefront; they stand between us and something we don't like to admit is even there anymore:

The cold. Oh, sure, we say it's there, but we don't believe it can get to us. But it can, if they don't drill for this oil and gas. If I had been them, doing what they did in twelve-hour, mind-killing shifts, day after day, month after month, I might well be amused to see someone like me get his arm cut off. (A man I know from that part of the globe told me, during the oil shortage of the early seventies, "Are you guys up there in New York cold this winter? Why don't you burn some art?")

But finding empathy in my heart for them made me no less eager to get off their platform and let them get about their business. I found myself standing high over the ocean on the white cantilevered helicopter deck, staring at the horizon one breezy cool October evening out in the Gulf of Mexico, watching the black dots that moved here and there among the rigs, trying to see which one was going to turn this way. I had developed a more practiced gait to step around and over and through the pipes and hoses, the coiled wires that grabbed at my ankles as I passed close by some sheer drop over the side to the sea.

When the helicopter finally came, there were so many people who wanted to get off that rig, it was like Saigon in '75, and the pilot wasn't sure he was going to be able to make the take-off, so he counted the luggage again, and then he counted us once more, and decided to give it a try. He climbed in and shrugged down into his belts. He hauled back on the collective, the machine groaned, and then the skids just barely cleared the deck, as we wheeled out over the ocean.

I don't know what state of mind I must have been in, but it didn't seem at all odd to me at the time, to risk crashing into the sea in order to get off that oil rig. I was on the chopper with several other mainland office types, who seemed to agree that anything was better than staying.

As we flew away, I glanced at the instrument panel to make sure we had a positive rate of climb. The pilot managed to get us to five hundred feet, and that was good enough for me, so I breathed a sigh of relief, as the oil rig receded beneath and behind us. When the crew boat had brought us out to the rig, I had watched it grow on the horizon, until it became real and menacing in the running seas, a dark and forbidding torture chamber, a dissonant unity symbolizing the cruel will of man to defy the elements in all his baleful audacity. Now it was with great relief that I watched that same rig shrink back to insignificance, where I could no longer see the gruesome details of its daily life, the whirling constant dervish of peril upon its slick and dirty decks. Soon it had shrunk to a simple geometric shape, mysterious and theoretical, and far enough away to contemplate. Before it disappeared altogether, it had been reduced to nothing more than a ghostly finger sticking out of the ocean mists, like that universal hand signal of brotherly disaffection.

Wire Walker

on the Circus

I was in a tent that served as a dressing room, watching Ayin de Sela, the wire walker, limber up before a show. The flaps were open to the breeze and sunshine, and circus people came and went, talking and laughing, juggling, and casually walking on their hands as if it were nothing out of the ordinary. In a grassy area off to one side, a man built and climbed two stacks of bricks, picking up first one brick with the left hand, then one with the right—all while standing on his hands, of course. I heard a soprano saxophone playing phrases of John Coltrane.

Ayin lay on a mat, folding and unfolding herself like a marionette. She stretched and twisted, writhed, and undulated, and then gently lifted her toe to her ear with her left hand and stood there, immaculate and motionless, doing a split in the air, until I had to look for the strings that held her. She was so small and still and beautiful that I was able to convince myself that she wasn't real, except for the tympanic beating of her abdomen as she breathed in and out. Her eyes were Mexican blue, a color that could at one moment look like the sea and at the next moment look like the sky. Sometimes they turned gray; other times, in pain, they were nearly green. Ayin let her left foot down. It touched the blue floor of the tent and planted itself there.

She bent at the waist and placed her palms on the floor. Her long, straight golden hair fell like a tent around her. She straightened to her full height, just under five feet. She took a breath. The membrane of her abdomen rose and fell. Then, without warning, she took off all her clothes and stood for a moment in thought, like Venus, appearing in a shell upon the sun-freaked sea. Her hair and skin were gold in color.

Even the saxophone stopped. The moment seemed to last forever, but it was only a matter of seconds—a girl, deciding what to wear—and then she slipped into another skin of gold and continued stretching as if nothing had happened. The saxophone player went on with his licks, and the drummer kicked in behind him, and the world went back on pitch once more.

■ ■ ■

A little later I sat in the audience on aluminum bleachers to watch the Pickle Family Circus, one of the few old-fashioned traveling circuses left in the United States. We were in Tucson, Arizona, and it was a hot October day just after noontime. The clowns had come out and sprayed the audience with water to wake us up and let us know they were real. The tumblers had tumbled, and the jugglers had juggled while the band played Thelonius Monk and Freddie Hubbard—good up-tempo jazz, soprano and trumpet and synthesizer and lots of crisp drums like a salad of iceberg lettuce.

The circus was only one ring, a big blue piece of rubberized canvas with a pad underneath to soften the leaps and falls, surrounded by a raised red circumference. Four people stood in a line, juggling sixteen clubs so fast that they made a white and creaming wave overhead. It was real and it was dangerous, and I could see when someone missed a throw by a little bit how the catcher recovered, adjusted the rhythm, and the whole thing went on, and how close to catastrophe it was by design and by divine inspiration.

Then Ayin came out to walk the tightwire. Her balance was almost too good. She moved, but the movement was so solid that she reminded me of a gyroscope on piano wire, except that she was so vividly an animal creature—I could see the lines of sweat coursing down from her scalp. Her close and elemental power was as formidable as that of an unadorned lion let loose in the ring. She was in her golden skin with her golden hair caught up and held in a shimmering ponytail. She sat on the wire, her legs stretched out before her, then stood from that position, a seashell-shaped fan in her right hand. The intense Arizona sun gleamed off of her arms and face, and the mountains and sky framed the armature of her body as it moved. She wore ballet point shoes and walked the wire on point, doing arabesque, plié, and every now and then, turning from her mask-like concentration to smile at the audience, but it was clear the smile was an adornment, an afterthought. As she moved, she went through a series of subtle but amazing mutations—machine, cat, bird, human—right before our eyes.

When she stood on one foot, on point, her copper arms went out to form a dihedral on either side above her head; and as she balanced, her arms tipped, one going down as the other went up, the way a bird of prey does in its long and soaring glide, watching for a tempting morsel of movement far down on the forest floor.

The Pickle Family Circus is not like the Ringling Brothers Circus in many ways, but one of the nicest of all is that the PFC (as its members often call it) is small. It is human-sized, and the performers are humans. In Ringling Brothers, everything is BIGGER THAN LIFE!!! Everything is impossible. In PFC the more amazing fact is that everything is natural, human, and very close. And it is all very possible. In fact, it's terribly real at times. Perhaps one thousand people at most can see a PFC show, seated in the three sections of bleachers and crowded on the grass around the single ring. The top of the arena is open to the sun, and only a tri-colored red-blue-yellow canvas wall separates us from the outside world and makes this a special place. This is a circus you can roll up and put in your backpack. And so when someone such as Ayin comes out and walks on a wire close enough so that you can see the holes in her shoes, it is terribly intimate. In the Ringling Brothers Circus, a tiny dancer high and faraway on a wire, appears perfect, not real. Ayin's work was the more breathtaking because she revealed herself and her secrets to us so willingly—we could hear her draw a breath, and we could see her lick her lips when they got dry.

She stopped on the small plywood platform at one end of the wire to put on a different pair of shoes, and for a moment, in her absent-minded concentration upon her task, she was just a little girl again, a blond girl with a ponytail, changing shoes. Then she coiled and leaped into the air from the platform and was nowhere, hanging in sunlight— I almost thought she'd take flight—but she came down upon the wire and stuck, and then she danced across as the band played jazz. She turned and hot-footed it back the other way now, as sure of her steps as if the wire were not five-eighths of an inch but as wide as the desert. And in the middle she leaped into the air again, and the audience saw and believed now in the astounding things that they were not allowed to know in their narrow lives in the outside world, these stunning revelations of fluid and flesh, of gravity and gristle.

Many of us cover our bodies, because they are nothing more than the unfortunate circumstances of our existence, a place to which we are condemned to live through no choice of our own. But for circus performers, the body is the total expression not only of art and self but of utter freedom as well. It is the freedom of fox and hound—and if Ayin de Sela is the fox, then gravity is the hound. She was liberated from the prison of her flesh only through the trial of her training, the falls, lacerations, peril, exhaustion, and pain—Ayin held hands with God in order to fashion her 103-pound body and to earn the gift of balance. Thus it makes sense that she would allow us to see her in her state of unadorned and absolute reality. In fact, she demands it. Ayin's nakedness was that kind of reality. Ayin was such a finely honed performer that she was naked even when she had her clothes on. I watched the audience comprehend that, and I heard them gasp when her act was finished—they almost forgot to applaud. They understood that what they had witnessed was not an act, it was a kind of reality from which they were guarded in their day-to-day lives. What Ayin did for them was not entertainment, it was a liberating revelation.

■　■　■

The Pickle Family Circus grew out of the performance-and-politics movement of the sixties in California, and most of the performers in it were in some way connected with values, ethics, and principles that reflect that lineage. Ayin's parents were, by her own description, hippies. Many of the performers over the years have had college educations, careers waiting for them (other careers), or some other great potential for a more traditional role and status in life. One of their most famous clowns, Bill Irwin, had a Guggenheim Fellowship and a MacArthur Award. Many Ph.D.'s can be found sprinkled through the PFC credits over the years (Ph.D.'s cast off like inventions that didn't work—a doctorate can't make you fly). Role, stature, salary, prestige could not compare with the raw, demanding reality of the circus. Most performers with the PFC were people who realized that life was too serious *not* to join the circus.

The Pickle Family Circus was also a circus in the grand old tradition of those that simply showed up in trucks on a bare spot of ground, and people leaped out and hammered great spikes into the naked ground and strung wire and cable and threw up tents. Soon the band was warming up, and the day was getting hot. A crowd had begun to gather around the periphery of the red-and-yellow-and-blue curtain of canvas that surrounded, like a twelve-foot-high wall, the single ring, over which was suspended a great metal contraption that was unmistakably intended for an aerialist's dangerous and death-defying act and could be seen from a distance sticking up out of the roofless tent like a taunt. That grand and many-headed creature had come to claw the ground with talons of steel and wave on wire tentacles its colorful banners at the Arizona mountains.

After walking her wire during the previous show, Ayin had disappeared through the dizzy rig (a colored canvas curtain that separated the back of the ring and the center split from the open-air backstage area) and returned to the ring in another costume. She became just another tumbler in the general commotion of the circus—scarcely recognizable as the same person—and during one misstep in the wild action of rolling and leaping and inverted flying-through-the-air, Ayin twisted her ankle badly. She came down hard, landed wrong, and a pain lit up her face as if she'd stepped on a scorpion. She said, "Shit!" and then caught herself, and although she was in a blinding fog of pain, she went on and finished the routine, in a kind of self-induced hypnotic trance that she was capable of using for her own protection.

■ ■ ■

At the act break, she went through the dizzy rig again and stumbled on her way to the Mad Moid (which is what they call the costume tent—there's a whole lexicon of circus lingo to learn). She was so suffused with the electric brilliance of her pain that she sat down and embraced it, and she wept.

Her sister, Miriam, who was twelve but had been in the circus longer than Ayin, came over to comfort her and said, "People don't believe you're real, because they watch too much television. That's why when you fall, they like it. They know you're real." In her appearance, Miriam was more Indio-Mexican than Ayin, with brown eyes and very dark hair, but her body was like a miniature of her older sister's.

After the show, Ayin sat on the blue floor of the Moid, rubbing her ankle and grimacing. She said, "I don't think I'm going to come back next year." I asked her why. "Because it's too hard," she said. She wanted to go study circus in the Shaloms Sur Mains school in Paris. Another de Sela sister, Sky, nineteen, who had joined the Pickle Family Circus even before Miriam, was studying there already. Ayin said that, although working with the PFC was extremely important experience and helped turn her into a professional performer, she had no time to practice—life was a constant race against time and entropy. Everyone here worked all day (and sometimes all night, too). When they weren't setting up the tents and main ring, they were tearing them down. When they weren't doing that, they were performing. When they weren't performing, they were rehearsing. And if they got any sleep, it was outside, in a tent, using an outhouse. I watched Ayin do her make-up sitting cross-legged on the floor of the Moid, working out of a fishing tackle box with a broken fragment of mirror. "We're homeless people," she said. Two months earlier a philanthropist had donated a kitchen trailer with a real stove and refrigerator, a little card table, two folding chairs, and two showers about the size of public-aid coffins, which sometimes even worked when the wind didn't blow out the pilot lights for the water heater. The performers thought they had died and gone to heaven. Over the years the best performers have always left the PFC. Being on the road with the circus is like being at sea in a storm—it teaches necessary survival skills. But to become a fine sailor, one must have calm seas, too, and time to think.

Ayin told me how she had gotten into the circus. "I was in high school. I was kind of depressed because I wasn't doing anything. And then I decided in about half an hour that the circus was what I wanted to do. I had had a lot of training in dance. I did a lot of ballet and then jazz dance, and I just decided." She spent five months training on the wire for no reason other than that she was drawn to it in an inexplicable way. She couldn't articulate what it was about the wire that drew her, but I knew. When I was seventeen years old, I had been drawn to the wire, too. For several years, I walked the slack rope and juggled and tumbled. I actually studied it for a while and got pretty good at walking the rope—that was my favorite. I dreamed of going away to the circus, but I never did. I still remember how it felt: It was like the snake and the bird. The rope was alive.

Some people are born in the circus, others are drawn there, as if by supernatural forces that they cannot explain. Three of the six de Sela sisters are circus performers, but their father is a schoolteacher. When they went, they went like tumbling dominoes. "We had a really strange childhood," Ayin told me. "We traveled around Mexico in a school bus. My parents were in love with Mexico. My father gave up his American citizenship when they tried to draft him, and then we just lived in Mexico. I was born in Mexico. And my father always used to do these funny things. Like he'd say, 'And now she will jump through the hoop of death!'" Ayin smiled, remembering her first performances as a child. "And I would jump."

She moved her foot in a circle from the ankle and cried out in pain. "Damn!" she said, looking at her ankle. "This is my first injury of the year."

I saw Ayin's eyes go far away as she rubbed her ankle, her leg stretched out on the blue floor. "The wire act is hard, because you focus so much that you run the risk of cutting out the audience."

Outside the open flap of the tent, I could see Lorenzo Pisoni, a thin, handsome, dark-haired teenager, running like a gazelle. Someone was chasing him with a paper plate full of whipped cream—the traditional pie-in-the-face. It was Lorenzo's thirteenth birthday, and he was on his guard, because he knew everyone was going to "help" him celebrate, especially after his stellar birthday performance out in the ring as a tumbler, hand balancer, and acrobat. Lorenzo was born in the circus. His father, Larry Pisoni, founded the Pickle Family Circus in 1974 with Peggy Snyder (Lorenzo's mother and Bennington College alumna) and Cecil MacKinnon (MFA from NYU). Lorenzo had been in it since birth. A baby photograph showed him in the arms of Bill Irwin, the scowling and ominous-looking Guggenheim Fellow clown. Lorenzo wore a button that says, "I'm Lorenzo. I belong to the Circus."

In a way, Ayin and her sisters had been born into the circus, too, but they had first to realize that their life was a circus, and then go join it. Lorenzo knew at the outset: Life is a circus; the circus is life. And the magic happens when the audience sits down and for a fleeting moment is vouchsafed the comprehension of that miraculous equation. The mysterious thing is how they can walk out of the bleachers and throw down their popcorn boxes and forget—how can anyone forget?

"I think it's going to rain," Ayin said.

"Don't say that," said Rosalinda, the lovely Puerto Rican acrobat and hand balancer. There was another show coming up in a couple of hours, and rain would ruin it. We were on the grounds of a school. It was a Saturday, and there were hundreds of kids and parents out there getting ready to have a big Arizona-style barbecue. But Ayin was right. I could see it tumbling in gray waves over the mountains in the distance out the open tent flap. "Well, I hope it rains," she said sullenly. "I don't want to do it tonight." But even as she was saying that, she was getting up to test her ankle to see if she could do the show. "Worse things have happened," she said and then told me about the night of the San Francisco earthquake, which had been less than a week earlier. The Pickle Family Circus is from San Francisco, and on October 17, when the city fell to the Great Earthquake of 1989, the circus was in a different city, but Lorenzo's parents were in San Francisco, along with other Pickle Family members. "It was five minutes before a show. It had been a really long season already, and we were all so tired. Of course, we couldn't get through on the phone to find out if everybody was all right, so we didn't know how anyone was. It was a terrible show. We all fell down a lot on that show."

Now she was up and testing her ankle, flexing and stretching. She cried out in pain. "I can't even do a plié." She suggested we go out to the ring. She was going to try to see if she could jump, and she said she'd teach me how to walk the wire if I wanted to try. I told her that I had only walked the slack rope, and she said, "Well, that's a different feel, but you can probably do this."

Walking out to the ring, Ayin seemed lost in thought and in pain. She said, "I feel ready to work up high—I mean really high. Women's wire acts are so wimpy. I'd like to do a cartwheel and a back tuck on the wire." The sun was now obscured by clouds. A drummer, sitting at his traps on the bandstand, was practicing the same figures over and over. A man stood juggling clubs to one side of the blue ring. Ayin stopped and looked at the wire, a gleaming silver-gray line of twisted steel strands, as straight as if it had been ruled with a graphite pencil. "I love the tightwire," she said softly. "I really love it."

■　■　■

Ayin showed me one of the essential tactics for staying up: Look at the far end of the wire. One reason that it is difficult to keep a traditional performer's rapport with an audience while on the wire is that looking at the audience breaks the gyroscopic effect of looking down the length of the wire. Keeping your rear end over the wire is another essential key to balancing. I asked her what to do if I fell with the wire between my legs.

She smiled. "Instinct takes over," she said. "It's happened to me," she added. "I skinned up my leg pretty bad, but that was all. I didn't . . . you know . . ." She made a knife-like motion with the edge of her hand, cutting at her own center of gravity.

The Pickle Family Circus doesn't believe in risk for the sake of risk. Its acts are very much grounded in reality, and the reality of life is that we all fall now and then; we shouldn't be sentenced to death for being human. That is one of the many deep, philosophical places where the Pickle Family Circus differs from the big commercial operations such as Ringling Brothers. The large commercial circus draws people in by suggesting its performers are superhuman and that if they aren't, they may well die—right before your very eyes.

What the PFC does is not a series of technological and engineering tricks. It is human beings interacting in amazing but real ways. The fact that they are human and not superhuman is a gift of revelation to the audience, which can see in the performance not the specter of death, but all human potential expanding before their very eyes, like rings on a pond when a stone is thrown in. Narrow worlds explode. Possibilities reveal themselves. People can do these things—and I'm people, too. People come away feeling connected to the action. In Ringling Brothers we peer into an alien world from which we are excluded except as observers. The Pickle Family brings new dimensions into our real world, and we keep that gift forever. The Ringling Brothers' wire is set so high as to guarantee that the performer will die if he falls. The PFC wire is set down low, so that you can see it's possible for a real person to walk it.

So I took my shoes and socks off and climbed to the plywood platform. The platform was scarcely a place of refuge, no larger than a dinner plate. The first time I put my foot on the wire, I could tell it was alive. I felt the singing of the strings in the ball of my naked foot, and I waited until my calf muscles found the pitch. Behind me the drummer was practicing that same figure over and over: Chick-a-boom. Chick-a-boom. Chick-a-boom. I could hear a violin from somewhere beyond the dizzy rig. The clouds were tumbling in over the mountains, and a slight breeze had come up, breathing cold on my T-shirt, which was sweated against my ribs. I understood that the wire would not stop its singing to accommodate my weight like a sidewalk. It was going to keep right on trembling, and if I wanted to make it across the twenty-two feet stretching in the sunlight before me to the other platform, I was going to have to get in tune with its restless animation. I stepped out into the air. There for a singing moment, we were one, the wire and I. And then I fell.

The wire was not set high enough to hurt anything but my pride, and there were pads underneath. The point of the exercise was not to risk injury. It was to balance the forces of nature with the forces of man. It would make no more sense to walk the wire up high than it would for the drummer on the bandstand to practice his licks on top of the Empire State Building. I fell many times before I got it, but I worked all afternoon, and I ultimately got it. (And the drummer worked with me, and he got it, too, and neither one of us got dead.)

I did as Ayin had told me, watching the other end, keeping myself centered, my arms in the air like the hawks I'd seen gliding in thermals above the mountains, their focus fixed far down the hill. The twisted steel was as delicate in its vibrations as a rosewood viola; but I was a mere scrap of trembling flesh, a strand of horse hair, which at any moment could be flicked off. Step by step, I went, and soon I felt my muscles—almost on their own—learning the wayward tune of the wire. I had to get my mind out of the way, which was the hardest part. I knew now why Ayin seemed so faraway when she was on the wire. She had to detach her mind from her body and let the bird within her fly. By doing this I understood a lot about the other performers, too. Jens Larson, who did a Roman Rings act. Or Lorenzo, who leaped from a teeterboard to the top of a man's shoulders (a man who was already standing on another man's shoulders). They were revealing a hidden reality to us: There is a bird in me. Now watch me let it go. You didn't believe it was there, did you? But you saw it, so it must be true.

So it was, through a spiritual transformation, through faith and revelation, that I was able to walk the wire. By the time Ayin returned from changing and from icing down her ankle, I was making it all the way across, from platform to platform, without falling, and I had learned something about the embarrassment of a fall, too. Falling is important, because the self is erased through coming to terms with embarrassment. It is part of the annealing process the performer goes through, a cleansing of self through stumbling. All our culture is filled with such symbols: Christ had to stumble while he carried the cross. The clown acts between the acrobatic performances are cleansing acts, in which the performer stumbles—the performance, is, in effect, nothing but a wash of embarrassment, laid out for the purpose of cleansing. The wire is as much a spiritual state of grace—what the modern usage might dub "an attitude"—as it is a special physical skill. Get the ego out of the way, and the human soul is a gyroscope, whirling inside the body and holding it up.

I had started to tell myself that it was like surfing or skiing, but the next day I was taking juggling lessons and said something about its being like learning music, and the juggler who was teaching me said, "Yeah, juggling is like everything. Everything's like everything." Anyway, I saw the assistant technical director, Hugh Tracy, walk the tightwire wearing construction boots, while drinking coffee out of a steel cup and eating a Danish. His mind was definitely out of the way.

It was late in the afternoon when Ayin came back, and I got down from the wire and she got on. She worked out, testing her ankle to see if she could do the evening show. She was framed by mountains, and when she went up on point, it was as if she stood atop Mount Lemmon. On the cradle (a sort of stationary trapeze) two women aerialists were practicing an act. One woman hung from the hands of the other high above us, slowly twisting and untwisting in a ballet of pure strength. When they were done, Ayin was still running across the wire, testing herself, and then the crew took the cradle down, and cables were falling all around us and even across Ayin's wire, but she paid no attention to anything but the gyroscope within.

"Want to see some stag jumps?" she asked. Then she leaped off the wire like an antelope, feet high behind her, and she seemed to hang in the air for a moment. Gravity stopped for her the way traffic stops when something amazing is happening at the side of the highway. Then, as if on her command, gravity commenced again, and she came down exactly on the wire. I calculated that during the year and a half that she had been with the Pickle Family Circus, Ayin had walked more than two thousand miles on the wire without touching the ground.

I watched her reach the end of the twenty-two-foot wire and turn to run again across its length and run back again and turn once more; and I understood something fundamental about her life and her pursuit: At the end of the wire, there is no applause. She cannot worry about pay, because there is no pay—no man-made currency can pay for this. Even if she has a home, somewhere, there is always no home. Because there is only the wire. At the end of the wire, there is still only the wire again, and at the other end of the wire, there again is the wire. That is why she cannot fall, not anymore than I could fall off the edge of the earth.

When she was finished she wiped the wire its full length with a cloth soaked in alcohol. She wiped it carefully, the way the musicians in the band wiped their instruments before they put them in their felt-lined cases. Then Ayin sat on the floor of the blue ring and stretched her ankle out and said, "I think live performance is dying." She squinted up at the tangle of cables strung around us, the roustabouts working to set up the next show. "I mean the little live performances." Then someone called her, and she was transformed into a roustabout herself, moving heavy equipment, limping as she did so, and apologizing for not being there to help sooner.

When she had finished her heavy lifting, I asked Ayin if she was going to do the evening performance. "Yeah," she said. "I wish I didn't have to. But I have to. I mean, it's totally up to me, but I have to." She looked up at the boiling sky and said, "I wish it would rain."

■ ■ ■

We were back in the Moid with its yellow walls and blue floor, and I had begun to believe that Ayin controlled not just gravity, but all nature. As she sat on the floor scraping the soles of her wire-walking shoes with a metal rasp, we could both hear the rain steadily ticking on the blue-and-red tent top, and she smiled a secret smile as if to say: *See? I did it.* The tent was dark, because the sky had grown dark with thunderclouds. A length of conduit was hung from the tent top to make a rack for clothes, and here and there costumes hung at random from the steel supports. A great spike with a great comic-book nail head the size of a saucer stuck out of the ground where the center tent pole was secured, and everywhere were boxes and suitcases spilling out hats and under-garments, make-up, shirts, shoes, and bits of crazy-colored clothing. An old and tarnished brass tuba sat inexplicably in the middle of the floor beside a silver C-melody saxophone and a table with pitcher, teacup, and vase, which I had seen a man balancing upon his chin ear-lier while he juggled three clubs.

Green grass poked through a slit in the blue floor between Ayin's legs, as she put her shoulder muscles into the task of rasping the rosin off of the soles in preparation for the night's act. She had to do splits on the wire, and the soles of that particular pair of shoes had to be slick. The other pair, the point shoes, required rosin for purchase on the wire. Then the rosin got on the wire and onto her other shoes, and after each show, she had to clean the wire and scrape the shoes.

The shoes had once been golden colored, like her costume, but now I could scarcely tell anymore. They were so worn that they were almost the color of the wire, a kind of grease-gray shade, and there were holes worn in them, and the elastics had been sewn on over and over again. I was watching her scrape, and I looked down at her bare feet straight out before her and saw a resemblance between them and the shoes. The wire is hard—it is steel—and flesh, no matter how hard you work it, is always and only flesh. In the end, the wire wins. Scissors cut paper. Paper wraps rock. Rock breaks scissors. Ayin's feet were scarred and callused and misshapen from walking two thousand miles on a steel wire less than an inch wide.

"I've got to get some decent shoes," she muttered to herself. She had had those shoes custom made in San Francisco for ninety dollars, "And they still weren't right." Shoes were a constant problem. She told me she'd ordered a pair she'd seen in a catalog for only forty-five dollars, "And if they work, they'll be the answer to my prayers." I had a suspi-cion that the shoes would never be just right, that it was going to be one of those things, like a saxophone player's reeds, a potter's clay, or the wind in flight.

All of a sudden, while both of us had our full concentration focused on one of her shoes, the strumming of the rain on the canvas increased, like a drum roll, lightning split the sky like a cymbal crash, and a tremendous wind came up and punched through the tent like a fist. I heard Ayin scream, and then the tent came down around us and we leaped out through the open flap. Suddenly, we were outdoors, and it was raining in earnest, and a cyclonic storm was whirling out of the mountains and taking us away. A show was on, but whose show was it?

Out on the grass behind the main ring of the circus, clowns were running and screaming. Thunder cracked through the chittering of human voices, and fifty yards away, where all the sleeping tents were pitched, I could see them lean and begin to take flight, as people ran toward them and then away from them, carrying suitcases and chairs and sacks of juggling clubs. Screaming, Ayin ran to her tent, a one-person silver-gray Eureka tent with a pretty maroon trim around its skirts. It was bent almost flat by the wind, and as we gathered her belongings from inside, the howling storm crushed it, twisting the aluminum poles, and Ayin cried out, "Oh, no! Oh, shit! Oh, damn! I hate this! What am I going to do. My stuff! My stuff!" Just before it collapsed, I looked inside, and it was neat, so neat, with all her tights and socks folded and lined up in an open suitcase—her bureau—and her bedroll neatly folded like a couch against one wall. Her sense of home and order was lovely. She had a miniature life in the Eureka tent, and now it was blown away.

Carrying her things—her home, her life—we raced among the running people and threw everything in trucks and vans and garbage bags and into the kitchen trailer. Then we ran about moving things, as lightning flickered in the east over the mountains. I watched Miriam try to run away with a make-up case, but it fell open, spilling little bottles and lipsticks and brushes everywhere. She looked at it and realized how funny it was—like something you'd do if you were planning this act—and she laughed, picking up the pieces in the rain. It was all so much like any other part of the circus, that a lot of people were laughing through their tears before the storm was over.

Then there was the pealing sound of a crack that at first we thought was thunder, until the great wall that separated the circus ring from the backstage area came down, tearing metal, crushing the dizzy rig, and the whole circus collapsed flat. It was the ultimate clown act—where everything goes wrong once and for all. All across the area now structures of nylon and canvas were folding up before the mighty wind, and before we had finished carrying everything to the trucks, the Pickle Family Circus was four acres of devastation, and night was falling around us in accompaniment to a thunderous driving rain.

Instinctively everyone gathered in the kitchen trailer, where Peggy Snyder was preparing to heat aluminum foil pans of lasagna as if nothing had happened. She had been through the eruption of Mount Saint Helens and gone on with a show. She had been through an earthquake in San Juan Bautista and a hailstorm in Modesto. Just a few days earlier, she had been in the Great San Francisco Earthquake of 1989. She knew that all life was just a series of clown acts.

I stood against the sink reading the stuff on the bulletin board and watching Ayin sit at the little kitchen table and run her hand through her soaking wet hair, which had turned darker from the wetting. "I'm freezing," she said, and one of the performers gave her a jacket, and Lorenzo sat in her lap. Across the room, Miriam communicated with Ayin through hand and eye signals. Eventually they both migrated through the noisy crowd of at least fifteen people jammed into the kitchen space, and soon they were seated together on the only two folding chairs, more secure in the comfort of their closeness.

Something on the bulletin board reminded me that it was Lorenzo's birthday. It was the day's schedule, headlined with "Happy Birthday, Lorenzo!" The schedule that followed told another story:

9:30–10:10	Wire/Aerial
10:10–10:40	Juggle I
10:40–11:20	Acrobatics
11:20	Rings/John
12:30	SHOW
6:00	Barbecue
7:30	SHOW
After Show	Dinner with Lorenzo

It was about six o'clock by the time everyone was gathered in the kitchen trailer, and it was pretty clear that the barbecue wasn't going to happen, although no one had said anything about canceling the show. In fact, the consensus was to wait an hour and see if they could put everything back together. A circus is all about human possibility: People fly like birds. Why wouldn't it be possible to put back together what the weather gods had rent asunder? But before that decision could be made, the sponsor came with word that the show was officially canceled. She was a very straight lady, a nice lady, jammed into that kitchen trailer, elbow to elbow with all those circus performers, thousands of pounds of honed and tuned and quivering muscle and sinew, steaming like horses from running around in the rain, and she looked a little bit scared as she asked them if they would like to come into the school gymnasium and have barbecued chicken with the people and maybe "mingle a little and do some hand stands or juggling or something like that?"

The performers all looked at one another with silent, wry, amused smiles or half smiles. There was a silence. Then someone said, "Do you want us to eat the chicken in costume and in character?" Laughter.

"Well, you can have dinner anyway," the lady said. "Please come and join us." Another silence. "See you in a while," she said and backed out of there, and then the trailer exploded in laughter and joking, and all the attention was turned on Lorenzo, because there was going to be a birthday celebration, come hell or high water—or preferably both.

Soon everyone was drinking San Miguel and Corona, and there was a Batman piñata and John the juggler was blowing up balloons, while someone timed him to see how fast he could tie them—maybe set a world record for balloon tying. Karen the juggler was throwing candy from a bag over the heads of the crowd, and Lorenzo was whacking at Batman (who was suspended from the very low trailer ceiling by a wire) with a wooden chopping board. Everyone ducked in the close space to avoid concussions and whatnot from the flying board. Cheers and screams accompanied the splitting of Batman's guts, whereupon more candy spilled out of him. Ayin and Miriam were the first ones to the floor to gather the Tootsie Roll Pops and M&Ms with peanuts. The lights went out and a collective "Ahhh!" went up from the crowd, but then someone switched them back on, saying, "Only kidding." No one would have been surprised by a power failure at that point.

Ayin said, "I've never seen the circus crumble so quickly." Meaning she had seen it crumble before, only not quite that quickly. They had all seen it crumble before. This was not the end of the world. Not even close.

Rosalinda, the Puerto Rican acrobat, said, "The last time this happened I put all my costumes in plastic garbage bags, and they got thrown away!" In other words, life is a clown act—if you miss that, you're missing the best part of the show. And one day you'll wake up and you'll be dead, and then what'll you do?

That night we sat on the floor of the great gymnasium of St. Gregory's School in Tucson, Arizona, and we ate barbecued chicken and pinto beans and drank Coke and Slice and ate brownies for dessert. I sat across from Ayin and watched her eat. She piled her plate high with pieces of chicken and then placed it between her spread legs on the blond glossy wooden floor with basketball lines lacquered on it, her back to the pale cinder-block wall. Then she bent her upper body over the plate like a ballet dancer stretching, and she ate eagerly, her delicate fingers picking apart the chicken, which dripped with barbecue sauce. When she was finished, she went back and got more chicken and did it again. The circus performers burn so many calories that they have to eat and eat, and yet they are exceptionally thin. The skin on Ayin's abdomen was as tight and smooth as the surface of an apple.

After dinner, two of the acrobats stood on their hands and then looked around: Is that enough? They laughed and walked away.

That night almost everyone got to stay in a nearby motel, due to the uninhabitable condition of the tents. By 9 P.M. Ayin and Miriam and Lorenzo were in the motel pool, practicing back flips off the side and inverted cannonballs to see who could shoot a water spout up onto the second floor balcony. Ryszard Ostrowski, the Polish acrobat (whom the PFC women called Mr. Macho), had decided that he was going to dive into the pool from the balcony. ("You can't miss," he said.) But cooler heads prevailed, and the stunt was postponed until daylight. Besides, Ryszard had had three scotches in a fifteen-minute period.

By the end of the night most of the water was out of the pool, and several people were walking around on the deck on their hands. Every now and then a regular motel guest would stroll past, stop, gawk, then move on. They didn't know what they were seeing—Miriam, this apparitional child-beauty, holding the toes of her right foot up beside her ear, standing on tiptoe—but they knew it was too close to the bone to investigate any further, and they ambled off, scratching their heads.

Watching Ayin play with Miriam and Lorenzo, I saw how really young she was. She was twenty years old, and in a very real sense she was much older than I was. But in so many other ways, she was still a child, too, just a few years out of high school, still living with her mother in San Francisco. Lorenzo and Miriam were thirteen and twelve, respectively, but ancient in their wisdom. I knew it was because they lived every day in that searing world of naked reality, the tremendous gravity of the circus, which the rest of us only visit for an hour or two, maybe a few times each decade if we're real fanatics about it.

■   ■   ■

The next morning Ayin was sad. The sun was shining all around Tucson, on the mountains and the town and the school and the cars, but the circus was flat, and Ayin's ankle was swollen worse than ever, and she sat in a chair—not on the ground as she ordinarily did—and looked very sad. She had a black silk scarf wrapped several times around her neck and wore a bulky black sweater—her light had vanished within those dark clouds—and she was glum about the prospect of doing anything stirring and beautiful today. "You're sad," I said.

"Yes," she said.

"Why?" I asked.

"Because I have to do today," she said. Then she added, perfunctorily, as if she were repeating something someone told her, "It's up to me if I don't want to push it." But we both knew that—at least at that moment, at 8:30 the morning after the storm had blown down the Pickle Family Circus, while the performers arrived and began pulling the pieces up off the wet ground and seeing how they might all fit back together like a puzzle thrown from its box—that really Ayin had no choice in the matter. "It's hard," she said, meaning life in the Pickle Family Circus, this old-time, from-the-heart, work-like-a-dog circus. "It's so hard."

John the juggler, so thin and youthful with light brown hair and glasses that made him look studious, came out of his tent in red Dr. Denton's and squinted around him for a moment at the destruction and went back inside. He was one of the few who had slept on the site. A woman emerged from another tent and went into the injection-molded plastic outhouse. I could smell coffee brewing in the kitchen trailer behind Ayin, who sighed and got up and stripped out of her sweater and picked up a big push broom and began to sweep the standing water off the blue floor of the Moid. I couldn't help thinking of

Wire Walker

Emmett Kelly, whose legendary sad-clown act involved sweeping the circle of a spotlight inward from the circumference until it closed in upon itself like the gravity of a black hole sucking the very light of the world, and it vanished to a point of light and then the whole tent was dark. So Ayin seemed to sweep the sunlight away with her sadness.

The tent structure, once the Mad Moid, lay in a heap a few yards away. Ayin put her back into the work, limping as she went, and then she stopped and called out, "Allis, do you have any more of those pills? I'd better try them to see if they affect my balance before I do the act."

It was only an hour or two before all the people working had put the dizzy rig back up again. Soon the backdrop was lifted into place, its structure repaired with a splint of wood, like a broken leg. Even the Moid went up again. Personal tents were put back together, and I could hear the saxophone player beginning to warm up on the bandstand. The sun had already gotten high enough to dry out the grass, and I saw a silver-gray hot-air balloon hanging motionless over the mountains.

Ayin sat again, putting ice on her ankle, calling to someone, "If you need me, I'll be there," torn between helping them and helping herself. She knew that she was going to have to quit the Pickle Family Circus and go to circus school. She did not know what her destiny was, but she knew the path she'd have to take. "My life has been so weird," she said, as if that explained her trajectory. She told me that her grandmother had a lot of money and would probably pay her tuition in Paris. "We were always poor, extremely poor," she said. "My father always took jobs that he liked, but they never made any money. But my grandmother married this horrible guy who had a lot of money. He was in public relations and did things like telling people that it was good for you to smoke cigarettes. He was truly an evil man, but he had all this money." She said her grandmother had several houses and one of them was filled with cats and dogs. Two of her six sisters were raised by her grandmother, "But my grandmother didn't like children. She used to tell my mother, 'I'd like to see you, but without the kids, please.' And yet she took two of my sisters away from my mother and had these maids raise them. I'm glad I wasn't raised by her."

She looked down at her ankle and cried, "I can't point my toe!" Then she sucked on the slug of ice she'd been using. The performers make ice slugs by freezing water in plastic cups. By stripping the cup back like a banana peel, they make a grip for holding the ice. "What's scary about spraining your ankle," Ayin said thoughtfully, "is that then you start moving your other foot all weird and then you sprain that foot, too. That's what happened to me last year. I had two sprained ankles all season."

Lorenzo came over, and they talked about the storm. "I thought we were in an earthquake," Ayin said. "The Moid was falling on me, and I was just screaming."

"I loved it," Lorenzo said. "Because you don't often get to act on your toes like that. Everybody had to run around and do things and think for themselves." It had been an impromptu catastrophe instead of one they'd planned, and yet they'd performed well. Everything was back together and no one was hurt. Well, almost no one.

Rosalinda had cut her finger pretty badly, and now she was walking around, naked inside the skin of her black elastic body stocking, with a big bandage on her finger, like a clown Band-Aid, trying to do a hand-balancing act and commenting on the paradoxical nature of her existence: "I risk my life every day and I slice my finger." Her partner lay on his back and put his hands up to the heavens. Rosalinda grasped his hands and rose effortlessly to a handstand, her toes pointed at the sun, her muscular body as still as if it had been carved out of solid carbon.

The crowd was arriving, and the band was starting to play. The day was going to be very hot. Ayin went out into the ring and sat on the wire, balancing without thinking, just draped there as if she sat on a park bench. Hugh came over and suggested she cut the toe work to save her ankle. "That would be a dinky act," Ayin said. She thought about her options. "I should either try it in the first show or not try it in the first show." She meditated on that for a moment longer: Her face contorted as she saw more clearly her lack of options.

She stood up on the wire like a marionette, drawn up on its strings from above; then she danced lightly across the wire, her face now relaxed as if in sleep. It is impossible to walk a tightwire without relaxing. If you don't relax, you fall off. Her steady state on the wire seemed to violate all the laws we internalize and accept as fundamental. It was only the sinewy reality of her animal nature that kept us tuned to what she was, this amazing creation out of flesh, a mute and thinking being.

Yet in another way, what she did was a skill, which she had practiced and learned, like the violin or the jitterbug. It was not magic. Not anymore magic than transforming a lump of clay into a human head.

I watched her arms wave smoothly, rhythmically back and forth above her: She was gliding now like a bird in soaring flight, tilting with the vicissitudes of the wind. Behind her, Karen was juggling clubs in a pouring white cascade, and the saxophone player was doing arpeggios, which sounded like the juggling of golden bubbles in the air.

Now an accordian started up from behind the dizzy rig. Lorenzo stepped out into the ring and looked at the sky for a moment in concentration, then did a back flip as if it were just a nervous tick, something he did while thinking about something else.

"How is it?" I asked Ayin.

"It's pain," she said, slipping across the wire, backlit by the immense gray mountains, sliding and dancing and turning on one foot with the green mesquite and the blue sky behind her. "It's just pain."

The War on Drugs

on a Coast Guard Cutter

We flew east out of Opa-Laka, past Bimini, and then down the Great Bahama Bank, looking for smugglers. We were in a Coast Guard Falcon interceptor jet, a sleek white bird with an orange slash on the side and a fine blue accent, a symbol recognized by outlaws throughout the Caribbean. The day was bright, and ice cream cumulus rose with the summer heat, building into grand confections. The copilot talked over the radio to Slingshot, the radar service. Slingshot fed us information on suspect aircraft, and we chased them down. Once we acquired them with our on-board radar, we could navigate to the target. When we had the bad guy in sight, we'd fly "right up his gazops," as one pilot put it.

"Slingshot, Redhead four-two," the copilot called, using our code name. "Request bogie dope."

The Slingshot briefer came back with a description of the suspect aircraft. "Turn right two-zero-zero for intercept," Slingshot said.

"I have a Judy, fourteen miles," our on-board radar operator called over the intercom from his scope far in the back of the plane. The term *Judy* meant he had our target on radar.

"Your ball, sir," Slingshot said, and we were on the chase.

We turned to intercept the unidentified aircraft, whose altitude was 3400 feet, speed steady at 140 knots. Since Slingshot had been tracking him, he seemed to be circling, which probably meant he was preparing for an air drop. A traditional method for smuggling drugs involves an aircraft dropping waterproof bales into the sea. High-speed boats (Scarabs, Cigarettes, Makos) then pick them up and take them to Florida.

"I have him locked on radar," our on-board radar technician said.

Sitting in a passenger seat in the cabin, another officer was ready, his video camera pointed out the window, to put our smuggler on tape for additional evidence at the trial. Our plan was to sneak up beneath and behind the smuggler aircraft and identify him. Then we would video tape him as he dropped the bales of drugs into the sea. We would call reinforcements to pursue the Go-Fast boats.

Tracing silver contrails around the skirts of building cumulus clouds, we emerged into sunlight between the ranges of mist and caught sight of a black speck disappearing into the mouth of a billowing white leviathan.

"Tally-ho," the pilot called, meaning he had the suspect aircraft in sight, and he throttled up. The plane climbed out toward the black dot that was appearing and disappearing among the magnificent cumulus clouds. Beneath us the sea spread out in splashes of color. The shallow waters created geometric patterns of pale greens and blues, dotted here and there by rocks and cays, each one another hiding place for drugs. In olden days, pirates hid treasure here. "Bimini used to be the Casablanca of dope," a helicopter pilot told me, "but now it's all yuppies."

"Eight and a half miles, two hundred and eight knots." Our radar man warned us that we were closing fast on the bad guy.

"I've got him," the pilot said, and we thundered right on up his twin-jet pipes, spitting fire, just in time to realize that we had intercepted a navy Seahawk helicopter out on covert maneuvers over the silent, secret sea.

"What's he doing out here?" the copilot said.

We peeled away, surfing out along the cloud ridges, full throttle, and left him in our wake.

Before going out to hunt drug smugglers, I had received many official briefings, both on the war on drugs (the wider war, which has grown out of administration policy in Washington under presidents dating back at least to Richard Nixon) and on activities at the front lines of that war, the area that extends like a cone of confusion from Florida outward to encompass Cuba and everything from Cozumel to Venezuela.

It had sounded so simple in the briefings: With an armada of vessels, both in the air and on the sea, from exotic German-made spy planes to French helicopters and jets, from navy ships and Coast Guard cutters to fast boats and hydrofoils—with the men and women of the Drug Enforcement Agency and Customs, the CIA, FBI, air force, and the Bahamian Police, we would go out there and chase down the drug smugglers, board and search them, and bring them and their cargo back, thereby preventing dangerous intoxicants from entering the country.

At lunch in the Coast Guard officers' ward room, the conversation turned to cocaine babies, infants born to mothers using cocaine. An officer explained: "What we're doing is saving the next generation." Throughout my travels along the front lines of the war on drugs, I heard that refrain repeated. The war on drugs is a holy war. In all such jihads the leaders must compel themselves and their men through zeal, not through reason.

A helicopter pilot who was involved in rescue operations at sea said, "Nothing makes you feel better than bringing someone back who's really hurt and seeing them get better." Then he thought a moment and added, "Or busting someone with a load of dope, and knowing you're saving some kid back home from that stuff." Over and over again, I heard the two equated: Arresting "dirtbags" (as suspected smugglers are called) was the equivalent of saving a life.

I went out chasing drug smugglers to see for myself. I went as a war correspondent to the front lines. I flew in the jets and helicopters. I sailed in the cutter *Padre* from Key West down the Bahamas to Cay Sal off the Cuban Coast and then up to the Marquesas, where Melville jumped ship in 1842. I went on an aerostat ship, a great vessel with a dirigible tethered on a three-thousand-foot Kevlar line with radar gear aloft, capable of seeing one hundred miles (only a god can see that far, so therefore we must be gods). I even chased across the open waters one evening at sunset in an Avon, a small, rigid-hulled, inflatable boat with a sixty-five-horsepower outboard.

Out in the middle of the great ocean, with no land in sight, flying fish glided before our rubber bow. Skidding the waves at thirty-five knots, I watched our mother ship, *Padre*, disappear behind us. The ocean swallowed us up, and then it swallowed the big orange sun, too, as if to show us, with intense and visceral finality, how small we were. Then the sky opened up and shed its cargo of stars. Inside all of this, we sought a 135-foot Panamanian freighter with twelve hundred pounds of cocaine on it. We were searching for a raindrop with a speck of white

The War on Drugs

dust upon its surface. We were joined for battle by another Coast Guard cutter, two aircraft orbiting overhead, and the aerostat radar blimp ship somewhere between Havana and the Dry Tortugas. To the great baleen of the sea, we were nothing more than plankton.

■ ■ ■

As the Coast Guard cutter *Padre* steamed out of Key West, headed straight for Hurricane Flats and the Tropic of Cancer, that first and simplest problem with our jihad became immediately apparent to me. As I stood on the bridge with eight thousand Paxman diesel horsepower trembling through the steel ship beneath my feet, I could see that we had a veritable armada of sea-going vessels coming at us, and we could not—quite naturally—see inside their hulls. Clearly, we could not stop everyone. Only chance would tell us which boats were dirty and which were clean.

The captain, young and fair and blond, in a crisp, sky-blue shirt and a sea-blue baseball cap with "USCGC *Padre* WPB 1328" stitched in yellow upon the crown, watched hopefully through binoculars. He took a few names from the sterns of boats and had the quartermaster look them up in the FOLIO file, a ring-bound oracle as thick as the Koran, filled with the names of boats suspected of carrying intoxicants.

As the gunner's mate put it, "It's a pretty Herky job," short for Herculean.

At sunset the lights were turned down in the pilot house, and the officers on watch put masking tape over all the annunciators to bring the light level even lower. A soft red glow was all that was left—that and the chatter of radios—and all those elements blended with the eerie sense of menace on the heaving swells in the groaning boat.

Our patrol had all the trappings of a military operation. Talk on the bridge was often of "cross training" and "evolutions." The scramblers were military equipment, as were the 20 mm cannon on the forecastle and the M-60 machine guns ("Rambo Specials") bolted to the port and starboard railings and the locker full of M-16s and shotguns below. As in any war, everyone out there who was not one of us was, *ipso facto*, one of them.

■ ■ ■

on a Coast Guard Cutter 139

I passed the time with the crew in the pilot house. The center of attention was the radar scope, which gave us a picture out to about twenty-four miles so that we could spot other ships. Throughout the night we intercepted boats and identified them by the names on their sterns. Periodically, one of us would go down to the galley on the lower deck and bring back a thermos of coffee, some honey-nut granola bars or chocolate chip cookies, and we'd sit in the pilot house watching the scope or studying the darkness out the window with binoculars. The radar was like a computer game. It had all sorts of trackballs, knobs, switches, and dials with which we could plot the course of target vessels; and then the demon in the machine would, like a trained dolphin balancing a ball upon its nose, calculate how long it would take us to intercept and how close we would pass to the target at that point in the space-time continuum.

The pilot house had a powerful air conditioner, which kept the room refrigerated for the sake of the electronics in the ET room below, where all the computers were kept. By comparison, the open bridge was a comfort, out under the stars with the hot breeze and the unreeling plenitude of night. At one point during the long watch, the quartermaster came out to give me a quick lesson in astronomy, pointing out the Plieades, Taurus, and Orion, with its stars Bellatrix and Betelgeuse (which he pronounced "Beetle Juice").

We spent the night that way in silent contemplation of our fate, broken only by occasional radio checks and the humor of the crew to cut the creepy silence of our stalking. "Did you get your subscription to *Gay Apartment Living* yet, Burt?"

"If you see women's underwear hanging all over the Anti-Gravity Room," the boatswain told me, "don't be surprised. That's just Cox." The Anti-Gravity Room was the forward berthing area. In heavy seas it heaved around so much that the men became airborne in their sleep.

The gunner's mate, a large, intelligent man, with a quick, dry sense of humor, said, "Sometimes we come home covered with bruises."

Earlier, Guns had explained to me how they test drugs for purity on the high seas. "When we get the dope, we pull out this old sixties long-hair hippie from below, and he tokes up on it: 'Yep. This is the real McCoy, all right. 1978. Brought out of El Dificil on a pack mule. Transported in a sixty-nine Dodge truck.'"

■　■　■

Dawn: A treasure of reflection on the sea, like a pirate's chest, rose with the sun. South and east we saw the wreckage of the clouds left by storm, fleece and flotsam-gray and the boiling rain on waves a nearby mile away, and the bloom of sun emerging from the newly turned celestial soil. A pink cloud flew from the radar mast like the ragged flag of the renegade nation between Key West and Cuba.

A shimmering silhouette in the morning-silver-burning sea, as the fishing vessel *Sea Farmer* materialized out of the buff and tarnished waves. The captain said, "Ah, I know *Sea Farmer*. Everybody and his brother has looked at *Sea Farmer* lately." He looked with his binoculars and added thoughtfully, "The only thing that bothers me about *Sea Farmer* is all the antennas." Indeed, the small fishing boat looked a bit like a porcupine.

Four seal-gray dolphins paced us, leaping and dancing off our port side as we cut along at twelve knots, headed for Aerostat 3, the radar blimp ship. As the sun rose high, the sea turned black as farmland, ploughed in neat rows by the farmer moon and skimmed with a scum of haloed light. Our white ship was led by a color guard of iridescent blue flying fish, which beat the water with their tails to get airborne and then fanned out in flocks before our bow and vanished in the waves a hundred yards ahead.

Long before we could see the 190-foot *Gulf Sentry*, the Aerostat 3 MAP boat, we saw the faintly moss-green blimp, like something out of World War I, among the tumbling clouds. Those Mobile Aerostat Platform (MAP) boats were the centerpiece of the war on drugs. Similar blimps blocked the four passages from South to North America, along with Coast Guard cutters and navy Femrons (lethal-looking thunder-gray hydrofoil ships with cannons and great missile tubes as big as telephone poles—potent delusions come to life, science fiction dreams of war). But as sophisticated and useful as a radar blimp can be, the technicians told me that any boat wanting to avoid it could simply install a $150 Fuzzbuster radar detector and never fear again being tracked by the Aerostat blimps. Moreover, the communications used by the Coast Guard were used by the smugglers to locate the Coast Guard ships by a procedure called Direction Finding. "They may not know what we're saying," the captain said, "but they can easily tell where we are and avoid us." And no matter how much technology the United States was willing to build and cast like nets upon the sea, someone—a real person—still had to find a boat, sight it visually, sail up next to it, and walk onto its deck in order to catch any smugglers or bring home any drugs. With our telescopes we may see the stars, but we cannot hold them in our hands.

It is not surprising then that most busts on the high seas come about because someone involved in the drug deal tells the authorities. "Intel," they call it, or: "Our spooks say . . ." Of course, the radar eyes are always watching, but they rarely turn up anything real. I was told that a Coast Guard cutter, like whaling ships of old, can stay out for two years without making a single seizure.

In order to sail from South America to Florida a boat must go through one of four main passages. Between Mexico and Cuba is the Yucatan Channel. Between Cuba and Haiti is the Windward Passage. Between the Dominican Republic and Puerto Rico is the Mona Passage, and between Puerto Rico and east of the Virgin Islands is the Anageda Passage. Five MAP boats, all accompanied by cutters, blocked those passages. The Aerostat provided a radar umbrella (with a radius of sixty nautical miles), and the cutter circulated around it, with its own, smaller radar coverage (typically twenty-four nautical miles). Military aircraft came and went as needed.

Until recently, drug planes from Colombia flew straight over Cuba to drop their loads, and Cuban Navy vessels escorted them into Cuban ports to unload and pass cargo to fishing vessels or Go-Fast boats for the ride to Florida. Cuba was a critical refueling link in the chain. But events have changed. Castro recently executed certain military officers for aiding drug dealers. Drug planes have been flying around the eastern edge of Cuba, not over it, ever since one plane that went over Cuba was met by Cuban Mig fighter aircraft. Now intelligence insiders aren't sure if Castro is for or against drugs. But the *Padre* captain believed that Castro executed his military officers for political reasons, not for dope, and everyone on the boat seemed to believe that Cuba was still a player.

Whatever Cuba was doing, there was no question that the Coast Guard presence had made the passages less attractive for everyone. But to the budding nation-states that were the giants of the drug-smuggling world in the closing days of the twentieth century, to the towering multinational businesses that ensured a steady supply of herbs and intoxicants to the United States, that expensive and desperate American blockade was little more than a minor nuisance. Even inside the military command structure, with its hyperactive propaganda machinery churning out hopeful statistics about the war on drugs, there was agreement that most of the drugs no longer came in air drops to little Go-Fast boats.

By the time I got to the war on drugs, it was generally agreed upon in higher intelligence circles that the big drug suppliers had shifted their operations to alternate routes and more sophisticated means. Containerized cargo was the modern way, both on large ships and in airliners, and those did not come through Florida but through Europe. There was no pretending that we could "seal off" European or Canadian supply routes, and so the military didn't talk about them much. Statistics were being produced by the ton to show that the war on drugs in the Caribbean was going well, having some effect, but in 1988, the Coast Guard seized only 149 vessels. Since 1980, only 1453 vessels had been taken, and not all of those seizures resulted in convictions, and some of those vessels had to be returned to their owners.

Summarized, the productivity of the Coast Guard in capturing cocaine was as follows: In the eight years from 1980 through 1988, the Coast Guard seized an average of 182 vessels per year bearing 57 pounds of cocaine per vessel, or 10,374 pounds of cocaine per year. Put in other terms, each year, the Coast Guard's entire anti-smuggling effort prevented about $207,500,000 worth of cocaine from entering the United States. That may seem like a lot of money, but it is an illusion of scale. For example, a single money launderer who was arrested was found to be processing more than $200,000,000 each year—and that was back in the seventies, when drug smuggling was not quite as sophisticated as it is today. Gonzalo Rodriquez, one of the big-time drug entrepreneurs (though not the biggest), had an income of $20,000,000 per month, or $240,000,000 per year. In other words, what the Coast Guard has been seizing each year for the past eight years does not even amount to the income of a single big-time drug smuggler. And there are many of them. Too many to count.

One day, standing on the bridge with the captain of the *Padre,* I saw him watch the sea and shake his head. "There's a heck of a lot of ocean out there," he said. It was one of those moments when I thought he was beginning to realize the magnitude of the problem. And yet he kept on.

In a briefing the day before we shipped out, one of the officers told me why he was so concerned about stopping cocaine traffic. "One, maybe two passes with a crack pipe, and you're one hundred percent addicted," he said. "It burns out a part of your brain, and it's gone. You can never feel pleasure again, and so you go back again and again for that hit of crack. You're lost."

. . .

We had tied up at Key West on the 199th birthday of the Coast Guard after our long and fruitless meanderings at sea. Just off dockside, there was a grassy area and pavilion, and the celebration was under way, with barbecue and beer and rock-and-roll. Sailors from other ships were there, turned out in wild civilian shorts and Hawaiian shirts, and the girls were laughing and making over them. The wives and children of the *Padre* crew had come, some from very far away, expecting to have Daddy home for a week or more. The *Padre* mariners stepped onto land with that peculiar lurching walk of men who had been a long time at sea, and they crouched down to let their children crawl over them and cover them with kisses.

We were taking on diesel oil, and I was watching that pretty, domestic scene, when I saw the captain run down from the bridge, jump off the ship, and proceed at a sprint toward the Ops shed. Everyone knew something was going on, and when he came back, he called the crew away from their families and huddled them on the fan deck. I was asked to wait on the open bridge, out of earshot. He was taking a vote to see if the crew wanted to go back out, and a few minutes later he came up and told me that the boat had received a new mission.

"I can't tell you what we're doing unless you come along," he said.

. . .

Once we were safely under way and there was no danger that I could communicate with anyone off the boat, the captain revealed our mission: A 135-foot Panamanian freighter was steaming northward to drop twelve hundred pounds of cocaine over the side as it passed nearby an American lobster boat, the *Michael James*, which was DIW (dead in the water) one hundred miles west of the Dry Tortugas in the Gulf of

Mexico. He said, "We've got to run hard and it's a long way." Two hundred miles, to be exact.

So it was with the twin aluminum Paxman diesels going full chat, we put land behind us so fast that it was alarming. Florida simply vanished, as if swallowed by a wave. By four in the afternoon, there were huddles of men on the open bridge and in the pilot house, and the narrow walkways and corridors of the ship were bustling with people. The captain stood in the pilot house and chewed his cuticles and stared at the horizon, talking about tactics and selecting his boarding team for the bust. Something about the pace before had made the *Padre* seem like a cruise ship, almost a vacation for me. But now the rock music and television in the galley were turned off; the men were outfitting themselves for battle; and the atmosphere had taken a grim turn. Even the engines (which I only now realized had been loafing along before) seemed to pulverize each nautical mile, thundering out their twenty-eight knots and causing the great steel hull to tremble beneath my feet. High atop the bridge, the ensign lines were whining in the wind. Behind us the white wake split the blue sea all the way to the horizon.

■ ■ ■

Running dark in darkness at 21:09, talking to the Falcon jet somewhere over the sea, the radios were buzzing with garbled words and static, and the dim lights made all the men in the pilot house look like the walking dead, the forms of ghosts. The aircraft had spotted a ship, and now we ran for it, diverting from our previous course. I was standing on the open bridge with the captain when we overtook the vessel, and with the sea shuddering and lurching beneath us, we both trained binoculars on the skeleton lights of the dark boat. I have to admit that I felt my heart leap inside my chest when I read through my trembling glasses the word "Panama" on the stern of the ship. Her name was *Tenkei*, and soon our quartermaster below was calling her on the radio as we closed in.

"Light me up," the captain said, "and light up my stripes." By stripes he meant the orange and blue Coast Guard symbols on the hull.

All over the cutter *Padre* lights went on, a candlepower demon apparition on the waves, which must have terrified the *Tenkei* crew if they were watching. Also, if they were bad guys, the captain and I made perfect targets, standing there in the spotlight against the black curtain of the sea.

The quartermaster talked with the *Tenkei*'s master. She was a freighter bound out of Houston, Texas, for Dakar, Senegal, on the continent of Africa. She bore a load of tallow.

"Wish him a good trip and thank him for the information," the captain said as we put our binoculars away and doused the lights. He said he knew immediately that he had a merchant ship. Divine inspiration was his job on the mythic, battered sea.

Now the Falcon jet overhead reported that it had no other sightings, not even the lobster boat, *Michael James*, which was supposed to have been dead in the water west of the Dry Tortugas. Both boats, which were earlier spotted by a Customs' plane (and by the cutter *Cherokee*, steaming slowly north from somewhere one hundred miles south of us, and which was not fast enough to effect the interception), seemed to have vanished. We were all aware of the fact that the *Michael James*, a wooden boat only sixty-five feet long, would not be easy to pick up on radar. We were even more acutely aware of how things simply vanish at sea, boats, people, celestial visions . . .

The engineer of the watch came through the dark pilot house to tell the gunner's mate he was making exterior rounds. "Okay," Guns says, "but make sure you wear a vest and hold on tight. We're screaming." They understood that to fall over the side at night was to vanish. The sleek and oily sea, the churning, pleated whiteness of the wake, would snap a man in two. Not the captain in the air-conditioned pilot house, nor gunner's mate, nor quartermaster would ever hear the cry. A man would perish beneath the yawning vastness of the stars.

Somewhere high above us, metaphorically, if not in reality, someone was directing the operation and processing intel. *Cherokee* told us in the middle of the night that the Panamanian freighter—the real one— was sixty miles from *Michael James* and traveling north at five knots. We were put under the command of *Cherokee* and now did her bidding. "We're chopped to *Cherokee*," they said.

Customs launched an aircraft, and when we found it on radar in the dead of night, it was moving so fast that we knew it could be nothing else, but still we turned our stern to its approaching beacon, preparing

The War on Drugs

for a collision in case it happened by chance to be a navy Femron, whose top speed is classified. Of course, whatever it might have been, we would likely have been killed in such a crash.

The captain called a meeting in the mess to select his boarding party. He leaned against the stainless-steel milk machine, next to the television and VCR, and he looked tired as he instructed the men in how he wanted the operation conducted. It would be a standard Coast Guard boarding with the usual checks to be completed (checking for life vests, and so on). And by the way, the men were to dress out in flak vests, Browning 9 mm pistols, handcuffs, and Asp riot batons and to get some sleep before we moved any closer to the bad guys.

"Johnny," he said to one crew member, "you stay. We've got to get you out on the range a few more times and make sure you can kill somebody." He thought about that for a moment, then added: "And that you want to."

The boatswain was the most experienced member of the crew, except for the captain, and he and the captain were very close. In the dark early hours of the morning, they stood up in the dark pilot house discussing the quarry they hunted. They both seemed quite excited, evidently since what we chased sounded a lot like a recent case: the *Barlavento*, a 180-foot Panamanian freighter that had come north carrying cement. Everyone thought the dope was going to be under the cement, but it wasn't. It was inside a false fuel tank, which was inside a real fuel tank. The Coast Guard surface-effects ship *Shearwater* took thirty-three hundred pounds of cocaine off of her. In order to board a foreign vessel, the Coast Guard needs permission from the host nation. Many drug ships bear the flag of Panama. That is not surprising to anyone who has read the Senate Subcommittee report on Terrorism, Narcotics, and International Operations.

Panama has no income tax and has complete secrecy surrounding bank transactions. Noriega's administration, according to the congressional report, was "substantially funded with narcotics money." The Panamanian military guarded shipments of drug money from the United States and according to Noriega's accountant, Ramon Milian Rodriquez, "helped the Medillin cartel launder billions of dollars through Panama, meeting airplanes filled with cartel money from Miami at the Panamanian airport, guarding the money as it was loaded into armored cars, and delivering the money to the Banco Nacional de Panama."

Interestingly enough, during that time—through the early 1980s—the U.S. State Department knew about Noriega's drug dealings based on what Norman Bailey of the National Security Council called "clear and incontrovertible evidence." Nevertheless, the State Department did nothing to stop Noriega and in fact frustrated other U.S. efforts to combat his drug-smuggling operations. In 1987 the administrator of the DEA wrote Noriega a warm letter commenting on "our close association." A top official of the U.S. attorney's office in Miami quit because of the duplicity of the American government in its stance toward leaders such as Noriega. Yet, when it was politically convenient to do so, the United States mounted a military invasion of highly questionable legality in order to bring Noriega to trial. Cynicism and corruption have tainted the war on drugs at its very core. The war is not a war on drugs but a struggle of politics and power within the United States Government itself.

■ ■ ■

Now two targets were pinging hard at fifteen miles. It was very dark out, and the night was muggy and still with the incipience of rain, but inside the pilot house the air conditioner was freezing us in the low green-and-red glow of lights. The tension was palpable. Those two ships were just the size and shape of the ones we wanted, and one appeared to be DIW. "Come on," I heard the captain's voice say to the radar screen, "don't be a tease." Earlier I had heard him describe a run we'd made, where we ran and ran all night after a ship that was nothing—clean, a commercial fishing boat out of the Bahamas. "It's like you take her out, you spend all this money on dinner, and then you don't even get in the door."

As the tension built, the humor began to take bizarre turns. "I'm going to make rounds outside," an engineer on watch said.

The gunner's mate said, "'If we go outside can you kiss me?' Is that what you said?"

"No, that's not what I said," the engineer said with disgust.

"Run around the deck four times and then jump on my face," Guns said. "But do it in a manly way."

"You are sick."

"Let's see," Guns said, looming over the charts to figure our time to intercept the targets. "We'll spend six hours boarding them and then two hours beating them up . . ."

Now Aerostat 1 and *Cherokee* and *Padre* were all closing on the suspect targets out in the dark waters. A faint slime of light played upon the waves. Even at twenty-eight knots, distance moved slowly beneath the boat, and much of our time was spent waiting, watching, listening to the eight or ten radios hanging on brackets overhead as they bubbled and babbled incoherently. Two men, far off, had been speaking in Spanish for an hour, incessantly chattering about banalities. Why don't they shut up? Don't they know a war is on?

Another aircraft passed and was gone before we could spot it. Cox was on top with a night-vision scope that illuminated the whole world in an eerie green light. Now on the high bridge, lightning clouds built castle walls around us, and the ship was luring phosphorescence out of the dark waves in a wide and glowing wake. Creaming through the air, our boat seemed to fly on a cold tail of fire, and our dark flags ripped the clouds.

As we approached within eight miles of the radar contact, we were rapidly reaching the point where we had either to engage and board or break off. Yet no one could find him with binoculars, not even with the night-vision scope. This was truly our Flying Dutchman, then, the mystery ship of legend, of the fabled thirty-thousand-ton haul. Surely this was the bust we were looking for, if only we could find the thing that was pinging so hard on our radar scope. It was right there, we all could see it in orange light on the round radar screen, but nowhere in the darkness of the sea night would it reveal its shape.

I stood up on the open bridge straining my eyes as the steel bow of the boat slit the sea. Then I heard the captain's voice call up the stairs from the pilot house: "All right, guys. We just found the *Cherokee*."

"Shit." It was our sister ship we were tracking all along.

■　■　■

We finally found the *Michael James*. Actually, *Sitkinak* found her one hundred miles east of where she should have been and boarded and searched her and found nothing. She was not a sixty-five-foot lobster boat, but a fifty-foot shrimp boat, which may sound like a faint distinction, but is something like mistaking a Boeing 727 for a Piper Cub. On the second evening of the chase, *Padre* intercepted the *Michael James* and took over from *Sitkinak*. It was dark when we overtook the two boats heading into Key West at nine knots. The only part of the *Michael James* that the boarding party had been unable to search was underneath the ice in which the fisherman had put their shrimp and yellowtail catch. District 7, headquarters for the Coast Guard bosses, ordered us now to take *Michael James* into Key West and complete the search.

By that time we knew we had nothing. We were going through the motions. The master of the *Michael James* was cooperative, and none of us thought the boat was dirty—certainly not the crew of *Sitkinak*, who had searched her, for if they had smelled the least bit of dope, they would have torn the boat apart to get that decal of honor on the side of the *Sitkinak*'s superstructure. Our crew would have, too. No, it was experience that told those men they were escorting a clean boat back to Key West. Somebody higher up had a reason for wanting the boat in Key West, but it was not because there were drugs on board. We knew something else was going on—that we were small pawns in a large game—and that we would never know the true magnitude or meaning of our moves.

■　■　■

America's war on drugs is more dangerous to Americans than drugs. The propaganda about the effects of drugs, which is necessary to conduct a war, serves only to mislead people about compulsive disorders. The misinformation allows more people to become compulsive drug users than otherwise might if reliable information were available. The anti-science bent of the war on drugs prevents the research and treatment of a treatable medical condition. The war on drugs constitutes a public health hazard.

The war on drugs is a convenient cover for carrying out hidden plans, such as a military build-up in the Caribbean, a limitless and unquestioned increase in police powers, and a costly (and profitable) increase in manpower and technology for government. In the meantime, more drugs of better quality are available in the United States than ever before, while our civil liberties are falling by the wayside. We are no longer (for example) protected from illegal search and seizure or from self-incrimination.

The war on drugs has created a new criminal class. People who are otherwise law-abiding citizens are filling up the jails, and more jails are being built in order to handle the overflow. The war on drugs arbitrarily punishes certain members of society who are no different from other members except that they have developed a medical problem with pot instead of with tobacco or a medical problem with cocaine instead of one with alcohol. That's like saying we'll treat those suffering from emphysema and punish those suffering from cancer. This situation is doubly dangerous. It fosters a lack of respect for what is and is not legal, since even the casual and uninformed observer can see that it makes no sense. Marijuana is still smoked openly in public places in blatant defiance of the law. In other words, it erodes respect for all law and thereby weakens the fabric of society.

The war on drugs is a convenient political tool. In its character it is not unlike the Nazis blaming the Jews for everything. We blame the drug dealers—crime, poverty, the spread of AIDS, and Communism— it is all the fault of third-world drug dealers, who are portrayed on television as the worst of the bad guys. In an official Coast Guard briefing, I was shown a slide of two Latinate people in handcuffs after a raid on a boat. In order to identify them, the officer conducting the briefing said, "There's two dirtbags." It is okay, on shows such as "Miami Vice," to push aside the Fourth and Eighth amendments in order to shoot a drug dealer full of holes. On that pretext, we are building up our military presence in the Caribbean and Central America, where some members of Congress have tried to keep us out. Then when we turn our backs, our own government deals drugs anyway, or helps the drug dealers—as it did in Cambodia, Laos, and more recently for Noriega and the Contras. More routinely, shipments of drugs are allowed to cross the Mexican border undetected and to be distributed in the United States during undercover operations—all in the course of State Department business as usual. At the same time, we are about to institute the death penalty for drug dealers, a move that may threaten to turn the United States into the world's largest banana republic.

That's the way it is on the high seas: Last night the spooks overheard what they thought was a drug boat being boarded, and they called wanting to know if it was us. It wasn't. But there has been a lot of piracy on the high seas, with pirates boarding drug boats after the drugs are gone and then taking the money from the sale and scuttling the boat and feeding the crew to the sharks for chum. The occasional radar target that disappears from our screen may be lost that way (while we stumble over our sister ship). Whole boats, whole crews, are swallowed up and vanish without a trace. One day we passed a shoe, floating in the middle of the ocean, and we all wondered what it meant, and we all knew we'd never know.

We took the shrimper *Michael James* to the Coast Guard dock in Key West and sent some of our men down into the wooden ice holds, and they dug up the shrimp until they could see the floor and satisfy themselves that nothing could be hidden there. And then we sent the shrimpers on their way.

Watching the boat, one of the Coast Guard boarding team had said, almost as a lament, to himself, "Where is the dope? Where is the dope?"

Another had come up beside him to watch the shrimp boat. "The dope is in the Ops Center," he said.

I met with an officer running air ops out of Miami. He had flown Cobra helicopters in Vietnam, and he sat me down and said, quite earnestly, "After Vietnam they told me that we had lost that one because we didn't have the support of the American people behind us. Okay, fine. Well, then tell me this: We've got the support of the American people behind us on this one. So how come we're still losing?"

The War on Drugs

Firefighters

on Fire

When the lieutenant at the firehouse gave me my turnout gear, the first thing that caught my attention was the hat. I think that's what gets us as kids, isn't it—the hat? When Lt. Bob McKee of the Chicago Fire Department handed it to me, I was surprised at how heavy it was, as if it had a steel liner. As I looked it over, I just knew it had a tale to tell. The fire hat is no mere hat; it is a protective machine of black reinforced battering-ram material, bristling with the bolt shafts and nuts that hold its parts together. The cracked white shield on the front was emblazoned with "Squad 1," and the regal brass topknot was bashed in from what must have been a stunning blow. The flip-down eye shields were smoked over and smeared with a black paste like dried India ink. The dense black crown and brim of the hat were spattered with melted tar and plastic and solder, as if its previous owner had been walking through a wall of burning pay phones.

There was an inner lining of webbing and leather with soft Kevlar fabric earflaps that could be turned down (against the cold, I assumed) like that cap my mother made me wear in the third grade. But when I got inside my first real fire, I found out that the earflaps were meant to be turned down against the heat. At one point I took off my gloves, and the heat burned the hair off my hands. Hair is always the first to go, and it goes in a flash—eyebrows, eyelids, flat top—and if you stick around, then the ears themselves burn off. I heard the men talk about the Greenmill fire, in which a firefighter got caught in a stairwell when the stairs burned out from under him and left him hanging by his fire coat up there, turning like a pig on a spit. One officer told me, "When we got to him, his head was the size of a cantaloupe." He lived.

Running at night, then, with those thoughts clear in my head, I became acutely aware of how alone I was. My children were at home, covered and protected in bed. If anything went awry, they wouldn't know. One night we ran to a fire at the Drake Hotel, and when we got there the smoke was so thick that we couldn't see down Walton Street. I had eaten many business lunches in the plush lobby of that hotel, and now I was going in with turnout gear as the guests were being evacuated. It was eleven at night, and some of the women we saw were fresh from the shower, loping down the main lobby stairs in their beige Drake Hotel bathrobes, with wet hair and the startled look of ponies. My black Kevlar coat was heavy on my shoulders. I felt the iron weight of firefighting equipment in my leaden gloves. I saw them look at us in amazement as we went (Lieutenant McKee and I and big Bob Kuehl and others) down a stairway to the basement and passed incredibly into a thick shroud of smoke that smelled like electric death.

Down there all was quiet. The walls were light-colored tile. It was a service corridor, but it looked to me like morgues I'd seen. Lights flashed through the smoke. I could hear the pry bars and pike poles clanking. Dull explosions in the distance made the hair stand up on my arms, and I was sweating in waves beneath my coat. We were all coughing, trying to see, but there was only smoke and the tile slabs, which seemed to close upon us, and room-service carts to trip us, and a terrible maze, where every sign points the wrong way.

When Bob Kuehl, six feet six inches, 265 pounds, on one side of me, and the muscular black man named Al, on the other side of me, were both taken to the hospital, overcome by the toxic fumes, I understood how serious the trouble was I had gotten myself into. The old Irish firefighter named Red began screaming at me, saying I should never have come down, and who the fuck did I think I was, and who was going to carry me out if I got killed—and of course, he was right, but there I was. I wondered how I had gotten in so deep so fast, but the answer was alarmingly simple: one step at a time.

Although it involved dozens of pieces of firefighting equipment and hundreds of people, the Drake Hotel fire, in the end, was not the one, not the big one. It was a mess, to be sure, but it was not the Moment of Truth. For each man and woman that moment is a different place, a different time, and it comes in a form we cannot imagine.

Each of us dies differently, as each of us lives differently. I could see it at night, at the long picnic-style table in the firehouse dining room. Firehouse corned beef is a Chicago classic, with boiled potatoes and cabbage and carrots. Lieutenant McKee refused to eat "that Irish shit" and instead piled boiled potatoes on his plate and mashed them with a quarter pound of butter. A young firefighter took a look at the slices of corned beef to try to figure out what it was, then took two pieces of rye, added mustard, and had a sandwich. A big paramedic piled his plate, twice, with everything, and ate half a head of cabbage. As I watched them eat and talk and laugh around the long table with the television blaring a pre-season football game, I could see the death in each man, just as I had seen it out on the bulletin board up near the business end of the firehouse. The men passed that bulletin board each time they went out on a run.

The bulletin board (behind dirty glass in a painted wood frame in a corner by the old radiator) contained departmental memoranda with bad Xeroxes of the haphazard Polaroid IDs taken in harsh light with sharp shadow and coarse grain. The faces all had that shocked, dumb look we have when they snap our IDs, that stunned moronic look of gaping solemnity that we get from waiting in line. And beneath each photo was the canticle: "It is my sad duty to inform you . . ." followed by the name and company and the location of the fire at which the man died and a date for services. They were not all grunts, either. There were lieutenants and captains and even the occasional bigwig in there. Tommy O'Donovan fell off snorkel #4 on a still alarm. Both Mike Tally and Mike Forchione died at 2847 North Milwaukee on February 1, 1985.

Big Bob Kuehl and Lieutenant McKee each lost an uncle in the same fire on the same day by a freak accident. The two men older were fairly high ranking: one at the academy and the other in charge of investigations. They heard about a fire while they were having lunch. They did not have to go, but a good fireman lives to get to a fire, and so they went. They were the only two men who died in that fire.

Each time I passed that bulletin board I wondered: Why do they do it? Each photograph showed a man who died at the peak of living. Not many people get that opportunity. Most people die in bed.

But one of the most telling facts I learned about firefighting was that on each day of the year, on each run, each man must renew his pact with the element of fire and his dedication to his work. It is not like the military, where someone puts a gun to their heads, literally, and says, "Charge!" No officer tells the men to go into a fire, and if one does, Kuehl said, "You always say, 'Teach me, Sir. I don't understand. Come in here and show me.' And if he won't go with you, you don't go either." And so for every moment of truth in that great big tinderbox world, there is a moment of transcendental truth for each firefighter, in which he must decide for himself: Is this the fire of all fires? Am I the chosen one for this fire? Can I go in there and live? And if there are children in there: Am I willing to die for them? The truth—the deepest and most amazing truth I discovered—was that Lieutenant McKee and Bob Kuehl could always answer those questions.

More than once Lieutenant McKee told me that he was bothered by the fact that civilians (as they call people who are not firefighters) think that the fire department is always wrecking things. "We come in and break your windows and wreck your roof, that's what people think." They don't understand, he said, that in order to fight a fire, you have to ventilate it. "The fire has to go somewhere, and if you don't let it out the other side, then it's going to come back on you. Windows are the cheapest things to replace."

More important, the civilians don't understand the gestalt test that a fire is. We see what we want to see in a fire. The resident sees his home burning up, and when a fireman breaks a window, the homeowner sees a man breaking a window. But the fireman sees a dangerous puzzle, and when he breaks a window, it is like a chess master moving a pawn.

■ ■ ■

The firehouse I was assigned to, Engine 5, was built in 1928, in the days of Al Capone, under Chicago Mayor William Hale "Big Bill" Thompson. It was a downtown firehouse, set back in a light industrial neighborhood west of the Loop, an architectural treasure of stone and brick with overhead doors and a brass plaque in front. The inside walls and supporting pillars were faced with a gleaming, glazed, sand-colored institutional tile all the way up. The ceiling was elaborately decorated in the grand Chicago style of the day, with impressive moldings and

Firefighters

dentils in deep patterns, each ten feet square. But decades of wild-growth technology had brought in the makeshift modern age beneath layers of telephone wire, jury rig, new paint, gaffer's tape, and conduit that made up the routine necessities of firefighting in the big city. Unit performance awards were stuck haphazardly behind the conduit that was hammered into the old concrete walls. The pipes ran up toward the ceiling, changing from silver to white where the ceiling paint took over. A cheater speaker hung on a nail above the red phone, and a faded old decal above the lieutenant's desk said: Up Your Chimney!

At the front of the house, near the lieutenant's battered gray metal desk, were the communications lines by which the company and squad were called to a fire. There were several telephones, several speakers, a radio or two, and the joker line, all above a makeshift formica counter with bundles of wire hanging down in hag-brown, tangled tresses. Nearby was the dirty old army-green steel card catalog listing the alarm boxes around the city and outlining which engines should respond to them and in what order. The card file was desk-high, and its top was made of blackboard slate. Whenever a call came in, someone (who-ever was near) wrote the address of the call on the blackboard, held down a button that prevented the firehouse bell from ringing (it rang automatically unless someone was there to stop it, a safety device in case everyone went to sleep at once), and then decided what code to ring, if any. Three bells, for example, would send the ambulance.

The whole operation had a temporary, thrown-together quality about it, as if we were just making do, just barely holding the rising tide of chaos at bay, just enough to get our shift done, until the experts arrived. I had the feeling at every moment that our position was embat-tled and that we were about to be overrun by the enemy. But who was the enemy?

There had been attempts to modernize the Department, but it had resisted change. Perhaps it's better this way. The original system, still in use, was elegantly simple: A man in the central alarm station would press a switch that said "Engine 5" and he would talk into a micro-phone. Then a big speaker right above the telephones in our house would carry the words directly to the man on watch. "I always knew who I was talking to," said the officer at the alarm center. A backup system called the joker line operated at the same time. If one system failed, the other would get the message through. Hundreds of miles of cable underneath the city carried the signals. A few years ago the Chicago Fire Department contracted Motorola to build a modern computer system for communications, which they did for many millions of dollars, and as the man on alarm watch told me, "It didn't work worth a shit. I never knew who I was talking to, and it took twenty-five seconds to get the thing cranked up."

Half a minute might be forever in a fire. So now the Chicago Fire Department has a building with $7 million worth of unused computer equipment in it, and alarms are sent the same way they were sent over one hundred years ago—and the system works pretty well. When the call came in, we heard a human voice, and all it said was the address and what type of call it was (for example, a still-and-box alarm).

The first time I heard a call, I nearly missed the whole thing. Lieutenant McKee was sitting at his metal desk at the front of the house. It was summertime and the overhead doors were open. Some of the guys were sitting on black Naugahyde chairs outside, nearly in Des Plaines Street, with the downtown traffic rumbling past. The garbled voice said something over the speaker, an address, and then the joker line clacked out its series of numbers—5-5-1—and Lieutenant McKee stood up slowly and said to me, "We're going. That's us." The way he said it was so casual, so matter-of-fact, that I didn't know what he meant at first, until I saw a couple of men getting onto the rig, and I understood he meant going in the fire engine. I had somehow envisioned a scurrying of rubber boots, men sliding down the poles they kept so meticulously polished, the rush and noise and urgency that people in a burning building must feel.

I shrugged into my turnout coat, which felt like it was made of tire chains. It had reflective yellow stripes running around its girth so they could find us if we passed out in the smoke. The collar was soft corduroy. I kicked off my shoes and jumped into the hip-length rubber boots that were turned down to the knee, and I put on the ten-pound helmet and the gauntlet gloves. When I went to climb onto the rig, I realized how very heavy I had gotten. I had to pull myself up, like hauling a sack of sand up a rope; and then we were starting out the door, four guys in the back with me. Lieutenant McKee was in front with the driver, big Bob Kuehl. And we were lurching and bouncing down the road with the immense diesel engine strumming the steel beneath us. A strap hanging from the ceiling operated the big air horn, and Lieutenant McKee kept it busy—a great, grand, irritating, bleating, squealing bellow that fell like Armageddon upon the sleeping buildings of the city.

Running in the city, there was not so much a sense of speed and emergency as there was a sense of mighty, unstoppable momentum. The big red engine was forty feet long and carried a long silver ladder and a snorkel basket on top, and the interior cabin of steel and black upholstery, where I sat with the firefighters, was the size of a respectable Manhattan living room. Our seats were each backed with an aluminum rack that held the yellow-painted steel air bottles and breather masks we would use inside of fires. In addition to that, the truck was laden with miles of hose, dozens of pike poles, axes, sledge hammers, pry bars, and every manner of rescue equipment from cutting torches to "Jaws," a pneumatic device the size of a shark, which could be used to open an automobile like a sardine can. All this, then, was sent hurtling down the street at forty miles an hour, diesel-powered, air horn bleating furiously, its cries echoing off the glass-and-steel cathedral towers around us, as morning traffic dipped and swam in the windshield. I had the distinct sense that it mattered little if those high-colored fishes got out of our way or not: Moby Dick was coming through. I remembered Bob Kuehl, who drove the engine, telling me about a guy in a Lincoln Continental, blocking the way to a fire one day. Bob leaned on the air horn, and the driver gave Bob the finger. Bob just rolled right over the Lincoln and pushed it out of the way. The insurance company called, evidently not in possession of all the facts. "This man says you hit his car," they said. Bob said, "Yeah, I was driving a fire engine, and he got in my way."

But it was during those first few runs with Squad 1 in Engine 5, as I became aware of the fact that there was no real sense of urgency, that I began to understand how firefighters can go from being such ordinary people to being such heroes in such a short span of time. And the answer was: one step at a time. By very small increments. Michaelangelo carved his famous statue of Eve one little chip of marble at a time. It was just an ordinary rock before that. We get into the worst trouble that way, too. One moment we were pushing a column of noise down the street, cozy and protected in our berth, and the whole world was making way for us, and along the street all the women going to work were stopping to turn and look at us, touched with empathy and under-standing. (They say no one gets more affection from women than fire-fighters, not even fighter pilots. I've worked with both, and I believe it.)

But the next moment we were in the blazing doorway, looking into the unknown. One more step wouldn't kill us, we always knew that. It was never the first step into the void that killed you. Was it the second step, then? Probably not. And yet, somehow, by otherwise imperceptible increments, things got worse—they always did. It was a law of nature.

■ ■ ■

Lieutenant McKee was typical in many ways. He was one of five brothers, "And only one of them was smart enough to avoid becoming a firefighter." His father rose through the ranks to become a battalion chief over a thirty-year period. When I ran with him, Bob McKee was thirty-eight and looked young. He was under six feet tall, powerfully built, with brown hair and blue eyes, a quick laugh and a knowing smile. When I'd ask him a very direct question, one that probably ought never to be spoken out loud, he would look at the ceiling and get very quiet and then smile in a certain way, like I had touched upon a secret that he didn't want to tell. But he was so good-natured that he couldn't disappoint me, and he'd tell anyway.

One night we were out under the stars on the concrete apron in front of the firehouse, sitting in old chairs, our feet up on the red fire hydrant, and I asked, "Have you brought many children out of fires?"

He gave me that look of his, but there was no little smile as usual. He just looked blank. "Not many live ones," he said.

McKee and Kuehl had worked together for years and were as close as two soldiers in a trench. In fact, they had both been Marines, though not in the same place, and now that they were together, they made something of a Mutt and Jeff team. Kuehl, an immense and powerful man, towered over Lieutenant McKee. When I'd ask either one of them a question that demanded a personal or thoughtful response, they would get around their embarrassment by telling the story to each other instead of to me, so that I could listen in. But like so many men I had met over the years who were in naturally hazardous professions, they did not like to speak directly of the hazard in a way that acknowledged that it was there. For if they acknowledged that it was there, then they'd have to be fools to do anything other than avoid it. But their profession was to confront the hazard. So what could they make of their lives, when its most central and definitive professional act was to do something that others would consider foolhardy?

No, certain things had to be kept at a respectful distance, and then they could be approached sideways, by small increments, until one was square in the jaws of the dragon. And when I made them talk about it directly, they told stories and they laughed and laughed, as if it had been the funniest thing in the world, to be almost burned alive.

They talked about the way you approach a fire, the signs you're supposed to see as you come up to the building. Say there's smoke coming out, dense black smoke, but there are no flames. And say the windows are black on the inside, like they're covered with soot, but there's a little glow of red deep in there somewhere. That is a fire that has burned itself out for lack of oxygen, but everything inside is superheated, ready to blow; all it lacks is some air. If you don't know what you're looking at, you might go up to the door and open it, and, like opening a can of coffee, break the seal on the vacuum. "Sometimes you can see the smoke pouring out around the window frames," Lieutenant McKee told me, "and it curls right back and is sucked back inside."

That is a backdraft.

And if you open the door unaware, it can pull you right in with it, like an undertow. As you are dragged inside, kicking and screaming, the missing ingredient, oxygen, is sucked in, too. "When you do the wrong thing, you find out real quick," McKee said.

One night, he went to a tavern that had been built on the back of a three-story apartment building. The fire had started in the tavern area and burned down until there was no air left. "When we got there, it didn't look that bad, some smoke coming out. I'd gotten the line laid out, and I was standing by the door putting my face piece on. I opened the door, and next thing I knew, I was laying fifteen feet away. I had no idea what happened to me. We went from solid black smoke to a building completely involved in flames in about two seconds. The worst thing was there were two guys going across the roof when that happened. That was not a great day." Luckily, the two men had just gotten to the three-story apartment building when the roof vanished beneath their feet and flames shot into the sky. They scrambled up a fire escape.

Each type of building, each type of fire, has its own way of killing you; and just when you think you understand them all, one turns on you with a new trick. Like the lion tamer in the cage, the firefighter must approach a fire with the knowledge that it is never tame. You can make it do tricks, but you can't turn your back.

Those big old brick industrial buildings, three or five or seven stories high—every big city has them. They were constructed out of immense pine timbers that used to be available before we cut down all the forests, virgin growth out of prehistory, dripping with resins. When they burn, they go fast. The sappy wood burns bright and hot, like· nature's own acetylene. The firefighters are aware of the irony of the rehab business, in which old factories are converted into dwellings for the over-privileged. Those buildings are firetraps. Even if he had the money, no firefighter would live in one. They're too dangerous.

Once the timbers get going, the load-bearing walls of brick and mortar come crumbling down around the fire engines and men. Lieutenant McKee's brother was buried by a collapsing wall. He was working with Bob Kuehl at the time. "And I just happened to walk away at the right moment," Kuehl said, "and he didn't." He miraculously survived, although, as Lieutenant McKee said (putting his hand out three feet above the floor, with that little smile of his), "He's about this short now."

■　■　■

We were sitting around the firehouse one day when the battalion chief came by and chewed out the lieutenant for leaving a fire. "But you told us to leave," McKee said. And the battalion chief blew up, denying that he had released anybody. McKee, a sensible officer, said he was sorry, but when the battalion chief left, he and Kuehl talked about how the chief had been acting a little strange lately, ever since the tire fire.

"The tire fire" was the way they referred to a big industrial fire at 2416 South Archer, which had involved three buildings and shut down the power to Comisky Park during the Chicago White Sox season opener and delayed three railroads. It was overshadowed in the news, because the very next day, while the tire fire was still burning, a landmark Sullivan building, housing numerous art galleries and millions of dollars' worth of art, was torched in Chicago's fashionable River North gallery district, and it was one of the biggest fires since *the* Chicago Fire. During the tire fire, the battalion chief had gotten himself in a bad spot and ended up in the hospital.

"He damned near got himself killed," Kuehl said.

"What happened?" I asked.

"He panicked," Lieutenant McKee said. He explained that the problem is that in big industrial buildings, it is very easy to get lost. In this case, there were two buildings of several stories each, with a mountain of old tires between. The tires were burning, setting both buildings on fire. It was a very big fire. The fire boat came up the Chicago River to help put water on it.

The chief had stormed through one building with a line, a hose, and came up, actually underneath the fire—in one building but below the level of the burning mountain of tires outside. When the building on the other side of the tires collapsed, it blew the fire back at him, sending him back into the building. Evidently, he lost his grip on the hose at that point. He went up a flight of stairs to the next level, and then he was lost.

"You ain't gonna burn up if you got a fucking hose in your hand," Lieutenant McKee said.

"The first thing they teach you in the fire academy," Kuehl said, "is that the hose is going to lead you to one of two places: On one end there's water, and where there's water, there's also air. You can actually breathe the air coming out of the end of the hose, and you can fight the fire with the water. On the other end is how you got in, so you can get out. So you never let go of that hose. It's your life."

"What happened to the chief then?" I asked.

"Fuck if I know."

"He panicked."

There were two of the chief's men down, critical, before it was over, and one of them wound up high above the fire on a balcony. They said the chief had been flaky ever since, blowing up at people, giving contradictory orders, forgetting that he'd released people from fires. It happens. You get too close to the flames too many times, and not only can you get burned, you also can get flamed out.

Lieutenant McKee and Kuehl were still young and cocky when I met them. They had been saving each other's lives for years. It's enough to make you think you have nine lives, like a cat. At one fire Kuehl looked around and saw McKee standing on an 800-amp live wire that had been knocked down. "What do you say?" Kuehl asked. "He's got both feet on it. If he takes one off, he's going to touch the ground and get fried."

So he quietly, very softly, said, "Don't move. Now look at what you're standing on. Now jump with both feet at once."

A moment later McKee was going to go down a gangway when Kuehl saw the chimney above falling. "Don't go down that gangway," he said.

"Oh, I can make it," Lieutenant McKee said, and he ran as the bricks rained down behind him. As they told that story, McKee and Kuehl laughed and laughed until I thought they'd fall out of their chairs. "We saved the attic," Lieutenant McKee said.

"Yeah, but the first two floors burned out from under us!" Kuehl said. And they doubled over with laughter.

But after all the laughter, Lieutenant McKee admits that it bothered him that the battalion chief yelled at him, no matter who was right. He prides himself in doing the job right. Besides, his father was a battalion chief, and he knows that some day he'll probably be one, too. And although he knows he must rise through the ranks, as his father did— because it is his destiny and he was born to it—still he does not relish losing the familiarity of being one of the boys. "I'm just a poor boy who wants to go to a fire," he told me. "I don't want to sit behind a desk."

Late at night I found him at his desk with the big, black, red-cornered Squad 1 logbook in his lap, scribbling entries. Rock music, turned down low, played from a small plastic radio on the gray metal desk. Lieutenant McKee's chair was dirty and orange and ratty. He drank coffee from a heavy, old, chipped white ceramic cup such as the ones you'd find in a railroad dining car. His telephone was fire-engine red. The Sears Tower blinked from above us in the streaming August rain. If that tower ever burned, it would be Lieutenant McKee's fire: the tallest building in the world. He'd never even seen the inside.

This is probably the biggest secret in fire departments around the country: The real reason people become firefighters is to help other people. That is hardly ever spoken. It's almost a sacrilege to say it, because it sounds, well, it sounds kind of sappy, like you're some kind of do-gooder.

I asked him one day why he wanted to be a fireman, but it was a stupid question, and I knew it before I asked. Lieutenant McKee looked up from his book and said without a smile, "I like to wreck things."

■ ■ ■

We'd always get a run in the middle of something. We'd be talking or doing a chore or eating, and the call would come, and then we'd get into our boots and coats and we'd rumble out onto Des Plaines Street and down the avenues of the city. We were running one day to the Chicago Hilton Hotel, and in the cab of the fire engine there were two young guys on my left and two old guys on my right. I knew the older guys, Bernie (the Irish guy they called Red) and Wally. They were there all the time, had been for years. The two younger men were from other houses, temporarily assigned to Squad 1 while someone was on vacation or out sick or (in this case) injured by falling bricks in a fire. I noticed that whenever we ran, the two young guys and I got all dressed up right on the way out the door. We snapped the hasps on our Kevlar coats and did up the Velcro closures. We got our air bottles all strapped on and put on our gloves, and we were ready. But Wally and Bernie just hung there on the seats, heads down. Bernie would chain smoke cigarettes, and Wally would just sit and look out the window, as if he were on a very long train ride. Every once in a while, Bernie would enliven himself and scream something out the window, especially if he saw another firefighter or a pretty woman. He was a wild red-headed Irishman with a foul mouth and a crazed glint in his eye, and a typical Sunday morning greeting to a brother firefighter might be, "Hey, motherfucker, lay off the cocksucking cheeseburgers!"

It was the middle of the afternoon, but we had obviously gotten Bernie up from his nap, what with the bells and all. Kuehl commented that Bernie could sleep just about anywhere, and Bernie said, "I could sleep with my dick slammed in a door."

The Hilton wasn't really burning, although maybe a trash can was, and we sat in the rain for a while, smoking and joking, and then we were dismissed and rolled away into the city smoke and haze. As we left, Bernie leaned out the window and screamed at one of his fellows in a shrill voice, "Ah, they'll make anybody a fucking engineer!"

Rolling down the avenue, Red caught sight of the chief in his red

LTD Ford with a firefighter for a driver, and he yelled out the window at the firefighter: "Hey, how's the chief's golf game, cocksucker? Maybe we can get you a job as the chief's caddy when you get shit-canned outta that buggy." The derision was not aimed at the man but at the fact that he was driving a red Ford with the battalion chief in it. He was not in a fire engine, and he was not going to walk into a fire. He was going to sit in a buggy with the chief. I understood: Riding in that silly little red LTD was, well . . . degrading. Riding in the fire engine was the thing. The *real* thing.

The fire engine was an amazing object of art and engineering: It was, for one thing, as big as an old-fashioned locomotive. But it was also worked into a blazing red luster of enamel and filigree with chrome fittings and brass pipes, and then hung all over with buffed steel attachments, battlements, and gear, so that it looked like a rock-and-roll battleship when it went clattering down the lane. Now, leaving the Hilton Hotel fire, this amazing machine pulled up next to a UPS truck. The driver looked over, and we were just about face to face with him. Our windows were open. He smiled and said something in greeting and then lit up his cigarette with a Zippo. When the flame appeared, Al, the young black fireman sitting across from me, screamed at the top of his lungs, "Fire! Fire! Fire!" The UPS driver was so startled that he dropped his cigarette in his lap and turned pale, and the firefighter across from me laughed and laughed as we pulled away from the traffic light, our diesel engine churning up the wet air with an oily soot. "I done scared him," he said.

■ ■ ■

Firehouse humor: They call the big beer cooler the Baby Coffin. And they have different names for different kinds of dead people. Dead ones they find in fires are Crispy Critters. Ones that have been dead for a long time, like gangsters in somebody's trunk, are called Stinkers. There are Floaters and Headless Horsemen and Dunkers. McKee and Kuehl were reminiscing about the times when they were lying around or swimming (they can do that because the squad has a scuba team, and so the whole squad can go swimming on the excuse that they're practicing scuba diving) or doing something else sinfully lazy in the middle of the mean work week, commenting to themselves how the regular working slobs were out there getting their asses packed on the rock pile, and they all smiled and laughed at one another, saying, "What a fucking great job," when the call came in: Assist police. They dreaded that call: Assist police. That meant do the dirty work for the cops. "That is a definite shit detail," Kuehl said.

The police were down on the first floor in the apartment building, and they didn't even want to go near the apartment. So Kuehl and McKee went up. They were those kind of guys, the Special Forces of firefighting: They'd do anything. There was a stinker in the bathtub, and he'd been there for a while. The soup in the tub was green, a kind of green that's not on the Sherwin Williams color chips. So they wrapped the corpse in a tarp—which in itself was no easy task, because his arms and head were falling off like a chicken that's been in the pot too long—and then they put it in the elevator and pushed 1 and let it go down alone: Little present for you, guys.

The firefighters have to risk their lives fighting fires, but they also get the lowest shit work in the city, like picking up the dead. Kuehl picked up a lady one day who had crossed against the light, in front of a truck. She slipped, and the truck ran over her head. "When I grabbed her hair to pick up her head, it was actually stuck to the road with suction." And then he made this suction cup sound with his mouth.

They get called to the highest places and the lowest. They get called when someone has jumped or wants to jump. One morning the call came, and we all got into our turnout gear and jumped into the rig and wound up in the lobby of the Leo Burnette Advertising Agency, a brand-new building in Chicago's Loop. Beautiful women in expensive clothes and guys wearing silk ties and eighty-dollar haircuts swished past us as we clanked in our bulky protective clothing there in the green-marble lobby with its buffed chrome fittings. We were like sooty armored animals who had stumbled into the china shop. We smelled like high noon in hell, and the women who passed us smelled like heaven. They looked at us with this mixture of awe and shock, respect and disgust, for they knew they were looking at the only real heroes left in America, but we were so grubby and awkward, our appearance so rude, it just didn't add up. This was definitely not what the Leo Burnette Agency would do with a fireman's image.

We went to the roof and did a hero-like thing. There were two window washers on high ladders, and they were stranded on the side of the building, forty-eight stories above the city, and the Chicago Fire Department saved their lives, pulling them off with ropes. As I hung over the side of the building, I saw the look on the face of the worker who was being hauled up to safety by the firefighters. He was dangling there on what looked like spider web, five hundred feet over the street, a straight drop, and the city beyond was wreathed in the summer green of the park by the glittering blue-silver lakeshore. The tops of office towers floated ghostly above the pointillist city, and in the middle of it all, like Breughel's *Icarus*, was this redneck window washer, his face as white as a lamb. I could hear the electric commuter train rattling past in the loop below, and I could see our red fire engine like a matchbox toy with the firemen in black with yellow hornet stripes, walking briskly in the mist. The lake and the park fell away into haze, and the single man dangled like a doll on a yellow thread with five firemen holding the end and nothing but the moist and empty air to catch him if it all came suddenly unwound. When they pulled him clutching and gasping onto the roof, ten hands were on him—nobody here was going to let this one get away—and the window washer stood pale and shaken and thin in his seed cap and green T-shirt. He stammered, "Thanks. Thanks, guys." And that was all.

When we came back down through the lobby, it was strange to see this other side of life, the luxury, the opulence, the riches, the goodies of society, and know that it was forever out of reach. Firefighters save all this for the rich people. They save it equally for the poor. They save your life just the same if you are the president of Leo Burnette or the window washer. Yet the biggest rewards of society are forever out of reach for them.

■   ■   ■

More than once Lieutenant McKee thought his life was over. He has come near panic, he said. The worst time was in an old industrial space, one of those old firetrap buildings of exterior brick and timber joists. Lieutenant McKee had gone to an upper floor to reconnoiter while the others fought the fire down below. He wanted to see if the upper floors were involved so that they could plan their tactics. But then the upper floor was engulfed in smoke, and when McKee had gone in far enough to look around, it turned out to be one of those new office mazes divided into cubicles, with desks and computers and false walls, long zigzag corridors, and dead ends. Before he knew it, he became turned around, and he was lost in the labyrinth. He understood, yes, this is how it happens: You get into the worst just the way you get into the least, one step at a time. And at each step he took, he knew he was getting in deeper.

The smoke was rolling over him. He had started to hear the crackling of fire, the tinkling of glass, as things began to break. There was heat coming from over there in the darkness. The smoke was choking him, and he heard human voices, possibly from an air-conditioning duct—somewhere. He had no line to follow, no hose, and he could not even find a real wall to follow. It was all fake barriers that came apart in his hands, and he fell over them as he blundered this way and that. It was then that his superior breeding—son and brother of firefighters that he was—came to the fore. He told himself to calm down, to take charge. Panic has no place in a fire. There are always clues, if only we can read them. You have to think your way out like a detective. Okay, no hose to follow out. How else can I tell which way is out? Something must tell me, something. Smoke was all he could see. All right, how about smoke. Smoke has to go somewhere, right? It has to go out. And how does it get out? When I approach a fire, I see it pouring out the windows. That's it!

He looked to see which way the smoke was going and followed it. Soon, he was at a window, and in another minute he was off the floor and had been reunited with his company. Another man might have panicked and died in there.

Firefighters talk about fires the way musicians discuss the symphonies they have played over and over. And the fires are different the way the symphonies are different in the hands of different conductors. "You know that place where it's allegro and there's a key change? That always screws me up."

Then there are attic fires in frame houses. Old frame houses in big cities are almost always made with hollow walls, so the fire can start in the basement—or anywhere—but it's going to go to the attic, because heat will rise through the hollow walls. And it's such intense heat, that it starts a fire up there early on. So Lieutenant McKee and Kuehl always find themselves, sooner or later, trying to save an attic. It's a part of their lives, and they pride themselves in their ability to save attics (not that the attics are worth anything, or serve some useful function in society once they are saved; these acts are pure, without ulterior motive—in their own strange way, they are sport or even art). McKee and Kuehl have a technique. They feel they can read the fire, sense its moods, and outfox it.

One day they arrived at a fire. Another company was already there and had lines all laid out, but no one was going in. As Lieutenant McKee and Kuehl came up, the other company officer told them, "You can't make it in there."

Lieutenant McKee took a look at the fire and said, "Let me just get by you here for a second and see what I can do." And he and Kuehl went on in, Kuehl holding the pipe, or nozzle, and Lieutenant McKee holding the hose behind him. One technical note: They didn't have their breathing masks on. They had air bottles, but they were wearing cheaters, which are simply mouthpieces like scuba regulators and offer no eye protection. (Strictly speaking, cheaters are forbidden by the Department, but there are always three levels to every institution: the administrative fantasy, the staff reality, and then there's how ordinary people really do things.)

Later McKee would say, "Those little frame houses are small but they're hot." And he and Kuehl would laugh and laugh, sitting out under the stars and sipping coffee. They nearly lost their eyesight from using cheaters.

"We showed them, didn't we?" Kuehl said.

"Yeah, we showed them. We put it out, but it nearly put us out."

"It was either put it out, or resign from the Department after that."

They crawled into the attic, literally on their bellies, and the fire flashed over their heads and got behind them. "It took about two years to crawl thirty feet that night," Lieutenant McKee said.

"Yeah, Bobby Hoffa got burnt up that way. He walked through the attic to see what was up, went to the far window, and yelled down for them to send a line up. When he turned around, it was nothing but fire."

"Yeah, I'd like to hear the real story-story on that," Lieutenant McKee said, meaning that behind every story there's something else that will kill you. Or at least that's the way they like to analyze fires. If someone is hurt, they always believe that there was something done wrong, which, if they could just pinpoint it, they could avoid in a similar situation. In other words: That won't happen to me, because I'm too fucking good. No one truly believes in death.

I asked Kuehl what we should do when we're in an attic and it flashes over. That's when the fire gasses catch and burn through the air, over our heads, and start another fire behind us. "Just lay down," he said, "and stay down. It looks like lightning over your head in the smoke," he added, reminiscing about the attic fire in the frame house. "Going through those rooms was like going through the Seven Gates of Hell. But if you stand up, it'll take your head right off you. I was in one house once where a flashover came down a hallway. This other guy comes running down the hall shouting, 'Get out! Get out!' And here's this rolling, bubbling ball of fire coming down the hall. I'd never seen anything like that before in my life. We dove down the stairs, and I mean head first. Then we went out and had a cigarette," he said with a thoughtful smile, adding after a moment, "and we don't even smoke!"

"So what happened in the attic?" I asked.

"Oh, we put it out."

They say either "we won" or "we didn't win." On one fire they described (another frame-house attic), they said, "It was over our heads, coming out of the holes we had made, coming up behind us—we burned that one to the ground."

McKee described another one, when he was just a firefighter. He was going up the stairs leading a departmental lieutenant, when he shouted, "I think this stairs leads up to the back of the house."

And the lieutenant shouted back at him, "I know where the fuck it goes! This is my house!"

"We burned that one to the ground, too," McKee said. Again, he and Kuehl laughed and laughed, kicking their feet on the fire hydrant.

■ ■ ■

The moment of truth came for me on a sunny day when we were all down at Meigs Field, Chicago's lakefront airport, getting ready to go scuba diving. It was one of those days I'd heard the men talking about, when they're all saying to themselves, "What a great job." It must have been ninety-five degrees out, and jumping in the lake sounded good.

Kuehl had just gotten stripped down and was about to shrug into his scuba gear when he stopped. I saw him stop and look out over the skyline of the city: "Hey, there's a fire," he said.

We quickly got back into our clothes and jumped on the rig and drove across the city to the place where we had seen the smoke. There, in a humble neighborhood, we found a little frame house completely involved in flames. It seemed unimpressive as we arrived. It was just a few rooms, two stories, in a row of ordinary houses, and there was a big brown Cadillac blocking the fire hydrant. When I jumped down from the engine, Lieutenant McKee handed me a pike pole with a metal hook on the end and said, "Follow me." And we walked right into the burning building.

I had never done anything quite like that before. It seemed so simple, but it was then that I realized that fire is a living thing, a wild element, a manifestation of energy that eats the air. Fire can transform itself in the blink of an eye while you're looking the other way. It is a dragon, a bird, a wolf, a shark—and this one was in a feeding frenzy.

Lieutenant McKee ran, and so I ran to keep up with him, for the thing I feared most was losing him, because I had come to trust him completely. Before I knew it, I was going up a stairway. I recognized that stairway. I had lived with one just like it when I was a little boy, narrow, with a round wooden handrail, only this one was like the bottom of a back yard charcoal barbecue grill: It was glowing. We were encased in our protective clothing, but I wondered what a little boy in his pajamas and socks would do here: Everywhere I looked, everything, the walls, the floor, the ceiling, the woodwork, was glowing embers. Coiled snakes of smoke issued forth as if the wood had rotted before our eyes and maggots filled its blackened flesh. I was hit by wave after wave of heat that knocked the breath out of me, and when I gulped to catch my breath, I inhaled something noxious. It was not air; it was some superheated admixture of poisons. In all my lessons during all the nights and days with the firefighters, there was nothing that could have prepared me for this. I felt that I'd been dropped onto the surface of Mercury, and we were burning in a methane sea.

On and on we went, up the stairs and into the close little bedrooms where someone had lived. "Here, here!" Lieutenant McKee was shouting at me. I was coughing and trying to see what he was pointing at.

"Don't look up!" he shouted, so I looked up. He grabbed my head and pushed it down. "Don't! Look! Up!" he said again. "Pull the ceiling!" I didn't understand what he wanted of me until he showed me. He wanted me to use the lance I had in my hands: Shove it up with both hands until it poked through the plaster and lathe of the ceiling. Then yank on it until the ceiling came crashing down around me. *And don't look up*, because all that falling plaster and burning wood could blind me. It was then I realized that the fire was burning not only all around us but over our heads as well, and the man coming up behind me with the pipe was waiting on me to pull the ceiling so that he could open up with the water and put out the fire over our heads and keep it from leaping out to eat us.

I began jabbing furiously at the ceiling, ripping and tearing with the lance, and a great shower of lathe and plaster and conduit began raining down upon the hard helmet I wore. For the first time I understood the shape of the fireman's hat. I could no longer breathe, but breath seemed a peccant extravagance to wish for by that time. I was roasting in my Kevlar coat like a potato in tinfoil, but I pulled my way through the ceiling from one end of the room to the other, and the man behind me (whom I never saw) opened up the nozzle and showered the ceiling with water. We were engulfed in steam now, steam and smoke, and I was drowning in water, soaked from head to foot and covered with a kind of black paste. I was glad, though—glad because the water was cool and because the voracious oily dragon of flame was eating oxygen and water and not us. Now all I had to worry about was the steam that was burning my face.

I moved to the next room just in time to see that the outside wall had fallen into the back yard, and I took a moment to walk up to the edge and look down—actually, I went over to steal a breath of what I saw there: clear air. When I looked down, I saw the whole back yard was aflame with the rubble of cars and with stacks of truck tires and trash, burning in mystical rings of fire. The flames seemed to dance the whole world around—there seemed no end to it—and I remembered visiting the Prado in Madrid and seeing the gorgeous and hideous visions that Bosch painted of the world in flames.

Wondering how much more of the house was going to fall into the yard, I backed away from the precipice and returned to my task with the ceilings. I don't know how long I fought in there, wielding that pike with the man behind me spraying the flames overhead, but after a while the heat seemed to subside, and I was put to work poking holes in the roof above, through the attic space I'd opened up by tearing down the lathe. There were men on the roof, and when they'd see my pike going through a soft spot (soft because it had been burned), they'd chop a bigger hole with an axe, and someone would spray out the last lingering tongues of fire with a hose.

It was finally over. The whole place was encased and glued together with black paste. I came back down the narrow staircase, which had partly burned away while I was upstairs.

On the first floor, in the living room, I looked out onto the street and saw the crowd that had gathered to watch. A battalion chief grabbed me, and because I had a pike, he said, "Square off those windows, son." He meant the windows through which I was looking at the people. So I took my lance and I shoved it through the panes of glass, breaking them, and then I ran it around each square, raking the glass away with my pike and smiling out at the people on the street and remembering Lieutenant McKee, when I had asked him why he wanted to be a firefighter, saying, "I like to wreck things."

Rites of Spring

on Breast Cancer

When Carolyn discovered the lump in her right breast, it was no bigger than a pea. I tried to convince her that it was nothing. She'd just had a mammogram, and it showed nothing. Still, she continued to worry, feeling the pea-sized lump, touching it, looking in the mirror, frowning. All through that day and the next she was moody, inward-looking, despite my attempts to reassure her.

I said, "You worry too much. Dr. Silver would have felt that lump, and if it was something to worry about, he would have told you." If she had listened to my advice, she'd be dead now.

■　■　■

At H—— Hospital, where our two daughters were born, we had always felt a sense of well being. There were trees and it was quiet—almost like being out in the country. But the day we went in for her biopsy everything was different. She had a local anesthetic and the pea was removed and rushed to the lab to be frozen and put under a microscope while we waited in the sunny lobby. Carolyn held her wound and looked as if she might cry. I had brought along a little Dostoevsky to cheer me up during the long wait, but almost immediately her name was called, and we were put into a closet with two chairs and a stainless-steel table. Barry Silver came in and closed the door and put his hands behind him, palms flat against the inside of the door, as if to keep something out that was chasing him. When he told her, I felt a hard bubble form inside my heart. I turned to watch Carolyn's face, and I saw how determined she was. She planted both her feet and squared off as I'd seen her do on a sailboat, when the sea was pitching things about.

We were well aware that doctors are not philosophers, visionaries, nor rocket scientists; they are trades people. Assembling a team to treat a serious disease is like assembling a team to build your dream house. It is an arduous, treacherous, tricky process. We soon learned, for example, that if H—— Hospital had been up to date on diagnostic procedures, Carolyn could have had her initial biopsy done with a needle instead of a knife.

The diagnosis and treatment of breast cancer have changed a lot in the last quarter century, and a lot more in the last five years. Unfortunately, doctors don't learn about the changes quickly enough, and even when they do, they like to do what they're used to doing. That is why it may be a matter of some importance whether a woman lives in Chicago or, say, Salem, Illinois, when she happens to get cancer.

Women who discover lumps in their breasts are particularly vulnerable. It may be nothing. Carolyn's oncologist said, "Many women simply have lumpy breasts." So how seriously should they take it? Where should they go? How are they to know that they can ask for fine-needle biopsy (which costs less and hurts less than surgical biopsy and leaves no scar)?

Even after a correct diagnosis has been made, a woman has to decide who to turn to and how to take the advice she's given. Not so long ago, the only treatment for breast cancer was the so-called radical mastectomy. It involved the complete removal of the breast, along with lymph nodes and significant amounts of muscle as well. It was a cruel and crippling operation. (But people who had it lived on and on, and those who did not often died.) That procedure was replaced by the modified radical mastectomy, which involves removing all the breast tissue, including the nipple, and sampling the lymph nodes. It is still a devastating and disfiguring operation, which can leave patients with impaired functioning of the arms and persistent pain, to say nothing of the psychological effects.

In the past ten years, surgical trials have demonstrated that just as many patients survive if the tumor is removed and the rest of the breast is left intact. That procedure is called lumpectomy, and many women now elect to lose the tumor and save the breast. The National Institutes of Health (NIH) finally recommended lumpectomy two years ago, but only after persistent pressure from women who had learned enough to understand that they were the victims of unnecessary surgery.

Not everyone can have a lumpectomy. Even for those who can, it is not simple and it is not the end of treatment. During surgery a few lymph nodes are removed and sent to the lab to see if cancer has spread to them. Since the lymphatic system carries fluid throughout the body, the presence of cancer cells in the lymph nodes is a sign that cancer may have spread to other areas of the body. If no cancer cells are found in the lymph nodes, chances are good that the cancer has not gone beyond the breast.

Women with breast cancer have a 70 percent chance of survival, a chance that has steadily improved over the past few decades. If breast cancer comes back after surgery and treatment, the chances of survival become discouraging indeed: about 18 percent, the same as they were in the 1940s. Hence the recommendation that women undergo chemotherapy, even if it's only for the slight chance of doing any good. Today most doctors recommend chemotherapy, even for women whose lymph nodes show no sign of cancer.

Another question that arises concerns reconstruction and plastic surgery. Most male doctors can hardly speak to a breast cancer patient without talking about replacing her breasts. Perhaps more women with breast cancer need to ask if the prosthesis is a gift to them or a gift to someone else. On the other hand, some doctors may discourage an older woman from getting breast reconstruction because in his view, she is beyond the age where she ought to be concerned about such matters. Although Carolyn was only forty when she got breast cancer, one doctor, trying to convince her to get a mastectomy, told her, "What do you need breasts for? You've had children." It's all about choices and who gets to make them. Chances are that the uninformed patient will get her doctor's favorite operation. Fashion has as much effect on surgery as it does on clothing, cars, and buildings.

Finally, after a woman has been put through all of that, she may or may not be a candidate for some of the new cancer-suppressing drugs that are given following surgery, radiation, chemotherapy, and reconstruction. They're expensive, and there's no proof that they work.

■ ■ ■

"Get the best surgeon," people told us. But to concentrate on the selection of a surgeon was to miss the point entirely. Carolyn didn't need a carpenter first, she needed an architect.

Her name was Cassandra Botzek and her profession was medical oncology. She was perhaps the ideal doctor, a combination of scientist and artist, healer and scholar. She read everything, did original research, wrote books and papers, and saw patients nearly every day of her life. She had golden hands. She undoubtedly saved Carolyn's life, and she did it all on the first visit for about sixty-five dollars.

"Cancer means *crab*," she said, and curled her fingers into claws like crabs. Cassandra's hands looked as if they'd done hard labor but in the service of art.

Carolyn was given a blue paper gown to wear, and when Cassandra directed her to lift her arms, I could see her right breast through the large arm hole. I didn't know that it would be one of the last times I'd ever see it. I merely noticed how different Cassandra's examination was from those of the other doctors, all men, who seemed to grab the breast like a purse and massage it to see if it contained any coins. Cassandra's eyes closed as her fingers read the ancient text, divining, as if by Braille, the inner secrets of a living, breathing organism, pushing back against her gentle pressures.

Unexpectedly, Cassandra called in another doctor, a Dickensian figure, young, fine-pointed, aloof, who called himself DeMay, and whose expertise was fine-needle biopsy.

"She has breast cancer on the right," Cassandra told DeMay, "and I'm feeling something on the left." Then she turned to me and said in a level tone, "You aren't the type who faints at the sight of needles, are you?"

I said I was not.

"Because you can stay or you can leave, but I don't want you to faint."

I promised that I would not. I tried to look into myself to see what was there, where the black bubble had formed in my heart. I could still feel it lying in there, like something that had crawled inside me and died.

I heard Carolyn cry out in pain from the needle. It was the first cry I had heard her utter through the weeks, the first evidence that cancer is physical, not at all like the propaganda people we see on television, smiling bravely, fighting the good fight. A fight implies two opponents squaring off. Cancer is gunmen and ski masks, a blindfold and a dark car carrying you off in the middle of an otherwise ordinary day. Cancer is not a fight. It's biological terrorism.

Cassandra and DeMay left us alone in the examining room.

"What does this mean?" Carolyn asked me, and I could hear the fear in her voice.

I couldn't pretend I knew. No one had said anything about the left breast. The left breast had never been on the bargaining table.

A moment later Cassandra came back and said, "You've got cancer in that other breast," and I looked at Carolyn and saw her recoil toward the open window. It was spring, and the world outside wheeled with wind and green and bird songs. All at once I felt as if we were falling into that cool picture, and the room seemed terribly hot. Suddenly I thought: Maybe she's right. Maybe I am going to faint after all.

As my consciousness passed back through the window and into the room, Cassandra was asking if we did anything carcinogenic. Did we work with chemicals? I remembered putting Chlordane in the basement for termites in 1977. It was outlawed soon afterward for being carcinogenic. Was it leaded gas? Was it living in the city? Had we eaten too much fat or eaten too many Great Lakes fish? Was it PCBs or VDTs?

Cassandra had Carolyn on the examining table and was systematically going through her body, as if through a crowded closet, looking everywhere now for signs of cancer. I understood: If both breasts had cancer, maybe the Big Tumor was somewhere else. Cassandra was thinking: Maybe you don't have breast cancer. Maybe you have, say, liver cancer, and it's already spread to both breasts. On the other hand, if she had two primary tumors, one in each breast, then it may already have spread to other places in her body.

I sat in a chair beside the examining table, staring at the wall, waiting to hear what other horrible surprises Cassandra would find.

"Your cervix looks entirely normal," Cassandra announced after a few moments of rummaging around in Carolyn's innards. And then, *sotto voce:* "I'm doing a rectal now."

■ ■ ■

Ten percent of all women in the United States will get breast cancer, but that number, like all statistics, tells us little. Breast cancer research is not fantastically well funded, because it is not a disease that many men get (about 300 per year, out of 150,000 or so cases). The number of unanswered questions about the disease is frightening. Given the number of women who will get breast cancer, it is also scandalous.

Seventy-five percent of women who contract breast cancer have none of the risk factors that are commonly suggested by the research (high-fat diet, long-term exposure to estrogen, etc.). Critics of breast cancer research would like to see scientists asking what causes breast cancer, not who gets it or how to treat it. Those critics point out that cases of breast cancer tend to cluster geographically around polluted areas, such as Long Island, in New York. They would like to know if other hormones, not just estrogen, can stimulate the growth of breast cancer. Perhaps some of the hormones we put in meat are dangerous.

While survival rates for women who are diagnosed with breast cancer have risen, the rate at which new cases are developing has also risen (by about 32 percent between 1982 and 1987). Nothing kills more women between thirty-five and fifty than cancer, lung cancer first, breast cancer second. What causes it? And why is it on the rise? Those are the questions that we may not want to answer, because it might mean that we have to stop using pesticides and hormones in our food.

■　■　■

Our eldest daughter, who was eight, came home and said, "Mom, Annie said they were going to put plastic bags in your breasts. That's not true, is it?"

It was true.

We felt like displaced persons, refugees, as if our nation had dissolved, and now we were moving on to the frontier, and we had to be prepared for anything. I began to stockpile food in the basement—I'm not sure why. It seemed logical at the time, as if nuclear war might be the next step in this galloping progression. Carolyn had to meet and interview surgeons to decide which one she would hire to work for her, like hiring contractors for a remodeling job. I went along to take notes, because that's what I'm good at. Taking notes is a very effective technique in selecting a doctor. Doctors who grew nervous when I took notes were thinking about malpractice suits.

On our first visit to Tom Melhoff, Carolyn wore her triple-breasted

　　　　　　　　　　　　　　　　　Rites of Spring

navy jacket with three big rows of blue buttons, and waited with a secret smirk.

"How do you like my triple-breasted jacket?" she asked.

"It's very nice," he said, unsure what she was driving at.

"I need all the breasts I can get," she said, and Melhoff laughed. He got the job. After we had talked a while, he recommended she read *Love, Medicine, and Miracles,* by Bernie Segal. At first I was surprised at how many of the physicians we saw took the spiritual side of healing seriously. That was before I learned how little they knew about breast cancer. It was their subtle way of saying, "I hope you like to pray, because we don't know what we're doing."

■ ■ ■

All the physicians involved were now calling the tissues they saw under the microscope "ugly," which meant that Nature had gone wild in proliferating strange, prodigious, and freakish forms out of the Universal Substance. There are as many kinds of cancer as there are weeds in the fields, and they told us that neither of the ones Carolyn had, the left or the right, would fit neatly into any of the garden varieties. In other words, they could not say with any degree of certainty what the outcome might be. Even if they could have said it about one of the cancers, they could not hazard a guess about a case in which a woman got both. Neither could they tell us that a certain number of people with Carolyn's condition responded to this or that treatment, while another number did not. What we did with regard to surgery, what we did afterward—it was anybody's guess. It just so happened that all the research had been done (and all the articles written) about infiltrating ductile carcinoma, the most common variety of breast cancer. If you had another variety, they couldn't tell you much. You missed out on the NIH grants. You got the wrong disease.

One of our problems in deciding whether to have lumpectomy or mastectomy was that when the initial biopsy was done, the tumor was not inked. If a doctor is considering lumpectomy as a possibility, and if he does a surgical biopsy, then an attempt is made to cut the tumor out completely, to provide a clear margin between what is cancer and what is normal tissue. Then the specimen is stained all around (inked, they call it) to show that margin. If it had been inked, it would have been possible to tell under a microscope if the margin was clean or if the cancer was migrating out into the surrounding tissue. The problem is that many doctors still do not think of lumpectomy as an option.

One day after an exam, we were sitting there in silence with Cassandra, just looking at each other, waiting, listening to the cells growing, and without solicitation, Cassandra said softly, "I'm going to tell you something that the pathology department at H—— Hospital said if you promise not to take any retaliatory action."

We promised.

"The pathologist said, 'We believe as Dr. Rosen [of some famous clinic] believes that breast cancer is never a localized problem and that any woman who has it needs her breast removed. So we don't ink specimens.'" In other words, Cassandra explained, in the dialogue between factions, lumpectomy versus mastectomy, they were on the side of the hawks, the scorched-earth school of surgery. "It's one thing not to know. It's another thing to decide for people." She thought for a moment, then added to Carolyn, almost in a whisper, "I'd have 'em off so fast if they were my breasts . . ."

■ ■ ■

When word of Carolyn's cancer had gone out along the trembling web of filaments that connects everyone to everyone else, the phone calls began coming, letters arrived, packages were dropped at the door, and an outpouring of care and help and attention was paid. A friend from Santa Fe sent crystals by Federal Express in a medicine pouch. My brother gave me a crystal he called an Apache Tear, which was meant to absorb my grief. Books and tapes, cards and flowers came, and when Carolyn finally checked into the hospital, people began cooking meals for me and the kids; later when she came home, they cooked even more. In an odd way, for a time, the world was our family, and yet I sensed there was something amiss. We were not merely the recipients of neighborly largesse; we were part of a sacrifice being offered up to the gods. We were atonement.

People came to the door and looked inside our house as though they peered into the heart of a furnace. It wasn't until later that I began to understand the connection between people's fear and the political and social bramble that had grown up around the scanty facts of breast cancer. It all had to do with symbols. Somehow the medical world had become caught up in issues of cosmetics instead of health (and we had become caught up with them). Our discussions with doctors often seemed to revolve around the problem of having no breasts and the task of replacing them. Something seemed terribly lopsided in this strange world we'd entered, but in the midst of the crisis, it was difficult to tell what it was. It took me a long time to understand that the central problem was being unable to look beyond the surface. Our whole culture had the problem. Worse, instead of striving to understand Nature, we wanted to control it.

■ ■ ■

The surgeon, Melhoff, had agreed to try lumpectomy on both sides. He was a tall, thin, boyish fellow with blond hair, who made fine furniture in his basement with electric power tools as a hobby. He just smiled at me indulgently when I commented that it seemed paradoxical to be a surgeon and to play with instruments that could so easily cut off all his fingers.

The nurse in pre-admission put us in an intensely hot examining room, and at first we wondered if it was to sterilize us, as in an autoclave. Outside we could see the El coming up from downtown. It was a bright, windy day with giant whipped-cream cumulus rushing away to sea and people holding their coats and lurching between buildings. Everyone in pre-admission was wearing Reeboks and Nikes. A nurse with an Eastern European accent poked her head in and asked, "Do you have panty hose on?" I told her I didn't, and she gave me a look that would flatten a penny on a railroad track.

A resident named Barbara came in and took Carolyn's history (again) and then they talked about the surgery, recovery, exercise, risk, anesthesia . . . another gray area of mystery. The anesthesiologist puts you under by magic. No one knows how and why anesthesia works. Sometimes we go out on that tendril, and we do not come back. Carolyn wanted to know where the scars would be, and Barbara showed her, pointing with a pen. What kind of stitches would be used? Where would they show? Could she shave under her arm? Could she wear a bathing suit? Barbara said they would staple the incision in her armpit closed.

"Do you use street drugs?" Barbara asked.

"No," Carolyn said, deadpan. "We get them on the North Shore."

■ ■ ■

While Melhoff was attempting the lumpectomy, I was in the waiting room, watching the window washers in their safety harnesses, hanging on a thread. We're all hanging by a thread, I thought. The difference is that they know it. And now Carolyn knows it.

I could see the El tracks coming up Congress and running out to O'Hare. It was a remarkably clear day. Staring out the window, I realized what the central issue was. At the same time, I understood how scared I was. The central issue was that at any moment someone could come out and tell me that Carolyn was dead. How would I tell the girls?

When Melhoff finally called, I could hardly catch my breath it scared me so badly. He said that the left breast would have to go; lumpectomy was impossible, because there was no lump; the cancer had spread throughout the tissue. The right breast: He wasn't sure until the lab work was done. Melhoff and Carolyn had made a pact: "I want you to wake me up and tell me," she said. "I don't want to go to sleep thinking I'm getting a lumpectomy and wake up with no breasts." Melhoff was doing as he promised. Even though it was obvious that no lumpectomy could be done on the left, he was not going ahead with the mastectomy without letting Carolyn have time to adjust to the idea.

I got Cassandra on the phone shortly thereafter, and she had already been down to the lab to look at what Melhoff had cut out. She said, "This thing is huge," meaning what they got out of the left—the cancer that nobody had noticed at first. There was a five-centimeter piece "entirely involved by cancer. It will be important to know what's on the other side." I put the phone down. For a long time all I did was count seconds. I realized that I was waiting for something to explode.

We had expected Carolyn to stay in the hospital for a week, and she was home in a day and a half. Everyone assumed the worst, although it took me a few days to realize what I was seeing. Some of our friends were afraid to ask what it meant that Carolyn was home so soon. When someone asked if the cancer was "inoperable," I understood what was going on. I was shocked at how ready everyone seemed to believe she had come home to die.

When Carolyn walked into the house, workmen were there smashing out walls and putting up new wallpaper. The radio was trumpeting WXRT rock-and-roll, ladders and dust were everywhere, and plastic sheeting made a prism of pastel sunlight through the rooms. Some flowers had been sent and had died, and Carolyn ordered them removed; she was superstitious about dead flowers. She walked around wrapped in her coat, looking at the house as if it belonged to someone else, and then she sat on the couch, looking forlorn.

Carolyn had wanted to talk to one more surgeon for an opinion concerning the question of whether or not a lumpectomy might be possible, but she knew, really, and anyway the surgeon wanted her to bring one hundred dollars in cash before he would talk to her. He made his surgical consultation sound like a dope deal, so she decided to go ahead with Cassandra and Melhoff and their insistence that keeping any breast tissue would be extremely risky. The lab results had come back and confirmed their thinking.

■ ■ ■

The waiting room was white, and an intense white light came through a curving wall of glass blocks. Everyone wore white, and there were polished pine benches and a lot of dazed-looking people walking around in gowns and paper slippers, looking up and then looking down and not knowing where to put their hands. There were odd sounds— dinging tones and ringing phones, muttering voices and the U2 album, *Joshua Tree*, played faintly in the background. The place looked just like the admission area to heaven in a Hollywood movie. The music was good. The light was professionally done.

A nurse walked by, saying, "Oh, they screwed this up, that's a mistake. That's adding insult to injury," and walked on by. We didn't need to be reminded of the fallibility of people at that moment. Carolyn's mammogram was a not uncommon mistake. Cassandra said that half the time, just by feeling, she could find tumors that hadn't shown up on the film. And what about those doctors who had felt Carolyn's left breast for lumps without detecting the more widespread of the two cancers she had? When Cassandra found it, she said, "Don't be angry with your doctor for not finding this. If he hadn't suggested that you have a biopsy in the first place, you'd have come in here six months from now, and we wouldn't be having this conversation." With cancer around to set the stage, almost anything becomes a great line.

Cassandra said that the average doubling time of human breast cancer is one hundred days. That means that a one-centimeter lump you have on New Year's Eve will be half a foot in diameter by Christmas—well, not literally. But the advance of cancer is prodigious. It is interesting and frightening in retrospect to realize that if Carolyn had accepted the advice of the first surgeon and had allowed a mastectomy to be performed on the right side without further investigation, the cancer on the left would have gone undetected long enough to allow it to spread to other areas of the body. It is worse to think of the advice I gave her.

The chief resident for the plastic surgeon opened the door to our examining room and looked in. He said his name was Gabriel Kind. Brightening, Carolyn said to me, "Now this guy is really good-looking . . ." And to him: "Do you play trumpet?"

■ ■ ■

On television they always make anesthesia seem like this dream that we enter from a secret door, like Alice going into Wonderland, but it's not that way. I went up with Carolyn to see them induce anesthesia. The needle wouldn't go into her hand, and they wanted to stick it into her neck. "Wait a minute," I said. "You're not going to stick a needle in this woman's neck while she's awake." They all looked at me like I was crazy. They tried to induce with a mask over her face, but she just choked. It was like a bad executioner bungling the job. Panic is not pretty. They finally gave her an injection of some very good pharmaceutical-grade synthetic heroin (called Fentanyl) so that she wouldn't care what else they did to her, and I left, feeling sick and inadequate.

■ ■ ■

In 1811 Madam D'Arblay wrote an account of her own experience with breast cancer, which resulted in a mastectomy, performed at a time in history when the techniques of anesthesia had been temporarily forgotten by western civilizations. The surgery was done in her own bedroom.

> I refused to be held; but when, Bright through the Cambric,
> I saw the glitter of polished Steel—I closed my Eyes . . . A
> silence the most profound ensued, which lasted for some
> minutes . . . I did not breathe . . . Again through the
> Cambric, I saw the hand of M. Dubois held up, while his
> fore finger first described a straight line from top to bottom
> of the breast, secondly a Cross, and thirdly a Circle; inti-
> mating that the **whole** was to be taken off . . . When the
> dreadful steel was plunged into the breast—cutting through
> veins—arteries—flesh—nerves—I . . . began a scream
> that lasted unintermittingly during the whole time of the
> incision—and I almost marvel that it rings not in my ears
> still! so excruciating was the agony. When the wound was
> made, and the instrument was withdrawn, the pain seemed
> undiminished, for the air that suddenly rushed into those
> delicate parts felt like a mass of minute but sharp and forked
> poniards, that were tearing the edges of the wound . . .
> I then felt the Knife rackling against the breast bone—
> scraping it!—This performed, while I yet remained in
> utterly speechless torture . . . Twice, I believe, I fainted . . .

In the hospital waiting room, it was the dead middle of the week, and the street beyond the window was teeming with cars zinging past on the Eisenhower Expressway. The city was getting itself ready for the day. The mist of night still clung to the spires of downtown buildings as I contemplated the events taking place two floors above me in the panoptic mystery of a steel room. I felt Melhoff take up hammer and tong and drive a silver chisel into my chest. And yet even Madame D'Arblay's recovery was complete.

■　■　■

I was afraid to look for the longest time; I felt I'd turn to stone if I saw the mutilation. On the day of her mastectomies (how I hate that word!), I went to the hospital room where Carolyn would stay, and the aides and nurses were all so nice. "The room's not ready, but that's okay, you can go in. Do you want another chair? Can I get you something to drink?" At first I enjoyed the celebrity. But then one day (I can't say exactly when) I realized with a jolt that they were being deferential to me in direct proportion to how grave the situation was, and now their prostrations merely rankled.

I sat rigid in a chair by the window, and each time a cart or person passed, I jumped, thinking it was Carolyn. What would the living corpse of my wife look like? (For that is how I imagined it would be, as in *The Night of the Living Dead*.) Would there be blood all over? Would she be as pale as death?

When they brought her in on a steel cart, she had an IV needle as big as a pencil stuck into her neck, and I remembered how they had botched the IV the first time, jamming it into her hand, trying to find a vein. Tubes ran everywhere around her, as if she slept in a bed of shiny snakes, and her body looked so small, so flat, so thin, beneath the sheets and bandages, and her brown hair was matted and moist and tangled, as if she'd been shipwrecked here. Her face was pale, her eyes were swollen, her limbs were slack, and the gauze of death was like a gaudy dress upon her.

Yet she smiled.

I bent down to put my ear by her lips, and she said, "They have great drugs."

■ ■ ■

When the resident came in and peeked under the bandages the next morning, I averted my eyes and looked out the window at Chicago. Far in the distance I saw smoke and the scintillating of red strobes popping off the fire trucks. Someone out there was on fire. I felt a mirror of pain reflecting back at me.

After the doctors left us alone, Carolyn told me what she recalled of the operation. Melhoff met her in the operating room. He was wearing green scrubs and a surgical mask. "Whoa, was I up drinking late last night!" he said. "Am I ever hung over!"

A resident, washing his hands nearby, said, "You'd better have another one, Doc."

Another resident: "Hair of the dog."

"Yeah," Melhoff said. "Say goodnight, Gracie."

We had to be careful about how much we laughed, lest the snakes in her bed got excited and began biting.

Eventually she got up, and we took walks up and down the hall and met other people in the ward who made us feel lucky. There's always somebody else who's worse off.

She went home after five days in the hospital. Ten days after surgery, Carolyn, who is Catholic, was up and dressed and at the church for our eldest daughter's first communion. Life, as they say, goes on. And much too quickly.

. . .

I had to change the bandages at home. The doctors wouldn't come home with us. They had even given us some salve to put on the stitches, so there was no avoiding it finally, but we felt like two pilots trapped in a plane that was going down, saying, "No, you take the controls."

"No, you do it."

"No, you."

"Did you take a bath?" I asked.

"Yes. But I didn't look," she admitted.

"How did you avoid it?"

"I closed my eyes."

We were standing in the bathroom. The kids were at school. She stood by the sink before the mirror. She could not yet lift her arms, so I helped her off with her gown. I didn't want to be there. I hadn't realized until then how angry I was with her, irrationally so.

They had wrapped her like a mummy, around and around the chest with Kerlix gauze, and I unwrapped her the same way. It was awkward, and I kept thinking: This is a big mistake. I should not be doing this. Things will never be the same. I shouldn't be the one.

First she turned around while I held still, but the turning made her dizzy, so I walked the bandage around and around her. Even beneath the bandage her shape was different. The bird cage of her ribs seemed so frail now. She was like a child again—her long neck, her small head, her faint smile—I could see how afraid she was of what we were doing, and so I pretended that it was no big deal. I'd been to gross anatomy in a medical school. I'd been to the morgue. I once saw a plane crash with 273 dead people scattered in a field. I'd seen it all. How could a few stitches bother me? Still, deep down, I knew it was a mistake.

She held her head high, her chin elevated, proud, as I unreeled the last of her wrappings and saw for the first time the terrible thing that had been done to her, and the bubble burst inside my heart.

She was looking at the ceiling now; this job was all mine. I dropped the Kerlix into the waste basket and picked up the tube of salve, marveling at the horror of it, the profundity of what they'd done. If I hadn't been so afraid, I would have been fascinated; but as it was, I had to look closely enough at the black infestation of the wounds that traversed her chest from side to side and up and down, as if she'd been in a knife fight; and here the curling edges of her flesh met and meshed in the crisscross macramé of black thread. There was some dried blood. I felt myself dying from inside out. I knew I was a coward, and that in some essential way I had failed as a husband, as a friend, as a man. But still I pretended it was all right.

"What do you see?" she asked.

"It looks excellent," I said. "No sign of infection," imitating as best I could that medical school demeanor I'd learned from my father, the professor. But I knew that was not what she was asking about. She was asking, *Am I Still Here? Is it the same me you used to know?* She didn't know that it wasn't her who was in danger now. She was recovering. I was just beginning to get sick.

"You're fine," I said. "You're fine."

■ ■ ■

We asked Cassandra how the hair came out: One strand at a time? How did one lose it anyway?

"All at once," she said. "One morning you'll wake up, and it'll be on your pillow."

"Just like that?" Carolyn asked.

"Just like that," Cassandra said. I loved her for her directness. Carolyn said that she was more afraid of losing her hair than losing her breasts.

We learned that chemotherapy could be done at home, and we decided that if we never saw the inside of a hospital again, it would be too soon. The day before the first treatment, a truck pulled up to the house, a delivery boy gave me a cardboard box, and I had to sign for it. It was labeled "Caution! Chemotherapy! Handle with gloves. Dispose of properly." My immediate impulse was to dispose of it properly and promptly.

Of course, I opened the box to look. Inside were all sorts of fiendish-looking devices and potions, all zipped into Ziploc bags. It looked like the loot from a drug raid that the DEA would display on the six o'clock news. The miniature injection bottles, the "precision guide" needles, and the butterfly infusion set with mini-bore luer lock extension tube. A box of rubber gloves—fifty pairs—Jesus, this was going to go on and on, wasn't it? Alcohol wipes, a case of them. Then the chemicals themselves, each in its own syringe, wrapped in plastic, sealed in a transparent bag and labeled with warnings. One had this command: "Keep Refrigerated!" The other had said, "Do Not Freeze!" and featured a drawing of a penguin with a red slash mark drawn through him. Over the six months that Carolyn went through chemotherapy, she came to know the drugs as "Penguin" and "Do-Not-Penguin."

When the chemotherapy nurse, Kathy, was about to put the first needle in, Carolyn held up her hand to mark a pause in the onward-plunging events. "When we're finished with this," she told us, "we're going to be looking out these windows and the leaves are going to be turning fall colors. It'll be beautiful."

Kathy was a naturally pretty woman in a red dress, tall, large-boned, fashionable, with an air of friendly competence, partitioned off from intimacy by her long experience of people she treated who were going to die soon. (Most home chemotherapy is done for people who can't get around.) Carolyn asked to hold my hand, and I stood by the chair, compliant. As Kathy pierced a slim vein on the back of Carolyn's hand, Carolyn's fingernails dug into the back of my hand.

While Kathy worked, she asked a barrage of what seemed to me rather strange questions. "How often do you move your bowels?" and "Is it normal? Brown?"

"Well, I'll tell you," Carolyn allowed. "I was shitting up a storm when I was first diagnosed."

Kathy came once a month. It was spring and the doors were open, and people dropped by. A neighbor came in with a bouquet of lilies of the valley and a purple flower in a uterus-shaped vase. He kissed Carolyn, and the coiled snake wriggled on her arm. It was a windy, green, sunny day and he wore shorts and a T-shirt. He wished Carolyn good luck and left, and a little while later, while we were waiting for the Do-Not-Penguin shot, we saw him and his scientist wife out walking their new baby.

The suspense of waiting for Carolyn to get sick from chemotherapy took on a kind of comic quality after the first few times. Cassandra had warned us: Everyone is different. Some people get so sick that they have to be hospitalized. A few don't get sick at all. At first we wondered if Kathy had given her the wrong drugs. Carolyn didn't get sick and she didn't lose her hair, and people began to look at her the way the bad guys look at Superman in the old television series, when they empty their guns at him and he just stands there smiling.

Dr. Mitchell, the plastic surgeon, began inflating the breast implants. We would drive out to his office in Oak Park and Mitchell would examine Carolyn's progress, admire the work he had done, and then inject more fluid with an enormous syringe through the skin and into the receptacle that he'd inserted during surgery. Those injections didn't hurt, because there was no feeling in the skin beneath her arms.

By Kathy's third visit, Carolyn was sitting in the sunny room with her arm stretched out, wiggling her fingers and saying, "Gimme some more of that stuff. Haven't you got anything stronger?" The doctors had given her loads of sedative hypnotics, tranquilizers, and downers so that she could entertain herself in hours of sleepless anxiety, but she lost interest in them before she left the hospital, and they still sit on a shelf, gathering dust. I warned her that she'd never amount to much of a drug addict.

First Kathy would put in the butterfly set, which was an open IV line, in the back of Carolyn's hand. The back of the hand is bristling with nerves that sense pain—it is a tender area—and putting a needle into it is no fun. Kathy was very good at what she did, but even so, it was painful, and every time I watched Carolyn go through that, I could feel another door closing in my heart. Sometimes, when the needle didn't go in just right, tears would stream down Carolyn's face, but she would smile to show us what she was made of. She wasn't all steel, though, and I couldn't do what I did and remain unchanged. I always stood and held her other hand while Kathy did the injections. Another part of me died during that process. I could feel myself slowly being pulled free and drifting away.

The Methotrexate went in first, and then Kathy taped the IV down and she and Carolyn talked for an hour before the fluorouracil injection. That was the procedure.

Always, right after chemotherapy, she would want two things: To go somewhere and eat and to be entertained in some spectacular

Rites of Spring

fashion—a movie, a play, the demolition of a large downtown building . . . More than once we saw *Bill and Ted's Excellent Adventure.*

■　■　■

Now Carolyn is on some other drug, a sort of experimental therapy called tomaxifen, and recent pseudo-scientific rumor has it that this drug causes liver cancer or ovarian cancer, which is an exciting thought. Tumor tissue taken from breast cancer patients is tested for estrogen receptors, and those women whose tissue tests positive can use tomaxifen to suppress estrogen and possibly prevent new cancer cells from growing for as long as they are willing to take the drug. Like all drugs, tomaxifen has its side effects, such as hot flashes, depression, and the premature onset of menopause.

Cancer doesn't end like other diseases. It just goes on and on. It's a major change in life, and it stays changed, and it gets stranger as time goes along. Mitchell finished filling Carolyn's breasts to their maximum size, and then one day we went in and he took some of the fluid out to let the breasts sag down just the right amount—to make them look like breasts rather than balloons. Mitchell does fine work, if artificial breasts are what you are after. Now we were part of the system: The money was flowing at an alarming rate, and we had zoomed past the important questions and were now recovering, reconstructing, playing cosmetic games with gowns and bathing suits. We even went so far as to appear on a TV special as one of those happy couples who have "beat cancer." And in the hot lights, when the hostess turned to me and asked me how breast cancer had changed my life, I was suddenly seized by the nearly irresistible impulse to leap across the stage and strangle her on television. But I muttered something noncommittal about not wanting to be the Man of Steel anymore, and everyone laughed, and the show went on.

Mitchell looked at the results and said, "We're lucky. We're very lucky." He spoke of the results of his surgery in terms of winning and losing. He considered Carolyn a winner. "But you know, we could go in there and just remove some of that scar tissue . . ." As the conversation went around to new surgery, new general anesthesia, new knives, new sacs of blood hanging from a steel post by a bedside somewhere downtown, I could feel the world reeling around me as it tipped off its axis. Even if she didn't have the additional surgery, there would be surgery to remove the fittings through which Mitchell had injected the saline to fill up her breast implants. And then there would be the reconstruction of the nipples, a process not unlike the ritual scarring in certain African tribal cultures. That would be followed by the tattooing of an areola around the reconstructed nipple.

It's getting to be spring now, and since Carolyn's surgery was in the spring, this season has taken on a new meaning. It is a time to go through the annual hall of fire at the hospital: Iodine injections, bone scans, X-rays, and all the concentration camp tests that could be dreamed up in the thrall of dreams of greater profits—the barium enema, the tomography scan, the blood tests and needles and the basket of plastic snakes. Since there is no test for cancer, the strategy is to assault the walls of the citadel of flesh from all sides at once until a bright light will shine right through it.

Breast cancer is a family disease. Suddenly life is slit open, and you find everyone peering in, asking questions they'd never think to ask otherwise. For two years I was afraid to walk along the street in my own hometown, because no matter who I ran into, the question was the same: "How's Carolyn? So, any signs of . . . you know . . . ? All the tests are good? Great. Great. Glad to hear it." I became a prisoner of breast cancer.

One day Carolyn woke up with a pain in her hip. We knew that breast cancer metastasizes to the hipbone. Carolyn called Cassandra and told her about the pain. They were on the phone for a long time. Cassandra wanted to know exactly where the pain was, where it began and ended, how long it had been there, its quality, its size and shape, the time of day it occurred, and whether it was worse standing up or lying down. She told Carolyn she'd have to come in for more tests. There followed weeks of scheduling and trips back and forth to the hospital, driving downtown in the morning to wait for stainless-steel machines with lights to press their cold noses against her pale flesh. A few more twelve-thousand-dollar snapshots.

It turned out that the hip pain was not metastatic cancer but a sports injury because of Carolyn's tap dancing and ballet and swimming. We really knew how to sweat it. But I could see that it would happen again, and I knew I couldn't be the Man of Steel forever. The next spring would take us down to the city to turn over another card from the top of the deck, and there would be more syringes, more blood spilled, the bruises and tears, more careening along the singing high-way in the springtime when the jackhammers come out, traveling, traveling, always traveling toward the question: How many times can we do this?

The Platform

on an Aircraft Carrier

Sound isn't everywhere, like stink. It has a definite footprint—a paw print, actually, because there are places where it hits and places where it misses, and those places can be right next to each other. So when a jet lands on an aircraft carrier, at first—and this seems like a long time—there is no noise, just catastrophic events of metal against metal, and because we see them without sound, they seem unreal.

The jet appears on the flat gray horizon far out over the stern of the ship. At first it's only a dart in the sky, a needle-shaped darkness, like a cinder in the waxen sky. But as it draws closer, it begins to reveal a lethal geometry; the black origami trapezoid unfolds now as it turns in on the ship, and gradually resolves itself into an F-18 Hornet, blossoming suddenly in our field of vision, and crashing into the deck to catch the howling wire not twenty yards away.

As the jet lands, I can hear the wire singing and complaining like bad stage thunder made with a big sheet of barn steel. The tailhook engages the wire and plays it out two hundred feet, a hooked marlin leaping from the sea. Then suddenly, as the jet passes, an invisible fist of sound grabs my head and crushes it like a beetle's back. The catwalk shakes, and the air just seems to jell; it feels as if something's going to squirt out of my ears.

The pilot, Del Rio by name, recovers from the G-shock of taking the wire and manages to lift his hand again, grab the throttle lever, pull it out of afterburner, and taxi away. Now yellow-shirted directors swarm around his plane, as his hydraulic wings fold up in startling imitation of a bird.

As Del Rio is being chocked for refueling, he puts his head in his hands, miming agony and defeat, and holds up four fingers, showing that he caught the four-wire, almost an overshot, not a good score. He wears a wedding band and has a checklist strapped to his thigh. He unzips a calf pocket on his green Nomex flight suit, removes a flask, and takes a swallow of water from it. Now he waits, sweating inside the parachute and flight suit, strapped into his ejection seat, this human cannonball. Del Rio takes out a pen and writes on his kneeboard, businesslike.

I stand on the catwalk fifteen feet directly above, looking down into his lap. I watch Del Rio roll his neck around and around, limbering up for the next flight. He doesn't even look when another F-18 lands in front of him with a bone-shaking concussion.

As the new arrival retracts its tailhook, releasing the wire, the cable slithers back into position, each end sucked down into the black deck. When the jets catch it, the wire makes a whistling, whipping noise, like a bullwhip a split second before it cracks, testimony to the energy involved in the landing event, since the wire is braided steel, two inches thick. We can hear it as the jets land because sound is a creature with a paw print.

As the wire retracts, a black man in a green jersey pushes it along with a long steel tool as if playing shuffleboard. The deck is aswarm with crewmen in color-coded turtlenecks, wearing cranials and goggles and waving gloved hands in mute signals, waving, running, pushing machinery. The main jobs on an aircraft carrier are not done by pilots, those elite technicians. There are only a few dozen pilots, as compared with six thousand people on board a CVN (carrier) bound for battle. The average age is nineteen.

The purple-shirted "grapes" finish fueling Del Rio, and he puts on his oxygen mask and watches the man below his cockpit signal "breakdown," wiping his hands down each arm, as if brushing off lint, the signal that the aircraft chains have been removed. Silver-suited men stand ready with fire extinguishers as Del Rio taxies away.

Del Rio takes the cat. Men in colored shirts swarm the plane, pushing the control surfaces, setting the hold-back bar, and giving him directions to come forward slowly, slowly, to engage the shuttle that will launch him. A man runs in front, holding up a sign that shows his weight. Del Rio confirms so they can set the power of the catapult and not inadvertently dribble him off into the sea. In the center of the forward deck, between the two steam catapults, is a plexiglass bubble where the shooter waits like a captured specimen, watching for the signal.

Del Rio does his wipeout, moving the control stick through its full range of motion, flipping elevators, ailerons, rudders to confirm that they work. He finishes by snapping the stick back to neutral, and I can see the control surfaces shudder.

Del Rio pushes the throttle to full power, and a rooster tail of smoke hits the jet blast deflector (JBD) and coils up into the sky, and the sound twists like a tourniquet.

We're cutting through the water at thirty knots.

The yellowshirt gives the signal: One thumb up to the shooter, one to the pilot, kneeling. Del Rio salutes: I'm ready. Now he reaches up and grabs the "towel rack," a bar on the right side of the cockpit, just something to hold onto, because here it comes. The shooter in the plexiglass bubble beneath the deck has his finger on the button: Bye-bye, Del Rio.

Whiteout. Silence.

Now two blue eyes stare fiercely back at us from the sky. The sound knocks me to the deck, and I'm picking particles of Non-Skid out of the heel of my hand.

■ ■ ■

An aircraft carrier is a city, so the navy says, a city of six thousand citizens, with an airport on the roof, a nuclear power plant, a daily newspaper, hospital, post office, laundry, bank, shopping malls, gymnasiums, TV station, and unlike most cities, complete facilities for reworking jet engines and a very large number of things that explode. The navy will tell you that one link of anchor chain weighs 360 pounds, that the ship has two thousand telephones, and that it can distill four hundred thousand gallons of fresh water from sea water every day. (It doesn't taste bad, either.) What it doesn't say—not in so many words—is that for thousands of years men have been dreaming of machines with which to kill each other, machines of war, from the long bow to the battering ram to the catapult to the cannon to the tank. As civilization advanced, there seemed to be a galloping nightmare that kept pace with it, the more twisted and convoluted with each succeeding generation, the nightmare of killing all our brothers all at once. The aircraft carrier is

The Platform

the most complex, the most ample, vast, and stupendous machine ever dreamed up for the killing of other people, the destruction of their cities, and the scattering of their families to the four winds. It is a black and horrible terrifying machine full of the most unimaginable means of setting fire to people the whole world over and blowing them into such unidentifiable bits that their loved ones will find not even a scrap to bury. It is quite literally an engine of death, and it can race across the globe to do its grim work on a moment's notice.

■ ■ ■

When I walk in, a dozen new pilots are slouched in maroon Naugahyde chairs in a briefing room called Ready Nine. In a couple of hours, they'll have their first chance to land an F-18 Hornet on an aircraft carrier at night, and if they're nervous about it, they certainly aren't going to show it now. There's no need to get all personal and tell everybody how you're feeling here: It's going to be obvious when you fly. There's nothing like night carrier landings in a big old fifty-thousand-pound fly-by-wire fighter plane to turn your guts inside-out and let everybody see just how you're coping. As one pilot told me, "There's no place to hide up there."

Just as Mike Yankovich, the landing signal officer and flight instructor, steps up to give the 1800 briefing, one of the pilots comes in late. He's obviously just gotten up from a nap, and the side of his face is tattooed with sleep.

"Hey, got a little rack burn there," Mike calls. "Practicing for the luge run?" Mike is tapping his feet, laughing, fidgeting. He doesn't have to fly tonight, but he's more nervous than they are: These pilots are his students.

Mike is big and red-faced and youthful and smiling, with brown hair and green eyes and a square jaw that will end up in jowls if he lives long enough. He's come on board the *Carl Vinson* here, one hundred miles off the coast of California, because he's instructor and LSO for a group of new pilots who are involved in carrier qualification. They have to hop in an F-18 and prove that they can catch the three-wire on the deck of this ship more times than not. It's like learning to shoot an arrow through a soda straw.

Failure might mean a wave-off. Too many wave-offs might mean an embarrassing trip back to the beach. But every now and then everything balls together in a knot and gets ugly. Not long before I arrived, somebody got a high sink rate going, didn't get the power on in time, and hit the rear end of the ship. The impact cut the aircraft in half. One of the two pilots survived—the front one whose half of the airplane went skidding across the deck.

It isn't necessary to screw things up to get hurt. Events can overtake the pilot. Mike gave an example: "The launch bar breaks. The shuttle goes supersonic and hits the water brake. The water brake turns instantly to steam from all that energy and explodes. Deck plates come flying up, and you fly right through the deck plates as you take off. So you eject and land on the deck."

If the pilot does everything right and survives the random forces, too, then the prize is that he gets to live on a ship like this one for months at a stretch. Mike described it: "Eighty days, no port call, and after forty days, you get two beers. You don't know if it's Saturday or not. All you know is the Happiness Factor: How many days to port, and you hope it's not Dubai."

So why do it?

"Yeah, how come you do it, Mike?" one of his pilots asks.

"Penis envy," he says.

He flew in the Gulf War and wears a one-thousand-hour Hornet patch, so he ought to know.

Earlier that evening, down in maintenance control, I'd asked a blue-eyed mechanic with crooked teeth and a big red moustache the same question. He said, "I love this. It's a great job. Of course, in the Persian Gulf it's one hundred and twenty degrees on deck. We had fifty-five-gallon drums filled with water, and we'd dip our boots in them about every hour or so just to keep our feet from burning. The only difference between day and night out there is you can't see a fucking thing. By the time the deck begins to cool down, the sun's coming up again. All for one hundred and twenty-five dollars a month extra pay."

Mike begins the briefing at 1800: "Drink plenty of water before you walk, and take a leak before you walk. Remember, half the speed and twice the caution at night. Keep padlocked on those directors. The boss is very conservative about taxi speed." There is a big yellow crane on deck to lift airplanes that go astray and become stuck halfway off the side of the deck. There are two helicopters orbiting astride the ship during flight operations in case an airplane goes all the way off.

Mike outlines procedures for launching and landing tonight. Then he describes the catapult takeoff itself.

"It *will* scare the living shit out of you," he says. "If you taxi to the cat and you don't have a knot in your stomach, there's something wrong. It's like walking into a closet. You're going to go right off into a black hole. You're sitting there sucking liquid oxygen, you'd better have a plan. Because if you don't, you're screwed, and then you're fucked."

All of this is done in a casual, rapid patter, because they've talked through it so many times in training. It's a litany, almost a prayer now: *Deliver us from evil, amen.* . . . But this is the first time they'll actually have to land at night.

"The steam curtain comes up, and you lose the yellowshirt for a minute. You'll be a hero real quick if you have the fold handle in the wrong position, so check that. Spread 'em, five potatoes, and you're all set. Okay, wipe out, the engines come up, see that they match. The safety guys jump up and make sure the beer cans are down. Tension signal. Hands you off to the shooter, and then: head back and four G's. Grab the towel rack. Touch the ejection seat handle and make sure you're not sitting on it.

"If you lose an engine on the cat, stroke the blowers, twelve to fourteen not to exceed sixteen. Rad Alt: You see you're descending, the wiser man will grab the handle."

Mike describes going out to the marshalling area, so-called "comfort time," the twenty minutes each new pilot is allowed to feel out the aircraft, and which Mike said was pure torture. "All I want is to get the fuck back on the deck as fast as possible."

Then he comes to the inevitable subject of landing, saying that although take-off is optional, landing is mandatory: "You're at a quarter mile and someone asks you who your mother is, *you don't know*. That's how focused you are. Okay, call the ball. Now it's a knife fight in a phone booth. And remember: Full power in the wire, your I.Q. rolls back to that of an ape." In other words, you're most vulnerable when you're most stupid, and you're most stupid right after landing, because it's like riding a motorcycle into a brick wall.

■   ■   ■

on an Aircraft Carrier   201

We go to dinner before the launch. In the officers' mess we bolt some sort of stroganoff and fried pork chops and such things as I can't conceive of eating before a stressful flight. When we're done, a waiter comes by and everyone around the table says to him one word: "Dog."

When they finish ordering, the waiter turns to me. "Dog, sir?" he asks politely.

"Sure," I say. When the waiter leaves, I ask Mike, "What's dog?"

"Auto-dog. It's soft-serve ice cream," he said. "Like Dairy Queen."

"Why do you call it auto-dog?" I asked.

"Go over and watch it come out of the machine," he said.

■　■　■

Aircraft carriers were first developed by the British Navy. The *Argus* joined World War I in October 1918, too late to serve. Sopwith Camel fighters and Sopwith Cuckoo torpedo aircraft took off from her 565-foot-long deck. Just twenty-seven years later in February 1945, the U.S. Navy attacked Tokyo with eleven fleet and eight light carriers carrying more than twelve hundred aircraft and escorted by eight battleships, seventeen cruisers, and eighty-one destroyers—the largest assemblage of naval power in history. The first time anyone understood the true and horrifying significance of aircraft carriers was when the first wave of forty torpedo-bombers, forty-nine dive-bombers, and forty-three fighters took off from six Japanese carriers and attacked Pearl Harbor. Within thirty minutes battleships *Arizona, Oklahoma, West Virginia, California, Tennessee, Maryland,* and *Nevada* were either sinking or badly damaged. At the same time, many of the American aircraft parked on the island were destroyed by machine-gun fire from passing attack aircraft. Nearly twenty-four hundred Americans were killed.

It was only because the U.S. carriers were at sea and not in port at the time of the attack that the United States had even a scant hope of stopping the Japanese in its drive deep into the South Pacific and on toward Australia. Those surviving carriers, along with new ones that were built, stopped the Japanese offensive begun at Pearl Harbor and drove them from the Pacific waters.

Displaying many of the attributes of a tactical air force, the carriers had the amazing advantage of being able to position themselves almost anywhere in the world and do their work not only at sea but to strike targets deep inland. Conceived of originally as escorts that would be used to facilitate the traditional battles between enormous gunboats, the aircraft carriers quickly proved themselves to be major strategic weapons. Between Pearl Harbor and V-J Day, U.S. aircraft carriers destroyed 12,000 aircraft, 6,500 in dogfights. (The United States lost only 451 airplanes in those aerial combat engagements.) Carriers sank 168 warships and 359 merchant ships, including 11 aircraft carriers, 5 battleships, 19 cruisers, and 31 destroyers. The United States lost 11 carriers during World War II.

■ ■ ■

The sun is low in the sky when we go out on deck to look at an F-18. Mike and I are standing two stories off the deck on the side of the aircraft, our toes hooked into the precarious footholds like rock climbers. We're already high—the deck is twenty stories above the surface of the sea—and everything is heaving slowly back and forth, up and down. I pick my way very carefully from spring-loaded handhold to vanishing foot peg, trying not to miss my grip on this gray titanium sculpture and go plunging to the deck. The deck is made of Non-Skid, a substance that feels like a mixture of cinders and broken glass embedded in epoxy. (I know how it feels from throwing myself face-down on it between the catapults, while F-18s rip overhead.) Now Mike is dancing around as natural as a monkey on the outside of that F-18, finding invisible footholds, walking on the wings.

I'm surprised to see how much the F-18 resembles some of the airplanes I fly, not so much in its equipment, but in its smell and feel and in the battered, greasy look of things. The interior of the F-18 looks like it belongs to a used Datsun. The seat fabric is frayed. The black plastic glare shield is ripped and patched with black goo and duct tape. This is no showpiece. It's a tool that sees a lot of use, like the little airplanes I rent at the local flying club. It smells like oil and sweat and old leather in there. It smells like my dad's old flight jacket, the one he wore in World War Two that still smells of fear after half a century.

Mike says, "Your whole goal is to kill people. The aircraft is nothing but a platform. All this other stuff, flying, carrier landings, cat shots, bingo profiles—it's got nothing to do with the mission. That's all just *technique*. Flying is not the goal. Flying is just something you do while you're killing people."

I ask him why he does it. The same question I'd asked in the briefing room, which I thought he hadn't answered seriously because the other pilots were around. "I always wanted to be a pilot," he says. "Sixteen years old, Williamsburg, Virginia, Kent County Airport, flying a J-3 Cub for fourteen bucks an hour, wet. I worked the line pumping gas. My dad was dean at William and Mary College, and everyone in my family was a musician. I was too dumb to get in any other way, so I had to get a football scholarship to the Naval Academy." He sighed and looked out over the ocean. "Yeah, I was the airport kid."

I tell him how dangerous the job seems to me, even just walking around on deck with the wires and jet blast and machinery and fire threatening from every side.

"Oh, this is nothing," Mike says. "During *real* ops, we get thirty launches and twenty recoveries all at once, and nobody ever says a word. It's called a Zip-Lip. Like in the Gulf War."

And of course, I ask, "What was it like?"

"The first day out there was so much triple-A, everyone was convinced that the enemy would run out of ammunition. It was solid from five to fifteen thousand feet." Mike flew above it, hitting what he could with missiles, while the B-52s did their carpet bombing from the stratosphere, the EA-6Bs fried microchips with their jamming pods, and the A-10 Warthogs fired uranium bullets, forty-two hundred rounds per minute. Mike doesn't make jokes about the killing part like I'd heard other fliers do: When you care enough to send the very best. That sort of thing. Mike seems to have a reverence for what he'd had to do out there, sending people into the unknown.

"The next night we went out, and it was the same thing all over again." A couple of times he had missiles come looking for him. The first time, he turned in on it and fired a flare, and the heat-seeking missile lost the infrared signature from his engine and chased the flare instead. The second time he slowed way down, dumped out chaff, and the missile "went stupid," wobbled up into space and blew up.

But after a few days, all the Iraqi radar was destroyed, and the flak concentration dribbled off to almost nothing. By the end of the war, the

The Platform

exodus from Kuwait on the main highway north had begun—convoys of vehicles five abreast. The U.S. military command waited until all the vehicles were out of the city and then laid down Gator anti-armor mines across the road to stop the convoy.

Some vehicles tried to go around but became bogged down in the sand on either side of the road. Other vehicles went around those, and they, too, became stuck in the sand. Soon there was a great wide barricade of stuck cars and trucks, and the traffic lined up behind it all the way back into Kuwait.

Kill zones were assigned.

Fast FAC F-18D night attack aircraft were sent out to play traffic cop, and eight aircraft every fifteen minutes were put on target. Mike was in there, mixing it up. "It was like shooting fish in a barrel," he says sadly. "They told us those were all Iraqis, and the vehicles were stolen. But it seemed a little excessive; they were just people, out in the open desert, and we'd just streak in out of nowhere and shoot them down." The engine of death had arrived. There were guys inside it, and they could see what was going on and reflect on it.

■ ■ ■

The pilots call it a *boat*. "Yeah, I lined up on the wrong boat a couple of times in the Gulf," Mike says. I ask what he did when he realized his mistake. "Oh, you just pretend you've got an emergency and fly away, because if you land on the wrong boat, you're practically guaranteed to have lunch with the captain while the paint crew goes to work on your plane to commemorate the event: Give you something to take back to show your skipper. It's difficult to live down."

The *Carl Vinson* is a Nimitz-class aircraft carrier. In essence that means that it's a nuclear-powered ship with ninety-five thousand tons displacement, as long as the Empire State Building is tall, and yet it can accelerate and maneuver like a Jet Ski. Sometimes late at night when the mission is done and we're down in the officers' mess eating mid rats (midnight rations), the captain turns north, and I hear comments around the table: "Whoa, where's my water skis?" Cruising at flank speed, the water boils up in a white froth all the way to the anchors. The exact speed is classified. They always say "in excess of thirty knots." When your chair tips over, you know it's well in excess.

It's difficult to get a sense of how big an aircraft carrier is. Out on a cruise with all its crew on board, a boat such as the *Roosevelt* or the *Carl Vinson* will serve twenty-four thousand meals a day. It's even more difficult to get an idea of what it costs. I asked the captain, and he said he had no idea. It costs $900 million a year to run a carrier battle group, and the U.S. Navy has a dozen of them.

Put it another way: If you earn one hundred thousand dollars a year from the age of twenty-five until the age of sixty-five, the U.S. Navy spends more money operating carrier battle groups in three hours and eleven minutes than you'll earn in your lifetime. A carrier battle group consists of an aircraft carrier with eight squadrons, including strike, strike-attack, anti-submarine aircraft, and early warning and electronic warfare aircraft on board. Accompanying the carrier are an amphibious assault ship (with a detachment from a helicopter combat support squadron on board), two guided-missile cruisers (with a detachment from an anti-submarine squadron on board), two guided-missile destroyers, two frigates (anti-submarine platforms, including a detachment of helicopters for anti-submarine warfare), one LPD amphibious transport vessel (for moving heavy equipment associated with amphibious assaults), and an LSD dock landing ship for amphibious assault (including elements of the naval beach group, elements of tactical squadrons, and assault craft units, with vehicles that ride on a cushion of air and are capable of making sixty knots over rough water). There is an oiler (AOR) for replenishing fuel, an ammunition ship (AE) for resupplying ammunition, and two SSN submarines protecting the carrier beneath the ocean's surface. There are Marine Corps expeditionary units spread out among all of those ships. The escort may change from mission to mission, but this is typical of a battle group's composition, and it would make a fairly good navy for a small nation.

In addition, should anything from the outside world get through all that, the Nimitz-class carrier itself has surface-to-air missiles and four Vulcan Phalanx mx-15 20mm cannons with six barrels capable of delivering three thousand rounds per minute. This so-called close-in weapons system looks like R2-D2 from the movie *Star Wars* and is operated automatically to put up what amounts to a lead curtain in the air around the ship.

A recent overall review of defense spending, intended to cut billions from the budget, glossed over the navy's assertion that it needs to keep a dozen aircraft carriers going. The navy has long insisted that it needs to maintain a permanent aircraft carrier presence around the world. The navy spends a lot of effort promoting that concept. As soon as we arrived on board the *Carl Vinson*, we were treated to lunch with a slide show presented by the ship's executive officer, Bob Willard, demonstrating how the carrier itself was nothing without the ships that accompany it: The carrier battle group. In addition, the navy claims that the groups must be refurbished and replaced with a frequency that seems excessive to some critics: An aircraft carrier's life span is said to be thirty years. The 1963 Chevrolet Impalas have lasted longer than that.

The mission, as defined by the navy, is "to be ready to employ her power anywhere in the world as directed by the president of the United States." If that seems a bit vague, the navy elaborates: "reconnaissance, long-range attack, anti-submarine warfare, and protection for other ships against airborne, surface, and subsurface attack." But the real mission seems to be to live with the memory of Pearl Harbor and its aftermath.

Keeping carriers on station in places with no home port, such as the Persian Gulf and the Mediterranean Sea, is extremely expensive. And the navy claims that it takes four carrier battle groups in order to keep one on station. Here's the thinking: One battle group is in place; another one is being rebuilt in the shipyard; a third is on home leave or in training exercises; and the fourth is in transit to relieve the first one. In other words, instead of spending $900 million a year for one battle group on station, the U.S. Navy claims that it needs to spend $3.6 billion a year in order for one carrier to do its job in one location. Many people argue with that idea.

Andrew Krepinevich, director of the Defense Budget Project in Washington, says, "It costs twenty billion for the battle group to defend the carrier. It costs another two billion a year in operation. You get for that princely sum a few dozen attack short-range aircraft. Question: Is that effective?"

No other nation has a navy to match that of the United States. Even so, the navy is about to begin building at least one new carrier at a cost of almost five billion dollars.

According to the navy, "The full range of implications must be taken into account when considering a carrier force of fewer than twelve ships." Gen. Norman Schwarzkopf said, "The Navy was the first military force to respond to the invasion, establishing immediate sea superiority. And the Navy was also the first air power on the scene. Both of these firsts deterred, indeed—I believe—stopped Iraq from marching into Saudi Arabia."

Robert Cowley, editor of *Military History Quarterly*, said, "Obviously carriers worked in the Gulf War. But then the Iraqis didn't have any submarines."

Famous military historian John Keegan says in his definitive book on the evolution of naval warfare, *The Price of Admiralty*, "Command of the sea in the future unquestionably lies beneath rather than upon the surface," and goes on to cite the Falkland Islands war of 1982. "The Argentine land-based aircraft and land-based missiles inflicted losses that narrowed the British aircraft carriers' protective screen of escorts to the slenderest of margins."

Krepinevich says, "I still think there's a strong burden of proof on the [Les] Aspin Pentagon." Aspin was author of the bottoms-up report that let the carrier issue slide. "They operate on the theory that we must be prepared to support military operations nearly simultaneously in two major regional conflicts. Additionally, we must maintain a forward presence in certain regions to deter, diffuse, or just moderate tension, to show U.S. resolve and influence. I have problems with requirements in both areas." Krepinevich says that history has shown that the chance of our having to fight two regional conflicts at the same time is extremely small in that it has never happened. "We ought to focus on the greatest threats and the most likely theaters. Neither is within this requirement. The greatest threats are down the road when we see the consequences of technology diffusion and proliferation of weapons of mass destruction to third world countries, when we're facing the Somalias and Bosnias of the world, and they have nuclear weapons. When third world countries have mines, ballistic missiles, and cruise missiles. They will be able to outrange carriers, and we may not be able to get in close where carriers work. Longer range systems will disrupt that capability. In the Gulf War the Iraqis used mines to good effect. They damaged Navy ships. They forced the Navy to stand off at a distance. The reason we didn't

The Platform

see Marines hit the beach earlier was that mines work. Combine that with submarines, and you have a very different conflict environment for the Navy. It's not clear that what we need is carriers. You may need subs to go in and take care of their subs and something to clear the mines. You may need a deep strike capability—the Air Force or Cruise missiles to take down those systems that the enemy uses to get at carriers. We have become too focused on the last war. We build carriers for 30 years, but we're not looking at what the world will be like in 30 years."

The U.S. Navy claims that it would actually cost more to reduce the number of aircraft carriers than to keep twelve in operation, because "We burn out our people and they leave; we use up the service life of our ships and aircraft faster than planned, and we end up with a force that is fundamentally less ready to meet the demands of future challenges. We've been through this before; our assessment is based on painful experience."

Bob Willard and I have coffee one morning, and he tells me with passion about his devotion to the concept of naval aviation and the carrier battle group. "The ships are with us to protect us. They form a protective bubble around the ship. Then when the time comes, the ship turns into the wind, and a strike package leaps over the enemy or surgically strikes the target, as in Libya." Each carrier has 85 planes. Four carriers bring 150 aircraft on deck to the party, with another 150 waiting in the hangar bay below decks. "With that we can sit off a coast for a hundred days and fly every day," Willard says.

Krepinevich counters, "Quaddaffi's tent was bombed by an FB-111 that took off from an air base in England. The Iraqi intelligence center was hit by cruise missiles from submarines. If forward presence is required, there are other ways to put it there." Indeed, submarines can do anything a carrier can do except track a moving target in real time.

David Isenberg of the Center for Defense Information said, "In Desert Storm the targets were telecommunications, radar, nuclear-biological-chemical weapons facilities, infrastructure, such as electric grids, and so on. All fixed targets. Subs can do that with cruise missiles. What they can't do is engage tanks and troops moving on the ground."

And so the debate goes.

Willard was recruited to play football at the Naval Academy, and he still has the clean-cut trim good looks of a player. A fighter pilot who worked his way up to the top of that profession with his own squadron, his mission in life now is to command his own ship. "I can't begin to describe to you the love I have for the science of fighting airplanes," he says. He says he loves the F-14 Tomcat, "the last of the stick-and-rudder airplanes."

Being on the ship and getting to know some of the people, I started to realize that the debate over carriers was not fueled by reason. In fact, it's not a debate at all, which is a contest of logic. No, it's something else. Being with these fighter pilots is like being with people who love Jesus: They just can't wait to tell you about it all the time. They don't want a debate. They don't want to hear that more people in the world are Muslims. This is *Their Thing*.

■ ■ ■

Night is beginning to fall. I emerge on the deck from the base of the control tower (called the Island), which contains the captain's bridge and the signal bridge, and mounted high upon it are safety lights that shine down on us and bathe everything in a sickly glow that makes us look like specimens preserved in formalin. I feel like a snail that has left its shell.

I find my way to the space between the two catapults on the bow of the ship and kneel with the crew in the grease and ash, wreathed in shrouds of steam, which wash us in hot waves. Men are running in every direction, and invisible blasts of infrared scorch our skin and clothing and grind the flecks of metal into flesh. Gauntlet gloves wave, and colored shirts run bearing colored, lighted wands—emerald, purple, sapphire, white—the keening siren, the twirling green beacon overhead; as among the darkened shapes of airships we scurry, putting our hands out to feel for the deadly jet exhaust that can send us tumbling over the side. There is no rail and no way to know which way to turn. A few get blown overboard by jet blast. The recovery rate is pretty good; most are back on board within a few minutes with only minor injuries, broken legs and such.

Flight operations begin by a seemingly telepathic concurrence that traverses the ship on invisible tendrils. Everywhere airplanes are taxiing, waved on by yellowshirts in headgear and goggles, while dozens of other crew members in their maroon or formerly white or green shirts,

The Platform

surge about the aircraft in colored waves, parting as the planes come toward them.

The pace quickens in the dancing of the men: The pilot runs his engines up to full power, and the craft stands shuddering and straining against a bar that holds it back. The exhaust hits the angled-up door of the JBD and shoots into the sky. Now everything is buffeted and scoured by sleeting particles of hot metal and surging waves of heat. The men in jerseys swirl their hands in the air, wave, jab, dance, and run, as if a lunacy has spread unseen among us, propelled on a hurricane of sound. Finally everyone settles on the deck and kneels and then freezes in a tableau, a fragment of Japanese theater: Some have their arms upstretched to the sky. Others point forward in the direction of flight. Some kneel, arm across knee, without moving, in attitudes of solemnity, and others spread their arms wide as if to receive deliverance from the black and swirling specter of radiant heat and noise and fire.

Suddenly steam blows the airplane away, and for a moment the sea and the ship upon it are oddly serene. The airplane is gone from the deck. We're steaming thirty knots, and the two helos are hovering out there. The ocean is so blue it looks almost purple. The deck heaves gently—hugely—up and down against the sharp horizon.

Now the jet tilts precariously above the bows, hanging for a moment, uncertain, before it catches itself and shinnies up a brown pigtail of smoke into the fading sky.

As the jet leaves the cat, it leaves a snail trail of orange fire reflecting from the metal rails.

I look up at the sky. The stars are beginning to rise.

■ ■ ■

I creep across the deck, among taxiing airplanes ready for the cat. Until reaching the cat, all the airplanes keep their wings folded demurely up, like birds grooming themselves. I pass the crewmen, who are hot fueling aircraft on the ramp between the cats and the Island.

The pilot above us put on his glasses with a fastidious air. Stenciled below his canopy is the name Torch Whalen, an inauspicious moniker, I note, as I move on. Even through protective goggles, my eyes are tearing; I can scarcely breathe from jet exhaust. Each time I step away from the blast of one airplane, I move into the eddying wind of another.

I most earnestly do not want to fall into the water in the dark. I don't believe they'll find me. I don't believe it at all.

I see a dashed foul line painted on the deck and step back from it just as an aircraft lands, and the wire snakes out, undulating at my feet. It's difficult to comprehend the energy involved in such a deceptively simple motion. They call it the wire, but it's a heavy cable, as thick around as a gasoline hose, and weighs so much that two men can barely drag it across the deck to throw it into the sea when it's replaced after one hundred landings. Yet when the aircraft hit, the wire comes alive like an electric snake, all silver and greasy in the twisty moonlight.

A light catches my eye. I turn to look back at the grouping of six airplanes.

I see men dancing in flames.

For a moment it appears they're warming themselves around a friendly bonfire, like students at a pep rally, as the flames climb up the misty stars and groom the airplanes underneath with a soft light. I see a fire cart race across the deck from my left, and men in silver flame suits run. People are sprinting now from all directions. Torch Whalen taxies his A-6 forward to get out of the way, and just as the swelling dome of flame is about to swallow the crowd and the planes, the men surround and smother it. It gives one last urgent surge, spins around the black deck, dancing to escape, and then vanishes.

Only later did I learn what had happened: Fuel had overflowed from a huffer cart, a low, yellow, tug-like vehicle that carries a jet engine to assist jets in starting.

Throughout the episode the catapults continued to shoot young men at the hazy moon.

■ ■ ■

I join Mike and we pass through the corridors of the ship. Mike plunges steadily on with an odd gait that is necessitated by having to step over the hatchways ("knee-bangers") every twenty feet. We pass through layers of aromas, of oil and sweat, grease and paint, and human beings. As we approach the galley, waves of heat billow along the length of the ship, bearing the smell of food just cooked but already rotting. Endlessly down the perfectly ruled length of the ship, the oval hatches line up. At one point we walk nearly an eighth of a mile without turning a

The Platform

corner, and after a while, as our stride falls into step and we all lift our legs together to cross the thresholds, and as seamen come toward us in mimic of our motion, it creates the illusion that there are only two hatches, one behind and one ahead, and they mirror each other, like the optical illusion in the barber shop, where we can sample infinity in the tricks of glass.

We pass the squadron insignias emblazoned on the doors of sleeping compartments—the Golden Warriors, the Jolly Rogers, Valions, The Bear Aces (featuring a crude line drawing of a woman's bottom), the Black Aces (a playing card, of course) and the Grim Reapers.* We see a skeleton flying across a red sky with a yellow scythe. There are lions, Indian braves, skull and cross bones—all sorts of totems such as little boys would use to keep girls and rivals out of their tree houses.

I'm touched by how like children they are with their *ad hoc* mythology and games of death. With the control they've been granted over their jets, the munitions they carry, the lives and real estate they are authorized to destroy, their responsibility is far greater than most captains of industry. And yet they call each other Hairball, Nutty, Eel, Cracker, Sea Dawg, and Stubby.

■   ■   ■

We make our way to the LSO platform by way of the passages below the deck, and on the way we pass the machinery that stops the airplanes above. Each of the four arresting cables disappears beneath the deck, where it joins its very own roomful of equipment half a block long and attended by two poor devils beset by heat and noise and stench and protected by nothing more than a set of earmuffs. Looking into the cable restraint mechanism was like stumbling upon a great, surreal guitar, a catabolic apparatus for reducing the very motion of the planets to the song of grease.

The number-three cable makes eight turns around a wheel, then eight turns around another wheel and then goes back and forth until it forms a fretted fingerboard of strands pulled straight and silvered with leaden tallow, all smoothed and flecked with metal shavings from

*I spent time on the Carl Vinson and the Roosevelt, and this essay draws on both experiences.

the ceaseless strumming motion. The airplane is a great aluminum finger pick, descending on all those tuned and tingling wires at 150 knots. Attached to the cable and wheels and pulleys is a piston as big around as the full moon, all chromed and slick with oil, penetrating a sleeve of gray-painted steel. The grease and the catastrophic arias of hydraulic fluid permeate everything in that suffocating room. Two men, one at either end of the machinery, monitor the flights taking place above. One of them, a huge black man in a filthy, smeared T-shirt and jeans rolled up to the knee, combat boots all blackened and caked with old soot, tips his head back and drains a Coke as an airplane hits the deck with a concussion that could reverse the poles of the planet.

The gleaming shaft plunges into its gray-painted sleeve like elephants uniting. All the cables strum a furious jangling note, as the entire apparatus absorbs the shock and energy of the thirty-ton airplane up above, which comes to a complete stop from 150 knots in only 315 feet. Here was the source of the sound I'd heard in the moment of silence created by the paw print of a landing jet.

Now the cables are waving, loosening, rising and falling across the fretboard of the instrument, and the screeching of hydraulic fluid dies away, as the appliance resets itself. The cables run, whirring, into their sleeves and then snap tight like a zither, vibrating away their excess energy, and come to rest, once more, trembling and taut and ready.

One of the men is named Grubbs. The word is stenciled on the breast of his filthy green T-shirt, as to comment upon the situation. I ask him how it's going. "We slept more during the war," he says, and I head on up the stairs to catch up with Mike.

■   ■   ■

Now we stand with two dozen guys on the LSO platform, a spidery lattice affixed precariously to the outer skin of the great rolling ship. One step more to my right: A twenty-story rush to the streaming, moon-freaked sea. I stand for a moment to watch as the ship rips the sea guts out with the cleaving of its steel prow, and they curl and eddy in boiling knots of bile below.

A plane lands, then immediately skitters away into the sky again with a roar of afterburners. In the silence that follows, Mike says, "I hate night touch-and-gos. It's like kissing your sister. It's like practicing bleeding." As LSO, Mike talks to the pilots. He has to be able to tell if they're in the groove or not and to wave them off at the last second if something isn't right.

The night is huge out here at sea. The clouds are low. Through thin spots in the ragged fabric, the crescent moon sheds soft and sooty light. Now and then the fabric bulges and splits and spills a profusion of stars down on us.

Tremendous shapes move on deck in a darkness that is splashed orange by sodium vapor lamps. The deck is like a huge and broken trapezoid of stolen sky, a broken scrap of frozen sea, populated with ranks of pad eyes like starfish in rows. I happen to be standing next to the flight surgeon, who leans in on me and shouts, "The only place more dangerous than right here tonight is Bosnia!"

Another jet lines up and isn't doing well, weaving back and forth. Mike says, "Look out. Here comes Ray Charles," and does a dance on the LSO platform, rocking his head around like a blind man singing a song. Mike hits the pickle switch and sends the plane away. Another one comes in.

Each new landing throws up a tremendous smell of burning rubber.

All fire. All burning. Blue night. Blue sea. Blue lights, white stars of deck lights, cold wind, whistling thunder. The stars seem to race away through holes in the clouds, and among the stars now I see the dark shapes of aircraft creeping through the ragged shreds as they make their way around the pattern.

"Shit hot!" Mike says, as someone takes the three-wire. There are four wires, and hitting the three-wire gives the best score. A one-wire is bad, because you're just that close to a splatter.

The next plane bolters, as they call it when the hook misses the wires entirely. The airplanes hit the wire at full power just for this reason: The wheels crunch into the deck, the rings of fire open behind the tail, and the aircraft goes off the other end. We all turn in time to see the plane sink before it catches the air again and begins to rise. When he's gone, Mike says, "Boy, did you see him *settle?* He'll be picking the seat cushion out of his asshole about now."

■　■　■

During a break in the action, the pilots all gather around a Marine on the LSO platform, and he breaks out his stash of Tootsie Roll Pops, which he'd hidden in his flight suit. When the planes begin to land again, the pilots on the platform have lumps in their cheeks, and they're all intense and focused, but they look like boys at a little league game.

When it's all over, we go down to mid rats and eat stale food and drink grape Kool-Aid, and everyone seems to fall in upon himself, eating with grave concentration. We could hear the scream of hydraulic fluid up above as the airplanes continued to catch the wire. I remark that it might be hard to sleep with that noise.

Mike tells me that he became accustomed to sleeping through a whole launch sequence during the war—eighty-five airplanes thundering off the deck over his head as he lay in his rack, snoring. "Then coming home, I find myself running out into the back yard to stomp a cricket to death because the *fucking noise is keeping me up!*"

■ ■ ■

I wait for my flight home, standing on a catwalk outside the ship's gray and trembling elephant skin. I look down through a hatch at the play of light on the inky royal ocean. A Sea King helo passes me at eye level, thundering freakish patterns on the surface of the sea. Fishing boats dot the water in the distance, and thunderheads build high and gray on the horizon. A many-layered sky of varied blues and whites and grays and broken shades of tinted pastel smoke makes a backdrop for the whales that rise and fall beneath the waves. Above my head the jets take off and land with a cyclonic rush of steam and kerosene. A lone airman comes walking down a staircase on the catwalk toward me from the deck above. He is tall and blond and looks lost. He hangs on a length of fat black cable near me, fidgeting, uncertain. He doesn't seem to see me. Then he passes into the ship, looking serious and focused on something invisible.

I'm wearing my cranial and goggles as I go up on deck to board the plane that will take me home. It begins to rain. The drops are picked up by the turbine wind and flung at me like bullets. The Cod C-2 carries passengers facing backward and has no windows, except for two portholes covered with heavy screen. I sit in darkness, feeling the rumbling of the engines as we taxi about. The interior walls are laced up and across in a crazy pattern of wires and tubing, as if this cave has been the home of mechanical snails that trace these baffling hieroglyphics. Yellow lights placed here and there in steel fixtures cast a dim illumination on the highlights of fleshy painted steel. We taxi. The whole ship shakes. Then at a shout from the crew, I am given to understand that we've taken the cat and are about to be shot off the ship, and I put myself straight in my chair. I put my head back. I straighten my neck and wonder about my sixth cervical vertebra, which sometimes gives me trouble.

I'm flung against the harness so hard that the web belts cut into my neck, and I can feel myself being choked as I hang there. My arms shoot straight out ahead of me, and I am powerless to bring them back in, though I want to reach my straps to relieve the pressure on my neck. I strain to pull myself back, but I'm paralyzed. I'm dimly aware that I've been in an explosion of some sort, but I'm too busy choking to fix it, and then it's all over.

Silence.

I hear a clunk beneath us, as I'm thrown into my seat. We must have hit a wall, I think. It's so quiet. I know that something has gone wrong with the launch. Maybe they'll try again.

I turn and see (faintly through a latticed porthole) the whitecaps of the sea, diminished by our altitude. Amazingly, we're aloft. My hearing begins to return, and I realize that what I took to be silence was simply momentary deafness from the blast of the catapult. The engines are strumming the air. We're on our way home.

Vera and Art

on the Farm

In 1990 I was working on a book called *One Zero Charlie*, about a small airfield on the Illinois-Wisconsin border. I moved into a cabin on Wonder Lake, a mile from the field, to write. I had spent an intense summer flying aerobatics there with my pilot friends, Gerry and Mark and Howard and Jan, who had a passion for the sport of inverted flight, but I was glad when summer came and the season was over at last, because it gave the air around Galt Airport a chance to cool. Already four pilots had died. It's just the way the sport worked. People died like that every year, and I felt that we all needed time to sit still and contemplate what we were doing.

I went up to Art's house one morning and found him in the kitchen in his blue pajamas, sitting at the round Formica table reading the newspaper. Some weeks earlier I had asked him if he would mind gathering together all the photographs of the airport and the family that he could find and letting me look at them. He said he'd see if Vera could find some. "There must be a bunch, I know that," he said.

When I came in, he stood up, saying, "I've got those photographs you asked for."

"Great," I said, sitting down and preparing for a long session with him, in which we would go over every detail of the photos for clues to the history of his airport. Art stood up and went to the sideboard. It seemed that his palsy had grown somewhat more pronounced in the last year, and I noticed that he had taken to wearing a hearing aid, although he'd never had any trouble understanding the questions I'd asked him. He rummaged around in some papers and came back to the table with three tiny black-and-white snapshots. I looked at them, then I looked expectantly at Art. He smiled ingenuously. I said, "Art, is that all?"

"Is that all?" he asked. "Well, that's the whole story right there." One photograph showed a military Jeep, piled high with someone's belongings. Another showed a few old-time, rag-tag airplanes tied to a fence by a big oak tree. And a third showed Art and Vera, forty years younger, in the act of turning from the altar just after being wed.

"See," Art said, pointing, "there's the Jeep we came in. And here we're getting married in Woodstock. And this here, that's the airfield with all the airplanes. Well, not *all* of them, but enough to give you the idea. What more is there?"

He then fell to talking about a time when they were out plowing, four tractors in a row, and they stopped for lunch. They unhooked one of the tractors, and three of the men stood on the draw bar to ride back for lunch. "It was a neighbor's tractor, and he had taken the fenders off of it. Well, it was fine when we were going straight, but as soon as he made a turn, I was swayed over like this, and I got caught in those big treads of the tire. It pulled me right under." The enormous treads of the tractor tire were like hands, picking up the slight, almost frail, frame of Art Galt and stuffing him under the freshly turned soil with their rolling black momentum. It ripped his ear off and ran over his arm, but his arm happened to fall between the treads. "Luckily, the guy who was driving didn't put the brakes on or it would have ripped my arm off," Art said. As it was, he had to have his ear stitched back on.

I told him that statistics seemed to suggest that being a farmer was far more dangerous than being a pilot or for that matter almost anything else. In response, Art showed me his hands, which were deeply scarred. "This one here," he said, "is where I slipped off the roof and grabbed something on the way down." He fell and was hanging by the gutter when Lee came along.

Art called out to him, and Lee asked, "What do you want me to do?"

"For Christ's sake, put a ladder under me," Art said.

He said that Vera was every bit as much a farmer as he had ever been, too. She was always in there working right alongside him. In fact, one day she was out on the tractor discing up some peat with a cat, and a local man happened by to talk to Art. "Who's your hired man?" he asked.

"That's my wife," Art said.

Vera came in, as if on cue, looking tall and elegant in her long white chenille bathrobe. "Good morning," she said.

"Good morning, Butchie," Art said. "Did you swim?"

"I just played around," Vera said and drifted off into the next room.

Art picked up the photograph that showed the airplanes tied to the fence and stared at it. He began to reminisce about Hal Staehling, who was killed when his Harvard SNJ ran out of fuel on the way from Hebron to Galt—a distance of less than five miles—and that reminded him of the war surplus that Hal used to sell, which reminded him of the war. Art said he met the Russians on the Elbe, and he laughed. "Those dumb shits. They'd buy anything with a luminous dial." He sold his watch to some Russian soldiers for a good price, although it was a worthless trinket. Somehow the connections began linking in Art's brain, one to the next, and the war made him remember why he was there in the first place, and inevitably the specter of his father raised its ugly head once more.

He began plaintively, like Hamlet, as if his father might still hear him. "If I'd have been a boob or drunken or no good, maybe I'd think differently, but I never did a thing wrong. My grandfather was a lawyer, my father was a lawyer, and they wanted me to be a lawyer, so I became a lawyer. I flunked the bar the first time, but I became a lawyer."

He told me that his family had a fruit farm in Michigan, but it was a gentleman's farm, more a dude ranch than anything. They had horses and the family went there every summer from the time Art was eight until he passed the bar. He and his brothers used to hook horses together and pretend to have Roman chariot races. They'd ride standing on their backs. Life had been fun back then, and Art never forgot how it felt to be on the farm.

"Go back to the beginning," I said.

"How far back?" Art asked.

"All the way," I said.

"Well, all right, if you want me to."

■ ■ ■

Art was born April 9, 1912, in Evanston, Illinois. His mother was from a wealthy family in Winsockett, Rhode Island. Her father made his fortune trading grain by the carload from Omaha, Nebraska. Art's father was Arthur Galt, a powerful Chicago attorney, whose father, Asaria Thomas Galt, was the attorney for the Chicago *Tribune* in its heyday.

Art went to grade school at Evanston's Lincoln School, where Marlon Brando would later be a student. The Galts lived at 1013 Judson, the corner of Greenwood Street, two blocks from the edge of Lake Michigan. Art was a sickly child and was held back in school by illness of the vaguely defined sort we read about in novels. Even Art doesn't know exactly what was wrong with him, except that it had to do with his stomach. It's entirely likely that the doctors of his day didn't know either, although they cut him open from neck to navel at an early age and ran his bowel for him, resulting in a lifetime of adhesions.

At the age of eight, he was put in a Montesorri school, a rather progressive concept in 1920. Art was recovering from his illness and managed to move through three grades in six months. He attended the Miller School on Dempster and Hinman for the summer. Then he returned to Lincoln School in the fall of the next year at age nine and continued through the eighth grade there, holding his own from then on, although, he is quick to point out, "I wasn't a very good student." He continued to have stomach trouble. "I was a weakling," he said, as if it had been something he'd heard so many times that he had come to believe it, even now, despite the obvious contradictory evidence of his accomplishments. "It takes me a while to absorb things," he said. "One of the things I did not absorb was spelling."

The family moved to Astor and Division streets, "The Gold Coast," Art recalled with disdain. Arthur, Senior, coached him in Latin. "Hic Hoc Hic Hujus," Art said, mocking his father even from beyond the grave. Art was enrolled in Francis Parker, a private high school for teenagers from wealthy families. He managed to plow through four years of Latin and achieve the positions of being both president of the football team and of the student government.

He recounted an incident in which a teacher read a poem and asked what the structure of it was. Art said it was iambic hexameter, and the teacher asked the class in general, "How many of you think that's right?" There were no hands, because everyone was certain that the teacher was mocking Art. The teacher then turned and said, "Well, Mr. Galt, as sometimes happens, the majority is wrong and you and I are right." Art was eighty years old when he recalled that.

Art went to Williams College at Williamstown, Massachusetts. He took an additional four years of Latin in college. In spite of that, Art recalls, "I was a dumb shit." More correctly, he was independent: Art only studied what he liked, and he managed to fail the same European history course twice. He had to go to summer school at Northwestern to make it up. On the other hand, he made A's in geology.

Although he weighed only 135 pounds, Art played football and lacrosse and was on the wrestling team. Despite Art's efforts to win his father's approval, Arthur, Senior, refused to come to his graduation.

■　■　■

As Art entered law school, his life seemed to grow more unhappy by the day, as he looked to the future and saw the bleak enterprise of working for his father's firm, under his father's disapproving scowl, enslaved eternally by censure and indifference. Art hated the law and law school. A photograph of him from that period shows an unhappy, grim, determined young man in a stiff collar and tie with dark hair and smooth face, looking into a future as desolate and humorless as a row of accounting figures.

After passing the bar just before World War Two, Arthur, Senior, as expected, put Art to work in the office, but he was no more than a glorified office boy. Art said, "He never gave me any authority to do anything." Arthur had vast real-estate holdings, and he put Art in charge of a single apartment building, but even there Art was unable to make decisions without his father's approval. Art was working on the street level, while his father was in the protected atmosphere of the office, and he could see that people were cheating his father behind his back. Art attempted to warn him, and perhaps thereby to show Arthur, Senior, that he could be useful, but the old man was convinced that his son was an idiot, and he ignored his advice. Art, the first-born son, the scion of the Galt empire, felt helpless, worthless, ignored. He practiced law for a time, but it seemed nonsensical to him: "People never asked you what to do. They got themselves into trouble and then expected you to get them out."

The phone rang, and Art went to the wooden stand by the kitchen door, where a five-button phone sat blinking. A fly swatter hung on the wall above it. Art stood in his blue pajamas, bare feet on the green linoleum floor, looking out the window at the sunny day and talking on the phone. It was nearly noon. On the sideboard were recent color photographs of great-grandchildren in a chaotic collage. On the wall an Elgin Regulator pendulum clock was scything time away like a machine slicing some delicate confection. The Borden's Elsie Cow cookie jar stood graceful and tan on top of what must have been the first microwave oven ever produced for general use, near the enormous stainless-steel Chambers stove.

■ ■ ■

When Art sat back down at the table with me, I said, "Well, Art, the thing you've never told me is this: What exactly made him disown you like that? I mean, there must have been something other than just you being sick when you were a kid or not measuring up. There must have been something."

Art looked me dead in the eye, and I felt for a moment as if my own grandfather had come back to life and were telling me the stories about coming across from Mexico to the States during the Revolution. In fact, I realized that there were a lot of similarities between Art and my grandfather, Agustín.

Then Art told me about a couple who had three children and who had come to work at the Galt mansion in Chicago. The woman did the cooking and cleaning and sewing for Mrs. Galt. The man did all sorts of things, including driving Arthur's car and gardening and fixing things. The housekeeper was a young woman, only two years older than Art at the time that she came to work there. And she somehow struck Art as the purest heart he had ever known. In the dreary and hopeless picture of his future, she marked the first real bright spot. He and the housekeeper became fast friends. In that intense world of isolation created by his father's indifference, she was someone Art could talk to. Art had stood around yawning in his tuxedo at the society dances, where he was supposed to meet his blushing bride, but he had just been bored by the society girls, the debutantes. For whatever reason, he had found a kindred spirit in the housekeeper, someone he could talk to.

Then her husband left her, and she was thrown into the world with three children and only her wits to support her. She worked for Mrs. Galt for a time, sewing and doing other chores, but she needed more to make a go of it with the children, and she had to leave.

Her name was Vera Davis, and she and Art had fallen in love by that time. When Art announced to his parents his intention to be with Vera, they thought their son had taken leave of his senses. Art took it one step further: He was going to marry the housekeeper. "Mother wanted me to marry a girl my own age who was a virgin," Art said, "but that's the way she was raised. And she supported me anyway.

"I tried to win the family's approval for her," Art told me with a sad smile, "but it evidently didn't work out." It was Art's typically understated way of expressing the shock, horror, disappointment, and fury that proceeded from his announcement of his intention to wed the housekeeper of the great and powerful Arthur Galt.

■ ■ ■

The Second World War was on when Art entered the military. Arthur, Senior, insisted that Art at least enter as an officer at a rank befitting his station in life. Art started as a private, much to his father's mortification, and worked his way up the way everyone else did.

With tears in his eyes, Art told me, "He decreed that I should not be buried in the family plot in Graceland."

Before Art left to go into battle, his father told him, "It would be just as well if you'd spill your blood on the battlefield as come home."

Weeping, Art said, "I wouldn't tell that to my worst enemy, let alone my eldest son." He wiped his tears with the sleeve of his blue pajamas and said, "I don't think there's anything in my life that's affected me as much as what my dad told me when I was going overseas." He grew quiet for a moment. Sunlight angled into the kitchen, and we could hear airplanes taking off overhead every now and then. "Then I suppose I did a few things that I wouldn't have done if I'd thought a little more of myself," he added. "But someone was watching over me, so I came back."

Art was in Germany through 1944, 1945, and 1946. He commanded a company of seventeen tanks, although he claimed he wasn't qualified. The army simply ordered more tanks and took Art from a

Recon battalion and put in him charge. He reminisced about the slow 76s he had used and then the giant and speedy 95s with which they were replaced.

At one point, they had taken 125 German prisoners, and Art was trying to sleep when he heard moaning and went to see what it was. The sound was coming from two badly wounded Germans. So Art drafted four of the fit German soldiers and gave them stretchers to carry the wounded. He took a light machine gun and pointed it at the Germans, saying that they would be the first to go if they tried to escape. Art and his men gave them first-aid and took them to the hospital the next day. The doctor said they would have died if Art had not brought them in.

"Once a guy scared the shit out of me," Art said. The radio frequencies were garbled, and Art couldn't tell what was going on in the battle, but he saw smoke, and he could hear the guns. He left the company in the charge of a sergeant and went to look. He walked on foot through the tanks and infantry to find the fighting. He was moving through German farm country now, and suddenly he became caught up in the beauty of it. He had always liked farm country, and this was some of the most beautiful in the world. All at once the fighting, the awful, crushing tedium and desperation of war, seemed far removed. As he strolled along, daydreaming of what it would be like to have his own farm, he suddenly became aware of a German soldier pointing his rifle through a picket fence and motioning for Art to raise his hands and surrender. Art was about to drop his weapon, realizing that he would be killed when he did so and that the farm he dreamed would never become reality. Then he noticed that the man could not swing his weapon left or right because of the pickets, so Art jumped left and ran. The soldier tried to aim to shoot Art down, but found that his rifle was stupidly jammed in the fence.

"I went back and got a squad of men and tried to find the bastard, because he scared about ten years out of me, I'll tell you." But the German soldier was gone.

Even after what Arthur, Senior, had said before Art left for the war, Art tried to write down his feelings and send them in letters to his father, thinking that perhaps it would finally make the difference, if only his father could see the aching humanity of the position he was in and his harrowing human reactions to it. If only his father could see compassion and bravery—if not in Art himself, then at least in the men around him—and see that his son had a capacity to observe and appreciate it . . . But Arthur, Senior, corrected Art's spelling and sent the letters back to him in the European theater of war.

■ ■ ■

During the last few days of the war, the Germans and Russians met on the Elbe. Art took his tanks up and secured a position. Those were his orders, and he passed them on to his men, but they didn't want to go, because it was the last day of the war. They said, "What the hell do we want to get killed for on the last day of the war?"

Art said, "Deciding who to send in was always the most difficult thing. You can't send in your best man, because you can't afford to lose him. You can't send in your worst, because he's too dumb. Then you look at this guy, and you say, well, he's got kids. Then you look at the next guy, and you say, hell, he's got a new sweetheart. Finally, you just do it yourself."

So Art told his men on that last day of the war, "All right. I'll walk out in front of you guys and see if there's anybody out there." Art walked with his rifle before him in front of the rolling tanks, while the men he led marched behind in the shelter of the armor plate. As he told me that, there were tears in his eyes once again—and I could see the pain of his desperate efforts to give his father what he wanted—the blood of the son, who otherwise was no good. Weeping, Art told me that he was hoping that he would get killed that day and not have to go back. He still thought that he had to go back and be a lawyer and live forever in the tenebrous shadow of his father's scorn. He had not yet conceived of Galt Airport and those wonderful ramshackle buildings, that audacious and contrary monument to his father's iron will, Art's own topsy-turvy empire, built in defiance of the old man's millions, the gleefully scattered debris of Art's life and work spread around for God and everyone to see, as if only this—acre after acre of happy chaos, along with the joyous skyward-leaping machinery, the wild Sunday hangar parties in praise of a different god, with voice after celestial voice calling across the airwaves, "Galt Airport, Galt Traffic, Galt Unicom, Galt, Galt, Galt"—as if only such an outrageous concatenation of improbable, insolent, and frivolous elements could finally and properly answer the old man's vicious, willful, and intractable power.

■　■　■

When Art returned from the war, he was changed as people always are by war. For one thing, he knew that although he might live forever under his father's influence, he wasn't going to live under his contemptuous gaze. Art reaffirmed his intention to marry Vera and moreover to move to the country and be a farmer. His father tried to talk him into being a gentleman farmer, to get someone else to do the work and to own the operation outright, as Arthur, Senior, had with the fruit farm and horse ranch in Michigan. "But I wanted to do it myself," Art said.

Art got out as soon as he possibly could. He couldn't even wait for spring. It was just after the war, and there were no automobiles to be had, so they bought a surplus Jeep, and on that January day, they rattled up the old roads—Art and Vera crowded in there with kids and equipment and even piled on top with more perfectly good stuff and in the back a used disc for cutting the earth, which Art had naively bought at the farm show in town, figuring it was a farmerly thing to own; and anyway, it had seemed like a perfectly good beginning to his collection of Perfectly Good Stuff. On that sunny, icy day they arrived in the driveway of the old Schranz farm, Art unloaded the people (but not the belongings) from the army Jeep, and he stood back a few feet with his Kodak Brownie camera and, with his shadow protruding into the frame like the shadow of his father protruding into his life, he snapped a picture of the mud-green vehicle and the white-painted house in the background.

Art and Vera were wedded January 22, 1950, in the Methodist church in Woodstock.

Art's father came out to visit only once. "It was a tangled mess of nettles and bramble and wilds then," Art told me. "I hadn't drained it or anything." Arthur, Senior, never came back, and he never saw the airport. He believed people were not meant to fly. "His brother was killed by food poisoning on a train, so he didn't think much of trains, either," Art said.

Art said, "I was hoping that before the final date things would be settled between me and my father, but they were not. He died when he was ninety-three. Mother died when she was ninety. The only thing I ever did against his wishes was to marry, and I was thirty-eight when I married, and I thought it was about time for me to decide some things on my own."

Art visited his father all through a long illness before his death. He bought his father a remote-control television to make it easier on him. Those gestures did nothing to soften the old man's heart. Arthur Galt, Senior, had $53 million when he died, and his eldest son was not a beneficiary. Indeed, rather than leave his son something, the estate demanded that Art pay back a $400,000 loan his father had made for a family business venture. "But it didn't mean a damn to me," Art said. "None of it."

■　■　■

A couple of weeks before his birthday, Art and I went for a ride in my Bellanca Citabria airplane. There was no particular reason for the flight. I was waiting for the weather to clear so I could go on a business trip to Michigan, and I had decided to go up and take a look—see if what I saw in the air bore any resemblance to what the government weather briefers had been reporting. I happened to mention to Art that I was going up for a weather check, and he laughed, reminding me that he used to say the same thing to the kids who would come around begging rides.

"Yeah, I'll go," Art said. Just as we were taking off, the sun started to come out, and as we flew toward Lake Geneva, Wisconsin, the great swirling mists parted, and rays of sunlight burned down through the fog to the fields of corn and beans just beginning to turn faintly green, and the smaller gleaming lakes took on the cast of smudged-over melting pots in the foggy wetness that blew and drifted across the land. Here and there snow was still visible from recent squalls.

As we flew along, Art kept up a running commentary on what he saw below. One cornfield was planted in an odd way, with geometric bald patches scattered throughout, and Art said, "He must've jammed when he was planting." We passed over a nursery, and he remarked, "That fellow sure has a lot of trees planted." Out over the endless rectangles of crops, he looked down for a long time in silence, and then said, "I've been here forty years, but I never get tired of looking at it. Isn't it beautiful?"

As we were coming back to the field, he looked down and saw the shadow of our plane following a highway, and he laughed, "Isn't it fun when you can see your own shadow? I like to make it follow a road. It's kind of a game." I understood that Art Galt had made an amazingly clear-headed decision about his life, as if someone had given him a glimpse into a crystal ball. Yet at the same time, he had made the decision the way a child does: He chose something that made him happy.

When we had landed, we left the airplane on the ramp and stood near the parking lot, talking. He told me that he had a spot all picked out at Greenwood Memorial Park with a gravestone, "And it even has my date of birth on it," he informed me with a smug smile. "All we have to do is put the other date on it and it's done." He said he had arranged to rent a coffin. "I'd rather be buried in the ground and let my parts be scattered naturally," he said, "than have somebody dig me up——" Here he aped what I took to be an archaeologist digging up his skull one thousand years from now and brushing if off. "Oh!" he said in a high voice, "this would look pretty good in the museum. Let's take it!"

■ ■ ■

We crossed the parking lot. It was a cold, beautiful day. We stopped near the back of the shop, and I could see Lloyd's burned-up Starduster peeking out at us from where it rested among the thistles—one of the pilots we'd lost to the business of aerobatics. Art stood there thinking for a while, and then he said, out of nowhere, "You know, my family wanted me to marry a virgin and all, but I really love children, and if I had done as they wished, then we might not have had any. Vera and I tried to have children and she was all right certainly, but we couldn't have any. So she got tested and I got tested, and they said she was okay, but there was something wrong with my stuff. So it's a good thing that I married someone who already had children, or else I wouldn't have had any."

■ ■ ■

The annual Galt Christmas party took place on a low IFR (instrument flight reading) day with a brisk wind from 230, fog and drizzle. The airport was closed for the party, generally about 1 P.M., because wine was served. But there would be no flying, anyway. It was one of those days when the airport manager even let the line boys off of work.

People were laying out a spread that looked elaborate enough for a Lithuanian wedding when I arrived that morning. The Christmas bunting was already hung, and a few people were working on the preparations. Carla, the office manager, was running out the door as Greg, a line boy, arrived with the trunk of his car full of drinks, and Lee, a factotum, was loading the Coke machine for the Free Coke Day—the machine was left unlocked and everything was on the house. Out the window I could see Greg sling a bag of ice over the air conditioner that was permanently bolted through the wall near the cash register and wrapped in plastic for the winter.

There was a slightly mournful note as people gathered for the celebration, because one of the oldest of the old-timers of Galt had died suddenly over the previous few days, and everyone seemed a little shocked, despite the fact that Cal Vyduna was old and had had heart trouble before. Cal had a partnership in a Cessna 210. He had been one of the two-hundred-dollar-cheeseburger crowd flying out for lunch and flying back for no particular reason. Mark, an insurance salesman, was calling it a bohemian suicide. Mark was talking to John Fountain, my partner in ownership of the Citabria, who had just arrived for the party. "You know what I mean," Mark said, as he hung his thin frame on the counter from the sales clerk's side, sipping coffee from a styrofoam cup and glancing expectantly out the window now and then as if watching for planes by long habit, though there was nothing going on out there except freezing drizzle accumulating in shining layers on the wings of parked airplanes. Mark was one of those perennial hangers on at the airport, who seemed to stay at the bar drinking coffee and only occasionally to actually go flying. He had dark curly hair and a slow drawl, thick with midwestern nasal twang. "That's what we called it back in the neighborhood where there were all these old bohemians. They'd wait for the first good snow, and then they'd go out and shovel like hell. Drop dead of a heart attack, like Cal. And he was sure an old bohemian." John and Mark stood at the counter and talked about Cal, while Lee and Greg and Carla carried party supplies past them into the briefing room, which had been set with folding cafeteria tables. I was surprised to learn that Cal had never had a pilot's license or a medical certificate. "Nope," Mark said, "he always flew with someone else."

"And yet nobody was more enthusiastic about aviation," John said.

Vera and Art

"He flew all the time," Mark said.

They speculated about what would become of Cal's half-ownership of the C-210, which was probably worth sixty thousand dollars. There were many people at Galt who wanted to share a C-210, but not many who could afford it. John wanted it badly. He had flown with Cal many times, and he liked the airplane. Mark, too, had his eye on the plane and seemed more likely to make a bid for it. John was retired and didn't travel enough to justify owning such a fast, expensive airplane. Moreover, his wife, Mary, was thinking of retiring from her job as a bank officer, and if she did, they'd probably spend half the year somewhere else for the weather and the golf. John had told me that Mary didn't like flying and wouldn't be inclined to travel with him in a light plane. John had made vague intimations to me of trouble with his health, saying he was seventy-one, after all, and he could lose his medical at any time; although he wasn't willing to say precisely how that might happen, there was the hint that he knew something that frightened him. The fact was, although he had had a few health scares from time to time, he was in great condition. He flew upside down three times a week in our Citabria. Pulling G's that way, he'd probably live to be one hundred.

"I thought Cal looked kind of pale Sunday," Mark said.

"He didn't look like himself," John said.

"He said he wasn't feeling up to snuff."

"He told me that, too," John said. "You know, he wanted to go flying, and I had a family commitment and told him I couldn't go. Then later on I felt badly, because I knew how much he wanted to go and I just couldn't. I ought to have gone."

"Yeah, he said the same thing to me," Mark said. "I couldn't go, because I was hanging drywall. I should have left the drywall and gone flying with Cal. Now I feel bad about it. I guess he must have been getting sick right then, the way he looked. Pale."

"Pale."

■　■　■

People began to arrive in numbers at about 1:30. Bob Russell, the airport manager, was there with his girlfriend, Kathy, and he was relating a story about the new automatic weather-reporting systems that were being installed at airports to replace the old human weather observers. One such device was installed at Hibbing, Minnesota, and a snowstorm erected a big snow sculpture directly in front of the sensor. Well, the blizzard blew on past, and the high pressure built in behind it, but the instrument continued to report a quarter-mile in blowing snow throughout the next day or two of perfectly clear and sunny weather. Airliners and commuter airlines cannot even begin an instrument approach when the weather is reported as a quarter-mile in blowing snow, so they all had to divert until someone cleared the snowdrift away from in front of the machine, which was dutifully reporting what it saw.

The Christmas party presented an unsettling scene, all the people, whom I generally saw only one or two at a time, separated in time by days or weeks or months, now gathered in one place. It was as if we'd all been in a movie, and now the cast was having a party and we were reverting to our real selves, whoever they might be.

Steve, Carla's husband, and Chance, their son, sat on the black pretend-leather couch together, and Chance was saying, "The only thing that'll make this worth it is if I win the ride." Chance was willing to endure even the Galt Christmas party for a chance to go upside down with smoke in the Eagle. There was to be a raffle, and first prize was a ride in a biplane. Steve, whose leg was still bothering him more than a year after he broke it falling from a ladder, put his foot up on the coffee table to ease the pain and swelling. Jim Liss, a mechanic, was at the bar, giggling to himself. And on the Pancho Barnes wall beside him was the newly framed portrait of Gerry, Mark, and Howard, looking like a parody of aviators in their Ray Bans, with their hardware all spread out before and behind them. They were the top aerobatics competitors.

Brad Campbell came in. He was a young advertising executive with D. D. B. Needham in Chicago, and his father, a pilot, had been killed in an aviation accident when he was young. Brad had just gotten his license and was determined to learn aerobatics. I had taken him up a few times, and he flew well and had no trouble with vertigo or nausea. He introduced the woman he was with and announced that she had just had her first ride in a small airplane a few days earlier.

"How'd you like it?" I asked.

"Great," she said.

"I'm trying to convince her to take lessons," Brad said.

"Well?" I asked.

"I'm considering it," she said.

Someone raised a glass and called for a toast to Cal, calling him one of the most dedicated people in aviation and saying, "We'll miss you, Cal." There was a general murmur as Carla rushed around trying to make sure that everyone had a glass of champagne before the toast was completed.

By three o'clock the rooms had become so jammed and smoky that it was impossible to breathe or move. Everyone was eating and discovering, one person at a time, that there was no mustard or mayonnaise to go with all the cold cuts and rye bread. There were big plastic tubs of cookies and great aluminum tins such as are used for baking turkeys, which had been filled with rolled up slices of ham, cheese, and sausage meats, loaves of bread, gallon jars of olives and pickles, tubs of cheese dip, bags and bags of tortilla chips, and a gallon jug of Mexican jalapeño *salsa*. Art found the smallest children and made sure that they had the pick of the cookies. But there were so many people that Art eventually found himself wedged in a corner near the picture window, laughing at the spectacle, saying, "These are the people who used to jam into our kitchen in the old days. Vera and I would come home from church, and we couldn't even get in the door."

■ ■ ■

After a while, not even Art and Vera could stand the smoke and noise, and they drifted outside, where a group of pilots were standing around in the snow, breathing steam and talking with their hands. We stood around for a while, getting our breath and catching cold, when a buzzing overhead alerted us to a machine in the clouds.

"It's one of us," Russell said facetiously.

"And it's a little one, too," Liss said.

"Boy, he's crazy," another pilot said.

"What's he doing up there in this weather?" Art asked.

"Landing, I hope," Liss said.

"Or not," another said, a comment on the poor quality of the electronic instrument approach to Galt.

Several of us went inside to stand by the flight desk and listen for the announcement on the radio. In a few minutes we heard the

TRACON at O'Hare handing off an airplane to our local frequency, and he was cleared for the VOR-A approach at Galt. A ripple of muffled approval and disapproval ran through the crowd, as if to say, "Whoever is coming in with that crummy VOR approach in this weather has got to have some pretty hot credentials as a pilot." We all knew what it took to fly into a little field like this on the slender filament of the electronic signal from a facility more than fifteen miles away at Northbrook in a single-engine airplane with no back-up instruments on a spitting, foggy, snowing, uncouth day like that. For a while, the room grew quiet, as we divided our attention between the radio and the end of the runway where the airplane would appear. Finally, Russell picked up the binoculars and trained them on the place where the misty tree line met the lowering clouds, and eventually a tiny speck appeared, trumpeting its triumph in bleating, crackling waves of noise, and amid fumes and blowing mists, it squatted on the runway and glided easily up to the gas pumps. A tall thin man in a sleeveless down-filled vest jumped out and in an instant he went from hero-size to human size, making it all the more confounding to explain how he had done what he had done: Come out of the clouds on a big day such as this in a little machine such as that.

He and Russell knew each other and immediately engaged in a conversation of technical talk about the flight just passed, a kind of verbal secret handshake of the IFR club, in which they acted very nonchalant about how it really was up there. "Oh, no, no problem, tops about six thousand, trace of rime ice on the way up, but there weren't too many bumps, got handed off sixty miles out, and they wouldn't give me lower, cleared me for the approach five miles out at four thousand feet, but no sweat, you know how it is with O'Hare TRACON."

"Yep," Russell said.

Then they went into the briefing room where the party was and sat down to talk more seriously about the deeper matters of IFR flying, but as the pilot removed his down vest, I could see the diamond-shaped patch of sweat that had soaked through his shirt. You don't sweat like that on a day like this unless you're shooting the VOR approach at Galt with ice bullets being shot at you by invisible battalions.

I went back out and found Art and Vera standing together, watching their house back across the ramp and parking lot, beyond the

Vera and Art

wrecked B-17 and the tangle of old asparagus and new weeds. Vera was dressed in black and looked youthful and radiant with her relaxed smile and bright eyes and her hair done stylishly. I had seen her earlier, drifting around the room without seeming to move her feet, blissfully looking this way and that in the air above all the heads, as if she were having a vision that none of us could see, and I had remarked to myself that she was beautiful, and I could imagine what she had looked like when Art met her. Now she and Art simply stared back from the airport to their yellow house by Greenwood Road, as if they looked back on their whole life and saw all its parts revealed. They had built a farm, and it had turned into an airport.

"We ought to consider having it at the house next year," Vera said. "There's more room."

■　■　■

A few days later, I was up at the house with Art, and while he pushed some mail around on the kitchen table, examining it carefully, I stood at the sink, looking out the window at the airfield. An airplane rolled toward me, as if on a suicide mission, and then magically rose away and went over my head. I turned to the refrigerator. It was decorated with children's magnetic alphabet letters in primary colors. They held news clippings and photos and a few bits of paper to the white porcelain surface. There was one message written in pencil on a square white piece of note paper in a hand that I recognized as Art's palsied penmanship. It had been rubbed and smeared, and I had to stare at it for a few moments before I could decipher what it said. Then it became clear to me, and within the stark purity and the brevity of its four simple words, the whole crazy place suddenly made perfect sense to me.

It said, "Butchie. I love you."